SANCTIFIER

THE SHATTERED CITY
BOOK TWO

MEG SMITHERMAN

ROSE & MOTH BOOKS

The Shattered City Duology

Destroyer

Sanctifier

The Iceblood Duet

The Frost Queen's Blade

For everyone who lives for party and ballroom scenes in their fantasy books. I might have overdone it this time, but I overdid it for you. Don't forget that.

INTRODUCTION

EXCERPT FROM THE INTRODUCTION TO "MIND & MAGIC: A TREATISE ON THE EXISTENCE OF DEITIES" BY AGNES WHIDFORD

From the Cornelian Tower Archives, single printing. Lent to the private library of Lord Heron IV, and subsequently lost in a house fire in 1303 AH.

There has always been a certain set of scholarship that argues in favor of the existence of gods. I refer not to the temples in various states of disrepair throughout the Continent, nor to those who pray, whether at home or at chapel. I refer, instead, to *recorded* histories. Unexplained events have occurred with some regularity throughout the course of human history, and only until recently, with the growing popularity of the concept of *science*, have scholars begun to dismiss such texts as "fanciful."

I find such dismissal troubling and seek to refute it. There was a time when all of Navenie, in addition to its more superstitious neighbors, believed in gods, magic, and monsters. While the existence of flying lizards with webbed wings was never confirmed, evidence of the gods' interference in human lives is vast, largely consistent, and, based on the various accounts I will discuss here in great detail, undeniable.

Take, for example, Festra, a particularly meddlesome

deity, whose most notable act was to set several towns on fire, as legend has it, simply to prove a point. If we are to take these accounts of violent interference with mortals at face value, assuming one has read the relevant text,* Festra seemed to have a fascination with passing on his power to mortals and setting them loose upon the world.

And so, when we look at the diary of Festra devotee Winifred Castlecombe, who awoke the morning of January 24, 279 BH, with the ability to shoot fire from her hands, we ask not, "What does the concept of Winifred's fire represent," but rather, assume that the fire is real and ask instead, "What did Festra want her to do with his fire?"

* See: *Divine Atrocities* by Julian Dacre, publication pending.

PROLOGUE

S imon Delara was late.

Usually, he arrived precisely on time — at least, he made certain to *appear* as if he did. In fact, he typically arrived early, hiding in some alcove or outside a door, with the express purpose of eavesdropping. It was fascinating the things people gave away when they were waiting, thinking themselves alone or with trusted company.

If Simon were to arrive late, it would encourage a client's mind to wander toward him, his doings, what might be causing him to tarry.

So he was never late.

Well… *rarely*.

The delay had been a sudden interruption from someone unavoidable. Irritatingly scruffy and brooding, and decidedly unwelcome, but not avoidable.

He went as quickly as he could without appearing to hurry. His step was jaunty, the heels of his silk slippers tapping a staccato on the marble floor of Regent Sigrun's great palace. His copper hair, styled to unnatural heights and impeccably coiffed, bounced jovially in the lamplight. And a finely tailored frock coat, embroidered with green and fuchsia, swung daintily as he went. Under one arm was tucked a case of black leather lined with wine-colored velvet. And nestled inside was, of course, his beloved lute.

He knew he looked a delicacy as he flowed through the halls, brushing intimately past courtiers in lace and velvet, some whose secrets he knew and some he didn't. But every face was familiar to him, every name filed away in the banks of his memory, orderly and precise. This was the craft of a minstrel — to know everyone's business and use it to his best advantage.

Outwardly, he swept along with carefree ease, his sensuous lips curved upward invitingly. But he was late. Inside his impeccably formed ribcage beat a restless heart. Inwardly, he ground his teeth, swore, bit at the inside of his mouth — a habit he had fought long and hard to drop and in which his beloved sister continued to indulge.

Ru... he couldn't spare the time to worry. Not now.

At last, he came to his client's chambers, a sprawling suite in the royal wing of the palace. Not for the first time, he wondered how the woman had managed to secure such opulent and — frankly, presumptuous — rooms. She was somewhat new to the regent's court, having only arrived that year, but somehow, quite quickly, she had come to ingratiate herself with the most influential members of the aristocracy. Even Simon hadn't been able to learn a single detail about the woman, and there was nothing that aggravated Simon more than not knowing everything about everyone.

And more than just the usual personal details, Simon was desperate to learn not only how this woman had climbed the social so quickly, but *why*.

Yet after weeks of prying, she remained a mystery to him, a bit of toffee stuck between his teeth, a wayward lock of hair he couldn't quite tame. No matter who he questioned, manipulated, or overheard, there was only this answer: *she's just that charming, I suppose.*

When Simon had nearly come to the end of his quickly fraying rope, the woman herself, Lady Bellenet, had summoned him to perform for her. In her private rooms, no less. But now, by the cruel hand of fate, Simon had been held up. And in doing so, he'd missed his opportunity to hover at the edges, lurk in the shadows, to overhear things not meant for him.

Fucking hell, he might have said, had he still subscribed to the oafish idioms of the middle classes. Never mind that he held no title, that as a merchant's son, he had come from a family situated firmly in the middle. He was a minstrel, a dealer of information to anyone who paid the right price. That in itself was title enough.

Fucking hell.

He would exact his vengeance on the man who had delayed him later — for this and several other reasons. But now, he had work to do.

The painted doors to Lady Bellenet's suite were ajar, a welcome invitation as much as a warning — *break my trust, and the doors slam shut.*

Simon paused at the threshold, hearing voices within. He was already late; let them wait one more moment. This might be his only chance. He made a practiced show of checking his hair, fluffing his neckcloth, and smoothing every wrinkle in his attire. To anyone passing in the hall, or perhaps even sensing his presence from within, he was no more than a vain musician ensuring he looked impeccable for a performance. And though his cunning reputation preceded him, he liked to think that at his best, he fooled even the most astute members of court.

Because this was part of the performance itself, a step in a dance he knew well. As he ran long fingers down the front of his waistcoat, as he adjusted the delicate gold chain of a pocket watch so that its drape was just the right length, just the right amount of curve... he listened.

Voices drifted out from Lady Bellenet's room, but they were so low that he couldn't make out a single word. He was about to push through the doors at last, when a name caught his ear. The sound of it pierced him dully.

"Ruellian Delara... ?" The rest of the sentence was an incomprehensible murmur, but he had heard enough for his hackles to rise. Why should this lady, of anyone, be interested in his sister? Perhaps she was interested in archaeology, but it wasn't terribly likely. Only abominable bores like Hugon D'Luc cared about such dull things as ancient pottery.

Simon craned his neck, trying to hear more, but it was useless.

"Where *is* that cursed minstrel?" a deep and feminine

voice said, loud enough now that Simon could hear quite clearly. "He's three minutes late."

And Simon was through the doors, breezing in like a confection of silk and charm. As he sashayed in, he nearly collided with a woman on her way out, dressed in finery.

"I'm terribly sorry," he said, bowing.

"It's all right," she said, her tone distant and uncaring. Simon saw now that he recognized her — Countess Odeline. He had performed for her often in the past, though not recently.

"My lady," Simon said, treating the countess to his most inviting smile, "how long has it been? I do so miss our musical evenings. Please, don't hesitate to call upon me when the mood for melody strikes."

He had known the countess to possess great humor, and she dearly loved to laugh. But she merely blinked in response, her gaze glassy and far away. As if she'd never seen Simon before in her life. He turned and watched her depart, unable to keep his brows from drawing together in confusion.

Blinking quickly, Simon revived himself — he was not here for Countess Odeline. He turned, smiling brightly, and dropped a hideously intricate bow before Lady Bellenet. When he straightened, he caught her gaze and held it. He knew that he radiated warmth, an unassuming beauty, despite the strange encounter at the door.

Everything about Simon Delara was practiced. Rehearsed.

"My lady," he said, "a thousand apologies for the delay. My lute was afflicted with a string that simply refused to sing true. If you must have me executed as punishment, I should warn you that I would enjoy it terribly. Facing eternity at the hands of such a lovely woman… how could I complain?"

Lady Bellenet's cupid's bow lips curved in a slight smile, a froth of gold-brown hair piled above her youthful face. "God willing, we won't need to go so far as that. And how is the string now, Mr. Delara?"

His smile widened, and he bowed again. "She sings with the utmost purity, my lady."

"Good," said Lady Bellenet. "I expect nothing less from Mirith's most recommended minstrel. And what will you be performing for me?"

"Whatever will please your ladyship most," said Simon, setting his lute case on a velvet bench and flipping it open with deft fingers. The instrument gleamed within, shining honey wood, inlaid with mother-of-pearl flowers along its curves. Removing it gently from its velvet case, he hefted the lute with practiced ease and strummed a chord.

"You may not be familiar with the song I crave," Lady Bellenet said, lily-white hands folded in a taffeta lap. She was perched in a throne-like armchair, her back facing a tall window that looked out over a red-drenched sea.

Simon knew the sunset illuminated him strikingly, setting his coppery hair afire. But even that couldn't free him from the barbs in the lady's eyes.

She tilted her head ever so slightly, her sharp gaze trained on Simon's face as if she expected to find something there. But greater women than she had attempted to see through his mask, and all had failed.

"Tell me the name of the song," said Simon, playing a soft chord as he spoke, "and I shall do my utmost to ensure that your ears are caressed with the tune you so desire."

She smiled faintly, her eyes devoid of any pleasure. "Tell me, do you know The Song of the Sun Gate? A traditional Mekyan folk tune, nothing I'd expect anyone here to have heard."

Her expression was all soft apology, but Simon felt the sharpness in her tongue as if it were steel against skin. He had expected the mysterious Lady Bellenet to be fierce, a force to be reckoned with, but there was more to her than a simple gift for charm.

"My lady," he said, "you underestimate me. We Mirithans may have an obsession with science and progress, but only the hardest of hearts could not be swayed by the stories of the ancient gods. The Song of the Sun Gate... I haven't heard it in years, let alone played it, but I'd be obliged to hang up my minstrel's hat if I didn't know the tune like the back of my hand."

Lady Bellenet inclined her head slightly, a silent acknowledgement and the cue for him to play.

So he did. The notes came effortlessly as always; he was a skilled musician, his fingers deft, his musicians' muscles blessed with long memory. As he played, he schooled his features, kept his eyes light, his smiles soulful and indulgent. But on the inside, his gut churned, his heart hammered, and try as he might to stop it by sheer will alone, a sweat broke out on the back of his neck.

Lady Bellenet knew something she wasn't telling him. Simon wondered whether the woman hadn't known he was waiting, listening. Wondered whether she hadn't left the doors ajar just to ensure that he heard his sister's name.

Worst of all, this was no simple song request from a bored lady of the court. It was a brutal song, a vengeful song of death for those who disobeyed their betters. Simon had spent enough time at court to know that every song he played, every request from a noble, alluded to something bigger. This one was a warning.

And Ru was in danger.

CHAPTER 1

Lord D'Luc came in the mornings.

When they first returned from the Shattered City, Ru had been eager to prove herself impervious to him, to make it clear that she couldn't be cowed by his threats or manipulations. She had called herself Destroyer, taking up the mantle in a moment of anger, spurred by a thirst for vengeance.

But as time passed, she found that her rage was beginning to gutter.

Because Lord D'Luc came in the mornings.

His arrival was always heralded by a sharp knock on Ru's door, his very presence a reminder that this was not *her* room — it was his, just as the artifact was his, and the Tower. The professors, the academic leaders and keepers of the Cornelian Tower who had sat at the head of the kingdom's scholarly pursuits, were bedridden, all afflicted by a mysterious sickness. And who but Lord D'Luc was so conveniently placed as to keep the Tower in their stead?

Ru was already awake and dressed when the knock came that morning. She had attempted to do something with her hair, which amounted to pulling it out of her face and securing it with a piece of velvet ribbon.

"Good morning, Delara," said Lord D'Luc, smiling brightly in the haze of morning light.

Ru hated the way he affected her, even now. His beauty was simply unavoidable, a fact of science. Anyone seeing him in that moment, with the rising sun reflected in his pale gold hair, would have been struck by the vision. There was an air of ethereality about him, and while he was tall, he remained trim, elegant, angelic. Full lips and a sharp jaw, light eyes, and a dimple when he smiled — these were the trappings of a man whose soul, Ru believed, was rotten through.

She wanted to slap that dimple off his perfect face.

"*Good* is subjective."

"Charming as always," he said, holding out his elbow for her to take. She did, already knowing the moves to this dance. They had played it out each morning since returning from the Shattered City, less than a week ago.

Less than a week since Fen's disappearance, since Lord D'Luc wrested the artifact from her and claimed it as his own. Ru's pain remained so present and acute, Fen's betrayal lying so heavy on her heart that it could have been only yesterday.

As the pair moved through the front vestibule, Ru frowned. "Not your rooms today?" she asked. Thus far, their breakfasts had been taken in Lord D'Luc's private quarters.

"I thought we ought to enjoy summer's last gasps," he replied, rings flashing as he pushed open the Tower's great front doors.

"Aren't the others coming?"

"You mean the Children?" he said. "Not today. I want you to myself."

Ru bit the inside of her already-raw lip, tasting the tang of blood.

He led them out of the front courtyard through an arch in a hedgerow, along a curving path of flagstones, until they came to what appeared to be a picnic. A blanket was laid out on the browning grass of Ru's least favorite courtyard, and the usual array of breakfast foods was arranged pleasingly in a tableau. Ru imagined Inda, Ranto, and Nell — the trio of Children who served as Lord D'Luc's ever-present servants — unfolding the blanket, laying out all the food, even arranging cushions to sit on. The image would have made her laugh had she been with anyone else.

"It's a bit cold for a picnic," she said, her woolen skirts whipping in a stiff breeze.

"The sun will warm you," he said, in a tone that put an end to the matter. "Sit."

He held out a hand to help Ru onto an overstuffed cushion. She settled herself fitfully, her nose and fingertips already uncomfortably cold. The bright sun hung low on the horizon, and it was far too late in the year for any warmth to be found in its light.

Lord D'Luc settled himself across from her, seemingly unperturbed by the chill air. Even lounging on a cushion, he managed to appear immaculate.

"To what do I owe the pleasure of seeing you balancing precariously on a pillow?" Ru asked.

Hugon's blue eyes narrowed slightly. "So disagreeable when hungry, Delara. Do eat."

"Why are we having a picnic?" She reached reluctantly for a jug of coffee.

"I've told you."

It was always like this — a stalemate, a stand-off. Ru poured herself coffee and took a small sip. It was lukewarm. Likely on purpose, to upset her. Everything Lord D'Luc did was to upset her.

Lord D'Luc watched her movements, cat-like.

"Well?" she said, setting down her coffee. "What probing questions do you want to ask me today?"

His lips quirked. "I think I'll start with a reminder."

Wind rustled the hedges, the carcasses of dried-up flowers breaking free and billowing outward across the courtyard. Ru shivered. "Of what?"

"Your purpose here. With the artifact." His lips curled upward as he spoke, his tone mirthless. He reached for a pastry and took a delicate bite.

Ru narrowed her eyes. He was well aware she would never forget what he expected of her. "When you lie to me," she said, "You say you want me to bring about a scientific revolution. Isn't that right? Thinking somehow that if you push me to breaking, the artifact will reveal itself to you. And then you'll be at the forefront of some intellectual movement in Navenie. But when you're being honest…" She paused, waiting for an admonition, but he only watched her thoughtfully.

"When I'm being honest, Delara?" The question was soft.

"A cleansing fire. A new Destruction. All in the name of some ancient god who doesn't exist. *Festra*. Do you really believe—"

He lifted a finger ever so slightly, cutting her off. "What I believe is irrelevant. These are the facts. You will use the artifact to bring about a great scientific breakthrough. A cleansing, just as Taryel Aharis once did at the Shattered City. As you did not long ago, an echo of his ancient deed. And I will continue to lead you in this direction, no matter how you rail against me. Fate has spoken for you." He studied her with sharp eyes, as though trying to see past her walls. "Why not accept that Festra's will cannot be ignored any longer? That this artifact was shown to you, and you accepted it. That you were *made* to burn the world and bring about its rebirth. The circumstances lay it out so clearly."

"Festra is a character from myth," she said. Frustrated, wanting distraction, she popped a blackberry into her mouth and bit down. It was overripe and too soft and tasted of earth. "I wasn't *made* for anything."

Lord D'Luc made a noncommittal humming sound.

She crossed her arms, hugging herself against the cold. *I decide my own purpose*, she wanted to say. But even that seemed to be a dream long abandoned since the artifact would not free her from its grasp. Even now, she could feel it in her mind, a distant hum, a whispering echo of its true nature. It was a constant reminder of Fen's betrayal — it was his heart, after all. And Ru was connected to it, unable to escape it, though lately, the artifact's voice had been quieter. As if it were sleeping.

It was enough to ruin anyone's appetite. Surveying the spread of food, Ru found she was no longer hungry.

"Delara, have you ever been in love?"

She leveled an incredulous look at Lord D'Luc and saw that he was serious.

"Well?" he said.

Ru couldn't fathom how she was supposed to answer the question, or why he would ask it. Up until now, their breakfasts had been one of two things: a painful interrogation, or a heady scientific discourse. It was all about the artifact, naturally.

He seemed determined to make Ru feel terrible. She often left their breakfasts with tears in her eyes, questioning her own motives, her intelligence, her place in the world.

Lord D'Luc had never asked about love before.

"That's a pointless question," Ru said finally.

The lord leaned back, bracing himself with a hand on the blanket. "I'm a man of science," he said. "But I'm also a man of faith. I know that you are intrinsically joined to the artifact, even though I cannot see it. So why not ask of love? Is it not another sort of joining?" He popped a piece of fruit into his mouth and chewed.

Ru wracked her brain for some hidden meaning. Surely he couldn't guess that she had loved Fen, or been close to something like it. With knowledge like that, who knew what emotional torments he might devise for her? And anyway, Fen was gone. Her throat tightened.

Then, apparently oblivious of her inner turmoil, Lord D'Luc said, "Solve an equation for me."

Ru sipped her now cold coffee, waiting.

"Tell me, how does one differentiate between science and magic?"

"*One* doesn't," said Ru, unable to hide her exasperation. This was a topic they had covered many times in the past few days. "We lack the tools to quantify magic, but as you *know*, my theories point to it being rooted in physics. The movement of particles we can't measure with our technology."

"And how," said Hugon, his hair lifting and falling about his ears in the chill wind, "would one differentiate faith and magic? Love and science? Are they, by necessity, separate entities, mutually exclusive yet existing in harmony?" His neckcloth, usually starched and stiff, had loosened in the breeze and ruffled against his chin. "And if they were laid out before you, would you know the difference?"

Ru stiffened. "That's conceptual."

"The artifact itself, I'd argue, is a concept." Hugon's blue eyes were lighter in the sun, and his smile remained. "So is joy. Love. Death. I know you're familiar with the latter."

The lord had never ceased to be magnetic, despite the darkness that rose often in his eyes. And even this, a jab at the deaths Ru herself had caused, felt to her like a beautiful knife in the ribs.

She sighed deeply. Her nose had gone numb. "If I participate in this obscure banter will you let me go inside?"

"Naturally," came his elegant reply.

She glowered; at least she could be petulant if nothing else. "I'm not sure my answer will even make sense to you. I don't believe you've ever been in love. You lack the required selflessness."

The lord's eyes flashed. "Tread carefully, Delara. My methods thus far have been gentle."

Gentle. As if his cruel words, being under constant guard, Children monitoring her every move, were gentle.

In some twisted way, Ru almost *liked* pushing him, seeing how close to danger she could get before one of them backed down. It was a rapier dance, a thrilling game that left her breathless, tripping on the edge of a tumbling dark.

"I don't *know*," she said. "I don't know if I've been in love. Love isn't quantifiable, anyway. I suppose you think we can measure feelings if we try hard enough, assign an emotion to the artifact, conduct studies in that way. 'Oh look, it's feeling a bit peckish this afternoon! Ah, how joyful the stone is feeling this morning.'" She glared heartily at Lord D'Luc.

He smiled right back. "As always, you seem to know my thoughts before I speak them," he drawled. "Why not? Why shouldn't we hypothesize that the artifact, inanimate as it is, might feel emotion? I know you have some connection to it, though you continuously evade me when it comes to the details. Couldn't such a connection be based in emotion, in love?"

Ru remained impassive. Only her breaths gave away

her true feelings, the fact that she had wondered the same. "Speculation doesn't become you."

"Evasion isn't your strong point," Lord D'Luc shot back with a half-smile and a tilt of his head. "The stone reacts to you, and you alone. I've held it, touched it with bare skin. What you share with the stone is more than physicality. And as a man of science, I mean to understand it. Furthermore, I mean for *you* to harness it. You'll succumb to me regardless."

"How do you intend to manage that?" Ru asked, her tone clipped. But even as she spoke, her breath quickened, and the picnic spread began to smear into a colorful haze. Her fingers clenched in her skirts, curling into fists. "Needles under my fingernails?"

Breathe in, then out. She shouldn't be afraid of this man, and yet he filled her with a growing dread that wouldn't abate. Every morning she woke with a curdle of fear in her belly, and every night she lay awake with visions of his sneer, his sapphire eyes, kaleidoscopic in her mind's eye.

"Needles?" said Lord D'Luc, his gaze heavy. "I shouldn't need to go so far as that. Your friends are very loyal."

It was all he had to say. The meaning was clear. Ru could fend for herself; she could take anything he threw at her. Because she had to. But Archie and Gwyneth…

Breathe in. Breathe out.

Ru tried to wrap her mind around the thought, her friends in danger. Cowering at the tip of a blade that Hugon D'Luc wielded. He was a monster in the trappings of an angel.

In, then out.

Would Hugon D'Luc go so far as to harm students of the Cornelian Tower? She had to believe he wouldn't, not yet anyway. Surely there was a limit to how far he'd push her before he broke himself instead. Her heartbeat slowed, and her mind began to clear. The threat was a ploy. Just words. A desperate man, grasping at straws.

She had to believe it.

Ru held the lord's gaze defiantly, refusing to show her fear. "And what about you?" she said, conscious of every one of his movements, the set of his jaw, his hands. He was a viper lying in wait in the grass, likely to strike at any moment. "Have you been in love?"

He smiled bitterly and stood, elegant as ever. He held out a bejeweled hand to Ru, and she took it. She had no other choice.

"I thought you said I lacked the selflessness," he replied, and they stood facing one another, close enough that Ru could see flecks of grey in his blue eyes. She studied his face, looking for a threat. But all she saw in those fine features, just for a moment, was a young man in pain.

Ru said, "I can't take you seriously when you talk about love."

He offered her his elbow, leading them back to the Tower. "Immaterial. I have never needed you to take me seriously. I only need you to acquiesce."

~

THE TOWER MESS hall was off-limits to Ru. Not by any decree, but because she couldn't bear to face the other academics en masse. Their gazes followed her and stuck to her like burrs, screaming silent judgment. In their minds, she was the reason things had gone wrong. She was the reason the professors lay sick; she was the reason Children and King's Guards roamed the halls of the Tower as if it were Hugon D'Luc's personal estate.

Ru Delara: first, a laughingstock, and now, a harbinger of some unknown doom.

Skirting past the mess hall on her way up to her room, Ru avoided the unfriendly glances from her peers. She kept her head high and her eyes straight ahead, but their unseen gazes, the jarring cold of their disdain, felt heavy on her heart. Some even hated her, she could tell. Grey Adler, her long-time academic nemesis, was chief among those who wanted her removed from the Tower. The academics might even have done it if it weren't for Lord D'Luc's official takeover, signed and sealed in a letter by Regent Sigrun herself.

Lyr, a tall and large-featured King's Guard, met Ru just inside the Tower. He was her bodyguard now, whether to keep her safe or to watch her movements, Ru couldn't guess. Likely both, but at least his intimidating presence kept the academics at bay.

"Want me to grab you breakfast?" he asked, when it became clear Ru wasn't going into the mess hall.

She paused. The smell of toast and sausage, eggs and jam, filled her nose. Her stomach, at long last, began to grumble.

"Don't you want a cinnamon roll?" suggested Lyr, raising his eyebrows. "Warm, sugary, nasty—"

"Fine," Ru said, unable to resist. "A cinnamon roll, then."

"It'll give you a stomach cramp."

"My stomach is used to it."

Lyr shrugged. "Not very good for the brain, all that sugar."

"Lyr," Ru said, almost laughing, "Don't suggest cinnamon rolls if you don't intend to deliver on them."

He grinned. "I'll bring some up to you."

Once back in her room, a plate of gooey cinnamon rolls in hand, Ru settled herself on the bed. She ate methodically, fingers sticky with icing, and tried to forget about the artifact, Lord D'Luc, and Fen… no, *Taryel*. The unspoken name filled her lungs like black smoke.

If she could forget him, she might feel peace. At least for a little while.

CHAPTER 2

S ummer was waning in the kingdom of Navenie. Warm nights had given way to chill evenings, and flocks of waterfowl cut southern-facing Vs across dusky skies. Clouds of fireflies in the Cornelian Tower's courtyards diminished by the day until there were only a few left, dancing sparsely under the night. The trees caught fire slowly, some yellow, others hinting at a bright flaming red soon to come.

Inside the Tower, fires burned longer, and hot drinks became the new favorite. Mulled wine, toddies, and cocoa reigned supreme where once fruit cordials held sway. The loss of daylight wasn't a reason for sadness in Navenie; it was a time to gather blankets, candles, and lamps; to pull loved ones closer, and enjoy the warmth of a long evening by the fire.

But such homey comforts were lost on Ru. They couldn't push back the cold dark that threatened her heart, storm clouds boiling up from a horizon, inching across her sky.

"Stop it," said Gwyneth, slamming a book shut to release a cloud of dust.

Ru coughed. "Stop what?"

Gwyneth narrowed her eyes, an expression that didn't quite seem to fit her sweet, soft features. She set the book irreverently on top of a row of shelved tomes. Her full attention was focused on Ru. Many young men would have given plenty to be at the center of Gwyneth Tenoria's attention. She was delicate, beautiful, and nonthreatening, with brown eyes, curling blonde hair, and a nose that belonged on a porcelain doll.

Gwyneth said, "You know what I mean."

Ru retrieved the book from where Gwyneth had haphazardly placed it, tucking it under one arm. "Terrible library etiquette," she said. "If any of the professors caught you…"

"Well they wouldn't, would they?"

Ru turned her head sharply at the change in her friend's tone, remembering when she had tried to visit Professor Obralle. It was not long after their return to the Cornelian Tower. She had been watching the professorial wing, taking note of when the Children were likely to be gone, tending to unknown tasks about the Tower. And when she was sure that the professor's rooms were unattended, Ru had slipped inside.

Professor Obralle had seemed to be asleep, her eyes flitting nervously behind closed lids. Pink hair lay in tangles over her pillow. But her pulse was steady, and she had no fever.

Ru had only enough time to wonder what could make a person lie unwaking and helpless for so long before she heard voices in the corridor and fled.

"Yes," said Ru, vaguely aware that she was meant to be carrying on a conversation. "I suppose not."

"You're doing it again," Gwyneth said, almost apologetic. "That empty, terrible look in your eyes."

"Sorry," said Ru, "I suppose being emotionally tethered to the cursed heart of a murderer takes a toll."

Someone on the other side of the library sneezed.

"Keep your voice down," Gwyneth hissed, hunching over as if they were being hunted through the stacks.

Ru made a noncommittal sound. She had nothing to hide, not from the academics anyway. They had already decided to hate her, or they hadn't. Ru rambling wildly about Taryel's heart in the library wouldn't change much of anything with no Children nearby to overhear.

Ru had done her best to put an end to the artifact's hold

on her. What had it ever given her but pain? Where once the tether to Fen's heart had felt something like tenderness, now it was only a reminder of his loss. She had tried night after night, alone on the parapet walls or wandering the courtyards in the small hours, reaching out to that unseen thread and hoping to snip it in two.

But it was impossible. Always the thread slipped from her imagined fingers, unbreakable. As if some part of her, a part she refused to fully acknowledge, wanted to keep the connection in place. Perhaps that lonely part of her was comforted by the artifact's presence, its soothing hum against the fabric of her mind.

Sometimes, when Ru was teetering just on the cusp of sleep, her mind about to free-fall into the abyss of unconsciousness, she was glad to have him there with her. The man she'd lost forever.

"Some people," Gwyneth hissed, snapping Ru out of her reverie, "might prefer not to broadcast the fact that we've brought *Taryel Aharis*'s crusted-up heart into the Cornelian Tower."

Despite herself, Ru smiled. She hadn't laughed much lately, and the urge to do so surprised her. Her always downturned mouth had become a constant frown, as if finally reaching the pinnacle of what it had been created to do: brood.

"Sorry, Gwyn, I'm distracted."

"I hadn't noticed."

"What are you two doing back here?" another voice cut in. It was Archie, strolling between shelves of books as if he owned the place. Hands in his pockets and an impatient expression on his aristocratic features, he came to a stop at Gwyneth's elbow.

"We're looking for books, genius. How else are we going to unravel the mystery of the professors' cursed slumber and wake them from it?" Gwyneth was in a mood now, Ru could tell. "And be careful, Ru's brooding."

"Old news," Archie said airily. "Anyway, haven't we read every last book in the blasted Tower by now?" He spoke in the clipped, elegant manner of the Mirithan highborn upper crust, which he had never been able to shake despite his efforts to get rid of it. He was continually embarrassed about the fact that he had been born wealthy and privileged, when all he really wanted was to live a bohemian life of scholarship. "What's new, is the artifact acting up? That bastard Fen Verrill weighing particularly heavily on your heart?"

"Arch!" Gwyneth's admonition was hushed but fierce.

He shrugged.

"He's right," said Ru, self-consciously pushing a dark tuft of unbrushed hair behind her ear, her hair hanging in disheveled waves down her back. She no longer put thought into her clothes. Today she wore a simple dress and a woolen waistcoat that she hadn't noticed was buttoned up crookedly until Gwyneth pointed it out. "It's everything. Fen, the artifact. And..."

"It's not your fault," said Gwyneth, laying a soft hand on Ru's arm. "What happened at the Shattered City... none of it."

"He betrayed me." Ru's voice was low and hoarse. "I let him... I let him use me. His heart called me to that dig site, and I didn't do a thing to resist. I murdered people. I've failed at every attempt to make things right. And now they're going to make me do it again, and I *can't...*" her eyes burned.

"Yes, we're all aware," Archie said, clipping her jovially on the shoulder with a fist. "Good ol' Ru, our own little Destroyer."

Gwyneth's glare could have melted a glacier.

"What?" Archie said. "She needs more laughter in her life."

"Of *all* the jokes to make."

"It's fine," said Ru, pushing past them, suddenly impatient to get back to her room, back to reading. When she wasn't working to stop Lord D'Luc and his control over the professors, to stymie his plans for her and the artifact, she felt worse than ever. She could only continue on if she believed, somehow, that she was actively trying to fix what she had broken.

As if she could bring Lady Maryn, the archaeologists, and the King's Guards all back to life. It was too late to save them, but if it were within Ru's power, she would do whatever she could to prevent more losses.

Ru heard Gwyneth and Archie exchanging hurried, hushed words behind her as she left the library. It was a familiar sound, the murmur of caring friends who didn't know what to do or how to help. *It is fine*, Ru reminded herself as a surge of loneliness took her. *You'll think of a way out.*

As Ru came into the hall, Lyr peeled away from the wall and began to follow her. The steel of his chest plate clanked softly as he walked.

"You look like shit," he said.

"How kind of you." Ru didn't bother to look back at him.

"I have news," he said, his voice low. "You won't like it."

Ru turned sharply. "Simon?"

The guard shook his head. "D'Luc. Called me to his office yesterday. Asked me to… spy on you."

"He *what?*" Ru stopped in her tracks, causing mild chaos as a cluster of academics nearly collided with her and Lyr and had to veer around at the last second.

Lyr glanced around, presumably for any nearby Children. They were fixtures in the Tower now, come from the palace and seemingly only loyal to Lord D'Luc. Lyr glowered down at Ru. "No need to yell. I'm not going to. Just thought you should know."

"Wonderful," said Ru, staring into the middle distance. The Tower had once been a bastion of education and study, free from the societal rules that confined those outside its wall. But for Ru, it was now little more than a prison. The regent was in Lord D'Luc's pocket, or compromised in some other way. There were no other reasons she would have signed the Tower over to him.

It made sense that Lord D'Luc would want eyes on Ru, to keep her in line. She was an asset, the only one who shared a connection with the artifact, the only one who could use it. But he underestimated the loyalty of Ru's friends.

"I'll feed him false information," Lyr said, leaning down, his voice barely above a whisper. "You can trust me."

Even though she didn't need it, the reminder was a balm. "Thank you, Lyr," she said. "I do trust you."

They began to walk again toward Ru's room in companionable silence. Ru had grown accustomed to the guard's gruff silence, his disapproving grumbles. He was one of the few comforts that remained to her now.

"Do you sleep anymore?" he asked, as they approached the dormitory wing.

She did sleep, but it was restless. Shallow and hot, and full of dreams. They were painful dreams, or tragic ones, or simply re-enactments of events that had already happened and Ru wanted to forget.

"No," she said. "Not really."

"You want a strong spirit," he said. "Knocks you right out."

Ru paused, considering the possibility of a rum or brandy, her hand on the doorknob of her room. At that moment, Gwyneth and Archie caught up to them, their arms laden with books. They were breathing hard, eyes bright.

"You can't just run off without us," Gwyneth said, shifting under the weight of several heavy tomes. "We're here to help."

Ru said nothing and unlocked her door, ushering her friends inside. She gave Lyr a small nod, then closed the door behind her.

"Right," said Gwyneth. "I've brought all the books I could find that might explain the professors' shared state of catatonia."

"She found two books that mention catatonic states in medical patients," said Archie, setting down his stack of volumes before he set about lighting a fire in the hearth. "In *passing*, might I add. Because, and I *told* her this—"

"*Arch*." Gwyneth cut him off. "Discounting books out of hand just because they're not scholarly—"

"You could have gone for any number of books about, I don't know, trepanning. Instead, you picked up the ones about dreams."

"I don't suppose you've noticed, but we're experiencing a bit of an *unprecedented* moment in history—"

"Yes, well, if we're ever to find out how in the hell D'Luc and the Children managed to turn the professors into living vegetables, if we even believe that…"

Ru let the sound of her friends' argument fade to background noise. She had heard it before. She quietly picked up the nearest book, settled herself in a chair by the fire, and began to read. Rather, she *tried* to read. She found it difficult to focus on anything for long. It had only been a few weeks since the revelation of Fen's true identity, but every time Ru was alone, she thought about him. Every moment in solitude was a slow and subtle agony.

The recollection of Fen in the spectral city, holding the artifact, telling Ru it was his heart… it stole air from Ru's lungs. She bit the inside of her lip where an angry sore had developed from her anxious tic. But where the artifact's touch had once been so vivid in the past, its comforts warm, it now lurked at the distant edges of her consciousness. It was almost silent but for the occasional, distant thrum of energy to remind Ru of its presence.

She hated that she missed the stone's loudness, the way it had always pushed past her emotions and made its presence known. And she hated that she missed *him*.

Taryel, the Destroyer, a man who had flattened an entire city in a rush of dark magic, centuries and centuries ago. A man who had, inexplicably, survived the blast and become frozen in time, a twenty-six-year-old whose memories spanned centuries. No — she missed who she had *thought* he was, Fen Verrill, the man whose heart had called to hers, who would have protected her, maybe even loved her, if given a chance.

When Archie and Gwyneth grew tired, when they were finished reading and concluded that nothing productive would be achieved that night — if ever — Ru would wait until she knew the Tower corridors would be mostly empty, and she would wander somewhere lonely. Somewhere isolated, where no one could ask her what she was doing, or exude disappointment when she failed. And with Lyr at her heels, she would try again.

She would try desperately, anguished and enraged, to sever her bond with the artifact. And she would, as she always did, fail in the attempt.

CHAPTER 3

Lord Hugon D'Luc had a depthless capacity for cruelty, but Ru was violently stubborn. And both were reaching their limit.

It happened in the morning, six weeks after that hellish night at the Shattered City. Instead of Lord D'Luc, Ru opened her door to see the staring, empty gazes of Inda, Ranto, and Nell. Lyr stood behind them, looking apologetic. "You have been summoned to demonstrate," said Inda, her tone as devoid of emotion as ever, and that was all.

Ru followed the Children with a sick knot in her stomach. Lyr had been dismissed, and she was alone.

She hadn't been asked to demonstrate these six weeks. She had thought that maybe Lord D'Luc had given up on it as a means of understanding the artifact. But she'd been wrong. She remembered how it had been before, how speaking to the artifact with her mind had led to a loss of control. But without opening that line of mental understanding between herself and the artifact, Ru could not make it do what Lord D'Luc no doubt wanted — destructive darkness.

The dungeon was horribly cold. Lord D'Luc waited there alone. He smiled when Ru and the Children arrived, holding out a hand in a facsimile of a warm greeting. "Good morning, Delara."

She walked to the small wooden table that stood, as it

always had, at the center of the dungeon. On its surface lay a smooth black stone, slightly misshapen, the size of a man's palm. Ru couldn't help but move toward it, this beautiful thing that had brought her so much pain.

"Now," Lord D'Luc said, "I'd like you to summon darkness from it. Like you did at the dig site, like you did here, once. Ranto, stand over her. If she loses control, if the darkness begins to spread unchecked, knock her out."

Ru spun, her heart racing. "You can't—"

But Lord D'Luc's dark eyes flashed. "It was not a request."

Ru swallowed hard and said nothing.

For the first time since learning what the artifact truly was, since losing Fen, since becoming a prisoner in her own home, Ru placed her palms on either side of the artifact. She closed her eyes. And she pretended to attempt to summon darkness from the artifact.

~

"YOU'RE NOT TRYING," Lord D'Luc's sharp words cut her like jagged glass. It had been days since the first failed demonstration. Half a dozen Children stood in the dungeon, watching. "You're useless, Delara. A disappointment. A failure, a joke."

"I'm trying," she gasped. A lie. Every day, she lied; every day, she made him believe that she was trying. But even that was painful, even that cut deep gouges into her psyche. The artifact was distant, almost petulant, and when she closed her eyes so close to it, she could feel it at the edge of her mind. Waiting.

"It's no wonder Fen Verrill abandoned you," hissed Lord D'Luc. "What could *you* have given him? In what world could you hope to please a man?"

Ru choked back a sob. He was right; he was right. Fen might have stayed if she were better, if she were more. But he had left her.

~

A WEEK INTO THE DEMONSTRATIONS, Lord D'Luc hurt her with his hands. He came at her like a predator, his fingers tight on her wrist, as he spoke low and threatening in her ear: "Do not test me, Delara. I know you're holding back. Accept that the artifact is your fate. You are no archaeologist. You are nothing. The artifact is all you have. Bring it to life."

She held back. She refused to give him power over her.

The next morning, Ru woke to find blue-black bruises on her wrist, and she wondered whether she hadn't already given up what little power she had.

RU'S TEETH rattled in her head. Spots of white light burst in her vision. Lord D'Luc's fingers were tight on her throat, her skull throbbing. He pushed her toward the dungeon wall and slammed her against it.

"You will not fail me again," he said, his words cold like blades. Then he dropped her, and she crumpled.

But even then, as she gasped and sobbed, trying to soothe her own skin with chilled hands, something in the lord's gaze caught at her. A wildness that wasn't cruelty, but fear. A reckless desperation. As if he, too, were being pushed to his limit.

They were feral creatures in the dark, threatening and cajoling until one of them lost their nerve or drew first blood. But Ru refused to be the one to do it.

Lord D'Luc could be the villain if he wanted it so much.

RU STOOD at the table in the center of the dungeon, her palms pressed to cold wood on either side of the artifact. In the lamplight, its smooth black surface shone like a warning beacon. At least two dozen Children watched from the shadows. This silent audience had increased in number by the day. Their emotionless gazes seemed to bore into her skull, and even when she turned away, she could feel them watching.

She closed her eyes, willing herself not to show fear. Her throat still ached where Lord D'Luc's fingers had closed over it, her head still throbbing from its collision with the wall the day before.

Lord D'Luc, meanwhile, appeared angelic that morning. His white garments and golden hair almost seemed to glow, even in that dank room.

"Well," he said, venomous. "What are you waiting for?"

So Ru pretended, as she always did. She made faces, clenched her teeth, and curled her fingers into fists. But as ever, she did not speak to the artifact. She wouldn't risk reopening that connection. Even so, it was still quiet, distant to her, as if Fen had taken some part of it with him when he'd left. Sometimes, she missed it, that rush of strange energy that might soothe or encourage her, depending on the moment.

Ru caught the lord's gaze across the dungeon, and in it, she saw a reflection of her own growing rage. He circled her, a cat stalking prey, until he stood just behind her. His breath warmed her ear. "You are still not trying."

"I am."

"I see clearly that you're holding back." He spoke quietly, but Ru caught the warning in his words. "How will you cleanse the world if you can't even darken a room? Again."

So, again, she did her best to pretend. The artifact remained sullenly dormant.

He moved quickly then, so quickly that Ru had no time to react, to fight back. Hooking his hand under her chin, he pulled her back to his chest, pressing his palm against her throat and tilting her chin so far back that breathing took effort. His chest heaved behind her; she felt every rise and fall of his lungs, every twitch of muscle.

"You disappoint me, Delara," he crooned. "I thought perhaps, after yesterday's fiasco, and the disaster before that, you might give up on this farce you've been trying to sell me."

"Farce?" she gasped. She was becoming lightheaded, her breaths increasingly labored.

Not bothering to reply, he spun her so that she faced

him, meeting his chill gaze with defiance. Her instincts told her to lash out, to strike with fists and feet. But he was far too strong and far too fast. Again, he shoved her to the wall. His fingers tightened below her jaw — a dance she was beginning to memorize.

"Let me show you," he said, his face twisted into a mask of white-lipped rage, "what will happen each time you fail me."

With that, he released her, and she slid to the floor in a sad heap. She held her burning throat delicately, her fingers cold and her eyes hot with tears.

She watched as he strode across the dungeon, footsteps ringing in the silence. She watched as he drew a knife from within his frock coat, glinting in the lamplight; as he took one of the Children by the collar, drawing her away from the rest. Things happened too quickly after that, a blur of events.

There was a flash of steel, a spray of blood on white robes. Thick arterial blood came down in hot gouts from the woman's throat until she was splayed on the floor in a pool of red. And Ru, cowering on the other side of the room, watched Lord D'Luc clean the knife. Watched him put it away and wipe his hands on a dainty handkerchief.

He came to crouch before her then, his eyes level with hers. His gaze was not steady; he was untethered, feral, ready to break. "Every time you refuse from now on," he said, taking her chin in his elegant fingers, "someone will die."

"Kill them then," she croaked.

Lord D'Luc was a monster, but even the most depraved had their limit. She believed he had just reached his.

Wordless, he yanked her roughly to her feet, his hands under her armpits. Then he held her tightly against him as her body shook, her knees too weak to hold her up, and waited. As soon as she could stand on her own, instinctively pulling away from his disdainful embrace, he took her by the shoulders, spun her around, and steered her to the table at the center of the room. To the artifact. She was too weak to fight him, too shaken to break loose from his grip.

"I gave you a choice in the matter," he said, thumb and forefinger tight on her chin, his other hand forcing hers toward the artifact. "I don't relish needless death. But you *will* comply, Delara, and I—"

But his words cut off, replaced with a sharp intake of breath.

It wasn't Ru's fault. He had pushed her, forced her. She had no choice but to stretch out her hand and pick it up, to feel the cold stone against her skin. Her body shook violently, and tears streaked her face. The artifact lay heavy in her palm.

"Good," he said, relinquishing his grip on her.

"Make me do it again," she said, enraged, her voice a warning. As she spoke, dark rivulets of inky blackness seeped from the artifact. "You so desperately wanted a Destroyer of your very own, *Hugon*. And now you'll get one."

He said something, a bark in her ear. Ranto, hovering nearby, surged forward. But Ru heard nothing. All she knew was blood. Blood on the floor, pooling near her feet. Blood on white robes. The sharp tang of iron. And the blank expressions of the Children, whose colleague had been cut down before them.

She held the artifact aloft, a death offering. A spherical cloud of darkness flowed from it.

Yes, the artifact seemed to say, as if waking in triumph after a long nap. *Now I'm listening*. But where once the black stone had stoked a fiery rage in her, now it seemed to freeze her from within. Her cold hatred was amplified, encouraged, absorbed, and reflected twice over by the artifact.

And like swathes of deadly smoke, its darkness inched ever outward, toward herself and Lord D'Luc and his staring Children. As if she were white-hot, Hugon dropped his hands and moved away from her. Before Ranto could get to her she spun, putting the table between them, the artifact held out before her like a warning.

Lord D'Luc held out an arm to stop Ranto, and his gaze was wild, terrified, broken.

"Put it down, Delara," he breathed, chest heaving. A sheen of sweat broke out on his forehead.

Somewhere far-off, as if a voice were speaking to her through the haze of a dream, Ru's bewildered thoughts echoed in her mind: *This is my choice. The artifact obeys me. I'm the Destroyer.*

"Make me do it again," she repeated aloud, advancing on Hugon. Her voice splintered like shards of ice. Darkness spread outward from her like ripples in an umbral pool. "I dare you. Make me do it again, and I'll kill you. I don't care who else dies, D'Luc, as long as you're among them."

"Put her down," came Lord D'Luc's cold words, and the last thing Ru saw was Ranto, descending on her.

Ru later learned that she'd lost consciousness on her own. Ranto had not needed to touch her. According to Lyr's stilted explanation, with details he could only have learned from Lord D'Luc himself, Ru had been blind for an hour afterward, and a fever took her briefly. She was allowed to rest for three days, during which time she saw neither Hugon D'Luc nor any of the Children.

After that, Lord D'Luc no longer asked her to demonstrate, and their breakfasts resumed as normal.

CHAPTER 4

CHAPTER 4

In her dream, Ru was alone in a windswept crater of black earth. And in her hands, resting in upturned palms, was the artifact. Its smooth, black surface caught the moonlight and reflected it in rivulets of energy that swirled around her until she was engulfed by sweeps of light.

And then, out of the darkness, came Fen.

He was as she remembered him that day he'd found her in the Shattered City, alone, clutching the artifact. His eyes were clear and honest, black hair blown across a stubbled face, and his smile caught Ru by the heart.

In the dream, he kissed her, touched her with hot and roving hands, made her breath catch in her throat. He drove her almost mad, pushed her to the brink of desire with his lips on hers, on her neck, everywhere that elicited a gasp. Anywhere that made her want him.

And she *wanted* him. Desperately, longingly, body and soul. She was feverishly happy in that dark, windswept crater. She had Fen. He had her. And they held his heart between them…

Until he pulled away, slowly as a glacier. And the moment she was every bit under his control, would have done *anything* for him, she caught his gaze, and he was no longer there. In his place stood Taryel. His eyes were like onyx, the artifact reflected in his eyes until there were no whites; fully black and staring, his smile turned to ice.

"What do you want?" Taryel asked. It was the same every night.

And Ru always answered: "I want you to take Fen's cursed heart away from me. I want to *forget him.*"

Instead of indulging her, ridding her of the stone's incessant weight, the Destroyer smiled. He moved further and further away from her. "But it's yours," he said.

And then he left, and Ru woke in bed, drenched in sweat.

A heavy darkness still clung to the shadows of her room. Checking the clock over the mantle, she saw it was a little past two in the morning. Then she heard it — the sound that must have woken her, a light tapping at the door.

Apprehensive, Ru opened the door to find herself face-to-face with Lyr. He held out a rolled-up piece of parchment.

"Letter," he said.

Ru blinked, her eyes still bleary with sleep. "At two in the morning?"

Lyr shrugged.

She said, "It's addressed to you." She peered down at the paper, trying to make sense of things. The dream still weighed heavy on her mind.

"For you, though," said Lyr. "Look."

At last, Ru saw the small initials written in delicate black ink next to the palace's official seal: S.D. A rush of warm relief flooded her chest as she ushered Lyr inside, closing the door behind him. Simon had written, at last.

In the wake of her relief came dread. But why hadn't he written sooner? Something must be wrong. Something must have happened. The last time she had heard from her brother, he had written to caution her about the Children. She wished she had attended to his words earlier, somehow. She wished she had left the Cornelian Tower, escaped the clutches of Lord D'Luc, abandoned Fen before he could betray her.

"Well?" said Lyr, shifting his weight from one boot to another. "You going to read it?"

Ru glanced up at him, his kind eyes watching her face with obvious concern. She relaxed slightly. She was grateful for Lyr, his constant presence, an anchor of normality in her life. Unrolling the parchment, she read it quickly, heart in her throat.

Dearest sister,

I do hope your handsome guard Lyrren has brought this to you immediately.

I'll try to keep things brief. As you can see, I'm alive and well as of writing this. And I've a new patron, whose name shall remain unwritten for both our sakes. There's something not right about the woman — she's beautiful, naturally, but her charisma reaches far beyond the norm. And she's aware of you, Ru. If that wasn't unsettling enough, she knows more about you than she should.

There is something rotten afoot at the palace. I can't say more without compromising myself and, by extension, you, but a wretched web of influence stretches from Mirith to the court of Navenie.

I'm safe, which ought to be obvious, but I know how you worry. Just promise me that whatever you do, stay at the Tower. Keep Lyr close. Keep Horrid Hugon closer. And don't do anything to draw attention from the Regent. My worst fear is that you'll end up here at court, embroiled in the horrific mess I'm currently trying to navigate.

Burn this, by the way.

Your loving and devoted brother,

Simon

Lyr yanked the letter out of her fingers before she could stop him. He scanned it with a frown that deepened with every second until he crumpled the parchment in his fist. Pushing past Ru, he went to the fireplace and tossed the letter into the burning embers.

"Lyr!" she hissed.

The King's Guard faced her, looking stormier than she'd ever seen him. "He said burn it."

"What if I wanted to read it again?"

"I'll kill Lord D'Luc for you."

Ru snorted. "Sweet of you, but no."

"I'll do it," Lyr insisted, moving toward her, large hand on the pommel of his sword. "I don't know what's going on at the palace, but your brother knows more secrets than anyone in Navenie. We can end Lord D'Luc's influence right here and now. Let me take care of it."

"I *think* that might draw the Regent's attention," Ru said, moving to sit on her velvet settee.

The King's Guard was still frowning deeply. "The Tower is safe for you," he said, "as long as D'Luc decides it is. He finds out your brother is prying into his business, he's liable to explode, worse than he has already. Just like he wants that magic rock to do. I'll kill him. You'll escape to Solmaria. I'll get you a horse."

"IIf Regent Sigrun is caught up in this, I don't think running to Solmaria will exactly absolve me of Lord D'Luc's murder, nor will it solve any of the bigger dangers at hand." She smiled despite herself. "I've never heard you use so many words in sequence."

His heavy dark eyebrows lowered over a fervent gaze. In the firelight, Ru became — as she sometimes did — aware of just how young Lyr really was. In his late twenties, he wasn't much older than her brother, or Fen… who, she reminded herself, didn't exist.

"I don't waste words," he said.

"Which I appreciate. But don't kill Lord D'Luc. Yet." She forced a smile. "I'll be fine, I just need to think. I need Arch and Gwyn."

"I'll get them," said Lyr, and turned to go.

"Wait," said Ru, reaching out, her hand extended in the firelight. Their gazes met, and she felt in that moment that if she had asked for it, the taciturn guard would have embraced her. He would have given her the comfort she sorely needed, a body to cling to in the dark. He was her bodyguard, but he was also a friend, and a generous one.

"Be careful," was all she said.

Lyr only nodded, a quick jerk of the chin, and then he was gone.

~

MORNING BROKE OVER A DREARY SKY. Gwyneth lifted a porcelain cup to her lips, sipped, and spat out the brown liquid with a sputtering curse. "Cold!" she gasped. "What time is it?"

"Sunrise," said Archie, sipping his own cold tea and wrinkling his nose. "More tea?"

Ru was sprawled on the carpet, doodling mindless sketches of the artifact in the margins of a notebook. She glanced up, blinking. "Yes, if you're making it."

She turned back to her notebook. Lyr had brought Gwyneth and Archie to her room in the night, both wrapped in their dressing gowns, eyes wide with confusion and obvious fear. Ru told them about Simon's letter, explaining that she was in likely danger, though she wasn't certain about the manner of the threat. The three had talked for hours, conjecturing about the palace, the regent's involvement, and Simon's new mysterious patron.

Their only conclusion so far was that Ru was safer at the Tower than anywhere else, despite Lord D'Luc's presence.

"I thought he stopped demanding demonstrations out of fear," Ru had said, around half past four in the morning. "But… maybe it has to do with whatever's going on at the palace. He's waiting for something."

"I don't like the sound of that," Gwyneth added. Her usual cheerful demeanor had faded in place of tightness around the eyes, a faint line between her brows. Her blonde curls were in slight disarray, the ribbon holding them in place having slipped loose sometime in the night.

"Sounds as likely as anything," Archie said. Like Gwyneth, he was a picture of exhaustion. "Perhaps a breakthrough here, before whatever plans he's laid in the palace can come to fruition."

"Or the other way around," Ru said. She couldn't help but imagine Lord D'Luc like a spider in its lair, legs curled in anticipation.

Suppressing a shiver, Ru reread the notes she'd made in

her notebook. They were messy and read like the scrib-blings of a madwoman.

"The artifact responds to emotion," Ru said slowly. "Strong emotion."

"Yes, we know that," said Archie, from where he was setting up the teakettle over the fire.

"Before the demonstrations, Lord D'Luc was asking me about… love," Ru said.

"A bit too philosophical for my taste," Archie said. "I thought he planned to use the artifact as a weapon. Now he wants to bring love into the mix?"

"I think he's losing his mind a little," Ru said. "Or, more likely, he wants me to lose mine."

A sudden rap sounded on the door. Before any of them had a chance to respond, the door swung open.

"Ah, you're awake," said a strangely dull voice. "Come with me."

It was Professor Obralle.

CHAPTER 5

Ru, Gwyneth, and Archie followed Professor Obralle through the corridors in stunned silence. The academics shot glances at one another as they went, the professor walking ahead of them, looking as healthy as ever. Even her hair was fluffy and pink, as always, and had been styled to look like a pumpkin on top of her head.

But something was wrong with her. The usually bright-eyed and talkative professor was subdued, her pace steadier than it had once been. Her eyes were glazed. And though Ru tried to think of reasons that might be — the professor had been sick, she would be tired, she would be recovering — Ru knew this had been no normal illness. And she recognized that horrible, emotionless gaze. She recognized the single-minded stride, the unsettling determination.

Ru and her friends had been too shocked to question and had simply followed the professor with sleep-deprived awe. But now that the sun had begun its ascent, now that breakfast smells wafted up from the mess hall, they began to murmur questions at one another, shrugging and making faces.

They passed one or two early-rising academics, whose wide-eyed gazes caught Professor Obralle and then Ru, Gwyneth, and Archie, all dressed in their sleeping clothes. Ru wondered what new rumors would spread from this strange procession, what new ire might spring up.

"Where are we going?" Gwyneth asked as the small group turned and began down a wooden staircase.

"You're looking, uh… shockingly spry, Professor Obralle," Archie added. "Are you feeling all right?"

The professor did nothing to indicate that she had heard them and continued on.

Ru remained quiet, puzzling it out. She was so distracted, she hadn't noticed where they were going. Not until the dungeon door loomed large before her. That door led to a place heavy and shadowed inside her, to memories she wasn't ready to face head-on.

"Wait," Ru said, stopping in her tracks. Archie and Gwyneth nearly walked into her, skidding to a halt. Ru didn't want to admit to her fear, so she said, "Where are the other professors?"

Obralle halted and turned, too slowly. Her eyes were like glassy orbs, as if sharply focused on something far away. "They are well."

Archie, Gwyneth, and Ru all shared a long look. The voice that came from Obralle's body was her own, but the tone lacked expression.

"But… you've all been sick," Gwyneth said as if she could set things right by saying rational things.

Professor Obralle blinked. "Nonsense." She turned to continue down the hall, but Ru and the others stood their ground. Obralle stopped and turned, gazing over her shoulder. "Come," she said.

"We're not going *near* that dungeon," Archie said, every bit the affronted aristocrat. "You and the other professors have been ill, to the point of being bedridden, for almost two months. We thought you'd never recover. And now you're *here*, acting as if it's nothing? Taking us down to the dungeon, no less?"

"Don't be silly," Professor Obralle intoned. "Festra wills it. Come along."

"I'm sorry, *who* wills it?" Archie spluttered.

Gwyneth's eyes went as wide as twin moons, her fingers grasping Archie's sleeve and twisting. "Did you say…"

"Festra," Ru breathed, taking an involuntary step back.

That name, the professor's empty countenance, the dungeon door behind her…

Instinct took over then, a rush of adrenaline that spiked her senses and made her desperate to run, to go back to her room and lock the door. But she managed to stand her ground.

Archie moved to her side. "Lord D'Luc put an end to demonstrations," he said.

Obralle stared at them all, and the lack of emotion on her face was horrifying. Then her eyes found Ru, and for a moment, they sparked with something different, something old and dark and feral. Ru had seen that tenebrous glint in the Children's eyes before when she had first coaxed darkness from the artifact. When they had seen what destruction she might one day sow.

"Come now," said the professor.

Ru reached for someone, anyone, and found Gwyneth's hand. She squeezed it hard, trying to calm her speeding heart. She thought inexorably of Fen, how he had always been able to calm her, to center her mind, to bring her back from the brink of panic.

As if hearing Ru properly for the first time in nearly two months, more readily and eagerly than even during the last demonstration, the artifact's presence roared forth inside her.

Gwyneth turned sharply at Ru's intake of breath, Ru's fingers tightening around Gwyneth's. "She can't go down there," Gwyneth said, almost pleading. "Please, Professor. The last demonstration… there's a reason Lord D'Luc put a stop to them."

Obralle only stared. "She must continue. For Festra."

Hardly registering Obralle's words, Ru gripped Gwyneth's hand as if it were the only thing tethering her to reality: Gwyneth's delicate bones, the heat of her palm, her skin against Ru's.

But Ru's mind kept faltering, veering away from the present moment. The artifact's voice, so sudden in its reemergence, was strangely *angry*. It felt like a pulse of vibrant energy against the film of her mind until her head was reeling with it. She had lost control of her breathing. Her thoughts were falling apart, fracturing.

Ru had always imagined that the artifact was tethered to her by an invisible thread, and in her mind's eye, she saw the thread go taut. As it did, her vision burst in black and gold and flashes of white. There was no comfort here, no reassuring presence as the stone had once been to her. There was only a reflection of her own terror and rage, unbridled with nowhere to go.

She squeezed her eyes closed for a moment, then opened them, trying to ground herself.

There stood Gwyneth, holding Ru still in a maelstrom of pain. There stood Archie, his form blurring into the background of Ru's terror. And Lyr, a solid presence that was fading fast… and finally, Obralle.

The professor's eyes were specks of unwavering night.

"I can't," Ru said. Her hands shook, her lungs were full to bursting. Dizziness swept across her senses. "Gwyn."

"She's *losing it*," Ru heard Archie say from far away.

Her friends' voices came to her as if from a great distance, fading in and out.

"Fen used to—"

"Don't mention *him*. Dolt."

"…taking her back to her room."

"D'Luc said… waiting…"

"What the hell is going on?"

That demanding voice cut through to Ru like a slap to the face. Lord D'Luc.

"I brought her here," said Professor Obralle. "Please forgive—"

"You're not supposed to be here," said Lord D'Luc, and Ru saw him moving toward the professor as her vision focused and blurred and refocused. He was dressed in white, golden hair haloing a savior's face.

"But," said Obralle, "My lady sent me to—"

"Never mind that," Lord D'Luc snapped. "Here's a new order. Go back to your room."

"Yes, Your Grace."

There was a strained silence as Obralle departed. Ru's

breathing began to steady as the professor disappeared from view.

Gwyneth's fingers were still curled around hers in a death grip. "Don't make her do another demonstration," said Gwyneth.

"I had no intention of it," replied the lord, an edge to his voice. "Delara, look at me."

Ru looked away, unable to meet his gaze. The artifact's rage was subsiding with hers, and along with it, the uncontrolled terror. But he was not the comfort she needed.

"*Delara.*"

At last, she turned to face him, and his hard blue gaze swept over her. Almost as if he were worried. As if he cared.

"Excuse me, sorry to interrupt, Your *Grace*," Archie's words were sharp as glass, the color high in his freckled cheeks, "but what the devil are you playing at?"

Hugon glanced at Archie. "Professor Obralle was confused. She and the others have only just begun to recover from their ailment. A brain fever." He turned back to Ru. "A miscommunication, perhaps."

"A brain fever?" Gwyneth echoed, eyes wide with anger and shock. "*Miscommunication?*"

Archie, too, was heaving with incredulity. "The professors have recovered? Just like that?"

"Just like that," said Lord D'Luc, smiling without mirth. "Now, if you'll excuse me, we're late for breakfast. Delara, shall we?"

Gwyneth opened her mouth to speak, but Ru held up a hand to stop her. She was tired of it. Tired of her friends feeling the need to protect her, to speak for her, tired of being a constant burden to them. She was a grown woman, wasn't she? An archaeologist, an academic, and so many other things that were not this unrelenting fear.

"Yes, we shall," Ru said. "Gwyn, Arch..." She gave each of them a hard stare, trying to show that she meant what she said, that Lord D'Luc didn't fully have her in his clutches. She hoped they understood that he never would. "I'll be fine."

"Of course you will," said Lord D'Luc, and she took his

elbow with cold fingers.

They left Archie and Gwyneth standing in the corridor together, watching Ru with such dire expressions she might as well have been lying in a coffin.

~

"I'D PREFER IT IF, in the future, you refrain from wearing a dressing gown to breakfast." Lord D'Luc's tone was light, but his pretty mouth curled in distaste as he spoke, pouring himself a steaming cup of coffee.

Ru sat across from him at the small table laden with breakfast food, bouquets of fresh autumn flowers, and a large jug of coffee. They were in Lord D'Luc's private apartments, a suite of rooms reserved for visiting royalty or dignitaries that he had taken as his own. Tall rectangular windows let in the morning sun behind her, warming her back and illuminating Hugon in a way she was sure he had intended — he glowed in his white silks, rings glinting on elegant hands, hair framing his ethereal face.

She ignored the comment.

"Tell me," he said, one finger circling the rim of his coffee cup, "what were Hill and Tenoria doing with you in the corridor this morning? Having a slumber party, were you?"

Ru stared at her eggs, fighting a wave of nausea as the smell of all that food, hot and waiting, overwhelmed her. "We weren't plotting to kill you, if that's what you were worried about."

He laughed. "So waspish when you haven't slept."

"Tell me what you did to Professor Obralle." She couldn't stop herself. The words had been hovering at the edge of her lips since she'd taken his arm, since two Children had laid out breakfast, since the lord had pulled Ru's chair out for her and poured her coffee.

"Was I not clear downstairs?" His finger froze in its circular journey around the cup's rim.

She caught his gaze and held it despite the rotting ache that sprung in her belly, despite the fear that coated her tongue when his full attention was on her. "Let's stop lying to each other, Hugon."

He grinned slowly. "I am the picture of honesty, Delara. You're the intellectual between us. Theorize for me."

Ru sighed. There was no fighting him; there never had been. "It's obvious you made the professors sick somehow. I'd thought you poisoned them to get them out of the way while you established control here at the Tower, maybe a wasting disease, but… your aim was never to kill them."

He sat back, pulling at his neckcloth to loosen it. "Go on."

"That wasn't the plan at all," Ru said, frowning slightly as she spoke, her thoughts spinning faster than her tongue could accommodate. "You didn't make the professors sick… you altered them. Professor Obralle wasn't herself. She was distant, glassy-eyed, and empty." *Like Inda,* thought Ru. *Like Nell and Ranto, devoid of humanity.* "The poison wasn't a delaying tactic at all," she continued. "You've made the professors into Children. You've weaponized them."

"You know I love it when you remind me just how clever you are, Delara." His voice was low, his eyelids heavy over shining eyes. A flash of tongue appeared at his teeth, and then he tapped his fingers on the table. "And then? Don't keep me in suspense."

Schooling her features into practiced neutrality, Ru shrugged. As if this conversation were nothing to her, a whim, a simple entertainment. "And then I suppose you'll have the professors sign the Cornelian Tower over to you permanently, enabling you to conduct your deadly experiments within its walls. No doubt the palace is already undergoing a similar transformation."

Her words didn't falter. But inside, Ru was gasping at this uttered revelation, holding back a new wave of horror. Simon was at the palace. His *letter…* She was used to hopelessness, used to self-hatred. But she much preferred it to the fear of what might happen to her brother.

"Are the professors… alive?" she asked, knowing how the question sounded. There was no such thing as the *undead.*

"Of course they are."

"But their minds are gone."

"Astute," said Lord D'Luc, still watching her with a subtle hunger. "Minds are pliable things. Easily redirected."

Ru grit her teeth until it hurt. "You didn't have to go that far. You could have just…"

"What, would you rather I… how did you put it? Drive needles under their fingernails?"

She was momentarily lost for words.

"I thought not," he said, leaning back in his chair.

"Their minds," Ru said, choosing her words carefully, "are they… repairable?"

He raised a brow. "I'm not sure what you mean. If you're asking whether you, personally, could perform some kind of brain surgery—"

"You *know* what I mean."

Lord D'Luc did her the honor of looking slightly shocked. "There's no need for that kind of tone. I've plenty of needles at my disposal. No. They are not… repairable, as you put it. Whatever delicate change has taken place in the professors' weak minds, it is decidedly permanent."

"And the Children?"

His mouth quirked as if he found this exchange amusing. "The same."

"You're unforgivable," Ru said, her voice shaking.

A shadow passed over the lord's face, and for a moment, it was as if his gaze were a thousand miles away.

"Perhaps," he said, in a raw voice that Ru had never heard from him before. And then he smiled, his expression shifting into an unreadable mask. "But I wish you'd give up on this self-righteous streak of yours, Delara. It serves no one. The professors are mine, as is the Cornelian Tower, and no amount of stubbornness from you will remedy that. Haven't you conducted experiments and drawn the inevitable conclusion? It's time to stop fighting me. You and I would be so much stronger together."

"I'm afraid I'm not as eager as you are to reduce the kingdom to ash," said Ru.

Lord D'Luc laughed. "Answer a question for me, if you will. How do you differ from Festra?"

The question caught her off guard. "He's a fictional god, for one."

"Humor me for a moment and assume that he's not. Assume that, like magic, spiritual figures exist in a very real, documented way. How does Ruellian Delara differentiate herself from this deity she so reviles?" He tapped his chin with a finger, playing at thoughtfulness, a cruel glint in his eye.

Ru knew where he was going with this. "I'm well aware of what I did. That doesn't make me a vengeful god."

"In a thousand years," Lord D'Luc said, low and crooning, "they will write about Ruellian Delara and her artifact. How she engulfed the Shattered City in darkness for a second time and miraculously survived. What would one call such a woman?"

Ru said nothing; her mouth tasted of blood where she clenched her teeth, gnawing flesh.

"A witch, maybe. A sorceress, a madwoman. But they are just as likely to label you a vengeful goddess." He watched Ru with keen, thoughtful eyes. "Is that not what you want? Secretly, desperately? Why else would you seek the stone and carry it with you? Why else would you study it? I see a hunger in you, Delara. I've seen it since the moment I met you. Why deny it? I can help you."

A deep, unwanted sorrow clawed at Ru. He voiced, so painfully, a fear that she tried hard not to face — that her own desire for knowledge, some unconscious need for scientific fame or even notoriety, had driven her to touch the artifact. Even as she tried to push away the thought, the artifact smoldered a distant but tender touch against her mind.

"You may be shocked to learn that I have no designs on becoming a deity."

Lord D'Luc actually laughed, a short bark of surprised mirth. "Now that you mention it, I wonder if we shouldn't alter the trajectory of our little experiments. As much as I adore our talks, we draw no closer to your being able to control the artifact. To *use* it in any meaningful way. The stone is your tool, not the other way around. I fear the route of scientific progress has dried up for both of us. So why not look to something else for motivation? Your desire for power, the dark desires you vehemently deny?"

"The method is irrelevant," Ru said, ignoring this last jab. He had already hurt her where it counted. "As much as you want me to re-enact the Destruction, I won't. Good luck with all of this, though." She waved her hands to indicate herself, the breakfast laid out before her.

A muscle feathered in the lord's jaw. "It's no use defying me. In the end, with or without your acquiescence, you will use the artifact to bring about the dawn of a new era. You will use it as it was meant to be used, and cleanse this world in fire. Whether you accept it or not, this is your destiny. Festra's will is your destiny."

"Did you ever once believe that the artifact could bring about a scientific breakthrough?" Ru asked, almost in resignation. "Or was that for my benefit?"

"Draw whatever conclusions you like," he said, leaning forward with a gorgeous, icy smile. "My only goal is to see you master the artifact and unleash its power. My personal beliefs are immaterial. Anyway, you ought to thank me. I have a surprise for you."

Ru went cold. A surprise from Lord D'Luc couldn't be anything good. "Lucky me," she said.

His smile widened. "Aren't you going to ask what it is?"

"No."

A flicker of impatience crossed his face. "Then I won't keep you in suspense. Tomorrow, we set out for Mirith. Regent Sigrun is deeply invested in your progress with the artifact and believes that you may find it easier to progress toward our shared goal at the palace. I look forward to seeing what we accomplish there."

Ru's blood turned to ice. So the palace truly belonged to Lord D'Luc. Regent Sigrun was under his power, probably rendered helpless in the same manner as the professors. Neither Simon nor any of her friends at the palace were safe. Ru knew in that moment that no matter where she went, the artifact would hold her in its stony grip. And as long as the artifact was hers, Lord D'Luc would not stop hunting her.

CHAPTER 6

Lyr found Ru on the Tower parapet that night. She hadn't been able to sleep, plagued by thoughts of her loved ones hurting, dying. Unable to rid herself of the sensation that she was falling unendingly into a pit of emptiness. And the only thing that awaited her at the bottom was her due punishment.

An evening rain was already beginning to frost on the parapet's stone walls. She stood in wet slippers, her dressing gown — which she had been wearing since the night before — and a blanket wrapped haphazardly about her shoulders.

She wondered what it might feel like to fall from that height, the wind in her hair and icy on her skin. Whether it would be freeing, the knowledge that this would finally sever her connection to the artifact. Whether it would satisfy her, knowing that she had cheated Lord D'Luc from his plans, his kingdom-wide destruction. And whether she might, at last, feel some infinitesimal measure of absolution.

"If you're thinking about jumping," Lyr said, "don't."

"I wasn't." The artifact was silent again, and she felt more at peace on the verge of self-destruction than she did at any other time. She said nothing, continuing to stare out over the shadowy courtyard at the moonlit road beyond that would lead her to Mirith in the morning.

"You'll need rest before the journey," said Lyr sensibly.

"I can't sleep."

"'Course not."

They stood together in companionable silence for a while, Lyr in full King's Guard regalia of leathers and steel plate, and Ru in her dressing gown and blanket.

"I won't let them harm you," he said eventually.

"I know you won't," said Ru, conciliatory, and a rush of memory made her breath catch painfully in her throat. The last demonstration, Lord D'Luc's quick strides across the dungeon, the flash of a blade…

"Whatever you're thinking about," said Lyr, frowning so deeply his eyes were nearly consumed by his heavy brows, "stop."

Ru finally met his gaze. "I should have died at the Shattered City," she said. "All of this… the Tower falling into Lord D'Luc's hands, the Children, Festra… it's all because of me. Because I found the artifact."

"You didn't, though."

"I *touched* it. I'm the one who woke it up, who set it off." *I should have known better.*

"You know that for a fact?"

She paused, pulling the blanket tighter around her shoulders. "Yes," she said at last. "What else could it have been? I was called to it, Lyr. Just as Fe— *Taryel* was called there. His heart wanted us to meet. It wanted *me* for some cursed, incomprehensible reason."

The King's Guard shrugged. "Just saying… I thought your studies hadn't come up with a conclusive answer one way or another."

"He *told* me," Ru insisted.

"Sounded like he was just as in the dark as you. I saw him reading all those books this summer. Wondered what he was so interested in that he wouldn't share with you, assumed he had reasons, but… he was looking for explanations."

"I know that," said Ru, shivering, her toes aching with cold. "But even then, he suspected something was… *between* us. He knew we were connected. And when he told me…" she shook her head. "I knew it, too. I don't just believe him. I know it for a fact. Because I can feel it, Lyr, right now, the tendon of magic that ties me to Taryel. And sometimes I wonder if it isn't the artifact speaking to me at all, but…" She winced as her teeth unconsciously found the inside of her lip.

"Taryel talking back," Lyr finished, nodding sagely.

Ru stared up at him. The smile he gave her in return was wan, almost sad.

"I'll meet you inside," she said quietly, turning back to the sleet-lashed view beyond the battlement. "I want to be alone."

Lyr left her, half-frozen on the parapet, gazing out once again to the south.

She had once believed in fate, in the hands of an unknowable universe gently guiding souls toward one another in an inescapable dance. *Festra's will is your destiny.* But neither Festra nor Taryel were part of her fate. She was Ruellian Delara, and what happened to her was up to her, and her alone.

She may be cursed by Taryel's heart, and Hugon D'Luc may have her wrapped around his finger. And maybe none of it made sense to her now, and perhaps she would never understand why Taryel had come to her as Fen, why the artifact had been uncovered, *why* it had called to her…

But she would not let it destroy her.

Leaning forward on frozen tip-toes, Ru braced her hands against the wall and leaned out until her chest was pressed against the frosted stone. She could so easily climb up, brace her feet against the stone, lift herself up to balance on the edge…

She could so easily fall.

A moment later, she was scrambling, her slippers fighting for purchase on the low wall, lifting herself by the arms. At last, she crouched atop the stone wall. The wind was stronger in her hair up here. The blanket, loosened by her climb, threatened to blow away altogether.

Ru remembered so clearly, as she often did, the words shared between herself and Fen that night at the Shattered City. Words that remained between them, cradled in blackened hands.

I am your punishment. In learning who I am, you've met yourself.

Ru had been used, she had been hurt, and she was now a faint vestige of the woman she had once been. She might have been able to fight harder, to rebel against Lord D'Luc more effectively, but her cruel conscience told her this was what she deserved. That she had earned this. She had murdered innocents, and no one had done a thing about it.

This is hell, Fen had said. *I've been here all along.*

And now Fen was gone. Only Taryel remained.

Far below Ru lay the flagstones of the courtyard, a long enough drop that there would be no hope of survival. She would die instantly if she fell, her organs ruptured, her skull crushed on impact. She was comforted by the thought.

Lyr had asked her not to, but surely he wouldn't miss babysitting her. He would be fine. Gwyneth and Archie would be better off. They had each other. Ru had no one. No one who understood.

Hot, bitter tears stung her cheeks. And with them came the memory, the one she tried so hard to forget. The last demonstration, blood on the floor. That woman, that nameless woman in a white robe... she was dead because of Ru. One of too many lives cut short because of the Destroyer.

But Lord D'Luc still lived. And tomorrow, they would leave for Mirith, for the palace, and Ru would be at the mercy of whatever horrors awaited. She wasn't afraid for herself anymore; she could not suffer enough to fulfill her penance. Instead, she feared what she might do. Who else might die. But if she were to go, if she were to gently press her own heart until it stopped, would it make up for the people who were already gone?

Leaning forward, Ru felt gravity and the wind doing their best to dislodge her from the wall. Her foot slipped, and she lost her balance, breath fleeing from her lungs as she hovered between safety and a long drop. All she would have to do is surrender; lean just a little forward, and—

All at once, a warmth bloomed in her chest. A distant,

thrumming flame. And with it came a gentle caress at the edge of her mind, from the base of her skull — the artifact.

Talkative today, she thought bitterly. But its warmth grounded her, and she leaned back, steadying herself enough to slide down from the wall until her feet landed on firm stone. She leaned back against the wall, breathing hard.

The artifact flared inside her, its heat billowing outward until her body was no longer frigid and numb. It was almost as if the artifact had known what she was contemplating, what she'd been in danger of doing. But whether the stone was acting out of some involuntary mechanism, a reaction that might only occur when she was in certain danger, or whether it — or *someone* — had known, and wanted her safe… there was no way to tell.

Whatever the method, resolve hardened in Ru. Her death solved nothing. She thought of Archie and Gwyneth, who did not deserve the grief her absence would have inflicted. And Lyr, who would have felt responsible.

Holding the blanket firm around her shoulders, Ru returned to the warmth of the Tower and Lyr's dour gaze. As always, the artifact's comforting touch was her only companion as she rolled into bed.

CHAPTER 7

The journey to Mirith would take days. Lord D'Luc, it seemed, had been planning this journey for quite some time. There was no way he could have pulled together such a convoy at the last minute, even though he had sprung the move on Ru only the day before. Three carriages were being prepared, a stream of silent Children moving between them and the Tower, packing trunks and food and blankets for the journey.

Ru watched the preparations from her bedroom window. She was fully dressed and packed but reluctant to make any further moves. What felt like a pile of rocks sat heavy in her gut. Nothing good awaited her in Mirith.

Someone knocked on her door. She could tell from the two heavy thumps in quick succession that it was Lyr. It was time to go. She slung her pack over her shoulder and opened the door.

"Morning," said Lyr. There were heavy shadows under his eyes, a weariness about him that she hadn't seen before.

"Is something wrong?" Ru asked, walking alongside him as they made their way downstairs. "Other than the fact that I'm about to be carted to the palace in a convoy like some prisoner of war."

Lyr shook his head slightly, not rising to the joke. "You're not traveling alone."

She frowned, glancing up at the King's Guard. "I would think not. Lord D'Luc and the Children…"

He shook his head again, more aggressively. "You'll see."

With deepening unease, Ru remained close to Lyr until they were outside in the clear dawn. A thin frost coated the courtyard, limning everything in a hazy glow. Ru usually loved winter at the Tower. It often snowed, and she loved to go out in the early morning before the powder was marred, before it had begun to melt. When it was just her and the muffled crunch of white under her boots. She savored the comfort of dashing back inside and sipping a hot drink by the fire while her boots dried.

There was something deeply comforting about the Tower when the nights were long and the fires were all lit. Some of her favorite memories were quiet moments, winter evenings, hot meals, and courtyards raucous with academics all bundled in their scarves and mittens.

She wondered if she would ever live one of those moments again, or if they would remain forever like that — as memories.

White robes and inexpressive eyes rushed past her in a blur as Children passed, carrying boxes and trunks to the carriages. Lord D'Luc stood at the first carriage, conversing with Inda and Ranto. The Children were as nondescript and grayscale as Lord D'Luc was vibrant and bright.

"Ah, very good," the lord said, seeing Ru approach. "You're both just in time."

Lyr grunted.

"What do you mean, both?" Ru asked.

Lord D'Luc raised an elegant eyebrow. "Didn't he say? Lyrren Briar will be accompanying us on the journey. Wouldn't want you wandering off and getting lost, now, would we?"

Ru should have guessed that Lord D'Luc wouldn't let her leave the Tower without his spy in tow. She bit back a smile. She had thought she would be spending the journey alone with Lord D'Luc and the Children, a torture in itself.

While Ru tried not to seem relieved by Lyr's accompaniment, Lord D'Luc turned to greet someone who had just come out of the Tower. "Ah," he said, eyes shining.

Ru knew that look. A serpentine, self-satisfied expression. She spun, heart in her throat. Archie and Gwyneth were coming down the steps toward them, packs slung over their backs. They were dressed for travel. Gwyneth's face was white as snow, her trepidation palpable. Archie, on the other hand, looked as if he was on his way to a particularly fascinating dig site.

"Good morning, Tenoria. Hill." Lord D'Luc ushered Gwyneth and Archie over to where Ru stood, still frozen to the spot. "Delara," he said as if he were bestowing a great gift upon her, "I've arranged for your friends to accompany you to Mirith. Won't that be *delightful*."

Ru ought to have felt relief at the sight of her friends. Happiness in the knowledge that she wouldn't be alone, that her journey to the palace, her time there, would not be in complete isolation. But all she felt was sick.

"I imagine Delara will find herself far more productive," the lord said, emphasizing the last word with a curl of his lip, "if her peers are nearby to keep her accountable. Wouldn't you say, Inda?"

Inda, dead-eyed and pale, watched the group with the usual lack of expression. "She must be kept accountable," she intoned.

Ru wanted to take her friends and run, to dash into the woods and hide, never to be found again. They had packs, they had clothes. They could hunt out there in the wilds, live off the land. After all, Fen had.

But it was a false hope. One day in the wilderness, especially with winter on the way, would find them dead or dying, and she knew it. Lord D'Luc knew it. And he also knew, perhaps more than anyone, that there was only one thing in the world that he could use to keep Ru in line, to do exactly as she asked, no matter how it might break Ru.

Gwyneth and Archie were not here as companions or as colleagues. They were hostages.

Ru, Gwyneth, and Archie were allowed to ride in a carriage together, though not entirely free from the watching eyes of the Children, who rode alongside and would intermittently peer into the carriage with staring gazes. Lyr rode on horseback, the glint of his armor and jangle of his horse's reins drifting in through the window, and Ru was glad of his presence. Lord D'Luc rode on a white horse ahead of the procession with Inda, Ranto, and Nell trailing behind on their own horses, while two more carriages laden with luggage and supplies took up the rear.

The frost had begun to melt slowly as the morning wore on, and muted sunlight glanced off the landscape as if it were made of glass.

"Isn't this an amusing jaunt," Archie said, breaking the carriage's uneasy silence not long into the journey. "Just what we all needed, a holiday to the court of Navenie."

"It's not funny," Gwyneth said. She was curved inward on herself as if for protection, her brown eyes even larger than usual, her features wan.

"Was I laughing?" Archie said.

Ru's attention, as it often did, wandered to the artifact. She felt it near, a telltale palpation against her thoughts, and knew it was with Lord D'Luc. He had confirmed its location when his hand darted inside his coat outside the Tower, as if silently noting its presence. Ru would not act on the vague impulse to pickpocket; she didn't have the skill, for one thing. And she found that she was relieved to be near it, to know that wherever the cursed stone went, she went too.

But the relief caught at her bitterly, an emotion she wished she could cleanse from herself. She hated that the artifact still held her like this, as if she were a bird with clipped wings, unable to fly even if she tried. Even if she wanted to.

"Simon won't be happy," Ru said, almost to herself. A mist grew in the air as they rode south, distant trees fading in and out of view as they went.

"And neither am I," Archie said, indignant. "He warned you to stay at the Tower no matter the cost, and here we are, trundling away from it at a nice clip."

"Why now?" Gwyneth said, hugging a tasseled cushion to her chest. "If the regent wants you at the palace, why not summon you sooner?"

Ru shrugged. "Ask me to interpret the will of Festra and I'll give you the same answer: Hell if I know."

Archie made a disgusted face. "Always with this Festra fellow. I was hoping that religious rubbish was a smoke-screen for some secretive and highly volatile scientific the-ory, but I've been proven wrong for what seems to be the first time in my life. *Being held in thrall by a religious cult* wasn't exactly on my list of things likely to happen this year, but everyone's fallible, I suppose, even me."

"You're not being held in *thrall*," Gwyneth said with ob-vious exasperation. "If anyone's in thrall it's Regent Sigrun, don't you think?"

"Lord D'Luc didn't poison the professors," Ru said, re-alizing she hadn't told her friends about her breakfast with Lord D'Luc the previous morning. "I mean, he *did*, but making them sick wasn't the goal. It was to… *change* them. He altered their minds, made them pliant, empty. Like the Children. He might have done the same to the regent."

Archie and Gwyneth shared a look.

"Good god," Archie said at last, running a hand through his caramel-colored hair. "I knew something was up, the way Obralle was behaving, but…"

Gwyneth's eyes shone with restrained tears. "Why would he do something like that?"

Ru shrugged. "To ensure his power. The professors will do whatever he wants, sign whatever documents. The Tower won't be a problem for him. And it *would* have been, had the professors been left alone. They would have made him stop the demonstrations, sent him back to Mirith. But now… he has free rein over the artifact. And me."

Archie nodded, his lips pursed in thought. "Of course the Children aren't actual devotees of Festra, the most ob-scure deity possible. They're slaves of the mind. How does one accomplish *that*?"

"I don't know," said Ru, twisting her fingers together in her lap, "but we need to find out. There must be a way to stop it from happening to more innocent people."

"Good luck to us," Gwyneth muttered. "We'll be nothing more than glorified prisoners in the palace. And who knows what Lord D'Luc means to do once we're there."

Ru stared out of the window, watching as the mist began to evaporate and pale sunlight lanced through it, burning away the cold wet. "Maybe it's not so bad," she said to herself, though she knew her friends were listening. "We couldn't find answers at the Tower. Something tells me we'll find them at the palace."

"I should damn well hope so," said Archie.

"And Simon," Gwyneth added, "he'll have more information, I'm sure."

"Yes," said Ru, distracted. Simon. She knew her brother. "He'll get us the answers we need, or presumably die trying."

"Let's not talk about dying," Gwyneth said, leaning forward to lay a warm hand on Ru's knee. "You have us. We'll sort this out. We'll be fine."

Ru turned to her, suddenly unable to contain herself, as much as she tried to remain calm. "Will we, Gwyn? You and Arch, maybe, if I stay in line. But I'm... *I* am already not fine. I went to the parapet last night, in the cold. I sent Lyr away. I climbed on top of the wall."

Gwyneth's eyes widened, and she reached for Archie's hand, but neither she nor Archie spoke.

Ru was grateful for it. She knew unwanted tears were forming in her eyes, just as the familiar stricture of shame and panic began to tighten about her heart. "I didn't... I wasn't planning to do anything, but I wondered what it might be like. To fall, to put an end to all of this. To make things right again, for all of you. And — no, don't say anything — I felt the artifact. Stronger, like it used to be when Fen was here."

"Fen," breathed Gwyneth. "Do you think he's here? Has he come back?"

"Fe— I mean *Taryel*," Ru said, the name still so painful on her tongue, "could be clinging upside down to the bottom of this carriage for all I care. I'm more worried about what it means if Lord D'Luc wants more demonstrations in Mirith."

Instead of immediately reassuring her as they were so

good at doing, Ru's friends sat in tense silence. They understood what it meant if the artifact was communicating with Ru again, if its influence on her thoughts and actions was returning. It meant that if Lord D'Luc pushed her again, if she fell into a rage like she had last time, none of them were safe.

~

THAT EVENING, they made camp at an old way station not far off the main road. There was a stream for the horses to drink from and posts on which to tie them up. The ground was relatively even and thick with grass, though the ravages of early frost had turned it brown. A circle of stones marked the fire pit, and logs were arranged around it for sitting.

Night was falling quickly. Inda, Ranto, and Nell began gathering wood for a fire while Lyr tended to the horses. Ru and her friends waited in the carriage, enveloped in blankets, until a fire was roaring between the stones.

Dinner consisted of meat pies, loaves of brown bread, and apple turnovers heated over the flames. Ru wasn't particularly hungry. She couldn't shake the mild nausea that seemed her constant companion now, an endless onslaught of dread. And when Lord D'Luc caught her eye across the flames, her stomach twisted.

"You will flourish at the palace, Delara," the lord said, his voice ringing clear in the strained silence. "The artifact's ultimate potential, its true power, will soon be unlocked."

As he said it, their gazes still locked across the fire, Ru felt distinctly that he was putting on a show for the benefit of the Children and her friends. She was far past succumbing to his ridiculous rhetoric.

Archie and Gwyneth remained quiet, eating their dinner and shooting Ru furtive looks. Ru only stared back at the lord, his sharp eyes still fixed on her. She said, "What do you expect me to do there? What do you think will be accomplished in Mirith that can't be done at the Tower?"

His mouth curved upward slightly. "You will have

much-needed structure. There will be oversight. And when you at last harness the artifact's power in full, you will be revered."

"By who, exactly?" Archie said, mouth half-full of pork pie.

Lord D'Luc's gaze darted to Archie. "Everyone."

"Their ghosts, maybe," Ru said. "Don't pretend the artifact is anything but a weapon to you. That *I* am anything but a weapon."

The lord's expression softened then. In a strangely distant voice, as if speaking to someone who wasn't there, he said, "Weapons come in many forms."

There was nothing more to say after that.

The Children, ever docile with piercing gazes, finished their dinners in silence. Ru picked at her food, stared into the fire, and tried to ignore the artifact's increasing chatter.

Its voice had grown louder as they traveled, and now it had come to a near fever pitch in its insistence. It pulsed against her thoughts, a warmth in her chest, and that unavailable flutter in her consciousness. *Look at me*, it seemed to say. *Remember me, I'm here.*

She tried to ignore the feel of it, the way it reminded her of Fen's hand in hers. She wished the stone would disappear. She wished it would consume her.

"Aren't you hungry?"

The question came from Gwyneth, who sat pressed as close to Ru as she could manage to stave away the night's cold. Even that close to the fire, the chill was inescapable.

"Not really," Ru replied, the thought of eating an entire pie turning her stomach.

"You'll be fine," said Gwyneth, putting her arm around Ru. "Arch and I will be with you the whole way. We'll figure it out. We'll make it right."

"Thank you, Gwyn," Ru said, and she meant it. She knew that Gwyneth's words were platitudes, meaningless in the dark. But she was relieved to be with her friends, even if their presence was just another means of controlling her.

Archie, on the other side of Gwyneth, leaned over and nodded in agreement. "If we die, at least we die together."

Gwyneth made a sound of exasperation. "What did I say about *dying*?"

"I'll try not to, but no promises," said Archie, taking a bite of turnover and immediately spitting it out. "That's *boiling*, good lord."

"Well, you did hold it over the fire for about five times longer than needed," Gwyneth said.

Ru smiled despite herself. "I'm glad you're both here."

Bedrolls were brought out after dinner and arranged around the fire. Lyr insisted on setting up his bed next to Ru, in case, in his words, "Anything comes wandering out of the woods and tries to eat you."

Lord D'Luc sat awake by the fire, facing the road, his hair shining almost orange in the firelight. His head rested on folded hands, elbows braced on his knees. Ru wondered what he was thinking about, whether it was the artifact, or even Ru herself. She wondered if he understood the concept of empathy. If he ever felt remorse.

She supposed, slipping into a restless sleep, that it made no difference either way.

∼

Ru woke in the night, heart pounding. Something wasn't right.

She reached instinctively for Lyr's form in the dark and found that he was gone, his bedroll empty. The sky was black and thick with stars, and the moon had set. Morning was hours away. Breathing hard, Ru listened. She didn't know what had woken her, whether it was a sound or a dream or something else.

She heard only the rustle of trees in night breezes, the soft breaths of Gwyneth and Archie in their bedrolls. Twisting around, she saw that the carriages were all there. The horses stood undisturbed at the edge of camp, and the bedrolls around the fire all appeared to be occupied, including Lord D'Luc's.

Lyr was nowhere to be seen.

And something wasn't right. Something was...

She squeezed her eyes shut at a sudden pain behind her

eyes, an ache, a pull. The artifact, calling her with precision.

Come to me.

Now wide awake, Ru crawled out of her bedroll, pulled on her boots and overcoat, and went into the forest.

CHAPTER 8

Ru's teeth chattered. She ignored the chill seeping into her bones as she pushed through cold, wet undergrowth, pine needles and dead leaves crackling under her feet. It was easy to find her way — she only had to let the artifact lead her.

Its call was clear and relentless. As if a burning thread were attached to her mind and the artifact pulled at the other end, urging her deeper into the forest. She knew it was incredibly foolish to follow the call, but to resist would be painful. Even as she pushed her way through the freezing wet, the ache behind her eyes lessened. She had felt the same pull on the day she first saw the artifact, on her way to the dig site at the Shattered City.

She could not refuse it then, and though she wanted to, though she *knew* better, she could not refuse it now.

And part of her was desperately curious to see where it led her. Would it be a living nightmare or a slow and gruesome death? She wasn't moving toward the artifact itself; she couldn't be. It was still with Lord D'Luc, safely in his pocket by the fire.

A vague thought fought its way to the forefront of her mind, her own logic — where was Lyr? Was he safe?

The thought fell away as quickly as it surfaced, the artifact's presence expanding and pressing outward inside her skull like a dull roar. Ru persisted onward through the trees, sharp branches catching at her coat and loose hair, wetness seeping in through her boots.

With every step, the artifact filled her mind like thick syrup, sticking to her consciousness until she thought of nothing but the black stone and continuing forward. Soon, the pain in her toes subsided to numbness. Soon, she began to forget where she was and why she was so frightened.

Then she tripped, her boot catching on an exposed root, and she would have sprawled face first in the wet earth, except something caught her.

Someone caught her. Strong arms, stopping her mid-fall and lifting her back to her feet, pulling her against his body. As the warmth of him extended to Ru, the artifact's fervor burst forth a thousandfold. An inferno of hot want crackled through every cell of her in a sudden crescendo until she was overwhelmed with it.

She stepped back, moving away from the man who had caught her. It wasn't Lyr. Of course, it wasn't Lyr. She didn't have to see his face to know, didn't have to meet that gaze in the dark forest. The artifact knew. Her heart knew, had already known… might have known since the moment she'd woken up by the fire.

He was breathing hard, and she recognized the sound of his breaths, the soft exhale in the night.

It was Fen. No, *Taryel*.

"You," Ru breathed, heart in her throat. She distantly felt as if she should be angry or afraid, but there was no fighting the artifact's enticement, its neediness. Not that she wanted to fight it.

Touch him, it said. Her vision spun.

She moved forward without trying, her hands pressed against his chest, his cold leather.

She turned her face upward to meet his gaze. He was taller than she remembered, but the shape of him was so familiar. Broad-shouldered but slender, pale in the darkness, and framed by black hair, black leather. An angular stubbled jaw, intense grey eyes; every part of him was etched in her memory, a series of pathways in her mind, and every nerve in her body lit up for him. Every inch of her skin yearned for his touch.

"Ru," he said, and his voice was low and rough.

Why should she not give in?

"Ru," he said again, a curse and a prayer. And then, as if he, too, wondered the same — *why not give in?* — he took her face in his gloved hands, gently but with such determination, and kissed her.

He fit into the crevices of Ru's isolation, filling her up until she burned with him.

If Ru had not been burning already, now the artifact's fire consumed her. She was lost in it. She was lost in *him*. He kissed her like a man given water after a journey through the desert. He kissed her as if she were the sun and he spun in her orbit. Teeth and tongue and caressing lips. Fervent hands on her face, in her hair.

Ru melted into him. She was coming home. This was where she *should* be. Hadn't she been born for this very moment?

Yes, came the artifact's response, flitting across her addled mind.

He pulled her closer, their bodies flush. And Ru couldn't stop the ache that bloomed between her legs, the want that clawed its way through her.

She opened her mouth to say his name, but his mouth swallowed her words.

"I have you," he said between kisses, whether as a warning or a comfort, she couldn't tell. She didn't care. Her fingers tangled in his hair, her breaths coming in short gasps.

She didn't care.

Then his hands were on her backside, and he was lifting her against him, her legs wrapped around his waist. He spun her, and in a moment, her back hit something solid — she didn't care what. His body was pressed against hers, his hard desire rocking against her own. Nothing mattered now. She was with him again. He had found her. The artifact had brought her here. Maybe even he, too, had felt its call. She clung to him; could not have enough of him.

"I missed you," he murmured against her neck, his breath hot on her skin.

He kissed her softly where jaw met throat, and she arched against him. The ache of her desire deepened, and she rolled her hips against his.

He growled something unintelligible, his body responding. His kisses grew deeper and more desperate. Almost as if he couldn't stop himself, as if the artifact was stoking his fire as well as Ru's.

"I missed you," he said again and again.

There was too much separating them, Ru thought. Too many clothes, too many words. As she began to lose herself completely, as her pleasure grew and sharpened, she found she needed something more.

"Fen," she murmured, a soft breath of a word.

And like starlight through a midnight cloud, that name cut its way to her heart, and she saw herself clearly in that moment. This wasn't Fen. This was Taryel, the Destroyer. The artifact had betrayed her. It had brought her straight to him.

As if feeling her stiffen against him, Taryel stopped kissing her. His chest heaved with pent-up want, just as hers did. But she felt it as if separate from herself now, the artifact's insistent lust, and pushed it away, disgusted.

"Put me down," she said. Her voice shook.

He paused, unsure.

"Put me *down*."

Obediently, he did, setting her gently on her feet. She leaned back against the tree, grateful for its steadiness.

They stared at one another for a long moment, and Ru saw that glazed look in his eyes. The artifact's influence.

Taryel's mouth fell open, and Ru knew an apology was on its way. She didn't want to hear it. Before he could say anything, she drew back her hand and slapped him full across the face.

"Fucking *hell*," he gasped, voice muffled by the hand he pressed to his face where she'd struck him. But the glaze had gone from his expression, his grey eyes clearing.

Her palm stung, and tears pricked her eyes.

"I deserved that," he said, his words tinged with surprise.

"Where have you been?" Ru spat, both angry and shamefully relieved at being near him again. The artifact's coursing fire was lessening, but not quickly enough. "How — Who do you— I should *kill* you, you know."

A smile pulled at the edges of his mouth. As if he was happy to see her despite her rage, as if… Ru tamped down her traitorous feelings.

"I'm sorry I kissed you," he said, though he didn't sound it.

"You *more* than kissed me. You had no right."

"I didn't mean to. The artifact, when we're this close to each other, it…" His gaze fell to her mouth for a moment. "You kissed me back."

He was still close enough that she could see his pulse at the softest part of his throat, evidence that he was alive. That he, like Ru, was made of blood and bone and muscle. And even though he was Taryel, a villain of legend who had lived centuries ago, he was somehow still just a man.

If she had been armed, Ru might have considered attacking him. But even with those thoughts came yearning. She imagined plunging a knife into his chest at the moment of embrace, of their bodies meeting and moving together, and she bit her lip. The pain cleared her mind, if only slightly.

Ru hated herself for feeling the way she did. Because, more than anything, more than anger or betrayal, one feeling would not relent — the feeling of coming home.

"I didn't mean to kiss you back," Ru said.

The corner of his mouth twitched. "Did you mean to make that *sound*—"

"I still might kill you," she said, cutting him off. "I'll call for Lyr."

"We both know you won't."

They stared at each other.

"Fine," Ru said at last, crossing her arms tightly as if it would protect her heart. "I won't kill you. Yet."

"We both know I should have died centuries ago, anyway," he said, cocking his head. "But not everyone gets what they want."

"What's that supposed to mean?"

He shook his head. "It means you're more than welcome to stab me through the heart if it will make you feel better. I'd probably enjoy it."

Sadness tinged his sarcasm, an apology wrapped in a joke. It was too much. It wasn't enough.

"You *left* me," Ru said. It wasn't the thing she had meant to say. She had meant to say, *Watching you bleed to death would be a pleasure, you murderous traitor.* But her churning emotions had other ideas. "Don't you understand that you betrayed me? Twice? You broke my—" She almost bit her tongue to stop herself from saying it. He didn't need to know how deeply he'd hurt her.

Taryel lifted a hand as if to comfort her, and she cringed away. Just one small movement, but it felt as if she had opened a depthless crevasse between them. He stepped away then, allowing her space. His expression was ruination.

"Ru," he said, and that familiar, deeply accented voice crushed Ru's heart with gentle fingers. "I know I've hurt you. But please, don't push me away. I didn't mean to kiss you, the artifact... I got caught up in the moment. Listen, I called you here for a reason."

She stared. "Called me here? *You* did..." She pressed a hand to her temple where the artifact's low hum still reverberated, "You woke me, you dragged me through the forest. You made me..." She went cold at the thought of his mouth on hers, the ache of her desire.

Her disgust must have been palpable. Taryel retreated further, a picture of contrition. "I didn't know it would affect us so strongly. I didn't mean..."

"I'm sure you absolutely *meant*," she said, seething. "By the way, you could have come at any time. You know I've been at the Tower. I haven't gone anywhere. It's been months, Fe—" She swallowed hard. Would she ever allow herself to accept that he was gone? "It's been months."

Taryel watched her with such heaviness, such weight, that she felt momentarily swallowed by it. His presence here. She had believed the only remaining hint of Fen was this painful tether to the artifact. And now, here was Taryel, the same man as ever, yet somehow infinitely different. Her shadow, the man who had offered her his traveling cloak, who had promised to protect her in every way, was truly gone. Only Taryel remained: immortal, something like a god incarnate, and the black hand of death.

And he had *missed* her.

Anger fluttered helplessly at her chest, a flame that would not be snuffed. Anger with him, but most of all herself. She had wanted this. Dreamed of this nightly. Was he not handing it to her? Was it not already hers?

At last, Taryel spoke. His words were low, hesitant, as if coaxing a wild creature from the underbrush. "If I had come to you," he said, "If I'd appeared at your doorway unannounced, would I have been greeted with an embrace or a knife in the throat? Be honest."

Ru clenched her jaw to keep her teeth from chattering, to keep herself from flying apart into a cloud of untethered particles. She *wanted* to hate him. But hate had begun to feel a lot like something else, something just as deep and far more painful.

"Why now?" she asked. "What do you want from me? I don't have the artifact."

"Of course you don't," Taryel said, as if she had brought up some random topic out of the blue. "Lord D'Luc has it."

Ru refused to let the anger go. "Did you kill Lyr?"

Taryel blinked. "What? No. Good lord, Ru, what kind of monster do you think I am?"

"Are you actually that delusional?" Ru said in a kind of wonderment. She was growing colder by the second now, her words punctuated by chattering teeth. "You revealed yourself as the Destroyer… you admitted that you *used* me to get to the artifact…"

"I admitted nothing even remotely to that effect," he replied, clearly growing angry along with her. "*You* stole the artifact from *me*, remember? But I suppose it's not up to me what happens to my own heart."

"I've yet to prove that outlandish claim," said Ru. "There's no scientific basis."

He regarded her impatiently, his black hair moving over his forehead in the night wind. "Unfortunately, I don't have a scholarly paper to present as my defense. But I know it's my heart. I know it because it called to *you*. No one else."

Ru moved away slightly, involuntarily, her back pressed against the frosted tree. She was suddenly afraid that if she got too close to him, she might fall into his well of gravity. Take him in her arms and never let go.

He moved toward her, slowly, panther-like in the heavy dark. His gaze caught and held hers, and she couldn't move. Didn't want to. "You have every right to hate me," he said. "But I know you believe me. Just as I believe that the artifact is my heart, that its magical transformation has kept me alive all these centuries."

"A heart already beats in your chest," Ru said through clenched teeth. "You can't have two."

"According to medicine, to science," he said, one corner of his lovely mouth curving upward. "But what about magic?"

She huffed an angry breath. "We're talking in circles. I don't care about your cursed heart right now. Where have you been? Why are you here?"

He sighed, glancing down. "I've been away."

"Away *where*, exactly? And you didn't think to come back, didn't think to explain yourself further? You didn't think at *all*."

"You've been at the Tower," he said, catching her gaze and holding it. "Within an arm's length of Hugon D'Luc and the Children at every waking moment. There are King's Guards at every door, walking the hallways. I couldn't just drop in on you any time I wanted. If I had appeared in your room in the middle of the night, you would have cried wolf. I needed you alone. And anyway, I've been… busy."

"Doing what?" Ru demanded, her self-righteous ire rising to a crescendo. While the artifact seemed to be doing its best to soothe her, its tendrils of unseen energy lapping gently at the contours of her mind, she ignored it. She let the rage grow. "Nothing useful, I'm sure. Probably hiding out like a wounded animal in some cave in the woods. Meanwhile, I've been miserable every..." She swallowed, steadying herself. "Every *second* of every day since you left. You don't know what Lord D'Luc is like. And the Children... they just watch him. He'll do anything to get what he wants. And they let him." Hot tears stung her eyes, and she blinked rapidly, trying to will them away.

Taryel's expression crumpled, a picture of remorse that Ru didn't want to see. It was too late for his feelings.

"I didn't know," he said, and the words were low, broken. "I thought he wouldn't possibly stoop so low, that he couldn't possibly be that cruel. I thought D'Luc's bark overpowered his bite. But I was wrong. You are so strong, Ru, but you should never have been forced to endure..." His mouth twisted. "I'm sorry. I'm a fool for leaving you."

"Obviously," said Ru, biting down on the instinct to let him comfort her. She knew he wanted to, but it wasn't his place. She could comfort herself. "So what changed your mind? Finished licking your wounds and now you've come to try your luck again and steal the artifact?"

He frowned, obviously disliking this characterization, but not contradicting her. That, at least, he knew not to do. "I've been planning," he said. "I couldn't risk returning to the Tower, for the sake of us both. I came tonight because I knew there wouldn't be many Children or guards. I knew I could call you, and you wouldn't be seen."

This made a small amount of sense to Ru, which frustrated her. She wanted so badly for every word he spoke to be a lie, to give her more reasons to hate him. She yearned to wallow in her anger. To hurt him as he'd hurt her. But his eyes were clear and honest. He was no longer the madman she had faced at the Shattered City that night when she had seen eternity in his eyes. He was so obviously human now, and vulnerable. Just as she remembered Fen.

Despite herself, her fears, and everything she knew of the man, her heart still sang every time she caught his gaze.

"Why did you call me?" she whispered. They were so close now that he could have lifted a hand and stroked her cheek with the back of a finger, drawing a long shiver out of her. She imagined it, wished for it, hoped he wouldn't dare.

"To take you with me."

"But the artifact…"

"We don't need it," he said. "We'll come back for it. It's useless to Lord D'Luc without you."

Taryel's presence, his body, the timbre of his voice… they were relentless against Ru's barriers, crumbling her walls bit by bit. She had missed Fen. She had *yearned* for Fen. But was Taryel truly such a different man than the one she longed for? Because here he stood, in the middle of the night, apologizing and ready to take her away. Away from Lord D'Luc, from the Children, even the artifact.

"But where would we go?" she asked as if this was a possibility.

"Home," he said. And he smiled, a genuine, warm smile, and he was as beautiful as Ru remembered him in the sunlight.

"*Your* home?" she said, incredulous. He had never mentioned a home; in fact, he had often said he had none.

His eyes lit up. "Ours. Wherever we go together, we'll make it home. Solmaria, or even Mekya. Rothen to the north, if you don't mind the snow. It's up to you."

She gazed up at him, warring with herself. The sting of his betrayal was still so sharp. But they were entwined, the two of them, and she knew it. Was it worth resisting, if only to be pulled back to him again?

"Ru," he said, pressing a thumb to her cheek, his fingers in her hair. "Come with me."

She hesitated. He would take her away from Hugon D'Luc. He would save her from the threat of a new Destruction. He didn't even want the artifact, he seemed motivated only to keep her safe.

But…

"I can't." The words tasted like ash in her mouth.

A brief, unfettered sadness crossed his face, and that alone broke Ru's heart all over again. "I won't hurt you like I did before," he said. "Ru, you can't go to the palace. You'll— "

Unable to listen anymore, she cut him off. "You can't

just disappear from my life, Fe—" She swallowed painfully, biting her lip. It was like speaking to a ghost. "Taryel. You can't just disappear and return whenever you like. I don't trust you. And my friends… Gwyn and Arch aren't safe if I leave. Lord D'Luc would only hold them hostage. He'd use them against me."

"Fen," Taryel repeated as if Ru had struck him. As if remembering a close friend's recent death. "You can still call me by that name. I'm the same man."

A tear ran down her cheek, stinging her icy skin as it went. "You're not."

She shook her head, pulling herself together. She could not let grief overwhelm her; couldn't forget that Fen was gone. In truth, he'd never existed. "I can't come with you. Any part of me that wants to, any part of you that wants *me*… it's the artifact."

"No," Taryel said, almost desperate. "It's not the artifact, it's—"

She pressed a palm to his chest to silence him, unable now to stop the flow of tears. "You don't matter to me anymore," she managed. "I don't need you. That night in the Shattered City, you showed me who you really are. What we had, it's over."

"Ru, listen to me."

"No, Taryel. I never want to see you again."

He watched her in silence for a moment, stunned. As if he hadn't seen this coming, as if he had truly believed she would take him in her arms and forgive everything. Forgive who he was. How could she, if she couldn't even forgive herself?

"Is that truly what you want?" he said.

She nodded, nearly blinded by her tears. She hated this show of vulnerability. He didn't deserve to affect her like this.

"I could force you to come with me. I *should*."

She inhaled shakily, meeting his eyes. "Is that what you want to do?"

The depth of his gaze was unsettling, and the darkness in it began to frighten Ru. "Of course it is," he said through clenched teeth. "All I want is to take you in my arms and flee. I could disappear with you, Ru. And no one would be the wiser. You'd be safe."

"Please don't," she said, her voice breaking. "Just leave me. We'll both be happier if you go."

"I'm begging you," he said. He held her gaze, clear grey eyes half obscured by the fall of his hair. "Come with me. If you go to the palace, I can't guarantee your safety. I can't guarantee—"

"I don't care what you guarantee or not," Ru insisted. "I'm not coming with you, Taryel. I don't know you. You're a stranger to me."

Pain stretched between them. Then Taryel nodded, the gesture stiff and formal. As if it took everything in him to speak the words, he said, "Very well, then."

He made a brief gesture with his fingers, and in a blink, he was surrounded by a sphere of black lightning. One moment he was there, his hair blowing in an unseen wind. And in the next, he was gone.

Ru finally let herself cry, wracking, painful sobs that filled her throat with phlegm and stung her face with tears. She knew it was the right thing to do. She knew that he was an enemy, another man she couldn't trust. Taryel was not Fen — he had his own motives and his own secrets. But in that moment, Ru felt she had just made the worst decision of her life.

CHAPTER 9

When Ru emerged from the forest, shivering and eyes stinging, she was immediately intercepted by a wild-eyed Lyr. He wore his overcoat over his sleeping shirt and trousers, and his dark hair stood up where he'd slept on it. He took her by the shoulders, stern as a worried father.

"Where the hell have you *been?*" he rumbled under his breath, careful not to wake the others by the fire. To Ru's relief, everyone else appeared to be asleep.

"Looking for you," she lied, her voice little more than a croak. "I woke up, and you were gone."

He scowled deeply. "I went to take a piss. When I got back, *you* were gone. You've been gone for nearly an *hour.*"

"Sorry," she said, thinking it best to play innocent rather than carry on a whispering argument in the middle of the night. "I got lost in the forest. It took me a while to find my way back."

Lyr's eyes narrowed, his already thick brows crowding together as he studied her face. "You've been crying. Why?"

"I haven't."

"You have."

She hugged herself tightly, exaggerating the chatter of her teeth. "It's the cold. It makes my eyes water. I'm going back to sleep." She made to step around him, but the tall broad man blocked her path.

"Cold doesn't make people cry," he insisted. "What happened? Did Hugon follow you? Is he—" he made to draw his sword, spinning toward the sleeping form of Lord D'Luc, but Ru put a hand on his arm.

"I was alone," she said, reluctantly grateful for the guard's loyalty. "I'm fine. I'm just... nervous about going back to the palace. And everything."

Lyr nodded, appeased for the time being. "Fine," he said. "Don't wander off again for fuck's sake."

Ru was surprised to find herself smiling up at the dour King's Guard. "I won't."

THE REMAINDER of the journey to Mirith, a total of three days by carriage, passed in a lackluster blur. Ru had no more nighttime visitors. Gwyneth and Archie kept her somewhat sane, distracting her with games and tame, silly topics of conversation. Even Lord D'Luc was blessedly quiet most of the time, only waxing poetic every night by the fire when he would regale the traveling party with tales of Festra or an eerie Mekyan folktale.

The artifact's voice was vague at the edges of her consciousness. Ever since Taryel's arrival and subsequent departure, it had lain dormant in her mind, sleeping. It had been Taryel's presence that had set it off, made it so insistent that night. There was no other possibility in Ru's mind, nothing more obvious than the fact that his nearness to her set the artifact alight.

The distant spires of Mirith appeared on the horizon just before dusk of the third day. They had made good time and would arrive at the palace just in time for bed. While Ru knew what lay in store for her in the palace, the sight of the city comforted her. It had been her home until she moved to the Cornelian Tower four years ago. She had missed its colors, its smells, the chaotic shouts of merchants, and the smell of pastries and strong coffee in the mornings. She had missed the narrow cobbled streets and alleyways, hung with drying laundry, like mismatched bunting.

But as they passed into the city and made their way

south toward the bay over which the palace sprawled, Ru's fleeting joy at the return to her old home dissipated in the wake of dread. The closer they came to the palace, the quieter her friends grew until the conversation stopped altogether.

Gwyneth and Archie were afraid; Ru could tell. Just like she was. The dread of the unknown seemed to congeal on their tongues, holding them hostage. Ru glanced at her friends, and they shared a look of unspoken support, of loyalty.

We have each other. We'll always have that, if nothing else.

The palace shone like a hulking beacon at night, lit by a myriad of lanterns both inside and out. Footmen in fine livery came to greet the carriages as they pulled up, helping their passengers disembark. Bags of luggage were gathered and whisked into the palace.

Ru watched everything through a haze of distraction. She kept wondering, despite herself, about Taryel. Where he'd come from, where he'd gone. She hated that her heart quickened at the thought of him. *He's my enemy*, she reminded herself. They were connected, that fact was obvious. But until Ru understood it, until she learned how to break it, that bond was nothing but a problem to be solved.

Gwyneth and Archie stood near Ru, watching as Lord D'Luc ordered the Children and footmen about with clipped, aristocratic words. When the carriages and footmen had gone at last, a pair of figures exited the palace through opulent double doors, the gold in their armor glinting in lamplight and the plumes of their hats swaying as they walked.

They were two women, one tall with dark skin and a no-nonsense gaze, the other pale, with a smile framed by curling brown hair.

"Sybeth," Ru said, the relief clear in her voice. "Rosylla."

"Here comes trouble," Lyr said, but his tone was jovial, and a crooked smile warmed his usually gruff expression.

The King's Riders strode forward and stopped to greet Lord D'Luc, who had moved toward them with a sweep of his frock coat, its embroidery catching the lamplight.

"Good evening, Your Grace," said Sybeth, giving him a stiff nod.

Rosylla beamed at Ru, even giving her a little wave while Lord D'Luc shared low words with Sybeth.

Gwyneth, Ru, and Archie smiled back, and for a brief second, Ru felt like a schoolgirl again, young and overwhelmed, grateful for any show of kindness or affection.

Then Hugon spun on his heel, gesturing impatiently. "Delara, Tenoria, Hill. The King's Riders will show you to your rooms. Delara, clean up quickly — you'll be dining with Regent Sigrun tonight." The words, harmless as they were, sounded like a threat in his clipped tone.

"Yes, sir," Archie said, not bothering to hide his sarcasm.

"Oh, and Lyr," Hugon added, ushering the academics past him, "you're relieved from duty until tomorrow morning."

Lyr bowed slightly, shot Ru a reassuring glance, then trotted off toward a side door in the palace. No doubt the barracks where King's Riders and guards slept, a place where Ru would have given anything to be just then. She imagined Lyr would spend the night laughing and sharing tales with his peers, drinking ale, and then falling into a simple, but warm, bed.

Meanwhile, she would be laced tight into a gown and expected to be on her best behavior. That meant smiling, charming the regent, pretending that everything was perfectly fine and that she wasn't at the palace for the express purpose of ending the world.

Lord D'Luc disappeared shortly after they entered the palace, leaving Sybeth and Rosylla alone to guide the three academics. As soon as he was gone, Rosylla slowed her pace to walk alongside Ru.

"We missed you," she said, still grinning as if Ru's appearance was the best thing that had ever happened to her. "It's been months since you were here. I'm sure your brother will be dying to catch up."

"Rosylla." Sybeth's voice was low, a warning.

Rosylla shot Ru a conspiratorial glance and murmured, "Sybeth doesn't trust Lord D'Luc."

"*Rosylla*," Sybeth said, sharper this time.

Ru smiled. They were still her allies, then. She wondered whether she might be able to speak to them alone soon, to get a better understanding of the situation at the palace. After all, Rosylla had been a friend to Ru since they had met, sharing sweets and coffee, on that fateful ride from Dig Site 33 to the Shattered City months ago.

"So you're the famous Rosylla," Gwyneth said, clearly noting tension and nudging the subject in a new direction. "Ru told us all about you, how kind you are. And you as well, Sybeth."

"Is that so?" Sybeth said, turning slightly, eyebrow raised.

"Sybeth and Rosylla are celebrities back at the Cornelian Tower," said Archie.

"A bit of an exaggeration," Ru said, laughing.

The group made their way through the palace, Sybeth remaining professional and alert while Rosylla peppered Ru with innocuous questions. *How was your journey? Was the weather all right? Did the carriage come equipped with cookies? Have you heard of the latest baking fad, a miniature cake that can be eaten in one bite?*

They passed through gilded hallways shining bright with crystal chandeliers, illuminating beautiful courtiers. The courtiers weren't shy in staring, wide eyes following Ru and her bedraggled friends from behind silk fans. Ru thought she heard some whispering her name, but she must have been imagining things.

Yet, something about the palace seemed strange to Ru, something different. She had been here many times growing up, with her father, and later to visit Simon, who worked and kept rooms in the palace. When they turned a corner into a particularly broad hallway, she realized what it was.

There were nearly twice as many guards. Everywhere. Guards at doorways, lining the halls at regular intervals, and even — she glanced back — following at a distance. The change was subtle enough that it had taken her time to notice, but now that she had seen it, the reality hit her like a hammer. The palace was a prison. Sybeth and Rosylla were a courtesy, a kindness extended to give her, more than likely, a false sense of comfort. The real guards were behind them, on all sides, around every corner they passed.

No matter where she went in the palace, Ru and her friends would be watched.

At last, they came to a relatively quiet wing of the palace, with lower ceilings and candelabras on the walls instead of oil lamps in opulent brackets. Sybeth stopped before a door painted dark green with a brass flower-shaped knob. She produced a key, unlocked the door, and handed the key out to Ru with an almost apologetic expression. As if she knew Ru was no more than a prisoner here. "Your chambers."

"Thank you," Ru said. Turning to her friends, she forced a smile. "I'll see you tomorrow?"

They said good night, her uneasiness reflected in their faces, and continued down the hall, led by Rosylla.

Sybeth remained with Ru. "I'll serve as your personal bodyguard for the night," she said. "Dinner is in an hour. When you're ready, I'll escort you to the dining room."

"I was wondering," Ru said, desperate to know what kind of information the King's Rider might be holding onto.

But Sybeth's sharp gaze cut her short. "Your brother is in residence," she said, and that was enough of an answer for Ru — Sybeth might not talk, but Simon would.

Once inside her chambers, Ru leaned her head back against the painted wood, willing herself not to cry. She was so tired, overwhelmed, and now she was meant to attend a dinner with the regent.

At least her rooms were gorgeous. Resplendent, actually. Too much for one woman. Ru stood in a small receiving room or parlor, with a great hearth and luxurious couches and cushions arranged around it. A harp stood in one corner, as if she might miraculously have the skill or inclination to play. There were two doors leading into additional rooms.

Glancing into the nearest one, she saw that the room boasted two large floor-to-ceiling windows and a wooden globe. The globe was so enormous that she could have easily fit inside it if she'd curled up. There were more arm-chairs and a sofa in this room, a desk, and a smaller hearth.

Crossing the receiving room, she went through the far door and found herself in the bedroom. Her trunk was already set at the foot of the bed, and when she went to the tall wardrobe against the far wall, found that her clothes had all been hung up, her shoes arranged in a neat row.

The four-poster bed would have easily fit a family of four, and was made up with blankets that appeared to be hand embroidered, featuring birds and tufts of leaves and berries in a complex pattern. Everything was too big, too elegant, too beautiful. Compared to this, her room back at the Tower was painfully humble.

She hated it. There was nothing comforting about this room, its gold-painted crown molding, its fine materials.

A soft knock and then a click jolted Ru from her thoughts. She spun, and was shocked to see a young woman standing in the room with her. A lady's maid, she realized — she had come in through a concealed entrance just beyond the wardrobe.

But this wasn't just any maid.

"Pearl," Ru said, smiling in surprised relief.

"Miss Delara," said the maid, a young woman with brown hair and pink cheeks, a friendly face that Ru sorely needed just then. She smiled and dropped a delicate curt-sey. "I hope your journey wasn't too long?"

"It wasn't long enough," Ru said. "Did you know I was coming?"

Pearl nodded. "Asked specifically to be assigned to you," she said, coloring a little at the admission.

"Ah," said Ru, momentarily chilled by the thought that Lord D'Luc had allowed this, just as he'd allowed Sybeth and Rosylla to escort her. Was it a game or an attempt to put her at ease, to make her more pliant? "That's very kind."

"I thought you might like a bath," said Pearl, her smile widening at Ru's obvious eagerness for just such a thing. "I'll draw you one fresh. Just through here."

Pearl led Ru into an adjoining washroom. Along with a

soaking tub and heaps of towels, a fire crackled in a small grate, and Ru saw a kettle beginning to steam.

The water, miraculously, was exactly the right temperature. Hot enough to make Ru's skin pink but not so hot that it burned. She inhaled deeply, lowering herself into the tub until her entire body up to the chin was submerged. Her hair spread out around her in dark rivulets on the water. She wished she could stay there forever, warm and half-floating, safe.

But she only had an hour. When the water began to turn lukewarm, and she was fully scrubbed and clean, Ru finally forced herself out of the bath. Wrapping herself in a towel, she padded back into the bedroom. Pearl had lit a fire there as well and was fussing with various beauty accoutrements at an elegant vanity.

"Ah," she said, hearing Ru enter the room, "just in time! I'll dress you for dinner, Miss Delara."

The gown Pearl had chosen was too beautiful. Too beautiful for Ru, who knew how foul she must look, even after a bath. Her hair was a wet and tangled mess, her eyes no doubt bloodshot, her skin sallow and dull from months of restless sleep. This dress was a work of art, something a queen should wear, not Ru.

"Maybe I should wear something…" She made a face, glancing at Pearl, "a little less… you know. Sumptuous?"

Pearl scoffed, shoving the gown at Ru. "Put it on. You'll thank me."

Ru sighed. She didn't have the energy to argue. "I'm going to look ridiculous."

The maid only shook her head with fond exasperation, helping Ru into the gown. It was dove-grey silk, embroidered with silver thread. The bodice, Ru thought, was lovely but far too low-cut. The sleeves, meanwhile, were long and trimmed with buttons of opal.

"There," Pearl said when she'd fastened the last button. "You're a vision."

"I'm something," Ru muttered.

"Sit down, we must do something about that hair."

Ru sat obediently, staring at herself in the mirror while Pearl brushed her hair, which had mostly dried in the time it had taken to get her into the gown. She watched as the maid twisted it neatly, arranging it on her head with practiced ease. Ru tried not to study herself too closely, tried not to scowl at the lines under her eyes, her tight lips, the ever-present crease between her eyebrows.

"Relax," Pearl said, draping a net of silver over Ru's hair, which was now coiled and arranged at the back of her head. "You've met the Regent Sigrun before, haven't you? And your friend will be there, no doubt."

The crease between Ru's brows deepened. "Lord D'Luc isn't what I'd call a friend."

"Not him," said Pearl, impatient. "Now spin your chair around, I need to paint your face."

Ru obeyed, wracking her brain. "Archie and Gwyn?"

"No, and stop *frowning*, you'll give yourself unsightly lines. Now pucker your lips for me, please."

Ru did, and she was rewarded with a thick swipe of red across her lips.

"There," said Pearl, standing back. "Let's look at the final product." She steered Ru over to an oval full-length mirror that stood in the corner of the room near the hearth, until now unnoticed by Ru.

Reluctant, and still trying to determine who her *friend* was supposed to be, Ru went to the mirror. She didn't recognize the woman staring back at her.

"You're a magician," she breathed, turning this way and that, admiring Pearl's handiwork.

Pearl watched her, beaming. "I told you the dress would suit you," she said, eyes shining. "Lord D'Luc had it specially made. He sent us all the details by pigeon, just so you'd have something to wear on your first night."

Ru's delight immediately faded, replaced by a cold resentment. Of course, Lord D'Luc had ordered the dress for her. Everything good in her life had to be marred by him.

"Are you all right?" Pearl said. "Too much traveling, I expect."

"I'm fine," Ru said, trying to smile, grasping helplessly for the joy again, the relief. But all she felt was cold. "You've done a wonderful job."

"Thank you, Miss," Pearl said, but Ru could tell she was worried.

"Really," said Ru, taking Pearl's hand. "I'm just hungry."

The maid perked up a bit. "Then it's a good thing it's time for dinner.

CHAPTER 10

Sybeth led Ru through the palace with an aura of dire reluctance. Ru could tell something was troubling the King's Rider, but she wasn't about to bring it up again. So the pair walked in silence.

The dining room wasn't far. Ru had almost expected it to be the same room she had dined in that summer, in an older wing of the palace, with dark wood beams and a cozy atmosphere. Instead, Sybeth took her to the wing with sky-high ceilings, where everything was gilded and painted in pastel colors, delicate and decadent, and considerably less inviting.

Ru hesitated at the doors, hearing lively conversation and music from within, the chime of crystal glasses, and elegant laughter.

"You're going to be late," Sybeth said. Ru glanced up at the tall woman. A glimmer of warmth shone in the King's Rider's dark eyes, and she smiled faintly. Reassuringly.

Taking a deep breath to steady herself, Ru entered the dining room.

She was struck immediately by light, sound, and smell. The room was bright, almost blindingly so, despite it being night. Chandeliers hung from the ceiling, crystal and sparkling, reflecting the dozens of candles and lamps that graced the room. Crystal goblets with long stems were strewn along a lengthy table, at which sat lively, finely dressed courtiers. Bejeweled hair shimmered in the candlelight, and rings glistened on dainty fingers.

"Ah!" said someone, seeing Ru appear in the doorway. "Is that her?"

"Don't *stare*," said another voice, prim and thick with excitement.

"It *is* her," giggled a third.

The room erupted in chatter even louder than before. But before Ru could turn tail and flee, Lord D'Luc appeared at her elbow. Even in a room of beauty, he shone the brightest. Ru found herself disgusted by it.

"Don't mind them," he said, only loud enough for her to hear. "They've been told of your arrival, the great Ruellian Delara. The palace has been buzzing in anticipation of your return."

"Lovely," said Ru, meaning the opposite. "Where's Regent Sigrun?" A cursory glance made it clear that the regent wasn't there yet.

"Arriving at any moment," replied Lord D'Luc. "Come, I'll keep the gossip-mongers at bay."

"How kind." She placed a reluctant hand on the lord's elbow.

"There's no need for sarcasm," he said airily, guiding them into the room. "You'll be much happier here at the palace. More fulfilled. The regent, I'm told, has made every allowance for your comfort and progress with the artifact."

Ru bristled but said nothing. The bright eyes of eager courtiers followed her across the room. One woman waved hesitantly, and when Ru raised her eyebrows in return, the woman flushed and pressed a hand to her breast as if she were ready to faint.

When they were seated near the head of the table, Lord D'Luc shot Ru a wicked smile. "Ignore the rabble. They're beneath you."

It was impossible. The courtiers were trying to be subtle, peering around fans or over glasses of wine, but Ru knew all eyes were on her. Whispers and soft giggles carried through the room.

"What's wrong with them?" Ru muttered, her palms beginning to sweat. "What did you tell them? That I'm some evil sorceress?"

Lord D'Luc chuckled, gesturing with a finger at a passing footman, who filled Ru's crystal glass with sparkling wine. "You are determined, as ever, to consider me your enemy. I've said nothing of the sort, nor would I jeopardize our studies in such a way."

"So what did you tell them, then?" Ru asked, eyeing her wine. She wondered if she should drink it to calm her nerves, or leave it to stay in control of her faculties.

"I told them nothing," Lord D'Luc said, lifting his glass. "It's well known in the palace that you are Ruellian Delara, Festra's chosen, and Keeper of his Heart. That with your help, we shall wash away the old and give birth to a new world. They're ever so fond of Festra these days. He's the latest fad amongst the courtiers."

Ru stared. "Fad? Keeper of *whose* heart?"

He smiled, conspiracy shining in his eyes. "Taryel's heart, obviously. Or weren't you aware?"

Ru sat frozen, a rabbit in the sights of a fox. "Aware...?"

"You needn't play coy any longer," he said, placing one finger on either side of her wine glass's crystal stem, sliding it toward her. "The artifact's nature is finally known to me, as well as every follower of Festra. It's no longer your secret to keep. And they are ready for you, Delara. All that remains is for you to learn how to ignite the artifact, show its power to the world in cleansing fire. The Court of Navenie stands with us in this endeavor."

"What you did to the professors..." Ru said, hiding the vague horror that had begun to throb in her gut.

The lord had the audacity to appear offended at her implication. "Don't be silly. Everyone here is in full control of their own mind. It's easier than you'd think to cultivate a new fad in the midst of a large group of bored aristocrats. All you need is a bit of charm, exciting tales of woe and romance, and so on. They eat it up."

"So you've created a new *religion*," Ru said in disgust, pulling her wine glass away from the lord's reach, clutching it like some kind of life raft.

"What you call it doesn't matter," he replied. "But it makes our work easier, doesn't it?"

Ru snorted. "You brought me here to play the part in some religious pantomime? How is that supposed to get me to control the artifact?"

The lord's lips curled in a slow smile. "You'll come to understand, once you've met her."

Ru shifted, heart in her throat, sweat clinging to her back where her corset pressed against her skin. "Met who?"

Just then, the surrounding laughter and voices faded, and in a moment, the room was silent. Ru leaned sideways for a clear view of the door as three figures entered the dining room. She watched in mute horror as they made quiet, polite greetings to the guests seated nearby.

Two of the figures were women, arresting in their obvious power. Ru knew the first woman well. Regent Sigrun was commanding in presence with graying black hair and dark eyes, dressed in the regalia of a military officer rather than a queen, and her epaulets shone in the candlelight. The other woman was a stranger to Ru. She possessed a sweet, youthful beauty, with a heart-shaped face and honey-brown hair.

But it wasn't these women who made Ru's heart stop, the blood in her veins slowing to a deathly crawl. It was the man dressed all in black, with hair to match. A deep frown creased his pale and stubbled face.

His eyes caught hers, just for a breath of a moment, and the artifact burst into life within Ru.

Lord D'Luc leaned close, his cheek only inches from Ru's, a smile in his voice. As if this were an intimate whisper between friends. "You should have told me that your tattered wanderer was Taryel Aharis. Imagine my shock when I learned. He's been instrumental in cultivating a sense of collective excitement about the artifact. It is rightfully his, after all."

Air ceased to flow through Ru's lungs. A weight pressed down on her chest until she couldn't think or move.

The seated courtiers, meanwhile, were behaving as if gripped by a ridiculous madness. Some of them almost wailing with jubilant glee, while others blew kisses toward Taryel and clutched their bosoms, delicate tears streaming down their faces. One man even fell from his chair, as if the arrival of Taryel Aharis had physically knocked him off balance.

Ru stared, almost wanting to laugh at the courtiers' behavior. Only her dread kept the mirth at bay.

Taryel moved through the room with the practiced ease of a gentleman, but his dour expression never changed. Ru watched in petrified silence as the brown-haired woman who had entered with him floated delicately to sit by the head of the table, seating herself across from Lord D'Luc. Ru wished she could crawl under the table and hide when Taryel Aharis, elegant and calm, sat across from her.

She looked away in anguish, as if ignoring him might make him disappear, might prove this night to be no more than a nightmare she'd soon wake from. She watched numbly as Lord D'Luc greeted the brown-haired woman with a kiss on the back of her hand. The woman smiled, her eyes shining in the candlelight.

In a devastated panic, Ru reached for her glass and downed its entire contents in one gulp, choking slightly.

As she set the empty glass down, fingers shaking, she risked a glance at Taryel. His gaze snapped immediately to hers, and there was such heat in it that her stomach twisted, her body responding in a way that was entirely improper at the dinner table. And the artifact, traitorous thing, only stoked the flame.

No, no, no, she thought, tearing her gaze away from his. *This can't be happening. He would have told me he was here. He had every chance to tell me.*

Confusion and betrayal came easily to Ru now, and she leaned into the feelings with abandon. She could almost still feel his body against hers, his lips on her neck. *I'm begging you,* he'd said. Yet here he was, at the very place he had been desperate to save her from. Was everything a game to him? *Why* hadn't he...

The soft pinging of silver on crystal drew Ru's anguished attention to the head of the table, where the regent stood holding her drink aloft. "Thank you for joining me tonight," she said, in resonant but distinctly emotionless tones. "I'm pleased to welcome Ruellian Delara, Archae-ologist…"

At this, a small clamor arose, excited whispers amongst the seated guests.

"And Keeper of His Heart," the regent continued, deadpan.

The seated courtiers reacted with continued enthusi-asm, some applauding loudly while others darted wine-addled and eager glances Ru's way. One woman tossed a dried flower toward Ru, who had to lean sideways to avoid it landing in her hair.

When the sound had died down, the regent continued, "We are pleased to host you once again, Miss Delara. I look forward to watching your progress with the artifact. Enjoy your dinner."

"To Ruellian!" cried one of the courtiers, and the chant was picked up across the room as a table full of aristocrats lifted their glasses in unison, drinking a toast to Ru.

Ru, meanwhile, wished fervently that she could fade into a mist and blow away. The regent was changed. She was one of the Children, in every way but the white robe. Her eyes as she spoke were glazed, her words without in-flection. Ru had already guessed as much, but to see it in practice…

In every way that mattered, Regent Sigrun belonged to Lord D'Luc.

And then, the regent's gaze drifted, almost aimlessly, toward the woman with honey-brown hair. As Ru watched, the woman gave a tiny, almost imperceptible nod. The regent returned the nod with a blank-eyed stare.

Cold realization rose in Ru's chest. She had thought Lord D'Luc was the only one holding the regent's strings. But this woman…

"Delara," Lord D'Luc said. His voice snapped Ru out of her trance. She turned to the lord, heart hammering. He frowned disapprovingly at her breathlessness, gesturing toward the woman across from him. "May I present Lady Bellenet."

Ru stared blankly for half a second before collecting herself enough to reply. "Good evening, Your Grace," she said, an obvious wobble to her voice. "I'm… honored."

Lady Bellenet smiled. "The honor is mine." Her voice was deep, sensual yet commanding. "I gather some things may have changed since you were last at court. I hope you find comfort here, nonetheless. There are so many fascinating things to do."

Ru inclined her head slightly in response. It was the most she could do, as her voice seemed caught in her tightening throat. Her gown was in danger of being ruined from the press of her sweaty palms. And Taryel's presence across the table from her, ever in her peripheral vision, was making her breaths too shallow, her skin too hot.

Lady Bellenet, either ignorant to Ru's suffering or choosing to ignore it, turned to Taryel. He raised one eyebrow slightly, returning the woman's gaze. "Taryel Aharis," said the lady, "I believe you already know Miss Delara, our honored guest tonight."

Taryel Aharis, Ru thought distantly, grasping at threads of reality. Then Lord D'Luc had spoken truthfully — he, and presumably everyone at court if the name was to be spoken so carelessly by ladies at dinners, knew that Taryel was alive, real. That the artifact was his blackened, fossilized heart. But did they truly believe it, or were they just playing along with what they thought to be a silly game?

Taryel turned to Ru. She longed for him, just as much as she longed to shove him headfirst into the hearth. She had thought she'd never see him again. That he was gone. To watch him abandon her, and *now…*

"Miss Delara," said Taryel, and even in the swell of anger, hearing her name on his lips was transcendent. "Lovely to see you again."

She wanted to melt to the floor, crawl under her chair and curl into a ball, dash back to her rooms and lock the door behind her. More than that, she wanted to drive her butter knife deep into Taryel's neck. But the artifact responded to her piqued anxiety with waves of comforting caresses, lowering her back to earth.

How dare you, she thought, glaring at him. *How dare you try to comfort me.*

Lord D'Luc said, leaning sideways, "Don't leave the poor man hanging."

"Good evening, Mr. Aharis," Ru said, biting out the words with a tinge of bitterness. She couldn't wrap her mind around these revelations. The wine was taking effect now, and combined with the artifact's comforting touch, she found herself, against her will, beginning to relax.

Lord D'Luc and Lady Bellenet shared a glance, but Taryel's gaze remained fixed on Ru.

"He used to go by a different name," said Lord D'Luc, lip curling as he glanced Ru's way for just a breath. "*Fen Verrill*. Perhaps you recall that he is a former member of Miss Delara's research team."

Lady Bellenet brightened at this, glancing at Ru with interest. "How fascinating," she said, as if she and Ru were in on some wonderful joke. As if she had not already known everything there was to know about Taryel and Ru.

The first course began to arrive. Conversation was suspended as footmen brought in bowls of spiced lamb stew. Ru took the opportunity to glance toward the regent.

The woman looked healthy and strong as ever, but now that Ru knew what afflicted her, the regent seemed smaller. A bright star, once powerful in the night, now diminished. The sight of her made Ru ache with grief for the woman who had ruled Navenie for many years.

But thoughts of the regent faded quickly, as Taryel's presence begged for Ru's constant attention. He seemed always to be watching her. She could feel his gaze hot on her skin. Lord D'Luc and Lady Bellenet seemed oblivious to it, engaging Taryel and Ru in lighthearted chat, asinine topics that Ru could not begin to care about — the rise in popularity of the pianoforte, or the higher cost of silk in winter, or an arresting book of poetry Lady Bellenet had recently read.

Ru nodded thoughtlessly along with the conversation, forcing herself to react in the way a cultured young woman should. She didn't want Taryel to know he affected her so deeply, that her stomach was in knots and her heart was a bleeding, gaping wound. Though he likely knew it already, could feel her somehow through their connection with the artifact. Even so, she kept her expression light, pretending.

But as dinner progressed, her thoughts were always on Taryel, and she knew that his attention remained on her. The air between them crackled with tension, unspoken words, and, in Ru's case, an angry, unwanted desire.

Did he see her as the enemy now? she wondered. Did he want her as much as she needed him? The slight curve of his mouth said he might, the glint in his eye, like a hunter watching a mark. The artifact began to encourage her, its comfort turning to a lustful heat until just a glance from Taryel had Ru aching with desire.

She relished and reviled every moment of it.

"Taryel," said Lady Bellenet, when the last of the dinner plates had been cleared away, and trays of tiny cubical cakes and coffee were laid out. "Do tell us about your previous studies with Miss Delara. Hugon speaks little of her, beyond the basics of her progress. What is she like as a colleague? As a woman?" She shot a brief, unreadable glance at Lord D'Luc.

Ru stiffened. Why not ask *her* what kind of scientist she was? Why not ask *her* what she meant to do with the artifact now she was here at the palace?

"Unnecessary to discuss the matter," Lord D'Luc replied, leaning back in his chair. His smile seemed stiff, uneasy. "The artifact is the key."

"The *heart* of the matter," added Lady Bellenet, with a knowing smile. "True, she is but a conduit. As Festra's will was done through Taryel…"

"His will be done through the Keeper," Lord D'Luc finished.

Ru stared, horrified at both the terrible wordplay and the fact that she was being ignored so blatantly. Lady Bellenet seemed strangely happy to make light of the artifact, its horrific truth. And worst of all, as Ru watched Lord D'Luc with Lady Bellenet, she realized that he deferred to her. He did not have the mindless look of a Child, but he bowed to her nonetheless. Lady Bellenet held his leash.

Likewise, Ru had thought Lord D'Luc was in control of the regent, but she'd been mistaken — Lady Bellenet was.

What kind of person was Lady Bellenet, then? A power-hungry fanatic, or something else entirely? The woman seemed almost girlish in her demeanor at times, yet she held the two most powerful people in Navenie in the palm of her hand. If she *was* a fanatic — and Ru was convinced she was — then Lord D'Luc's talk of both science and religion was beginning to make sense. He dreamed of scientific progress, but Lady Bellenet was Festra's devoted follower, and Lord D'Luc, in turn, was devoted to her. His eyes were always on her; his posture deferred to her.

Then Taryel began to speak, and Ru's thoughts fled.

"You asked about Miss Delara," he said, his voice catching her by the heart and twisting. "She was a pleasure to work with. Her mind is unlike any I've come across, even here at the palace. She is a wonder."

He caught her eye as he finished speaking. Ru's chest ached.

"You'd dismiss the King's Scholars so quickly?" asked Lady Bellenet. "Miss Delara is young. And practically a peasant."

Ru clenched her fists, twisting her gown with unspoken ire. Her skirt was definitely ruined.

"Why else would you have brought her here," Taryel said, ignoring the remark, "if you didn't find the palace's offerings to be lacking? Of course I dismiss the King's Scholars when compared to Miss Delara."

Ru's cheeks burned. She didn't know whether to be enraged or flattered.

Lady Bellenet laughed, scooping a sugar cube from a dainty tray with a tiny silver spoon. "You speak true, my lord. Miss Delara is here because she offers what the scholarship in Mirith cannot. She's the Keeper, after all." She tilted her head, regarding Taryel intently, as if he were the scholar of everything Ru. "Tell me, what manner of scientist is Miss Delara? Hugon has said little beyond describing her as a homely girl with a shockingly sharp mind."

A rising anger now threatened to take over, despite the wine. "Is she aware that I'm sitting right here?" Ru hissed, just for Lord D'Luc to hear. He had suddenly become her unwanted anchor in this jarring evening, a constant whose capricious manners were at least well-known to her. She didn't understand why Taryel was here or who he was loyal to. Why had he come to her in the forest, tried to run away with her? Was she nothing but a game to him?

But Hugon D'Luc... Ru understood him. At least, she understood enough to know that she couldn't trust him, that he had only her worst interests at heart. That was something known, a constant to cling to.

The lord turned just enough to catch Ru's eye, tossing her a sardonic half-smile. "Ignore it. Let them talk."

Lady Bellenet turned to Lord D'Luc and Ru then, their heads close together, and her eyes narrowed for the space of a breath.

Taryel, meanwhile, spoke as if Ru wasn't there at all, his intense gaze now fixed on Lady Bellenet. Ru reached angrily for a tiny cake, a sugar-spun flower perched on its top, and shoved it into her mouth.

"To work with Miss Delara," Taryel was saying, "is to work with the best mind in Navenie. Her methods are purely her own and second to none. She is an archaeologist by trade, an academic by instinct. Her sharpness of mind, the way she's able to see one thing and infer another, to predict an outcome before the chips have even begun to fall... she is not just a scientist. She is a magician. A sorceress."

At this last, his gaze flickered to Ru.

She could have caught fire and burned to ash, right there at the dinner table.

"How lyrical," said Lady Bellenet. She turned to Lord D'Luc, appraising. "Though, I don't see it. Hugon, would you agree?"

The lord paused in stirring cream into his coffee. "I wouldn't put it quite so rhapsodically."

Ru wanted to cut in, to make some scathing remark

that would wipe the self-satisfied expression off Lady Bellenet's face. Who did the woman think she was, treating Ru like a mute child? Calling her a peasant? Questioning her intelligence, worst of all? This, the same Lady Bellenet who would see the kingdom destroyed in cleansing flames. Yet here Ru sat, nothing to her but a topic of idle insult. Was that how they saw her, then? An ignorant girl, useless but for her connection to the artifact?

Ru wished she had the guts to fight back, either with words or even violence. She was utterly out of her depth. So she only seethed, strangely glad to stew in indignant anger rather than fear for once.

Taryel's gaze on her was steady but demanding, and even in her periphery, she was helpless to it. Even *he* had hardly spoken to her, hadn't given her so much as a hint that he was on her side.

I need to get him alone, she thought.

"Try the chocolate, too," Taryel said. His tone was quiet, and with those words came a soothing murmur from within Ru — the artifact, Taryel's heart, softening her ragged edges.

Lady Bellenet and Lord D'Luc were distracted, engaged in intimate, quiet conversation.

Taryel leaned forward as if to involve Ru in his conspiracy. "I requested the cakes especially," he said, "because I knew you'd like them."

Ru said nothing.

"It will make you feel better," he added.

"As if you know me," Ru muttered, reaching for one of the chocolate confections. Almost defiantly, she took a dainty bite. The cake was gorgeous, rich and decadent. Of course, the chocolate helped. She had always found comfort in bakeries and confectionaries.

He watched her, lips curving in a smile. "They're all the rage at court."

"Evidently," Ru said, "so are *you*. Care to elaborate?"

"Don't overindulge, Miss Delara," said Lady Bellenet, noticing the cake in Ru's hand. "You'll make yourself ill. Clarity of body is clarity of mind."

"Quite," said Lord D'Luc, as if he was used to agreeing

with everything the woman said. Her handsome little puppet.

Taryel rolled his eyes, his gaze catching at Ru's in some attempt at a shared joke. But she refused to be taken by his charm. A few nights ago, she had resigned herself to losing him forever. She wouldn't undo all that grieving; she couldn't. It would be too hard.

The soft haze of Ru's wine was beginning to wear off, and the sharpness of reality fell in to replace it. The stark knowledge of where she was, who she dined with, and why, hit Ru at the same time as a sickly stomach ache.

She stared at the tablecloth. It was white, patterned with fleur-de-lis and vines of grapes. Running her fingers over it, she could feel raised embroidery where the vines curled.

Voices rose and fell in the background, a fog of sound. In her mind, and spreading through her body like syrup, the artifact seemed to be doing its best to calm her. Or was it Taryel, somehow caressing her thoughts like he had in the forest? Either way, it wasn't working.

Breathe in…

"Are you ill?" The voice was clipped but urgent.

She turned to see Lord D'Luc's pinched features regarding her. She knew Taryel was watching her too but couldn't bear to look. He was too much right now. The artifact consumed her, overflowed in her. Everything was far too much.

Lord D'Luc's hand found her arm, pressing fingers into flesh. "Are you *well*?" Something in the tone of his voice was different, more present than a moment ago, harsher, almost… worried.

"I'd like to retire for the night," Ru said.

The cakes and wine roiled heavily in her gut, and the smell of coffee made her stomach curdle. The intensity of Taryel's gaze, Lady Bellenet's knowing smiles, the laughter of the courtiers at the table… it had all become grating. Unendurable.

At Ru's declaration, Lady Bellenet's eyebrows rose above girlishly wide eyes. "Oh?" she said. "Departing so soon?"

"The cakes," Ru said, forcing an apologetic smile. "You were right."

"We've much to discuss, you and I," said Lady Bellenet, "though I see that tonight is not the time. I'll send for you."

At this, Ru rose, unsteady on her feet. Hands shaking, she struggled to wrench her skirts free from beneath the table. The dress was creased and marred from her sweaty grip on its skirts. Disgusted with herself and everything around her, she turned to the door.

The sound of another chair scraping across the floor caught her short, and she glanced back.

Lord D'Luc stood behind her, offering an elbow. "I'll accompany you, Miss Delara."

She had no basis for refusal. The last thing she wanted was to raise a fuss. And whether she liked it or not, she could use a steady arm just then. Wordlessly, she took the lord's elbow.

Ru caught a flash of annoyance in Lady Bellenet's expression, and Taryel's stare was dark and deadly as Ru and Hugon made their exit, arm in arm.

CHAPTER 11

For the second time in her life, Ru was escorted through the palace by Hugon D'Luc. She leaned on his arm, hating every second of her reliance on him in her heightened emotional state, hating that the overwhelming feeling upon seeing him rise from the table behind her had been relief.

Sybeth followed several paces behind.

"You'll get used to her," Lord D'Luc said, after several long minutes of silence.

The casual tone in his voice, the unexpected familiarity, caught Ru off guard. "Lady Bellenet?"

"She has an exceptional mind," he added, thoughtlessly adjusting his arm around Ru's, steadying her, "which she often uses to get what she wants."

"How lovely."

He glanced sidelong at her, as if just now noticing the sweat beading on her upper lip, the way she had to lean on him for support. He frowned slightly and looked away. "She can be difficult to… understand."

"Her insults were shockingly clear," Ru said.

The lord shifted, his shoulders straightening and his expression smoothing, mask-like. "Lady Bellenet's actions are never without reason," he said as if reciting a line by rote.

"Just like yours," Ru muttered. She chewed her lip until

blood soured her tongue. "How long have you known about Taryel?"

There was a moment in which Ru thought he hadn't heard her or had chosen not to respond. They wove through the halls, past courtiers and footmen, under bright chandeliers, and past starlit windows.

At last, he said, "I could ask you a similar question. How many times have I asked about Fen Verrill, his powers, what he might do? And how many times have you evaded me?"

"His identity wasn't my secret to keep," said Ru. "That's not the point. You have no *right*—"

"What right do any of us have?" he snapped. "I suspected Fen's true identity not long after joining you at the Cornelian Tower. And when I saw that ghostly city from afar, Ordellun-by-the-Sea at night… of course, I was all but certain then. You must think me a simpleton not to have connected the dots. But it doesn't matter, Delara. A centuries-old god walks among us. The Destroyer, the hand of death. There are bigger things to worry about than your ego."

"He's not a god," Ru said through clenched teeth. "He's just a man who…" *Who what?* she thought. *A man who happens to be hundreds of years old? A man who leveled a city in a moment? A man whose heart belongs to me?*

"Gods and men are not so different," said Lord D'Luc. "What proof do we have that he is *not* a god? What my lady and I do here, spreading the word of Festra, enlightening those who would otherwise remain in the darkness, is for the good of all. And when you activate the heart, when you bring Festra's flames down upon us, the world will rejoice. Because Taryel, Lady Bellenet, and *you* will have made it so. Whether he is Fen Verrill or Taryel Aharis is immaterial. He inspires faith amongst the rabble."

Ru struggled to make sense of this. "He makes them swoon at dinner, you mean."

The lord scowled.

"So you've actually chosen the Destroyer," Ru went on, her tone dripping incredulity, "to be the figurehead of this religious cult? What is the point?"

Lord D'Luc exhaled through his nose. "Lady Bellenet prefers to think of him as a beacon of hope. And the point? It's you, Delara. You saw the courtiers at dinner, Festra's newest followers, people who see you as you *could* be. Taryel's consort, the Keeper of His Heart. It's romantic, aspirational. You may as well accept it, Delara — they admire you. They might worship you if given a chance. As they should."

Ru went cold. "Those people aren't believers, Hugon. They're not pious in the least. You know as well as I do that they're frivolous aristos, indulging in the latest fad. Festra isn't real to them. It's all a game. No matter what they believe, no matter what god they profess to follow, when I *activate the heart*, as you so nicely put it, they'll die. Along with everyone else." A lump formed in her throat. Without thinking, she breathed, "I don't want to hurt anyone."

The lord frowned, meeting Ru's gaze again. As if he were letting her in on a secret, he said, quietly, "If not the making of you, Delara, your mind will be your undoing. Try not to think so much."

They walked in silence for a few breaths. Ru struggled to contain her emotions, spurred into chaos by everything Lord D'Luc had said. That she and Taryel were meant to be worshiped by the poor palace courtiers, their visages twisted into a horrible farce of a religion.

But as they went, Ru's mind racing, she realized that the silence between her and Lord D'Luc wasn't strained or awkward. She found she was used to this, these moments between them. Their arguments, disagreements. He had been a constant presence, albeit unwanted, for months now. The realization hit Ru with a resigned sort of horror. She hadn't seen it until now, the way she depended on these moments with him. Had her life become such a nightmare that a conversation with an equal, jailor though he may be, was comforting?

"Are we almost to my room?" Ru asked, squeezing her eyes shut as a wave of nausea rolled over her. The evening had been too much for one academic to take, and her body was rebelling. "If I have to lean on your arm for one minute longer, I might actually lose my dinner."

"Charming," he drawled. "Just around the corner."

Ru glared up at him, the man who had held her in his iron grip for months. Hugon D'Luc had wounded her in ways that might never heal. Yet here she was, leaning on him. The only person who saw her as she was, the worst of herself laid out before him on display.

"Here we are," said Lord D'Luc, coming to a stop at Ru's door. "I hope you've access to your key. I'm not about to search in your pockets for it."

Unsteady on her feet, Ru dug out the key and held it up. He took it between two long fingers, unlocked the door, and pushed it open. Sybeth stood by, watching with the stern frown of a chaperone.

"Breakfast is at eight," said the lord, his cheek dimpling slightly. Probably in amusement at Ru's state — she was sweaty, sickly, and her face burned hot after walking in such a heavy gown.

"Good night," she said curtly and slammed the door in his face.

~

Ru had long since finished throwing up her dinner, crawling out of her beautiful gown, and rinsing her face and mouth with cold water. She lay now in her enormous bed, wearing the silk nightgown that Pearl had laid out for her. Her head was beginning to ache, but there was a full jug of water by the bed, and she made thorough use of it.

Sleep, however, would not come. Not that Ru expected it would — her stomach was still too queasy, and her thoughts strayed constantly to the one man she was desperate to forget. How was she supposed to sleep after seeing him? Not only was Taryel at the palace, only two short days after practically begging her to run away with him, but he was already well-acquainted with Lady Bellenet. *How?*

Ru groaned, rolling onto her side and burrowing into her feather pillow. Even with her eyes shut, in the darkness of her mind, she saw only him. His eyes, so familiar to her and yet belonging to a man who wasn't hers.

Taryel had betrayed her.

And yet... the artifact's sultry warmth coiled in her mind just as heat coiled in her belly, remembering the way he had looked at her that evening: With pure, unadulterated want. And her body, traitorous thing, had responded in kind.

And now, there was nothing she could do to stop her mind from wandering back to that feeling, watching Taryel's deft hands, the curve of his neck, the way locks of his hair sometimes clung to the edges of his jaw. The agonizing taunt of his gaze locked on hers.

In the quiet darkness, almost dozing, Ru wondered what she would do if Taryel came to her that night. If he knocked on her door, softly, and she answered it in nothing but her nightgown, a thin diaphanous thing that left little to the imagination. She imagined opening the door to him, *allowing* him to press his body to hers, to touch her, kiss her.

She let out an unselfconscious groan as she imagined him lifting her, hands on her waist, her backside, her thighs... and carrying her to bed. Would she let him if he tried? What if he were to draw a finger from her chin, down her neck, slowly, encircling her breast with a soft touch? And what if he bent down to tongue her nipple, laving, suckling obscenely, until the silk of her nightgown was soaked and see-through?

Her breath hitched at the thought of it, her hand sliding down between her thighs, pressing the heel of her palm to just above the most sensitive part of her.

What would he do next, then, after he'd had his fill of her nipple? If he were here, he would kiss her neck, sucking on her tender skin, one hand in her hair, holding her gently... the other hand snaking under her nightgown, grazing her thigh.

"Shit," she said aloud, biting her lip until it hurt.

Taryel wouldn't take things slow, not if he came tonight. He would use his fingers deftly, his mouth, his voice. He'd whisper in her ear as he plunged his fingers into her, kissing her mouth, her breasts… and then she'd lose control, her back arching…

Ru gasped as she came, her own fingers and the thought of Taryel pushing her over the brink of pleasure. But when she opened her eyes, she was alone in her room, and regret pooled in her chest. She lay there breathing hard, staring up at the ceiling.

You'd let him in, she thought. *In more ways than one, and you wouldn't think twice.*

She had ached for him since that night in the dungeon when she had finally let herself give in, when he had kissed her, and he had molded his body to hers as if they were meant to be; as if they were born for each other.

No, not that… she didn't want these memories, or anything real. She wanted the fantasy of him. She wanted *Fen*.

But as the haze of lust cleared further, she felt increasingly disgusted with herself. She let him in so easily, even in her fantasies. Taryel, D'Luc, Bellenet… all three were her enemies.

But her body, it seemed, had its own ideas.

CHAPTER 12

A grandfather clock ticked somberly in the corner. Ru watched its pendulum, latching onto that predictable movement as Regent Sigrun spoke.

"Miss Delara," said the regent, her tone as dull as the night before. "Are you listening?"

"Yes," Ru lied. She had been thinking about the clock. And her hunger. She had been awake since dawn without so much as a sip of coffee, and it was almost half past eight. And she was trying not to wonder why the regent was holding an audience here, in her study, rather than the throne room. Perhaps the lack of personality had made the regent averse to her usual pomposity.

"Good." The regent sat at a desk, which was the obvious focal point of the room. A King's Guard stood at the door, and a white-robed figure was seated to the right of the desk, holding a parchment — Inda.

"Agenda," said the regent.

Inda glanced down at the parchment. "You've done introductions. The schedule is next. Then, expectations." Her voice and manner were just as dull as the regent's. Ru felt as if she were meeting with a pair of automatons.

"Thank you," said the regent, exhibiting no hint of gratitude whatsoever. "Miss Delara, now that your work with the artifact has relocated to the palace, we are pleased to inform you that every resource, intellectual, academic, philosophical, or otherwise, is at your disposal. Your sessions will begin each morning at breakfast, led by Lord D'Luc. Demonstrations with the artifact will recommence when Lord D'Luc deems it necessary. Demonstrations may cease upon the achievement of your goal, which is..." Sigrun paused, and Ru thought she saw a hint of confusion cross that distant expression.

The regent had always seemed so strong, Ru thought. A powerful, empathetic woman. To see her mind erased like this was sickening.

Inda lifted her head. "Control of the artifact, and subsequently, the Great Cleansing."

"The Great Cleansing," said Regent Sigrun, never once acknowledging Inda's presence. She continued, her words an unending drone, "The Cleansing will be a joyous celebration of Festra's heart and his will. The heart shall, at last, achieve its full potential. Fire. Cleanse. A new world. It..." she blinked slowly. "It will take place on the winter solstice. No sooner, no later. You will wield the artifact as Festra has foreseen and decreed. You will fulfill your destiny at last."

Ru ground her teeth. "And if I refuse?"

Inda's gaze drifted to Ru, but she said nothing.

"You won't," said the regent. "You'll be under guard. You will not leave the palace grounds without an escort. You will not come and go without my knowledge. You will continue your studies as ordered. Your friends, I'm told, are here with you. And exceedingly loyal."

There it was, the threat. The same words Lord D'Luc had spoken back at the Tower. Ru deflated. She was a prisoner here, just as she'd been at the Tower. But now, she was watched by more than just Lyr, more than a handful of guards. The eyes of an entire court were trained on her. A smart move, she thought bitterly, if Lady Bellenet had planned it this way. Even if Ru slipped past the guards, every courtier in the palace would be aware of her comings and goings. They were obsessed with her. One of them had even fainted as Ru passed him on the way here.

"Where are you keeping the artifact?" Ru asked, grasping for anything that might give her leverage, any information that could help her.

"Safe," said the regent.

There was a long silence in which Ru wondered whether either of the women would react if she leapt at them with a burning ember from the fire. Instead of testing the question, she said, "Is that all?"

Inda blinked serenely.

"That is all," said Regent Sigrun. "You may go."

Ru needed no further prompting. She rushed from the room, aching for somewhere to vent her emotions. The artifact, thankfully, did not overwhelm her senses, though it boiled right alongside her.

"Hungry, Delara?"

The voice stopped her short, just outside the regent's study. Lord D'Luc leaned against the wall, arms crossed, watching her with a lazy smile. His cravat hung open, the top button of his waistcoat undone. Some distant and traitorous part of Ru reacted to the sight, wanting more of it. But she was used to pushing it away, dismissing her base instincts.

As she approached the lord, it occurred to her that he seemed different, somehow. His bearing was altered, more tense. The same man in a new mask. His smile just a bit strained, his body unable to lie still. He repeatedly tapped one elbow with a finger.

Refusing him might have been satisfying, but Ru was too hungry. She sighed. "You know that I am."

WHATEVER WEAK AND minuscule piece of Ru's heart that had softened toward Hugon at dinner last night, had seen him as a sense of unwanted comfort, was now completely gone.

After her meeting with the regent, she had walked with him through a maze of corridors and opulent, yet frigid, courtyards. He seemed content to breeze through these halls, his gold buttons catching the light and his hair moving pleasingly about his ears as he went. But when they finally arrived at his rooms, with breakfast waiting, he broke the worst news of all to her.

She, Ruellian Delara, was expected to speak to the court of Navenie.

"It won't be difficult," he said, leaning back in his chair. He had eaten almost nothing, simply watching as Ru made her way slowly through two soft-boiled eggs, toast and jam, and a rasher of bacon.

Ru sipped her coffee, washing down the last of her breakfast. With a full stomach, she felt far more equipped to deal with him. Even so, the artifact flickered angrily in the back of her mind as if spurring her on, and she couldn't help but lean into the feeling.

"I'm not doing it," she said, for the second time.

"The court deserves a proclamation from the Keeper. They *need* one. If the Cleansing on the solstice is to work as Festra desires, all of the court must be in attendance. You must entice them."

"You can't entice people into believing in a god," Ru countered, trying not to let her melancholy, her rising anger, affect her. "This announcement, this *event* you're planning, it's pointless. Have your lady poison everyone, or do whatever it is she does to make them pliant, and be done with it."

Lord D'Luc frowned slightly. "You see it as *making them pliant*. I see it as opening their minds to the truth. Lady Bellenet is not a usurper."

"I never said she was."

His eyes narrowed. "She is a guide. The sooner you accept it, the sooner you'll be able to focus all of your energy on controlling the artifact. On making it succumb to your will."

"Why would I do that when I know full well the result is a new Destruction?" Ru said.

Instead of answering, he gave her a long, disapproving look. "I expect you to wear something appropriate to the event. Something befitting a queen rather than a peasant."

She couldn't help but roll her eyes at that. "You and your lady need to coordinate better insults. I'll wear what I like."

"Even with Taryel Aharis at your side?"

Ru's stomach clenched.

"Will my friends be attending?" she asked.

Lord D'Luc's expression said he knew she was changing the subject on purpose. "They are free to do as they like."

Ru glared back as if to say, *you knew what I meant.* "Were they *invited*?"

"Yes."

"Will the artifact be there?"

"So many questions," he said, rising and offering a hand to Ru. "They'll all be answered soon, I'm sure. The festivities begin at dusk." He held her fingers in his, catching her gaze with hard sapphire eyes. "This will be your formal introduction to the court of Navenie. Your introduction as the Keeper of His Heart. Behave appropriately."

Wrenching her fingers from his grasp, Ru glowered back. The artifact's voice flared in her mind, a black flame. "I'll behave however I like, thank you."

He smiled. "You always do."

~

PEARL HAD JUST FINISHED BUTTONING Ru's dress when a sudden clamor arose from the window. The sun was nearly set, and the room was warmly lit with lamps and a lively fire in the hearth. Ru was on edge, ready to snap, and the sound made her nearly jump out of her skin.

Something had come in through the window, Ru thought. But her bed blocked the view, and...

"Goodness!" Pearl exclaimed, just as a man stood up from below the open window.

The man brushed himself off with exaggerated poise. His cheeks and nose were pink, and he delicately reached up to push a lock of coppery hair back in place. He grinned.

"*Simon*," Ru croaked, taken aback — not for the first time — by her brother's acrobatics. "Did you climb in through the *window*?"

"Obviously," he said, breathing heavily with exertion. "Didn't *quite* nail the landing. Did you really think me so foolish as to use the front door? Evening, Pearl."

Pearl only giggled, her cheeks going pink.

Ru's gaze darted between them. "Good god, Simon, if you've been…"

"I haven't seduced your maid," he said, "don't be silly. We're only friends, aren't we Pearl? Someone's got to look after you. Someone with style and taste. The characters you've taken up with lately… it boggles the mind." Simon managed to make even a grimace look dainty.

"I haven't taken up with any characters," Ru said.

"Mmm. *Character*, singular, I suppose. Now then, I've much to say and little time to say it. Pearl, won't you go and fetch us some tea?"

Still blushing furiously, the maid curtseyed and took her leave.

"You can't be serious," Ru said, following Simon into the parlor, where he availed himself of the entire sofa. He arranged himself luxuriously across it, like a lordling posed for a painting.

"About what?"

She waved her hands. "What do you think, Simon? Am I referring to that horrible shade of green you're wearing?"

"It's chartreuse…"

"I know we're all walking on eggshells here, but you came in through the *window*."

Simon was a creature of mystery, a stranger sometimes even to Ru, he was so deeply entrenched in courtly secrets. She had seen him leap out of a moving carriage, but to scale a wall as winter approached seemed foolhardy madness.

He only shrugged. "We've confirmed that I did."

"We're two stories high," Ru insisted. "Did you scale the wall?"

He pursed his lips. "Well yes, obviously. Keep up."

Lost for words, Ru studied her brother. His impeccably styled hair, his easy smile… even his shoes showed very little sign of damage for someone scrambling up palace walls for a lark. How on earth had he done it? Ru loved her brother but understood very little about him.

Simon moved over and patted the sofa cushion next to

him. "Now that tea is on the way, we simply *must* catch up. Before your little…" he grinned, "pronouncement."

"Pronouncement?" Ru echoed, not moving from where she stood, arms crossed.

"Don't be thick," he said. "Your formal introduction to court. I heard you're set to say a few words."

The raw glee on her brother's face made Ru absolutely furious. "I'm glad you think it's a joke," she said. "Do you also find it funny that Regent Sigrun has been compromised, that her mind is gone? That the palace is under the thumb of Lady Bellenet? That I am, in fact, a prisoner here? Oh, and let's not forget the most important bit… Taryel Aharis, the *Destroyer*, had dinner with me last night."

Simon picked at a speck of lint on his sleeve. "Why are you yelling at *me*? I've nothing to do with any of this. I simply live here." He looked up and patted the cushion again. "Anyway, I told you not to come. You should have listened."

Ru wanted to scream. "Stop being so… *Simon-y*, and just tell me everything you know."

"Sit down and I will."

Exhaling angrily through her nose, Ru finally gave in and went to the sofa, sitting stiffly at its edge.

"Relax, Ru, for god's sake."

She grit her teeth. "I'm two seconds away from throwing you back out the window."

The minstrel pursed his lips. "No need for threats. I'm on your side."

There was a clatter from the bedroom as Pearl wheeled in the tea cart. Neither Simon nor Ru moved.

"Well?" said Simon, waving a hand at the tea. "We'll need it for this conversation."

Narrowing her eyes, Ru stood and retrieved the tea from Pearl with a muttered thanks. She laid out the cups and sugar and milk, and, finally, the steaming jug of tea, her movements all by rote, her mind elsewhere.

At last, they both sat on the sofa, teacups in their hands. Ru was about to vibrate out of her own body. The artifact did nothing to comfort her, and she found herself looking to her brother desperately for guidance. For support, a rock to cling to. He was all she had, just then.

And he gave her nothing in return. His smile was calm and practiced, his fingers motionless against his cup. As if he were a perfect doll, wound up and set free to roam the palace, gathering tidbits of gossip as he went, unharmed and unaltered. Untouchable.

But Ru knew better. As a purveyor of information, talented in the arts of music, subtlety, and peril, everything Simon portrayed was an act, a disguise. His true heart, his raw emotions, they were something as mysterious to Ru as the inner workings of the artifact itself. He handled emotions with far more difficulty than even Ru.

"Ru," Simon said, and his expression softened. He reached out, placing a warm hand on hers for just a moment. It was all he was going to give her in the way of comfort, and she knew it. "Allow me to enlighten you," he went on, sipping his tea daintily.

"Please do," Ru said, resigned to the witty, surface-level dance that was a conversation with Simon.

"I came to warn you about Lady Bellenet," he said, managing to sound haughty even while relaying grave information. "But it seems you've already come to the correct conclusion. She's far more powerful than she seems. As you've no doubt witnessed, everything that leaves her mouth is a pretty lie, and everyone around you will be lapping it up like starving kittens being offered a bowl of milk."

"Then it's what I thought. She's the one holding the regent's leash. And Hugon is her lackey." Ru sat back, setting down her tea so as not to spill it in agitation. "But how is she gaining power? How does she change people, how can we stop it? And..." she bit her lip, hating that this was the most pressing of her questions, "why is Taryel here?"

"Ah yes, of course," Simon said, leaning back slightly, regarding his sister with a half-smile. "Your handsome rogue Fen, all grown up and revealed to be an immortal committer of genocide. How sweet."

"*Simon.*"

He waved a hand. "Oh, who cares about Fen, Taryel,

whatever his name is. I'm far more interested in discussing the tale of Bellenet and D'Luc, the delightfully deadly duo. Theirs is a story as old as time itself, isn't it? Two wealthy, attractive people join forces and start a cult defined by questionable fashion choices, travel to a new country, spread their ridiculous beliefs, seek out the reincarnation of their terrible god, dig up his heart, summon him here as some sort of annoyingly scruffy party trick, and… well, I suppose you know the rest."

Ru stared, fingers clutching the sofa cushions. The fire crackled cheerfully as her blood ran cold. "Did you say they… dug up his heart?" she said. "Lord D'Luc knew, or at least suspected what the artifact was, and he's been lying to me the whole time?"

"I thought you were supposed to be the intelligent one," Simon replied, a smile tickling the edge of his mouth. "Of course, he was lying. Why would he admit anything to you, a mere academic?"

"Shut up," Ru muttered, her thoughts a blur. "Then… he and Lady Bellenet came here together. From Mekya."

"So I've been told."

"*Overheard*, you mean," Ru said, raising an eyebrow. "So they came for the artifact. Somehow, they knew what it was and what it could do. But how? And Taryel…" her heart lurched. "Why did he come? Is he… loyal to Lady Bellenet?"

Simon leaned forward conspiratorially. "She believes he is. He's far too clever to fall for her special charms, fortunately for you."

"So, she really can turn minds like that?" Ru asked, her stomach roiling. "Do you know the nature of her power? Or how to stop it?"

"That," said Simon, "is a bit beyond my ability to learn. So far, anyway. I've yet to come across any evidence of her methods or limitations. She's very good at keeping secrets, Lady Bellenet. It's all very gauche if you ask me."

"But how did they know where the artifact would be buried?" Ru demanded, a thousand more questions bubbling to the surface. "If the regent ordered the dig at the Shattered City, has she been under their influence since then? I thought… but… I thought Taryel… he wanted me to come with him…" She chewed her lip and tasted blood.

"Ugh, not that," said Simon, recoiling slightly. "If you must insist on crying, please wait until I've gone. You know I'm no good at tears." Even so, he pulled a delicate handkerchief from within his waistcoat pocket and held it out.

Ru took it, blowing her nose.

"To be perfectly frank, I don't know any more than you do. Taryel's motivations are his alone." He leaned back as if to be as far away from strong emotion as possible. "I advise you to forget him, Ru. He's a knave, a rake, and so *old* for god's sake. I'd hate to be forced to duel him to preserve your honor, though you know very well I'd do it, and he'd die upon my sword. A situation I would rather avoid."

"Simon," Ru snapped, glaring at her brother. "I'm your sister. I can tell when you're lying. Why is Taryel here?"

Simon sighed dramatically, rolling his eyes to the ceiling. "Oh, *fine*. As far as I've been able to surmise, Taryel was never part of Lady Bellenet's original plan for the artifact. Until he stole the artifact from you, and those subsequent dramatics at the Shattered City, she thought Fen Verrill was nothing but a ragamuffin from the woods. I mean, he *is*, but he and I are—"

A knock sounded at the door, cutting Simon off midsentence. He and Ru shared a wide-eyed glance.

"That's my cue," said Simon, winking. Before Ru could protest, he leapt from the sofa and disappeared into the bedroom. Ru went after him, but by the time she got to the bedroom, he was already gone. A cold wind blew in through the window.

"Utter *buffoon*," she said through gritted teeth.

The knock sounded again, more insistent this time.

Heart in her throat, Ru opened the door.

"Delara," said Lord D'Luc, giving her an assessing once-over, and clearly finding her lacking. "It's time."

CHAPTER 13

As Ru and Lord D'Luc neared the throne room, the corridors became increasingly lively with bodies and noise. Courtiers made their way toward the great room as well, though considerably more slowly, gathering in clusters to stare or wave shyly at Ru, smoothing their skirts prettily. Footmen wove effortlessly between them, carrying trays of drinks and food as if this were nothing but a grand party.

One woman came up to Ru, her eyes alight, and placed a trembling hand on Ru's arm. "Miss Delara," she said, "where is your lover? We thought you might arrive together…" She glanced sideways at a pair of women who came sidling up to join her. "It's ever so *romantic*." The trio giggled in unison.

"I don't know where or *who* my lover is," Ru said, glancing accusingly at Lord D'Luc. "But perhaps my lord does?"

The three ladies turned their glowing attention to Lord D'Luc, who showed no evidence of discomfort. He bowed slightly, his smile handsomely charming as ever. "Fear not," he said, "the lovers will be reunited before long. Find a place in the throne room, now, before it fills."

Gasping and grasping one another's hands in breathless glee, the three women darted off through the crowds, toward the throne room.

"And what was that about?" Ru said, arms crossed.

"The court loves romance," said the lord. "Taryel and the Keeper of His Heart… it ignites the fancy, doesn't it?"

Ru's throat constricted. "What exactly is this pronouncement going to involve?"

"Nothing untoward," Lord D'Luc said airily. "A few words, that's all. Have you prepared something?"

Ru's stomach knotted. "The entire court is in attendance. And you've been conveniently hiding the fact that they all believe Taryel is my…" She bit her lip.

The lord sniffed. "Don't worry about courtiers. Hardly people at all."

Ru wanted to reply, but her nerves wouldn't let her. Ever since the artifact had come into her possession, there had been far too many speeches. Couldn't everyone leave her alone with her books? How was she supposed to accomplish anything useful in front of a crowd?

"Miss Delara!" came a bright greeting from across the hallway.

Ru turned, seeing Rosylla and Sybeth at the entrance to the throne room. Rosylla beamed, while Sybeth looked deeply uncomfortable. Both of them were dressed in starched uniforms, their buttons and helmets polished to a shine.

As Ru and Lord D'Luc moved to greet the riders, Lyr appeared out of the throng. He looked rested and well-kept, and his dark brown hair had been cropped shorter, his face clean-shaven. He looked every bit the King's Guard. Even in that crowded hallway, her nerves beginning to fray, the sight of Lyr was a wash of cool relief.

"Are you excited?" asked Rosylla, eyes shining.

Ru sucked on her bloody inner lip. "No."

Rosylla gave her a sympathetic look. "It won't be that bad, surely? I heard there's going to be a surprise announcement."

"Not a surprise if we know it's coming," observed Lyr.

"Oh, be quiet," Rosylla said with great affection.

Lord D'Luc stood by, fidgeting with his cuffs. "Delara," he said after exchanging vague niceties with the King's Riders. "Come. We're not going in this way. Avoiding the rabble." He gestured lazily toward the courtiers in the throne room, which was already fit to bursting with well-dressed aristocrats.

Ru craned her neck in search of golden curls or tawny brown hair and freckles, but she couldn't see Archie or Gwyneth in the chaos.

Lord D'Luc shot her a look. "They'll come."

That he had known what she was thinking set Ru further on edge.

Lyr followed dutifully behind as he, Ru, and Hugon left Rosylla and Sybeth in their wake, stationed at the throne room entrance. Lord D'Luc moved past the main throne room entrance, to a small door half-hidden by a tapestry. It would have been almost invisible if the lord hadn't pressed it at the right point, pushing it inward to reveal a narrow passage. Lyr took up his station at the door, while Ru went on with Lord D'Luc.

The passage opened into a larger sitting room, which was outfitted much like Ru's personal one — comfortable furniture, a roaring fire, and a tray of tea sandwiches and half-eaten pastries.

"Now," said Lord D'Luc, turning to regard Ru with a slight frown. "Do you have any questions before this begins?"

Ru stared. "Of *course* I have questions, Hugon."

His dimple threatened to make an appearance. "Spit them out, then."

Just then, another figure emerged from the passage. Ru's heart staggered at the sight of him, as if her world shuddered whenever he was near. She couldn't help the flutter in her belly, the heat in her cheeks.

Lord D'Luc glanced sideways at Taryel. "You're late. I was just about to brief Delara on her duties—"

"Duties?" said Taryel, coming to stand alongside the lord. Side by side they were a stormy sky and a bright spring morning, utter opposites in every way except for the shared, contemptuous glances.

"She's expected to make a proclamation," said Lord D'Luc, glaring up at the taller, darker man.

"A proclamation?" Taryel said with incredulity. "She doesn't even know what's—"

"I might *know what*," Ru interrupted, "if someone took the time to speak to me directly."

Taryel met her gaze coolly. "You won't be proclaiming anything, Ru. Lady Bellenet changed her mind."

"I hadn't heard…" Lord D'Luc said.

"That's because you're unimportant," Taryel said, tossing the lord a cheerful smile. "I am Taryel Aharis, the chosen avatar of Festra's will. Am I not?" He took Ru's shoulder then, guiding her toward another door on the far side of the room. "Ignore him," he muttered, just for Ru. "He's—"

"It's *time*," Lord D'Luc said from behind them.

"Right," said Taryel, stopping Ru before they came to the door and spinning her to face him. "Listen. There's going to be a lot of rhetoric out there in a moment. Even if you hate it, go along with it. Don't try to fight this, Ru."

As Taryel spoke, a subtle warmth swaddled Ru's heart — the artifact. No, Taryel, trying to calm her. To make her pliant, no doubt. She hated that it worked, that her breathing slowed, that she relaxed ever so slightly.

"*Go*," Lord D'Luc ordered.

Taryel flung open the door and ushered Ru through before following in her wake. For a moment, she stood stock still, her body a jangle of nerves even with Taryel's soothing touch. It was shadowy where they stood, dark after the brightly lit parlor.

"Stop panicking," Taryel said. "You're perfectly safe."

Ru jerked her shoulder out of his grasp. "*Safe* is a relative term."

But it wasn't physical danger Ru was worried about just then. It was eyes on her, the unknown; her tongue was dry and lead-heavy in her mouth.

A heavy curtain hung before them. So close, in fact, that Ru's nose almost touched it. She could hear voices, the low murmur of the crowd in the throne room, the swish of fans against sweaty faces. The regent's muffled voice carried over everything. Ru realized with a start that she was on the dais at the head of the throne room. And this curtain, she now saw, was one of the great crimson banners that hung behind the thrones.

Taryel took her hand for a moment, squeezed it tightly, then said, "She's just about to announce you. Go."

Ru hesitated. But even as she stood frozen, her feet refusing to move, her heart slamming against her ribs, the hazy warmth in her chest began to spread. It started in her chest, slowing the beat of her heart. It extended outward to her arms, her hands, further relaxing her tension. It spoke to her in wordless currents, a caress of energy that brought her back to herself, moment by moment.

Ru's shoulders relaxed, her jaw loosened, and she could breathe again. She could almost feel Taryel's self-satisfied smirk beside her. He had done his work.

Before the effect could fade, she strode around the banner and onto the bright dais.

"May I present to you," said Regent Sigrun's resonant voice, "Ruellian Delara, Keeper of His Heart."

Cheers and wild applause filled the room. Ru saw smiles and laughter, drinks being lifted in toasts, fans fluttering against the heat of that packed room.

"Taryel!" some of the courtiers cried out. "Bring him out!"

Ru thought she heard Festra's name, too. The court of Navenie was well and truly taken in by this madness.

Standing there in silence, the shining eyes of countless courtiers staring up at her, was worse than speaking at a Tower deliberation. Far worse. Ru stood just to the right of the largest throne, which appeared to be empty. This was the late king's throne, which Regent Sigrun had the right to occupy but she chose not to. She sat instead to the left of it, in a smaller, yet no less imposing, throne. Ru glanced sideways and saw the regent's usual plumed hat, her shining black leather boots.

But unlike the last time Ru had been in the throne room, there was an additional figure on the dais. Lady Bellenet stood to the Regent's left, mirroring Ru, and practically oozing celestial beauty. She wore a coronet of gold that looked like a sun rising from her hair.

The silence carried on for just a moment too long. And because Ru was more afraid of being at the center of awkwardness than at the center of attention, she said, "Hello."

Her voice was painfully small in that cavernous room.

Then, "Hello!" came the enthusiastic reply, sung from the lips of a roomful of courtiers.

It was then that Ru noticed, scattered about the room, some in groups and others hugging the sidelines, the Children. She hadn't seen many of them since arriving at the palace, other than Inda, Ranto, and Nell. But there were at least three dozen here in the throne room, watching Ru with hollow expressions.

Ru's skin crawled.

"We have long awaited her arrival," said Lady Bellenet, her deep voice spreading honey-like through the great room. Every face turned to her as the crowd murmured in response. "For we have seen Festra in his greatness, at the site of the Shattered City. And we have seen his heart. But who holds the blessed organ in her hands? Who will be the conduit between our mortal souls and the effervescent beauty that is our god?"

"Ruellian Delara!" shouted the courtiers.

Despite the artifact's ongoing warmth, ice began to form in Ru's veins.

"Who will show us the shining road to paradise?" said Lady Bellenet, almost chanting.

"Ruellian Delara!" came the disturbing response.

Ru felt as if she were in a nightmare.

"This is a day of beauty," Lady Bellenet went on, her tone bright and animated. "It is a pivotal day, in which we shed the selves we once were and take up new mantles. Too long has Mirith simply existed, persisted, survived. Should we not strive for more? Should we not strive to *live*?"

Roaring applause engulfed the room once more. A number of courtiers seemed to faint at this pronouncement, and more than a few exaggerated sobs cut through the din.

Ru tried to look passively pleasant, to keep the disgust from her face.

But Lady Bellenet continued to speak, gesturing broadly as she did. She seemed to glow in the light of the chandeliers. Even from that awkward angle across the dais, with two thrones and a regent in the way, Ru found herself captured by Lady Bellenet's words. She was beginning to understand how this woman had whipped the court into such a frenzy.

Even so, charisma alone didn't explain what had happened to Regent Sigrun or the Children. It didn't explain Taryel.

"Scientific progress, the study of the arts, literature, philosophy," Lady Bellenet was saying, "can only take us so far as a kingdom. As a *society*. Have you never yearned for more? Have you never heard a beautiful song, or gazed up at the heavens on a clear night, and wondered what awaited you in the after?"

Yes, Ru thought, and she was immediately embarrassed at her reaction. But she had. Who hadn't wondered what else lay beyond the known? It was those yearnings that had made Ru who she was, had driven her to study magic and archaeology.

"Have you ever loved someone, treasured a soul as true as yours, only to lose it?" Lady Bellenet continued.

Ru's stomach lurched. She sensed Taryel behind her, still lurking in the shadows. The man who had broken her heart.

"There is no pain to rival it," said Lady Bellenet, and Ru felt as if the words cut straight to her core. "You may still be healing. The wound may still hang open; your soul laid bare to the world. And every day, the winds of life ravage you, a tumult of mundanity and misery. And when you look up at the sky at night, perhaps you see not what is possible, but what you've lost. How little is left to you."

A cacophony of sniffles and strangled sobs broke out amongst the gathered courtiers. Ru blinked, hard, her eyes stinging.

Lady Bellenet stepped forward so that she stood just ahead of the regent. Ru could see her clearly, the lady's almond-brown hair hanging loose down her back. "But what if I told you," Lady Bellenet said, "that your pain was not part of you? That you were not beholden to it? My loves, you are not bound to misery. There *is* more to the world than what we see, what we feel, what is measurable by science. Have you not felt it in those joyous moments? Have you not heard it on the wind?"

Yes! Ru wanted to say, then bit her lip, hard.

"Together, we can find a way to eternal joy," Lady Bellenet said, raising one hand as if holding that joy within it, and Ru watched as every eye in the room fixated on her. "Together, we will discover the mysteries of the universe. We will journey together to paradise. You only have to choose it. You must simply give in to the will of your god."

That flicker of interest in Ru's chest vanished. She had been swept up in the drama, the rhetoric, without even trying. But the reference to Festra sent her tumbling back to reality. There was no paradise, no eternal joy in store for these people. Only darkness.

Only death at Ru's hand.

Movement from behind Ru distracted her from the applause that rose from the crowd, the clinking of crystal glasses, the cheers of enraptured courtiers. She turned just in time to see Taryel at last emerge from behind the crimson banner.

He was still dressed head to toe in black, but now he wore something new. Something that caught Ru's eye and held it — a shining circlet of gold, arcing across his brow.

He glanced toward her for an infinitesimal moment, and for a split second of eternity, the artifact roared forth within her, hot and beautiful and wild. And then it subsided like a violent tide, and he was moving away from her to the front of the dais.

Lady Bellenet raised her arm to greet him, smiling, as the courtiers and Children and footmen, every pair of eyes in the room, gazed up at him.

"Behold," she said, and all those gathered watched in breathless awe as he lowered himself into the king's throne, resting one foot on his knee, an elbow languorously propped on a crimson velvet armrest.

"Behold your god."

And Lady Bellenet fell to her knees.

CHAPTER 14

I t took Ru's brain several moments to catch up. She stared sidelong at the tall figure, as dark on that throne as death himself. But this wasn't one of Ru's fancies, some dire thought in the late hours. This was the court of Navenie. And Taryel had been declared a *god*.

Ru recalled Simon's words, gathering what she knew and attempting to understand it as she stood frozen on the dais. Taryel had never been part of Lady Bellenet's plan. Until recently, she had known him only as Fen Verrill.

While Ru hung caught in a moment of uncertainty and shock, the throne room reacted far differently. Shouts and cries broke forth through the din of applause. Courtiers embraced one another, faces wet with tears. Some tossed flowers up at Taryel or fluttered handkerchiefs desperately in his direction.

Good lord, Ru thought. Lady Bellenet's power, and the aristocracy's eagerness to leap from fad to fad, meant the courtiers had all unwittingly joined a religious cult.

Ru remembered the way she had felt when Lady Bellenet spoke of the night sky, of something more in the after. She had yearned in just the way Lady Bellenet had wanted, precisely because of Ru's deepest desires. Perhaps, in the age of science, there was a new vacancy that ached to be filled with faith. Centuries ago, the people of the Continent had been devoted to various gods. Their temples were strewn across the landscape, some in ruins and others well-kept. Ru had spent weeks in many such places, handling the remains of lives and faiths long faded.

But this was not faith. Lady Bellenet did not speak of salvation or joy, she spoke of an imminent genocide. Her gilded words were lies. And the winter's solstice was less than two months away.

Anger choked Ru as she thought of the beautiful books she had grown up reading, the Cornelian Tower, dirt under her fingernails, cracked vases at her fingertips. Theorizing and experimenting and uncovering more, *more*. Ru was proud of her kingdom, of the light it was shedding on the world. Mirith was the most scientifically advanced city in the kingdom — maybe on the continent.

And Lady Bellenet wanted to destroy it. All of it.

Ru hated her suddenly, more than she hated the artifact and Lord D'Luc and even Taryel.

"We must praise Ruellian Delara," Lady Bellenet said, as the crowd continued to hang on her every word, "the Keeper of his Heart. For it is she who speaks to our god, who loves him, who keeps him. It is she who will throw up her arms and bring down the light that shall cleanse our souls, that shall sweep us asunder, that shall carry us across the bridge to paradise."

Ru shifted, her unease ever growing. This was no longer the charismatic speech from before; it was a fanatic's chant. The Children gazed at Ru glassily. The courtiers were utterly swept up in the spectacle, almost frenzied in their fervor. Ru wildly considered making a run for it, but every exit would be manned by the King's Guards.

And Gwyneth and Archie... if they were here, she couldn't leave them.

So she stood and listened, trapped and utterly useless. Taryel was a god, and she was expected to end the world in his name.

Everyone in this room would be dead in two months. And Ru would be left standing at the center of a blackened crater that stretched across a continent.

Bile rose in her throat as sweat broke out on her upper

lip. The artifact's comfort had subsided almost entirely, and her breaths came faster and faster despite her attempts to relax.

Not now, she pleaded with herself. *Don't panic or faint in front of the entire court.*

But as Lady Bellenet continued speaking, her words becoming more and more feverish, Ru increasingly lost control of herself.

You can't throw up in the throne room, she thought desperately.

Fluidly as a cat, Taryel stood up from the throne. There was a break in Lady Bellenet's chanting, and as the eyes of the court shifted to focus on him, he said, "My poor lady is overcome by the power of Festra. Such is the strength of his love. Shall I accompany her to her bed, so that she may rest?"

The court erupted in wails and cheers. "Yes!" they cried. "Take her to bed!"

Taryel moved to Ru's side, his voice low. "The court thinks we're lovers," he muttered. "At the very least, pretend you like me."

Ru allowed him to put his arm around her, turning her gently away from the crowd. Every logical thought in her head hated this; wanted him gone. But her nerves betrayed her. The feel of his body against hers was horrifically perfect.

"How beautiful," Lady Bellenet's voice rang out, as Taryel steered Ru back into the shadows behind the curtain. "The Keeper and her god joined as one. As it should be."

As soon as they were back in the sitting room, Ru doubled over, retching. Nothing came out but spittle, and she clutched her stomach, eyes streaming.

Lord D'Luc, who had been lounging on one of the sofas, sprang to his feet at the sight of them. "What have you done to her?"

"Nothing, you thick-skulled lout," Taryel shot back.

"I'm fine," Ru croaked, wiping her mouth with the back of her sleeve.

"You're visibly not," said Lord D'Luc.

"She's fine," Taryel said. "No thanks to you."

Ru was shaking now, as everything she'd seen and heard in the throne room sunk in.

"She's coming with me," continued Taryel. "You haven't explained *shit* to her, as expected."

"I've been very clear," the lord said; the calm in his expression was a warning. "Delara isn't a child. She knows exactly what is expected of her."

"Both of you can kindly take a dive off the tallest tower in the palace," Ru spat, pulling away from Taryel. Her head was beginning to clear. "You're pathetic, the two of you. Would you like a pair of dueling pistols to clear things up? Or perhaps a pair of rapiers? I'd happily watch you gut each other."

"*One* of us would certainly face evisceration," said Lord D'Luc.

Without another word, too angry to respond, Ru spun on her heel and left them. She wanted to find Gwyneth and Archie. She needed to get away from these men, from this throne room, as far away as she could manage.

"Delara," Lyr said, as she rushed past into the hallway. It was quiet now, though Ru could hear continued chanting in the throne room.

"I want to be alone," snapped Ru.

"Sorry," Lyr replied, his long strides keeping him easily at her side. "Orders."

Ru made a loud, angry sound of frustration.

Another set of footsteps echoed in the corridor, hurried and heavy.

"If it's Taryel," Ru muttered, "would you mind stabbing him for me?"

Lyr glanced down. "This sword's more for slicing than stabbing, but—"

"Wait," said Taryel, breathless.

Ru stopped in her tracks, spinning to glare at the Destroyer. He was no longer wearing that horrible circlet, and his hair hung in loose black waves around his ears. She clung desperately to her rage, the only thing that felt real and true just then.

"What do you want?" she demanded.

He skidded to a halt, holding his hands up in placation. "I've told you, Ru. You're always welcome to stab me. Or slice." He risked a weak smile at Lyr. "I know you're angry."

"What an intelligent hypothesis, Taryel. Or should I call you Festra?"

He winced. "I can explain everything. If you'll let me."

Lyr crossed his arms in warning.

Ru sighed, a long, drawn-out exhalation, as if to rid herself of everything that had been said in the throne room. Even in her ire, she couldn't look away from Taryel. He was oil to her flame. He was inextricable.

"Fine," she said.

Taryel raised a hesitant eyebrow. "Fine, what?"

"Fine, I'll let you explain. But you'll have to do it now."

"Now?" Taryel asked. "Here?"

"You are the most wretchedly slow... no, not *here*," Ru said. "I need tea and a warm dressing gown. And to not be overheard by the entire court of Navenie. We're going back to my rooms."

~

RU WAS SITUATED on her sofa, wrapped in a fur-lined dressing gown, a cup of steaming tea balanced between three fingers. Her hair fell in a dark waterfall over her shoulders, and her slippered feet were drawn up under her for warmth. If she was going to face Taryel that evening, she would do it in as much comfort as she could manage.

Taryel, on the other hand, was perched stiffly in one of the armchairs opposite the sofa. He watched her darkly, blowing on his tea to cool it. She hadn't allowed him to speak until she was ready, and like an obedient dog, he had waited.

"Now," she said at last, sipping her tea, "you may talk."

"Everything I said back there," he said quickly, as if he'd been waiting desperately to say the words, "everything that happened in the throne room, none of that was my idea."

Ru raised her eyebrows slightly.

"...Some of it was Simon's."

Ru reached for the plate of cookies, which Pearl had

brought with the tea things. Slowly, deliberately, she picked one up and took a bite.

"Simon's idea," she said at last.

Taryel sighed. "The god thing—"

"You're an imbecile," Ru interrupted, "if you think you can blame any of this on my brother." She chewed her cookie violently. "Do you believe you're Festra then? Are you enjoying this? Did you *ask* to wear that stupid crown?"

Taryel sipped his tea, then set it daintily on the table between them, cup clinking against saucer. A muscle feathered in his jaw.

"May I have a cookie?"

Ru slid the plate out of his reach. "You'll be lucky to leave here in one piece, let alone with a cookie. Talk."

"Fair enough." He pushed black hair out of his eyes, meeting her gaze. "I'll start at the beginning, then. I've been living here, at the palace, for the last month. Don't look at me like that. I told you in the woods, there was nothing I could do while you were at the Tower. I wasn't myself for a long while. After I told you the truth of who I really was, I wandered in the shadows... I hid from the world. I knew I'd failed you at the moment you needed me most."

A painful lump formed in Ru's throat. "You lied to me. You abandoned me," she said in a near whisper. "And now you're *here*, playing god, like it didn't matter. Did that rescue attempt mean anything? Or was it just a way to confuse me?" She hated the way her heart threatened to break all over again. Just as it did every time she thought of Fen leaving her alone in the Shattered City. Alone with the Children and Lord D'Luc.

"Of course it meant something. I would have run with you, Ru." Taryel's voice was low and hoarse. "I know how this looks. I know you hate me. My heart—"

"You don't have a heart." The words were cold, but Ru needed him to know how he'd hurt her. She needed him to understand how alone she'd been, even in the place that had once been her home.

He sat back, running a hand through his hair. "Unfortunately, I do. But you know that."

"And I'm its *keeper*," she said bitterly. "I don't know

what that means, Taryel. Listen, I don't want to talk about the night you left. I want to know why you're here, now. Why you're playing this part. And why on *earth* my brother is caught up in your schemes."

"I finally came to Mirith because I believed it was the only place where I could be useful to you. To put an end to things. I came to your brother because I knew he was the only person with enough influence and information to help me."

"Help you do what?" Ru asked, though she guessed what he would say.

"Stop Lord D'Luc and Lady Bellenet."

"Then you knew she was pulling the strings from the start? And didn't warn me?"

"It wasn't like that," Taryel said, fingers white-knuckled as he gripped his teacup. "When I finally found the where-withal to make myself useful to you, I went to Simon. He already suspected Lady Bellenet of working with Lord D'Luc. Possibly even issuing orders from here in the palace. We only confirmed it recently, when Simon wrote to you. We didn't want to frighten you needlessly. We thought you'd be safest at the Tower, that we could figure out how Lady Bellenet was controlling the regent, put a stop to it, and you'd be none the wiser. But things have… spiraled out of control a bit, with Festra and everything. That's why I came to you in the forest. We knew you'd refuse to run, but we had to try."

Ru took a breath to steady herself and reached for another cookie. "Well, congratulations to you both. You've successfully accomplished nothing."

Taryel rubbed his face with both hands. "Don't look at it that way. This fad, this religion that's swept the palace… it's given me access. I played along from the start. Lady Bellenet made no secret of her belief that the Destroyer was Festra incarnate. And when I came to her, told her who I was, and confirmed the true nature of the artifact, she treated me accordingly. Put me on a pedestal before the court, allowed me to demonstrate my powers. And when the court was suitably enthralled, she began to let me in on things. Took me to dinners and balls as her right hand. It was a way in, a direct line straight to the source."

"And after all that," Ru said, incredulous, "you still have no idea how she's controlling people? Changing them? All of the professors at the Tower are gone, you know."

"I know."

"Then you also know it can't be undone."

He swallowed visibly. "I do."

Ru couldn't believe what she was hearing. "So for an entire month, you and Simon have been working to uncover the mystery of Lady Bellenet's powers, and all you managed to do was give yourself a fan club."

"When you put it that way it sounds a bit…"

"Laughable? Pointless?" Ru's mind whirled. The entire palace had known about the artifact, this secret she'd been trying to keep from Lord D'Luc for a month. She wanted to smash the plate of cookies into Taryel's remorseful face. "Why didn't you write to me immediately and let me in on this plan, you pair of meat-brained dolts?"

"I didn't want to frighten you," he murmured.

"As if I was having a grand old time at the Tower, performing demonstrations for D'Luc." Her voice caught in her throat, and she took a breath to still her nerves. "Now that I'm here, let me help you. I'm the Keeper of your horrible heart. If I can convince Lady Bellenet and Lord D'Luc that I've somehow relented, that I'm *enjoying* this newfound fame, maybe they'll let something slip."

"Simon won't like it."

"Well, *I* don't like being moved around on your ridiculous little board like a brainless pawn. He'll survive."

Taryel sighed. "If that's what you want, I'll have a word with your brother."

"I don't need his permission," said Ru haughtily. "Or yours. This is a demand, not a request. I'll bring a much-needed competence to your band of fools. Speaking of competence, how did you manage to learn about Lady Bellenet's plan all on your own? About Festra?"

Taryel blanched. "Do you remember when I left the Tower after we argued?"

"And you didn't come back until the night I tried to escape from Lord D'Luc? When you stole the artifact from me? How could I forget?"

He shook his head ruefully. "I know I hurt you. I'm sorry. But I left because I thought… I *suspected* that Lord D'Luc might be a disciple of Festra. I didn't say anything at the time because I thought it might be paranoia. I've dealt with them before, you know. It was centuries ago, but in Ordellun-by-the-Sea, there was a small contingent of those who followed Festra. I recognized signs, but I had to be sure, I had to confirm. So I came to the palace and did a bit of digging."

"You came *here*?" Ru asked. She couldn't imagine the regent admitting Fen Verrill into court without so much as an invitation, let alone letting him *do a bit of digging*. "How?"

He raised one hand and gestured with his fingers. For a moment, a tiny sphere of black lightning crackled at his fingertips, and then it faded and was gone.

She gripped the edge of the sofa, heart hammering in her chest. Even though she knew he had this power, every time she saw it, the truth of it overwhelmed her.

"Magic," Taryel said as if it were nothing. "I've traveled like this since I was a child. There were more of us, back then. Not travelers, but… magicians. Sorcerers, though not many people used those terms. It was a rare enough gift that scholars never conducted studies, or wrote any solid record of us. The magic of those days is now recalled only in superstitious metaphysical texts, or in folklore. Most at the time considered it a curse, including my family, who kept my abilities secret until I met the woman who taught me to hone my skills, to use them for the common good…"

"Althea," Ru said, remembering what he had told her at the Tower. A lifetime ago. "The witch."

He nodded. "Now you see why they gave her that name. I've spent centuries steeped in my own magic, learning and understanding it. In some ways, I'm more powerful now than I was as a mortal man. I can travel across the continent in an instant, where once I could only move short distances. But I've lost abilities, too. Now, other than pointless illusions or lighting a candle from across the room, that's all I can really do anymore — travel. And it's not without its limitations."

Ru sat back. "So you *traveled* to the palace to discover what Lord D'Luc was up to and found that he was worshiping Festra."

"And now we know he's under the command of Lady Bellenet. We also know they want to use you to bring about a Great Cleansing, but what they expect to gain from all this is still a mystery."

"Why didn't you tell me?" Ru asked, her voice cracking. "That night, when you came back… why didn't you just *tell* me?" She remembered it so vividly, the relief at Fen's return, the overwhelming desire, the way her chest had fallen open to reveal her wounded heart. How he'd stolen the artifact from her and fled.

He could have just explained.

"I'm sorry," he said, reaching out as if to comfort her, then pausing in the movement and dropping his hand.

She wanted him to touch her, desperately so.

"I hated you," she murmured. "I've spent every moment since you left… *hating* you."

"You won't let me forget it." His expression was broken, undone. "I was afraid to tell you the truth, terrified of what you'd think. I believed I could fix everything, that I could set things right if I was only given the opportunity. I thought…" he paused, holding her gaze as if to center himself. "I thought that if I brought my cursed heart back to the place where it had been wrenched from my body, that somehow I could… absorb it back into myself. Foolishly, I thought that by reenacting the Destruction, I'd be able to unravel the mystery of the artifact. That I'd understand what it meant, how it had been separated from me, why it called to *you*, why it brought us together. I meant to put everything right."

"Well, you've certainly failed in that regard. Nothing has been put right, and I'm still wondering why I can't get rid of you."

Taryel sighed, the lines of his face deeper than Ru remembered. A young man with centuries of loneliness behind him.

"I know," he said. "I should have been forthright with you. But I was desperate and frightened. I thought you were better off without me and my meddling. You were right to take the artifact. I'd have done nothing with it."

"So instead, you left me." Ru bit her lip. Her chest ached. She felt so distant from him, as if an ocean lay between their souls, despite only a few feet separating them.

"I was wrong. I made a mistake." He regarded her with stormy grey eyes. "That's why I came to you in the woods the other night. Everything I'd done was weighing on me. I couldn't let you come here, couldn't let you fall into Lady Bellenet's grasp. I would have taken you anywhere you asked. And I would have disappeared again if you'd asked. I would do anything to keep you safe."

At that, he reached out and took Ru's hands in his. She let him, her vision blurring with tears. His skin was rough and warm. She let him hold her like that, let him have that, because she needed it, too.

"I believe you," she said. "But it would have been too late."

"I know."

"You're the Destroyer. I should hate you for that alone, but I can't. I can't, or I'd hate myself, and… there's a part of me that doesn't. That part of me is just angry." She swallowed, shaking her head. "Actually, no. *All* of me is angry. I'm angry at the regent, Lord D'Luc, Lady Bellenet, *you*… but especially myself." She couldn't help the anguish in her voice. "But how could I have known? I didn't mean to kill anyone."

His chest rose and fell. "I know you didn't."

The moon was rising, and blue-white light angled through gaps in velvet curtains, in contrast to the orange firelight.

"What happened, Taryel? At the Destruction." Ru exhaled shakily. "Tell me that. Everything else you've done, I can wrap my head around. I don't like it, but I understand it. But the *Destruction…* I need to know."

He nodded, ran a thumb along the back of her hand, then let her go.

"It was nearly a thousand years ago," he said slowly. "But I remember as if it was yesterday. It was early morning in Ordellun-by-the-Sea."

CHAPTER 15

Firelight danced against the night's shadows, limning the room in warmth. It should have been cozy, but Taryel's dark form, edged in a fiery glow, only made Ru uneasy. She reached thoughtlessly for her tea, a small comfort in that breathless evening.

"The tale as it's told now," he said, in the cadence of a man lost in the memory of a story, "the Destruction, the Shattered City… it's mostly true. I was King Alaric II's sorcerer. He called me his advisor, but everyone at court knew what I was. My magic was a badly-kept secret, but I was too powerful to touch, the right hand of the king."

He sighed and shook his head slightly. "I joined him to change the world for the better. He was a monarch who ruled with cold rationality, a man who spared few thoughts for his own people. He wasn't quite a monster, but he was… lacking. And I believed that with compassion and my powers, I could mold him into a better king."

"Ambitious," said Ru, sipping her tea.

"More like self-centered," Taryel said, running a hand through his hair. "Naive. Wildly foolish, take your pick of descriptors. When I revealed to Alaric that I had magic, he was only too happy to bring me into the fold. He appointed me to the post of advisor by the time I was barely twenty-five. I was impulsive and emotional, quick to act and far slower to think. I made a mistake in putting my faith in him."

Ru listened so intently she hardly dared breathe, as if she might startle him into silence if she made any sudden movements. How many people other than Taryel knew the truth? A first-hand account of the Destruction, the moments leading up to it... she knew she couldn't afford to forget a single word.

"I was wrong about King Alaric II," Taryel said, and a darkness passed over his face, like a cloud passing over stars. "He wasn't a bad king. He was so much worse. A blind fanatic. A man who sought power above all else, for the sake of salvation. There were thousands of devotees in the city, so many. And they followed him religiously. He was their god incarnate."

Ru stared, teacup held halfway to her mouth. "Devotees? Of Festra, you mean?"

He stared at his hands, folding and unfolding in his lap. "Yes."

A god-king, a city's salvation, an impending destruction. Ru could see the faintest pieces beginning to fall into place, a pattern slowly emerging.

Reluctant, almost shy, Taryel looked up to meet her gaze. There was pain in his eyes that she couldn't begin to calculate, a depthless hurt that spanned centuries.

"I came to believe," he said, voice low. "I fell for the grandiose speeches, the promise of an eternity of light. Everything you heard in the throne room, the chants, the promises... King Alaric delivered the same rhetoric. And somehow, despite myself, I fell under his spell. I was a young man of sound mind, sensible, never before taken in by the concept of religion. But after only a few months with Alaric, I became devoted, a fanatic in my own right. I carried out his wishes in the name of his god."

Ru frowned, thinking. "You fell under his spell. Could King Alaric have wielded the same power as Lady Bellenet? There's clearly more to this than honest faith."

"Maybe," Taryel said, sounding unconvinced. "More likely I was weak, eager to please. Isolated, lonely. King Alaric offered me somewhere to belong, and... a lonely, desperate mind is easy to mold. It's easy to turn a blind eye when you want something that badly."

"But you wanted a compassionate king. Festra is in opposition to that," Ru insisted. "You weren't as weak as you want me to believe."

"I don't *want* to be weak," Taryel said, bristling. "I would have done anything... He used me, Ru. Coerced me. Convinced me that I would be the one to *save* the kingdom, to open the gates to paradise. I would be the one to cleanse the world in fire. You have to understand, the more time I spent with Alaric, the more I learned about my powers. I became intoxicated by it. Because I couldn't just travel, Ru. I could destroy."

Ru leaned forward, her tea and cookies utterly forgotten. Had anyone heard the full story before, in the history of Navenie?

Taryel, so wrapped up in the memory that he no longer seemed aware of Ru, stared into the past as he spoke. "I practiced this new power on remote beaches, in empty fields, even on boats on the water. Wherever I could reasonably avoid harming someone other than myself. But one day, Althea followed me. She'd been worried. I'd been avoiding her, caring only for my king and my god. I was blind to her. And when I realized she had followed me, that she was there with me in the woods... it was too late."

He looked up at Ru, his eyes red-rimmed, the expression of a ruined man. "I killed her. She called my name as I cast the spell, and when I turned to look... she was gone. Everything was gone: trees, ferns, every living thing. And in its place, a perfect circle of destruction lay around me. I nearly drew a dagger across my own throat that day. The only thing that stopped me was my hatred of King Alaric. He had pushed me to develop my talents for destruction. *He* made me Althea's murderer. And if I died, he would only find some other magician to *cleanse the world.*"

He spoke those last words through gritted teeth.

Ru leaned toward Taryel, an instinctive movement. She stopped herself just before her thumb touched his cheek. There was too much pain between them, still. Too little trust.

"After that, I played along," he continued, pain permeating his words. "I planned to do everything King Alaric asked of me, up until the moment I was expected to destroy the world. I meant to kill him, Ru. I meant to kill *only* him. My powers were powerful but volatile, and in my naivete, I was utterly convinced of my self-discipline. I was so sure that Alaric and I would be swallowed up in darkness, and that would be the end of it.

"Instead, I lost control. My own power was too much for me, and my rage was so great…" he hung his head, running shaky fingers through black hair. "I destroyed the city. *My* city."

Ru opened her mouth but found she had no idea what to say. A thousand years had passed, but she saw in Taryel's eyes that it might have been yesterday, the pain was so acute.

"I meant to save them," he said, and he looked at her with desperation, as if she were his absolution. As if she had the power to forgive. "Instead, I doomed them all. And this," he gestured to himself, "is my punishment."

Ru's thoughts were everywhere. She was horrified by what he had done, at how he could have been so thoughtless with such destructive power. But even as she judged him, she couldn't help but judge herself. She couldn't meet his eyes. Somehow his fate was tied to hers, and in a pivotal moment, they had both failed.

"You're not like me," Taryel said at last, his accented voice barely audible above the crackling fire. "I know that you believe our punishments should be equal. But you're innocent. What happened to you is my fault. My heart lured you to the Shattered City. *My* heart pushed you to do things you didn't want to do."

Ru lifted her head and saw that Taryel was watching her. "You know I'll never accept that," she said. "My actions belong to me."

"You had no idea what would happen."

"But I *knew* I shouldn't touch it. I didn't take precautions."

"Stop blaming yourself," Taryel murmured. "Put the burden on me, instead."

"Taryel…" she wanted to keep arguing with him, but even more, she wanted to reach for him. The artifact, that cursed thing, even now it made her long to feel his hands on her skin, his body against hers, his mouth caressing her neck. Desire flared in her in the wake of Taryel's truth, and it tasted bitter in her throat. "You should have told me sooner."

His brows drew together in a frown. "I know. But what could I do? The moment you learned who I truly was, you would have turned on me. Anyone would. And you had my *heart*. Ru, you were — you *are* — everything to me. The moment I saw you in the Shattered City, holding that stone... I was done for. I would have followed you anywhere, protected you from anything. I felt you here." He placed a palm on his chest. "And I knew that we'd been pushed together by fate, or the gods, or the stars in the sky. It didn't matter why or how. All I cared about was being near you. And when I..." he paused, swallowing thickly. "When I realized that the artifact was no longer part of the equation, that Ru Delara held my heart no matter what the fates had decided, I knew I had to make things right. So I left. And when I came back—"

"You stole the artifact," Ru cut in, her voice threatening to break.

"I was going to come back for you. After I fixed things."

"But you didn't," she half-sobbed, unable to hold back any longer. "How can I forgive you for that?"

"I don't know." He looked at her with a candid vulnerability that she had seldom seen on his face, an invitation to know him. "But I'd hoped you might find a way."

She bit her lip, refusing to cry in earnest. "Forgiveness is earned," she said. "I understand what you've done. I'm a scientist; I can rationalize it. But look at where we are. What's coming. I'm expected to perform a second Destruction, Taryel."

"I know."

"How can you ask for forgiveness until we've stopped it? King Alaric put this into motion, but if it weren't for you, Ordellun-by-the-Sea would still be here. You could have cut your losses and run."

"I know," Taryel said again. "Not a day goes by that I haven't regretted that moment. I am constantly thinking of all the ways I could have stopped those lives from being cut short. Please believe me when I say that however deeply you hate me, I've spent lifetimes hating myself more."

Ru had not forgiven him. She did not trust him. But she pushed the plate of cookies across the table, and wordlessly, Taryel took one, a faint smile hovering at the corner of his mouth.

CHAPTER 16

Gwyneth and Archie's rooms were adjacent to one another, not far from Ru's. Lyr showed her to them with bold defiance, neither of them knowing whether she was allowed or whether she would be stopped and returned to her room. But the King's Guards posted at her friends' doors said nothing as she and Lyr approached, despite the late hour.

When Gwyneth opened the door, Ru wasn't surprised to see Archie there already, half sprawled on a sofa, teacup in hand. The room was well-lit with a fire and oil lamps. Clusters of half-melted candles were scattered about the room.

"Thank god," Gwyneth gasped, pulling Ru into a bone-shattering hug. "Oh, Ru. We've been so worried. After that madness in the throne room—"

"You *were* there," Ru said, both relieved and embarrassed that her friends had witnessed the whole thing.

"Of course we were," said Gwyneth, dragging Ru inside and slamming the door behind her. "We didn't know what to think. Taryel is here, and he's... a *god*? I can't imagine what you're going through. We've been up all night, Archie's been pacing like a madman. Are you all right? Please say you're — wait, let me get you some tea. Archie! Get her some tea."

Ru was ushered to take a seat by the fire, and Archie, frowning slightly, shoved a welcome cup of tea into her hands. Gwyneth's large brown eyes were bright with concern, her usually pristine golden curls pulled hastily back with a ribbon. Archie looked his usual well-groomed self, although the telltale shadows under his eyes hinted at a night of little sleep.

"Thought you'd been consumed alive by an ancient god or something," Archie said, the joke falling flat in the face of his obvious concern.

"Or worse," said Gwyneth, seating herself next to Archie, "forced to demonstrate with the artifact. We saw you leave the throne room with Taryel. What on *earth* is going on? These horrible guards at our doors won't tell us anything, they won't let us leave. Ru, be honest. Are you all right?"

Ru curled her fingers around the near-scalding teacup, unsure where to begin. Last night's baffling dinner with Lady Bellenet? Her chilling meeting with Regent Sigrun? Her conversation with Taryel? They had obviously seen the spectacle in the throne room earlier that evening.

"I'm all right," Ru said at last. "But things are bad."

"Well, obviously," Gwyneth said breathlessly, as Archie nodded in agreement. "All that rubbish in the throne room about paradise and cleansing fire… they've built a pretty religion as a cover-up for a new Destruction."

"What's really sticking in my craw," Archie said, "is that Taryel got himself involved somehow. What's he up to? We asked around for Simon, you know. Couldn't find hide nor tail of him."

"Simon came to my room," Ru said, blowing on her tea to cool it. "To warn me that Lady Bellenet is behind all of this, and she's more powerful than she seems." She pursed her lips. "And Simon's working with Taryel, though I had to hear that from Taryel himself."

"They *what?*" Gwyneth gasped, teacup halfway to her mouth. "Is Simon mad?"

"Yes," Ru said, "but his madness is neither here nor there."

As clearly and efficiently as she could manage, Ru told her friends everything that had happened to her since last night's dinner. Taryel's appearance, the realization that Regent Sigrun was under Lady Bellenet's control, her meeting with the regent, breakfast with Lord D'Luc, and Simon's information. She wasn't sure why, but Ru found herself strangely reticent when it came to Taryel. As if their conversation earlier that evening had been something to hold close to her heart, or, more likely, she was afraid of judgement.

But Gwyneth's intuition was too strong a force. She eyed Ru over her tea. "You're strangely calm, Ru. Considering you just discovered that Fen... sorry, *Taryel* is at the palace, playing god with your brother."

"I wouldn't say he's playing god," Ru said. "More like—"

"Wait, I know that look," said Gwyneth, sitting up straight. Her gaze was hard and penetrating. "He's already halfway to charming you back into his good graces."

Ru snorted. "He's decidedly not."

"Yes he is," said Archie, narrowing his eyes. "You can't hide from us, Delara. Tell us everything."

"I'm not *hiding*," Ru protested. "He hasn't charmed me. It's just... I didn't know how to bring it up without you both looking at me like that."

"Like what?" Gwyneth asked.

"Like you're looking at me now," Ru said. "With obvious judgment and far too much worry. Just... it's really fine. When he came to me in the woods, it—" She pressed her lips together, realizing she had said too much. She hadn't meant to tell them about that night; it was too private, a tangle of emotions that she had yet to sort out.

"Excuse me," said Archie, his words dramatically clipped, "I thought you said *when he came to me in the woods?*"

"You misheard," said Ru, knowing it was useless.

Gwyneth's eyes were nearly the size of tea saucers. Ru couldn't tell if she was angry, scared, or both. "Ru," she breathed, "has he been... influencing you? Hurting you? Coercing you? You can tell us."

"This is a nightmare," Ru muttered, downing the rest of her tea. "He hasn't influenced me." She recalled the way he'd kissed her in the forest, hot and needy. She swallowed. "Not very much, anyway. I can tell when the artifact is reacting to him, and when it's me. I'm a big girl, I can resist the Destroyer, I promise." She glanced around the room. "Do you have anything stronger than tea, Gwyn? If I'm going to tell you what happened in the woods, I need a stiffer drink."

Ru told them everything in as little detail as possible without leaving out any important details. She relayed all of the information Taryel had revealed to her in her rooms, how he'd come to live at the palace, the truth of the Destruction. And when she finished, she was met with an extended silence.

Archie's face squeezed into a thoughtful frown, chin resting on intertwined hands.

Gwyneth, on the other hand, continued to stare wide-eyed at Ru with tear-wet eyes. "Ru," she said, placing a soft hand on her friend's knee. "Be careful. I know you said you don't trust Taryel, but… remember who he is. You're not rational around him."

"I know," said Ru, reassuring herself as much as her friends. "I don't trust anyone but you two, Lyr, and my brother. But listen. I came here because I think we can benefit from this ridiculous Festra fad."

"We're listening," said Archie, fingers steepling. Gwyneth nodded eagerly, eyes still bright with unshed tears.

"Why not play along? My brother and Taryel are already doing it. If I act like I've been taken in by Taryel, that I'm finally being a good little puppet, I'll be able to get closer to Lady Bellenet. Presumably, anyway. Maybe I'll overhear things, find cracks in the armor."

"Perhaps the religion itself is a front," mused Archie. "If so, the closer you are to Lady Bellenet…"

"The more likely we'll learn how her power works," Gwyneth finished.

"This Festra fad is only going to get worse," Ru said. "There's nothing to stop Lady Bellenet from turning everyone into Children, one by one, if we don't do something. She already has the regent under her finger. Who will be next? Me? Taryel? Something tells me that if we don't fight it, she won't have a reason to change us."

"True," Archie said, musing. "Though you step out of line, I'd wager it'll be Hill and Tenoria on the chopping block to teach you a lesson."

"Don't talk like that," Gwyneth said, visibly shaken. "Time isn't on our side, here. It's only a month and a half until the winter solstice. I say we do it."

"Play the parts?" Ru said.

Gwyneth nodded. "Archie and I will be the wide-eyed academics, dazzled by the pomp and elegance of courtly life. And Ru, you'll be the Keeper of His Heart, obsessed with Taryel and, by association, Festra."

"Woo them with your charm," Archie said, smiling.

"Yes," said Ru, "I'll draw from my deep well of charisma. Keep your eyes and ears open for anything that might hint at Lady Bellenet's powers or anything new about Festra. We still know next to nothing about the deity himself."

"Quite," said Archie, pouring himself a new cup of tea.

"Don't write anything down in case they search our rooms," added Ru.

"You can count on us," Gwyneth said, her face all soothing lines and soft eyes.

A lump formed in Ru's throat. She was grateful for her friends, their presence here at the palace, even though it meant they were in constant danger. She wondered if she could have done it alone, or whether she might have eventually lost herself in despair without them here.

"Thank you," Ru breathed, taking Gwyneth's hand.

"And you," Gwyneth said, forcing cheer, "are going to be the best Keeper of His Heart there ever was."

"I hate everything you just said," Ru replied, "but I'll try."

As she spoke, the image from her dreams, of Fen holding the artifact out to her, rose unbidden. *It's yours.*

Archie leaned forward on the sofa, somehow managing not to spill his tea as he caught Ru's gaze with sharp eyes. "Delara," he said, "you've got to really lean into this role. Use Taryel. Play him like a handsome, oblivious fiddle. Stare lovingly into his ridiculous, stumbled face. And if you *must*… even kiss him. I know it might sound horribly disgusting, but it's necessary."

Ru scowled deeply. "Thanks, Arch. Your wisdom never fails to awe me."

Archie folded his lips into themselves, his face taut, clearly suppressing a laugh.

Ru glared. "It's not funny."

"It's a *little* funny," Archie countered. "You, the love-struck god consort? Doing as you're told? Comedy gold, if you ask me."

Gwyneth said nothing, but it was obvious she was also trying not to laugh.

"Ha," said Ru. "You're both terrible." Getting closer to Lady Bellenet and Lord D'Luc was the last thing she wanted to do. But it was a good plan. And somewhere in the secret, needy part of her, the thought of being closer to Taryel made her heart swell.

"Right," Ru said, "Let's play."

"Shall we shake on it?" Gwyneth asked, thrusting her pink-fingered hands out over the tea things.

The three friends clasped hands, an awkward smash of fingers and fists, and Ru was surprised to find a laugh escaping her. She was trapped at the center of a religious fad, destined to destroy the world. But she wasn't alone. And destinies could change.

CHAPTER 17

Ru had always thought she was decent enough at courtly manners, at dancing and sipping daintily from crystal glasses. She had been all too wrong, according to Hugon D'Luc.

"Stop hunching your shoulders," he said for the third time that day. "You're a member of court, not some unknown merchant's daughter."

That's exactly what I am, thought Ru, throwing back her shoulders yet again and shooting a dark look at Lord D'Luc. He had been berating her all morning, nitpicking her speech, the way she walked, even the way she smiled. Though, she supposed, her smiles *had* been forced.

They were standing on the broad balcony of Count Leon's private quarters. Back inside, there was music and dance and drink — an exclusive party to honor Ru, though she felt anything but honored under Lord D'Luc's condescending gaze.

"Imagine what they'll say about Lady Bellenet," the lord went on, giving Ru a slow, methodical once-over, "when you prove yourself utterly useless as a courtier, let alone the Keeper they've so longed for."

Ru grit her teeth. "I'm not used to walking around like I have a stick up my ass." She regretted it as soon as she spoke. She was supposed to be playing along, but surely she could get away with a few snide remarks with Hugon

D'Luc. He'd likely be more suspicious if she became a pliant little mouse overnight.

He raised an eyebrow, leaning his elbows against the balcony railing. They were several stories above the ground, and a cold wind ruffled his hair. The tip of his nose was tinged with pink, and his eyes shone with amusement. "I must admit," he said, "I'm pleasantly surprised at the effort you're putting in, Delara. It's almost as if you care for once."

"I care about Taryel," she said, careful to walk a balance between saying what he wanted to hear and not laying it on too thick. "I care about the artifact and my friends. And if you truly believe that Festra is real, then… well, I've suspended disbelief for now. Perhaps it's time I set aside my rigid dependence on the scientific method."

"Time indeed," he said, reaching up to adjust his cravat, which had loosened in the wind. He seemed about to say something else, but remained silent as he tucked the cravat back into his waistcoat.

Ru shivered in her gown, which was terribly fashionable and far too low cut for the weather. Goosebumps stood out on her chest and arms. "Have you punished me adequately for slouching?" she said.

"You see it as punishment," Lord D'Luc said, pushing off from the balcony and holding out his elbow for Ru to take. "I see it as education. Shall we?"

They re-entered the party, a glittering little fete with miniature cakes and a wine fountain, all brought in for the occasion. Ru couldn't help but feel inadequate, as if somehow it was obvious that she didn't fit here. That Lord D'Luc had been right: she was nothing but a merchant's daughter.

"There you are!" cried Count Leon, practically dancing across the room to them. He was young and handsome, full of energy, with a tower of coiffed hair to rival even Simon's. He held out a hand to Ru, who had already been introduced, and took her fingers in his. "Ruellian, may I address you as Ruellian? Oh, Ruellian, how wonderful it is to finally look upon your countenance. How many times have I heard of your beauty, only for such pale words to be outshone by the real thing! Lady Bellenet never once intimated how… well… Taryel surely is a lucky fellow, isn't he?"

"Thank you, Count Leon," Ru said, forcing a gracious smile. "You honor me."

"Tell me," said the count, his eyes shining, "is it true that when you cleanse the world, we shall all be reborn in the land of paradise?"

Ru felt Lord D'Luc stiffen beside her. But she was ready for this; she had known what sort of madness she'd have to not only endure, but indulge. Despite a horrible sickness in her belly, Ru said, "I have been told that is true, that Festra will guide us to paradise. Who am I to question Festra?"

Lord D'Luc turned to her, his expression unreadable. "How diplomatic," he said, so only she could hear.

Count Leon, meanwhile, seemed to be on the verge of tears. "Oh, Ruellian. You may call me anything you like. You hold a miraculous power that none of us could have dreamed of until now. Oh, what a magical day! A glorious time!" At this, he turned and danced away toward the wine fountain.

Ru couldn't tell if he truly believed, or if he was simply caught up in the drama of it all. It didn't matter either way — he was going to die by her hand, just as every other courtier at the party would. It was a slow kind of torture, being made to meet these people, converse with them, and drink with them, knowing that she held their lives in her hands. And she had no idea how to stop them from meeting a horrific end, no idea how to save them.

Panic clawed at her throat. And deep down, something else, something angry and feral, churned in Ru.

"Ah, at last," said Lord D'Luc, apparently oblivious to Ru's inner turmoil. "Your god arrives."

The room went quiet as soon as Taryel entered. Even the chamber ensemble, which had been playing a lively dance, faded into silence. Ru's heart, against her will, seemed to stop as well. He was as arresting to look at as he had always been. Even dressed in the finest clothes, he managed to look as if he'd just come in from some dark and mysterious wood. His hair was wild and curled about his ears, his cheeks stubbled from days of beard growth.

His gaze found Ru's immediately.

Go to him, she thought, or rather felt, as the artifact bubbled to life within her.

"Well?" murmured Lord D'Luc. "Greet him."

Of course. It was all part of the play. Throwing back her shoulders, Ru made her way through the brightly lit room, past richly dressed courtiers and flickering candles, to stand before Taryel.

He watched her approach like a cat, wary and elegant. And when she dropped a curtsey, he took her hands in his and pulled her to her full height again, frowning. "Don't bow to me," he said. "I've said it before. You hold my heart, Ruellian Delara. I'm but a servant in your presence."

Ru's breath caught. His delivery was perfect. The low timbre of his voice, the way his breath caught when he spoke her name — an impeccable performance. She almost believed it.

"The *romance*," Count Leon exclaimed, surging forward. "The drama! You spoil us, Taryel, you spoil us! Your lady has been waiting, simply wasting away without you. Please, come, drink, eat, be merry."

The count bowed deeply before Taryel, and again before Ru, who had been subjected to his bows several times already. Taryel said nothing, but wrapped an arm around Ru's waist, guiding her. She hated the way his touch affected her, the solidness of his body close to hers.

It's all pretend, she reminded herself. *We're just characters in a play*. But her body, as usual, had other ideas.

By the time she and Taryel had made the rounds together, him murmuring in low tones and Ru laughing and smiling brightly, she was finding it almost impossible to keep her hands off of him. His arm around her wasn't nearly enough.

At last, he led her to a shadowy corner of the room, away from prying ears. They were visible to anyone who cared to look, but at least Lord D'Luc was on the far side of the room, sipping his wine and casting vaguely approving looks at Ru.

"Simon is throwing a fit," Taryel said mildly, his voice low enough that no one could hear him aside from Ru. "He wants you out of the palace."

"Good for him," Ru replied, leaning close. "Tell him I'll leave the second he can guarantee the court's safety while I'm gone."

"He loves you," Taryel said.

"And I love not murdering people. Stop frowning, they're looking."

"What would you rather I do?" he said, snaking an arm around her, his smile turning lascivious. "They'll love it if I kiss you."

"I'd rather set myself on fire," Ru said in a loving tone, smiling up at him.

He reached out a hand and tucked a stray lock of hair behind her ear. A collective gasp, then a flurry of eager whispers, broke out from amongst the partygoers. Most of them were watching Ru and Taryel, even as they danced and laughed together, their attention never left their dark god and the woman who held his heart.

"The court loves romance," Taryel said. "It's part of the reason they love me… well, Festra, so much. He's been sold to them as some vengeful creature who murdered thousands in defense of his lover's honor."

"How… utterly unromantic," said Ru, staving off a grimace.

"You're telling me you wouldn't burn down a kingdom for me?" Taryel asked, eyes dancing. He was teasing her.

"Not even a village," Ru said, allowing him to pull her closer until she felt the beat of his heart, the rise and fall of his chest. She pressed a palm to his waistcoat, as much to steady herself as to keep him at bay. "Not even a hamlet."

"What about… one person?" he leaned down, lips parted.

"I wouldn't burn anyone for you," she breathed, leaning back just slightly. "Don't kiss me."

Taryel's mouth hovered inches from hers, his eyes heavy-lidded. "They'll love it."

"Kiss my cheek," she said, relenting. "That's all."

When he kissed her, a soft brush of lips against her

cheek, the room erupted in titters and scattered applause. There was a muffled thump as someone swooned, landing heavily on a settee.

Ru's heart slammed in her chest; blood rushed through her veins like a furious river. She wanted him so badly it hurt. The artifact urged her, devious thing, as if it were just as untethered as she was, threatening to fall together into unchecked desire.

But she knew what was happening, understood the force of the artifact's will. And now that she knew it was pushing her, she could separate herself from it, just enough to resist Taryel. Though it wasn't easy.

"Now that's over with," Ru said, "I could use a drink."

Taryel fetched them each a glass of wine from the fountain, which took far longer than it should have as he was forced to stop and interact with several courtiers on his way back to Ru. When he finally returned with their drinks, Ru's heartbeat had thankfully returned to normal, her lust under control. Though she could see in Taryel's eyes that he had wanted to kiss her. That he still did.

"Does Lady Bellenet ever come to these things?" Ru asked, eager to discuss more useful things, to forget Taryel's lips against her skin.

"Rarely," he said, glancing around to make sure no one was listening. "She throws her own parties. I've surmised that she prefers to be in control of almost everything she does. And she's followed by a retinue of Children everywhere she goes. I've never been alone with her."

"Pity," said Ru. "If she truly believes you're Festra incarnate, she might actually reveal something about her power."

"It's not for lack of trying," Taryel said. "Whatever her powers are, if she has any, she keeps close to the chest."

Ru frowned, sipping her wine. She had hoped she might uncover something interesting at Count Leon's party, but so far, it had been one discomfort after another. Even the count himself had only spouted the same rhetoric Lady Bellenet spoke in the throne room.

"Are you all right?" Taryel asked, noting Ru's frown.

She forced a smile. "I'm having a wonderful time. The best night of my life. You?"

"Ru, I'm…" he reached out, fingers brushing the fabric of her sleeve.

But he never finished his sentence. Just then, Lord D'Luc appeared at Ru's side as if summoned by her discomfort. "Delara," he said, "it's time to go. One always leaves a party at its height, not its decline."

"Of course," Ru said, placing her hand on the lord's arm. She glanced back at Taryel long enough to hand him her empty wine glass. She felt his gaze on her as she made her way through the room with Lord D'Luc, boring into her until they were outside in the corridor.

Ru took a calming breath, savoring the cool, quiet air of the hallway.

"Well done," said Lord D'Luc, turning to regard her with hesitant approval. "You gave the rabble exactly what they wanted. It seems you were born for it, Delara."

"For what?" she asked, a cold dread hanging in her chest, ready to fall and engulf her.

"Your destiny," he said, smiling coldly. "To be Taryel's sweet little thing. You do seem utterly at home in the arms of a killer, don't you? Two Destroyers for the price of one. I can't wait to see your face when you do it. The whole of Mirith will be lined up to watch you."

Ru didn't ask what he meant by that. The wine she'd drunk tasted sour on her tongue, and her stomach roiled. Everything she had just endured, from Count Leon's prancing to Taryel's farcical kiss… it would all mean nothing if she couldn't stop Lady Bellenet. She would have put herself through hell for nothing, a hollow play for a theater of corpses.

CHAPTER 18

Ru had been at the palace for weeks. Lord D'Luc carted her from breakfasts to parties to intimate salons, never once taking her to the artifact. And though Ru tried to ask after Lady Bellenet, to find out what she might be doing, the woman was nowhere to be found.

"You would do well to respect her privacy," Lord D'Luc said when Ru asked — not for the first time — why Lady Bellenet hadn't come to speak with her yet, despite her promise at dinner that first night at the palace. "She has many other things to attend to."

"Such as?" Ru pressed.

The lord shot her a glance. "Persist in your rudeness, Delara, and you'll wish you hadn't."

"I only want to meet her properly."

She and Lord D'Luc were on their way to breakfast, and Ru was restless. She was finding it increasingly difficult to keep her thoughts to herself with Lord D'Luc, especially since they were becoming darker with every passing day. There were only so many times she could endure Taryel's arm around her, or Lord D'Luc's cold demeanor, or the bizarre excitement of another aristocrat, all while she feigned smiles and laughter and compliance.

Gwyneth and Archie meanwhile, occasionally attending the same parties as Ru, had seen and heard nothing of use. It was as if the court of Navenie were enveloped in some shimmering curtain, hiding the truth behind its gilded threads. And despite their efforts, none of them could seem to peer behind it.

"You will speak with her," said Lord D'Luc. "When the time is right."

"I might be dead by then," she said, her tone flippant.

He stopped in his tracks, studying her with a piercing gaze. "What do you mean by that?"

Ru started, taken aback by his intensity. Something in his eyes was different, as if a candle had blown out, revealing something wild and frightening in the shadowed dark. "I mean, the solstice is coming. If Lady Bellenet keeps avoiding me, I'll kill us all in the Cleansing before she gets a chance to properly meet me." She forced a smile.

Lord D'Luc stared past Ru into the distance, his eyes still horribly tormented. "I see," he said at last.

Disturbed, Ru was about to ask him what was wrong, when something caught her eye down the hall. It was a procession of Children, walking two by two, with candles in their hands. Ru's blood ran cold; she had never seen so many Children all together like this, let alone in a procession. There was something deeply primeval about it, an unsettling call back to a time forgotten.

"Where are they going?" she asked, surprised to find that she was genuinely curious.

"To Prayer," Lord D'Luc said, leading her away from the Children. His eyes were back to their usual cold, clear blue. "To offer their devotion to Festra."

"Are they really?" Ru asked. She hadn't imagined that the Children did anything on their own, let alone actually worshiped Festra.

"Yes, really," said Lord D'Luc, his practiced authority undercut by a glint in his eye. "But you know exactly what it's like to believe in something that cannot be seen or touched, don't you, Delara? Festra is as real as you or me."

"Can we go with them?" Ru asked, almost childlike. Perhaps if Lord D'Luc thought she was truly curious, that she wanted to believe, he would let her attend. Surely she'd learn something useful there, at the altar of Festra.

"Only the truly faithful are permitted to witness the

service," he said. "Don't tell me you've come around entirely."

"I'm still questioning," Ru said, "but maybe if I saw the Prayer, if I understood… I might reach my full potential at the Cleansing."

Lord D'Luc narrowed his eyes. "How very compliant of you," he said. "Don't think I haven't noticed how agreeable you've been lately. I'm almost worried."

"I'm not being compliant," Ru said, keeping her voice light, though her throat constricted with fear at the prospect of being discovered in her game. "I'm remaining open-minded."

He raised an incredulous eyebrow but only shook his head.

When they arrived at Lord D'Luc's rooms, as breakfast was being laid out by silent Children, Ru felt strangely off-kilter. Perhaps it was just the artifact, its voice so present now. Its absence had become her normality these last months. But now, it regularly yearned to be part of her, restless and loud against her mind. But something in the lord's countenance as she arranged herself across from him made her think it wasn't just the artifact affecting her.

As if responding to her thoughts, a spark flared in her chest. Anger, perhaps, or helplessness, lapping at her mind. She tamped down on it, forcing the artifact into the dark recesses of her consciousness.

Not now, she thought.

Lord D'Luc watched her quietly. She knew she looked exhausted, even with Pearl's help. She was increasingly tired and afraid, and with every new day came the growing realization that she was trapped here. Lyr's presence was cold comfort in the face of a palace full of King's Guards, and the looming threat of the solstice.

"Delara," he said, with a hint of exasperation. "Ask me. Whatever it is you're biting your tongue for, spit it out."

She returned the lord's gaze. She was still sharply aware of his movements, his moods. Just as she'd been at the Tower. But since coming to Mirith, he had not threatened her or pressed his thumbs to her throat. Instead, he had moments of strange emotion, like the flash of fear she'd seen earlier in the corridor. As if she were being shown glimpses of a monster beneath, or maybe even the true Hugon D'Luc. He gave Ru the impression of a caged tiger, fearsome but captive.

"You," she said, unthinking.

A self-satisfied smirk appeared at the edge of his mouth.

"Not like *that*," Ru added, "I mean… These parties. What are we doing, Hugon? How does this contribute to my control of the artifact? It seems aimless, frivolous. Are we waiting for something?"

"Why would you assume that everything is about the artifact?" Lord D'Luc replied, reaching for a pale strawberry. Even in Mirith, the fruit was out of season. The lace of his shirt fell back as he bit the strawberry, revealing a pale wrist. Ru thought she saw a discoloration there, perhaps a bruise, but he lowered his hand, watching her intently.

"With you, everything is about the artifact."

"Is it, indeed?" he asked, tilting his head. He had worn his hair loose that morning, soft golden waves caressing his cheekbones as he spoke. "If you claim to know so much, why ask?"

Ru sat quietly for a moment. She could lie, say some lighthearted half-truth, and turn the conversation away from her. But as she met the lord's cool gaze, searched the eyes that had so often reveled in her misery, she couldn't stop herself.

"Because I'm here now," she said, her words raw and honest. "I've shown you that I'm willing. I have no other option. Can't you see it? No part of me is intact. The Ru who defied you back at the Tower, she's gone. So be honest with me."

Another strange expression passed over Lord D'Luc's face for a breath of a moment. He seemed to have gone momentarily inward and found something lacking there.

"You're a woman of intellect," he said after a long moment. "What my lady asks of me, I provide. Do you believe that I, Hugon D'Luc, make any meaningful decisions in this place?"

Ru swallowed, struck silent by his words. Had she ever seen such clarity in his face before, she wondered, such honesty? "No, I…"

"For someone so adept at unraveling theorems, I would have thought you understood by now." He rested his chin on folded knuckles, never breaking Ru's gaze. "I do these things, Delara, I take you from party to party, I discuss philosophy and religion and science with you, because I have been instructed to. Don't presume to imagine that I enjoy it."

At a loss for words, she scrambled for some pithy response. And for some reason, in the face of this new Lord D'Luc, the man whose careful facade had slipped, she desperately wanted to be faced with the old version. The version of the man she understood, the cruel, science-minded lord with jeweled fingers and sapphire eyes. The man who had broken her.

But this was not a man she knew. This was a man who was bruised and tired, dark-eyed in the morning light. She didn't know how to speak to him. He seemed almost as much a prisoner as she was.

"I want to go," Ru said softly.

"Where?" he asked, slinging one arm over the back of his chair. Already, the curtain was falling back, his smile returning. "Where do you suppose you'll go that will bring you peace?"

Ru took a shaking breath. "I don't know."

Then he sighed, stood up, and offered her a hand. "I tire of you, Delara. I'll escort you to your rooms. And don't think for a moment that this conversation changes anything between us."

Of course not, Ru thought bitterly. It was impossible to know his motives, his desires. And so, despite that brief moment of honesty between them, she still knew nothing at all.

Distant music carried through the corridor as they walked back to Ru's rooms, a quiet melody that made her want to stop and listen. But the lord's gait was swift, and as they approached her wing of the palace, the music faded quickly, swallowed up by the clatter of courtiers' slippers on marble, of laughter and chatter, the echo of a door closing. Ru fixated on her shadow next to Lord D'Luc's, disappearing and reappearing on the floor as they passed a row of windows.

"You're worrying," said Hugon, the first thing he'd said since they left his rooms.

"I'm not." Ru felt right in contradicting him, even if his observations were astute.

"You are," he said. "There is a tightness at the corners of your mouth. A small divot between your brows. And your vice-like grip on my arm speaks volumes."

Ru relaxed her fingers. "How lucky I am to be the subject of your constant scrutiny."

The lord chuckled, patting her hand as if comforting a child. With the sunset framing him, Ru couldn't get a good look at his face. For a moment he was nothing but a shadowed silhouette. A suggestion, the shape of a man — and even then, she relaxed knowing he was back. The Hugon D'Luc she knew, the man she understood, an unwanted yet reliable constant in her life.

"There is a ball tonight," he said after a moment. "You're expected to attend."

"A ball?" Images of the Children spinning emotionlessly on a dance floor invaded her mind, and she almost laughed. "Why?"

They had come to Ru's rooms now, and Hugon turned to face her, his expression no longer hidden in shadow. He smiled, all teeth and mirthless beauty. "Why not? Surely, you're not above a night of music and dancing. The Keeper of His Heart could use a little fun."

"Will Lady Bellenet be there?" Ru asked.

Lord D'Luc only smiled, his cheek dimpling. "Be ready at nightfall. Your godly escort will be waiting."

As the sun began to set over Mirith, Pearl arrived with a gown. It had been sent by Lord D'Luc, with a note that read: "For Taryel's Sweet Little Thing."

Ru tossed the note into the fire.

Despite its origins, the dress was unlike anything Ru had ever seen. At first, it had appeared oddly plain, a garment of cream tulle and chiffon. But as she bent closer, she saw that the fabric of the bodice was intricately folded, fanning out like an opening cloud. The sleeves were elegant puffs of chiffon, cinched tight at the wrist above a few inches of skin-tight lace.

Laid out on the bed, next to the gown, was a golden sash embroidered with intricate swirls, and a golden sunburst crown.

"I'm not wearing that," Ru said, indicating the crown.

Pearl made a loud noise of impatience. "Miss, *please*," she said, holding up the dress. "You're going to be late."

So Ru, with both annoyance and a gnawing dread at what the crown implied, allowed Pearl to dress her. The gown fit Ru as if made for her, of course. And once it was arranged on her body, she saw that the sleeves fell off her shoulder, leaving her collarbone and shoulders exposed to the cold.

Pearl coiled her hair in lovely swirls, pinning it to the back of her head. She painted Ru's eyelids gold and brushed a warm rouge on her cheeks. When Ru looked at herself in the full-length mirror, she was amazed at the transformation. Pearl truly did work wonders. The gown was ethereal and soft, so different from the dresses Ru usually wore. It was the costume of a goddess, not a scholar.

"I feel silly," Ru said.

"It's a masque," Pearl replied, holding up a white and gold mask to cover the eyes, painted with golden swirls and framed with gold feathered wings on each side. "If you won't wear the crown, at least wear this."

Ru sighed, relenting, as Pearl tied the mask securely. At last, her look was complete. A stranger gazed back at her from the mirror, a dark-eyed woman dressed like an angel.

A knock sounded at the door, and Pearl went to open it.

And there in the doorway, not bothering to hide his gaze as it raked slowly over Ru, was Taryel.

CHAPTER 19

Desire, encouraged by the artifact, blazed hotly in Ru's chest. Even before the door had opened, she had known it was him. Taryel was dressed all in black, with dramatic gold embroidery spreading downward from his shoulders.

She was a goddess of light, and he was the god of death.

He held out a hand. "The evening awaits, Miss Delara."

Ru caught a spark of amusement in his eye, and she relaxed — just slightly. Could she allow herself to embrace the moment, to actually enjoy herself that evening?

Taking his hand, she found herself unable to look away from him. She hardly noticed Pearl's goodbye, the door closing behind her, her own feet carrying her through the corridors.

Courtiers, clearly on their way to the ball, made way for Ru and Taryel with small gasps and bright stares through their masks, whispering behind fans and gloved hands. Here came their god, his consort at his side. To Ru, rationally, everything about this was *wrong* — Taryel guiding her through the palace corridors, the bowing and scraping of the courtiers, their dainty clapping hands and cries to *kiss her*!

And yet, with her hand securely in the crook of Taryel's arm, she felt safe.

Ru was afraid to look up at him, afraid that if she did, he would say something and ruin the moment. She wanted to relax into the dream of him as the artifact glowed like a star in her breast.

When they came at last to the ballroom, Taryel paused. She felt his body shift before he turned to her. "Are you ready?" he asked so only she could hear. "It's going to be chaos in there. Worse than Count Leon's wine fountain party."

She bit back a laugh. "Of course I'm not ready. I was born for books, not balls."

"You were born to be Ru," he said, smiling. "That's all they want from you. Be yourself. Have fun. And if we learn something on the way…"

"Everyone keeps telling me to have fun," she muttered. "I'm not sure you people understand what that means."

Taryel grinned. "Come," he said, steering her with his hand on her back into the shimmering swirl of the masquerade.

Ru had been to balls, but she had never seen anything like this. Couples in rich, otherworldly gowns and costumes spun across the room; crystal chandeliers and the flicker of candelabra glinted like miniature stars in their jeweled hair, the rings on their fingers, their painted masks. Feathers burst out from hair that was styled sky-high, and bubbling wine flowed freely. A string ensemble played a lively gavotte.

She wanted to be swept away by the music, to dance with Taryel until they were in another world, one where her name did not spell doom for these people. Where she could just be a woman with the man she…

"Ru!"

Gwyneth's voice startled her back to reality. Ru turned to see her friends pushing through the crowd toward her. Archie's mask was perched on top of his hair, as if he'd worn it for a moment and had immediately become irritated by it. Gwyneth still wore hers, a pretty thing of spring flowers with a gown to match, but her fond smile and flowing gold hair made her immediately recognizable.

She curtseyed before Ru and Taryel, elbowing Archie until he bowed stiffly. Ru couldn't help smiling; Gwyneth was a natural charmer, born to play courtly games. Archie, meanwhile, couldn't have looked more uncomfortable.

"Put your mask back on, Arch," Ru said. "It will at least hide your glower."

"I keep *telling* him," Gwyneth said, sounding put-upon. Then she lowered her voice, moving closer to Ru. "Listen, the wine tonight is *flowing*, if you know what I mean. These aristos are loose-lipped and carefree. We haven't learned anything yet, but if there's a time to be poking about in search of Lady Bellenet's secrets, tonight's the night."

Taryel made a grumbling sound in his chest.

"Oh," Gwyneth said, gasping as if she'd just noticed him lurking behind Ru. "It's the god incarnate, Festra's avatar, Taryel Aharis himself, the *Destroyer*!" She pressed a hand to her bosom dramatically. "I didn't see you there. Please, my lord, won't you give us your blessing tonight?"

Gwyneth's carrying voice had alerted the nearby courtiers to their presence, and already clusters of eager ballgoers were making their way over to Ru and Fen.

"Yes, please, yes," said the nearest courtiers, bowing and curtseying. "Give us your blessing, Taryel and Ruellian. Bless this night! We'll simply *die* if you don't."

Ru's face heated as she shot an exasperated glance at Gwyneth, moving instinctively closer to Taryel. He was better at appeasing the masses, at playing the god. She smiled faintly as he bestowed some nonsense blessing upon the ball at large, and every courtier who witnessed it seemed to feign delirium for a moment, clutching at one another as if blinded by the glory of Taryel's power.

It was all Ru could do not to laugh. When at last the crowds moved back to the dancefloor, appeased for the moment, Ru stood on tiptoe to whisper in Taryel's ear. She had to clutch at his arm to keep her balance, enjoying the contact despite herself. "I'm going to mingle," she said. "Come for me later, and we'll dance."

He shot her a look, and the artifact flamed inside Ru. "I'd be honored," he said, taking her hand and brushing his lips across her knuckles. His gaze met hers, and somehow, she felt he wasn't pretending just then. "Until our dance."

Ru ignored the heat in her belly, peeling away from Taryel and entering the fray of the ballroom. If ever she was going to learn something useful, as Gwyneth had said, it would be tonight.

Almost immediately, she was swept up by the movement of the crowded room. Courtiers parted and made way for her as if she went. Someone handed her a glass of sparkling wine, and others offered her their hands — for dancing or praying, she had no idea — but she refused them politely, responding with smiles and soft words.

She was too close to the dancefloor, and there were too many bodies here. Ru wanted to get to the edges of things, where she might have an actual conversation with someone. At last, she found herself in a relatively quiet part of the room, away from the food and wine and dancing. A few other courtiers were here, sipping drinks or fanning themselves, resting after a lively dance.

Ru drifted toward a young man who looked particularly relaxed, his lips wine-stained and his mask hanging crookedly from his ears. When he caught sight of her, he beamed, raising his glass in a toast. He seemed not to notice as half of its contents sloshed over the edge and onto the floor.

This was exactly the sort of drunken reveler Ru had been looking for. "Good evening," she said, raising her own glass in greeting. "Are you enjoying the ball?"

"Enjoying?" the man spluttered, still grinning widely. "I am absolutely beside myself. Rapt. Overcome. What a reps… res… resplendent evening. I can hardly *breathe*, I'm so beset with joyous emotion."

Both disturbed and amused by the man's vehemence, Ru smiled pleasantly in response. "Indeed," she said. "Lady Bellenet's balls are something to be remembered."

"Oh, Ruellian," he breathed, "they are. Truly, they are. Have you danced yet? May I have this dance?" He held out a sweaty hand and stumbled slightly as he did.

Ru inclined her head politely. "Thank you, my lord, but my first dance ought to be with Taryel."

"Of course, the dark god! The giver of life. The bringer of death. What a *wonderful*—"

"I do wonder," Ru said, cutting him off, "if you might have seen the lady herself here this evening? I've heard rumors of her power but have never seen it. I thought perhaps, tonight..." she trailed off, hoping the drunk courtier would take it from there.

"Power?" He hiccuped, gazing blearily at a spot just past Ru's ear. Then he brightened, nodding excitedly. "Yes. *Yes.* She is the most powerful woman in the world, Ruellian. They say she lights up the whole chapel when they..." He swayed, and Ru put out a hand to steady him. "When they go to pray."

Ru's pulse sped. "What do you mean, lights up?" she asked, low and urgent. "Is that a metaphor?"

The man giggled. "Mega floor? What's a... matted door?"

"*Metaphor.* Never mind. What else do they say about her power? The prayers?" Ru glanced around, making sure no one was within earshot. But the ballroom was loud, and while courtiers turned to smile at her from a distance, no one was near enough to overhear.

"Everyone likes her," he went on, his voice lowering conspiratorially in the dramatic way only drunk people could manage. "But she scares me. Too happy. I saw her Children, they came out... too happy."

"What do you mean, too happy? Came out from where?"

"Not happy," said the man. "Em... pty."

Just then, a commotion arose from the entrance to the ballroom. A pair of ethereal figures appeared in the doorway, framed in golden light. Lord D'Luc and Lady Bellenet.

Heart in her throat, Ru murmured her thanks to the drunken courtier and drifted back into the crowd, gaze darting in search of her friends. She needed to tell them what she'd learned, vague as it was. But the room was so vast, and her friends could be anywhere. Ru was standing on her tiptoes, scanning the sea of masked faces and coiffed hairdos, when a white-clad figure appeared at her side.

"Your friends seem to be enjoying themselves," said

Lord D'Luc, glancing at Ru sidelong. "They greeted me a moment ago. They were disturbingly congenial, all things considered."

Ru bristled. "Of course they were. They're a lady and a gentleman, not feral creatures."

"And here I thought *feral creature* was synonymous with *academic*."

"What do you want, Hugon?" Ru said, turning to face him. His face was bare and unbearably beautiful in the low light, an unbidden thought that curdled in Ru's belly like sour wine. "I thought you told me to have fun tonight. Your presence is making it difficult."

He smiled. "Delara, you're the picture of affability tonight." He took her hand and dropped a delicate kiss to her knuckles, just as he'd done the first time they met. "My Lady Bellenet requires your presence," he continued, gesturing to the far side of the room. Ru saw now that a dais had been placed there, a pair of thrones upon it. One throne was empty — presumably Taryel's. In the other, sat Lady Bellenet. She was flanked on both sides by at least a dozen Children, robed in white and watching the ball with slack expressions.

"At last," Ru said, "she deigns to speak to me."

"Be respectful," Hugon said, taking her chin between his thumb and forefinger, "or it's *both* our heads."

Before Ru could react, he dropped his hand. She stood dumbfounded for a moment. He had been someone else, just for an instant. Was that the real Hugon who'd gazed at her, whose eyes had glinted in fear at the threat of Lady Bellenet? Then, he offered Ru his arm, and she took it, hands shaking.

From somewhere unseen in the ballroom, Ru felt Taryel's gaze on her. It was as certain as the roiling in her chest, the artifact's unease. Looking above the crowd toward the dais, Ru saw that Taryel had ascended to the throne and was watching her with a stormy expression.

"Come," said Lord D'Luc. "She's waiting."

Lady Bellenet greeted Ru with a warm smile. She wore a simple white gown, almost like the robes worn by the Children, with long split sleeves and an inner lining of gold damask. Her light brown hair was pulled back in a youthful braid, wound about her ears, and, like Hugon, she wore no mask. She looked almost like a religious illustration, a figure in a stained glass window. And when she pressed Ru's hand, smiling sweetly, the effect was almost motherly.

Lord D'Luc and Taryel looked on in silence as Lady Bellenet held Ru's hands, pulling her into her orbit. "Ruellian," she said in her deep, soothing voice. "You must forgive me. I've been quite busy as of late, though I have not forgotten you."

Ru didn't know how to respond. Suddenly her voice, her plans to play along, everything failed her. She felt trapped, alone, a beetle pinned to a board.

Lady Bellenet smiled conspiratorially, as if they shared some wonderful secret. "Oh, dear," she said. "I've offended you somehow. Let's remedy that, shall we?"

Again, Ru didn't know what to say. She wasn't offended, she was overwhelmed. Afraid. Her palms were sweating, her breaths shallow. Would Lady Bellenet make an empty husk of Ru as well? Would she turn them all, one by one, into mindless Children?

Lady Bellenet looked into Ru's eyes and seemed to understand something, or to know something, that Ru hadn't meant to give up. The woman smiled, her cheeks perfectly pink and round. "Tea in my chambers," she said, "tomorrow. We shall discuss everything."

Ru blinked. "Everything?" she managed at last.

"We must come to trust one another," Lady Bellenet said, her eyes wide and fixed on Ru's, as if speaking some great and obvious truth, "if you are to recommence your demonstrations with the artifact."

CHAPTER 20

Ru rushed a curtsey and fled the dais, clutching her glass of honey-colored wine. Lady Bellenet's gaze seemed to burn her as she made her way through the chaos of dancing bodies, music, and heat. Her heart was pounding, the artifact — Taryel — doing its best to calm her. But Lady Bellenet's cold words looped in Ru's brain. A reminder of what she was here to do.

Isn't this what you wanted? she imagined Hugon's voice, berating her. *You asked after the artifact, the solstice, Lady Bellenet, the Cleansing. Well, here you go. Time to prepare.*

Pausing at the edge of the dancefloor, Ru downed the last of her wine. It warmed her from the inside, and at last, the artifact's work began to do her good. She could almost feel Taryel looking for her, coming after her in the crowd. She hadn't meant to react like that, to let her fear overtake her so easily. She *did* want to study the artifact, to get close to it, to see what else she could pry from Hugon's lips as she played a willing Destroyer.

She had to find her friends.

"Ru," came Taryel's low voice from behind her.

"I don't want to demonstrate again," she said, spinning to face him. No one could have heard her but Taryel, the man so attuned to her that he seemed to understand what she was feeling from moment to moment. And even though she hardly considered him a friend, let alone a lover, Ru couldn't help but lean into the connection they shared, irrational as the urge was. It was one of the only things she had just then.

He took her empty glass, setting it away somewhere, and bent to speak in her ear. "You don't have to. String him along, just as you have been."

Her hands were shaking. She wanted the artifact ripped from existence. She wanted— But even as she thought of finally ridding herself of that connection, the one binding her to Taryel, she felt sick at the idea. As if her body, not her mind, were rejecting it.

I don't know what *I want anymore*, she thought bitterly.

"I learned something earlier," she said, dragging herself out from her inner turmoil and into the present moment. She needed to focus on stopping all of this, fixing it, instead of wallowing in her own confused misery. "From one of the courtiers."

"Did you?" Taryel said, sounding impressed. "No one will talk to me at all. They either swoon or cry or ask me ridiculous questions about godhood."

Ru couldn't help but snort with suppressed laughter. "Poor you," she said. "Listen, I need to find Gwyn and Arch. I think I know where we might see Lady Bellenet's…" she widened her eyes, "*you know what*. Have you seen them?"

"I haven't," he said, looking around the ballroom with ease due to his height. Then he turned back to her, his brows drawn together with concern. "Are you all right, Ru?"

She hesitated. This was an honest question, a genuine attempt to connect with her outside of their roles. "No," she said. The admission hurt. "Of course I'm not."

"I won't let them harm you," Taryel said. "I would do anything for you… you know that. Anything to protect you and, what did I call it? Your little rock."

Those words lit something in Ru, like a match in the dark. The artifact responded in kind, urging her to him. "Would you really burn the world for me?" she asked, a hazy desire beginning to spread through her body.

"I would burn a thousand worlds," Taryel murmured, his lips only inches from hers.

Ru imagined it, twin Destroyers, hand in hand at the heart of Mirith. She imagined the darkness spreading outward from them, engulfing the city, the kingdom. She saw their enemies annihilated, their friends too. She saw the Cornelian Tower, her father's house, the forests, and the rivers, all swallowed up in blackness.

He would do that for her a thousand times over.

Disgust choked her as she returned to herself, her head clearing. Taryel's hands were in her hair, on her back, holding her close. Her want was a throbbing ache, and she had almost given in.

"Taryel," she snapped, pulling away. "Stop it. You're… *doing things* to me."

He blinked as if waking from a sleep. "Oh," he said, rubbing a hand down his face. "I didn't mean… I'm sorry." He cupped her cheek with a warm hand. "It's hard not to."

She allowed this because in this ballroom, with all eyes on them, he was her god and they were playing parts. And because, though she would not admit it to herself, some part of her was weakening toward Taryel. Would it be so bad to let him in? To forgive him?

"I'm going to look for Gwyn and Arch," Ru said quickly, stepping backwards into the roiling crowd. "We'll talk later."

He didn't follow as she vanished into the crowd, wanting to lose herself in the movement of bodies and music and dancing, wishing fervently that she had more wine. As she stumbled through the press of gowns and frock coats, a blur of strangers in masks, she caught sight of something familiar. Golden hair, gleaming under candlelight.

A footman passed, carrying a tray of gleaming goblets. Ru took one and downed it in a single gulp, relishing the bittersweet burn as it warmed her from the inside. *Now* she could dance.

After that, Ru found herself almost inexorably in Hugon's orbit. At first, she made to move away, but as he smiled, his cheek dimpling charmingly, she wondered, *why not?* He would no doubt be good at dancing. He had revealed another part of himself earlier. Could she make him do it again? Could she pull forth more honesty from beneath that angelic facade?

"Delara," Lord D'Luc said, his voice a gentle croon. "There you are. I thought you might have run away to hide."

"And miss a chance to dance with you?" Ru said, returning the lord's smile. She held out her hand.

He hesitated.

"You told me to enjoy myself," she insisted. Faces blurred into formless colors as the dancers swirled around them. "I enjoy dancing."

Hugon's eyes narrowed ever so slightly, a faint sign of suspicion, and then his smile was wider than ever. "How could I refuse?" he said and took her hand.

He curved his other arm around her, resting his hand on the small of her back. It was a quietly intimate movement that felt utterly natural, and Ru suppressed a shudder. Hugon D'Luc would be the most difficult of all to fool. He saw her as she was, had seen her broken and her spirit flayed. He, more than anyone, knew all that she had to lose and how desperately she would try to hold onto it.

Sweeping her in his arms, he carried her breathlessly into the dance. And as they danced, he seemed to relax, his smile fading, but his eyes shining brightly.

"You dance shockingly well," said Hugon, "for an academic."

Ru allowed herself to laugh. "I have an accomplished partner."

The warmth of a thousand stars seemed to grow in her chest, her vision wine-blurred, her skin hot. She knew her heart was beating fast, too fast, but she ignored it. She was almost enjoying it, the shedding of their mutual antagonism. Hugon could have been a great friend had they met under different circumstances.

Perhaps, she thought as the lord's arm tightened around her waist, even more than friends. But Lord D'Luc was all sharp edges and deadly beauty. He was like a thorned rose, drawing blood at the slightest touch.

"We should have done this sooner," she said, her lips brushing golden hair. "It feels right, doesn't it?"

He seemed to stiffen slightly.

Ru leaned into him, her cheek against his, biting back her revulsion. It wasn't as difficult as it ought to be. The effects of the wine surged to her cheeks. "Maybe you were right all along. Maybe I've been a fool to ignore it, and destruction… death… they've always been my destiny."

"Delara," he said, pulling away from her, his eyes searching. "How much wine have you had tonight?"

"Hardly any," Ru said, smiling coyly. "Why, did I say something you disliked? I thought…"

The music stopped then, the dance over.

The dance floor became a chaos of talking and laughter, of courtiers looking for new partners. Ru and Hugon stood still in the midst of it, facing one another. Slowly and deliberately, he stepped backwards, separating them by mere inches.

"Whatever you thought," he said, his voice hard-edged, "it was wrong."

And there it was again, as she'd hoped — the curtain drawn back, the man revealed. She studied his face, his downturned lips, aristocratic nose, pale lashes framing sapphire eyes. There was a freckle above one of his eyebrows. She'd never noticed before.

"Hugon," she said softly.

"Thank you for the dance," he said, his movements stiff, his expression closed off once more.

Then he was gone, and Ru stood alone in the throng. When she spoke of the Destruction, of giving in to it, of dying… that was when he cracked, when Ru found herself able to peer through to the truth of him. Was he frightened, then? Afraid of what would happen if she didn't succeed?

Or was it something else altogether?

Deep in thought, she made her way to the edge of the dance floor. She felt strangely empty, despite getting Hugon to do exactly as she wanted. The room was hot and too crowded, and she became painfully aware of her mask. Constricted and annoyed, she yanked it off, setting it on a nearby dessert table.

"Are you all right?"

Ru turned to see a girl, a young courtier in ruffles of silk, smiling at her. She couldn't have been older than seventeen.

"I'm fine," Ru said. "Thank you. It's just…"

"The heat in the room?" the girl finished for her, nodding in understanding, her dark curls bouncing. "I fainted during a summertime ball, once. It was terribly embarrassing. I wouldn't recommend it."

Ru blinked, unsure how to proceed. This was the first courtier who had treated her as a human, an equal, rather than some romantic fantasy.

But the girl rattled on, unperturbed by Ru's silence. "I'm Georgina, by the way. My father's a duke, but he's off on business, so I'm allowed to attend balls as long as I go with a friend and leave by midnight. My father studied at the Cornelian Tower, you know, and has all sorts of books. He tells me not many people have books in their own homes. They're expensive to print, though I suppose you know that if you're from the Tower. Have you seen a printing press before? They're ever so fascinating! I could go on and on about books. Oh, I nearly forgot!" She brightened, reaching into her bodice and removing a tiny book from within. "I brought this for you. It's a book. Obviously. I know you're an archaeologist, which sounds terribly exciting to me, but Father won't allow me to go away and study. Not yet, anyway, not until I'm twenty. He wants me to learn about being a lady first, which is horribly boring, but there's no avoiding it. I'd love to study artifacts one day, or even magic. I hope you like it."

She held out the book expectantly, smiling brightly.

"You brought this for *me*?" Ru asked, still trying to take in everything the girl had said.

"Oh, yes," said Georgina. "I'm ever so intrigued by you. Father said this was the only known copy of *Gods & Glories* to survive after the Destruction. Isn't that fascinating? There used to be loads of copies, all of them were in Ordellun-by-the-Sea, except for this one! It's worth a fortune, you know. Father had it appraised. He gets everything appraised, of course. I thought you might like to read it if you're ever bored or tired of parties. There's a story about Festra in it. Isn't that terribly enticing?"

Plucking the book from the girl's fingers, Ru studied the cover. It appeared to be an illustrated children's book, but the painted leather cover was faded and chipped. "Thank you," she said. "But how will I return it to you?"

Georgina shrugged. "Just give it to a footman or a pageboy and ask that they return it to Georgina Brantforde. I don't know how they find anyone in this maze of a palace, but they do. It's terribly fascinating! I heard they use their own system of corridors and tunnels, ones that not even well-bred ladies like us are allowed into."

"Is that so?" Ru said, genuinely interested. "I'll have to investigate that claim."

"I hope you do," said Georgina. "I'd better go, or Father will have a conniption when he gets home. Last time I stayed late at a ball, he wouldn't let me attend another for a *month*. No dancing for a month! Not even a gavotte. Not a single gigue. Isn't that dreadful?"

Ru swallowed a laugh, utterly charmed by Georgina. "Thank you again, Miss Brantforde. I'll take good care of your book."

"I know you will," said Georgina, and she flounced off into the night.

Ru tucked *Gods & Glories* into her bodice, just as Georgina had done, not believing her luck. This would be the first book Ru or her friends had come across since leaving the Tower that mentioned Festra. And it had just fallen into her lap.

CHAPTER 21

The tinkle of silver against fine china, the bittersweet aroma of tea and honey, retreating footsteps on carpet, angled afternoon light through broad windows. Ru focused on her senses, the minutiae, anchoring herself in the moment.

"What preoccupies you?" The question was soft, unassuming in nature but not, Ru thought, intent.

She finally met Lady Bellenet's questioning gaze. The woman's youthful face was in full, radiant display that afternoon; her hair pulled back in a simple coil. She wore little makeup and a simple gown.

There was no reason for Ru's primal terror of the woman, the sickly swoop in her gut, and the tingle at the back of her neck. At least, Ru tried to remind herself of that — the solstice was not yet upon them. Weeks remained. And Lady Bellenet wouldn't harm Ru, not the conduit, the Keeper.

But Lady Bellenet frightened her despite all this. She was the woman who held the kingdom in thrall, who paraded Regent Sigrun about like a puppet, who held Hugon D'Luc's leash in delicate hands.

"My apologies," Ru said, hoping fervently that her expression was light and pleasant. "I'm still recovering from last night's revelries."

Lady Bellenet smiled proudly. "Wasn't it a feast for the senses! I do hope you enjoyed yourself. Though..." her smile faded slightly, "I wish you had stayed longer. There was a blessing in your honor."

Ru didn't know how to respond to that. An apology? An explanation? She wondered if it was even true, or if Lady Bellenet was trying to put her on uneven footing. "Was there?" she said at last.

"Indeed. We prayed and drank to your health. Wherever did you go?" Her smile was sweet but sharp. "I do hope Georgina Brantforde didn't exhaust you with her endless prattling."

A burst of panic filled Ru. Lady Bellenet had seen them talking. Then she must know about the book. She tried to relax; her conversation with Georgina had been innocent and mostly one-sided. It was only a book. What did Lady Bellenet care?

And then, like a fire being doused with water, Ru's panic disappeared. Her chest relaxed, her shoulders slumped. She was a churning sea reduced to calm waters in a moment. She took a long, uneven breath. Set down her teacup. *What does it matter?* she thought. *The artifact doesn't matter. Nothing does.* How comforting it was to simply exist, to feel nothing at all.

Lady Bellenet smiled. "How are you feeling, Miss Delara?"

Ru said nothing. She couldn't answer the question; she wasn't feeling at all.

With deliberate movements, Lady Bellenet sipped from her teacup, watching Ru intently. "I'd tell you not to worry, but I know you couldn't if you tried. See how lovely it is to let go of your cares? Your sorrows? You could be as joyful as my Children, devoting their lives to Festra, their god. It would be quite easy. I could leave you just like this. No fear or worries at all for the rest of your life."

"I see," said Ru. She couldn't think of any reason why it wouldn't be as Lady Bellenet said. Though when she tried to feel that joy the woman spoke of, there was nothing. Only a vast emptiness.

Lady Bellenet sighed and made a dramatic show of rolling her eyes and slumping in her chair. "You're ever so boring like this, aren't you? Fine, have your fears back.

Your sorrows and your terrors. You'll need them for the Cleansing, anyway."

Like a dam suddenly broken, rushing in a frenzied chaos, Ru's emotions came slamming back to her all at once. She gripped the edge of the table, overwhelmed for a moment by the force of it.

"Take your time," said Lady Bellenet, sipping her tea daintily.

"What did you do?" Ru said at last, her voice unsteady. She asked, but she knew exactly what the lady had done. She'd somehow taken her emotions from her and left her an empty shell, devoid of everything that made her *Ru*. In retrospect, it was one of the most unsettling experiences in Ru's life, though at the time, she'd felt nothing at all.

Lady Bellenet shrugged one shoulder dismissively. "Oh, just a simple tonic for the nerves. Though I hardly touched you. If I had used my full power, I could have made you sweet and docile with no hope of ever returning to yourself. It is my gift."

"Your gift…" Ru said, momentarily lost for words. They had done all that work to uncover Lady Bellenet's powers, and here she was, discussing them with Ru as if it were nothing.

"Quite," said Lady Bellenet, smiling a bit too gleefully. "How do you feel?"

Ru was still shaken by the experience, her throat tight, breaths unsteady. "I feel wonderful," she lied. "A tonic indeed. How did you do it?"

The lady's mouth pursed. "A lady does not reveal her methods. But it is not easy work, nor would I use it upon you lightly. What you felt was only a hint, a taste. I wouldn't want to lose you altogether, would I? But I needed you to see."

"See what?" Ru asked, tasting blood where she gnawed her lip. Lady Bellenet had called her power a *tonic for the nerves*. It was far more than that. If Ru had only experienced a hint of this woman's powers… she tried not to shudder at the thought.

"What I can do in the name of Festra," said Lady Bellenet. "How completely and how far I can spread his word before the glorious end." She leaned forward as she spoke, increasingly impassioned and bright-eyed. "This gift was bestowed on me by Festra at the moment of my rebirth. When my fear fled, and my pain was healed, he enveloped me and filled me with his love. His light. And when I was whole again, I had been imbued with… *this*." She spread her hands, her palms glowing faintly in the setting sun. "His voice, his love. They reside in me."

Ru's mind whirled. If she believed what Lady Bellent said, Festra had given her a power that would make it impossible for anyone to defy her. Ru suddenly wondered how many of the courtiers at the palace had been treated with this *tonic*.

"Then you truly believe?" Ru asked, studying the woman across from her. "In Festra, I mean."

Lady Bellenet laughed. "How could I not? I have seen him. You yourself have felt my power. And yet you still question."

"Taryel has powers," Ru said, unable to stop herself, "but he was born with them. They weren't gifted by any deity. Maybe you're the same and only managed to use your power later in life."

Lady Bellenet laughed. "An academic to the core," she said. "No, I was not born with the light of Festra within."

Ru bit her lip again. She had so many questions. She knew she shouldn't ask them outright — she should be playing along, drawing information from Lady Bellenet without her knowledge, but… something about the woman told Ru that she saw through Ru's game. That trying to deceive her would achieve nothing. So she asked, "Why do you believe that Taryel is Festra incarnate?"

"I believe nothing," Lady Bellenet said lightly. "I *know*."

"Of course, but how?"

The woman's expression turned inward, considering. "How do you know that you love Taryel?"

Ru froze, startled by this violation, the presumption of it. "I…"

"Did you perform an experiment?" Lady Bellenet asked. "Form a hypothesis? Did you make notes, sketches of the feeling, until the guess was proven and you were, at last, free to claim it as your own?"

"You can't experiment on emotions," Ru said flatly.

"And thus, you make my point for me," Lady Bellenet replied, smiling. "How do I know that the man you love is also the hand of Festra, the god who saved me from despair? It cannot be proven scientifically. Yet I know it. Because I feel it."

Something dark and writhing caught in Ru's throat. "... Do you love Taryel, then?"

Lady Bellenet laughed, and this time it was tinged with sadness. "Of course, child. I love him deeply. In the way a woman of faith loves her god. I am his sworn follower. *You* are the missing piece."

Ru swallowed. She knew the woman had summoned her to her chambers for a reason. Surely it wasn't to proselytize. "What missing piece?"

"The spark. The flame. The guide. When Taryel's heart ignites the world at winter solstice, in the Great Cleansing, you will be at its epicenter. The nucleus of a universe reborn."

"Yes," Ru said, growing impatient. Was this woman only capable of speaking in metaphors? "I'm expected to harness the artifact's power and cleanse the world. But what happens afterward? Won't we be... dead?" She paused. "Everyone but me, anyway."

Lady Bellenet only smiled serenely.

"Based on my experience with the artifact," Ru went on, "Taryel's heart I mean, after the Great Cleansing, I'll be standing alone in a scorched ruin. Where does paradise come in? You speak about rebirth, but all I know of the heart is destruction." She paused, noting her frustrated tone, and tried to smile placatingly. "Help me understand."

The lady's eyes shone. "There is more to this world than we know. There are places beyond the edges of our maps that may only be accessed in moments of great upheaval, pure devotion, souls and souls offered up to one god in a single moment. We, the followers of Festra, will pass beyond the gates of paradise as the heart ignites. We will not die, not in the way you understand it."

"How? Where?"

"The Isle of the Sun."

"There is no such place."

Lady Bellenet tilted her head as if listening to the gar-bled demands of an infant. "Fear not, child. When you have carried out your holy duty, Taryel will bring you back to us. And together, we will walk into paradise."

Ru's exasperation boiled in her chest. The deep well of rage that had been smoldering in her for the past week sent up a violent flame. "What does any of this *mean*?" she said. "You want me to do this *thing* for you, but you insist on talking in riddles. There is no Isle of the Sun. When I perform the Cleansing, everyone in the kingdom will die. I've seen what the artifact can do. You want a new De-struction, to murder thousands of innocent souls, because some made-up god *told* you to. I'm sorry, but it doesn't make sense."

Lady Bellenet's eyes went dark, and Ru realized too late that she'd crossed a line.

"Not... that I object to that," Ru said quickly, desper-ately hoping she hadn't given herself away altogether. "I'm sorry. Your gift shocked me. I didn't mean..."

"You do not need to believe," said Lady Bellenet, her voice slow and heavy. "And I cannot make you. But you have been chosen by Festra. You are holy. Even unbeliev-ing, you will be granted salvation."

A new, strange emotion rose in Ru then. A small crack in her chest broke open, and a pain that was both joy and sorrow flowed forth. *Salvation.* She was not innocent. She had killed before, senselessly, in great numbers. At her core, she felt that she was impure, tainted, broken. There was no coming back from what she had done, and no amount of apology or prayer could mend her.

What god, real or imagined, would ever grant her salvation?

Lady Bellenet held out her hand then, palm upward, as if offering some unseen gift.

And Ru, lost in the moment, small and afraid, reached out. Maybe the world was bigger than she understood it to be, and Festra was more than she could have believed.

What if there *was* forgiveness in his blessing? Could she refuse the possibility?

Lady Bellenet's fingers closed around hers, slowly, until they were tight and grasping, until Ru's hand cried out in pain.

The lady's eyes blazed.

"Remember what I can do, Ruellian. Do not defy me. Do not test me. Quieting a soul is as easy as snapping my fingers." Then she smiled, a beautiful, cruel curve of the mouth, and dropped Ru's hand as if it were a piece of discarded filth. "You may go."

CHAPTER 22

Ru tried to remain calm and collected in the aftermath of Lady Bellenet's threats, but she was shaken. The image of Lady Bellenet's dark eyes and glowing palm burned like a brand in her mind.

But Ru wouldn't find comfort that morning, not yet. Lord D'Luc waited in the corridor outside Lady Bellenet's chambers, leaning against the opposite wall. He wore pale green, a departure from his usual white and gold. His expression was strained, and shadows seemed to cling to his eyes and mouth.

For a moment, Ru was terrified and falling, unable to grasp at the beautiful walls on all sides, unable to stop herself from tilting over the edge and tumbling into desperate despair. There was no escape from this. She was alone. How could she stop Lady Bellenet when she was nothing but a prisoner herself? How could she save her friends, the courtiers, the world? All those Children… the professors… they were gone.

And then Hugon pushed himself from the wall and crossed over to her as Ru tried desperately to climb out of the darkness, to return to herself.

"She won't do it again," he said, as if he'd seen straight through to Ru's terror. "Not to you. I relieved Lyr, by the way. You're coming with me."

His tone was matter-of-fact and dull. Ru thought of the Hugon D'Luc who hid behind the mask, the one who showed himself to her only in flickers and glances. Was this him? Or some other iteration of the man? Today, he seemed to be not much more than a ghost.

"Let me guess," Ru said, deliberately hiding behind her sarcasm. "A demonstration."

Hugon gave her a long, inscrutable look. "Correct as always, Delara."

They walked through the palace in silence, Lord D'Luc leading by half a pace. With every passing moment, the world closed in on Ru. Her feet moved against her will. Crystal chandeliers threatened to swallow her up in a fractured reflection, repeating and repeating.

Lady Bellenet's words echoed in her head. *Quieting a soul is as easy as snapping my fingers.*

"Through here," Hugon said, stopping at a heavy wooden door.

Ru stared at it, imagining what might lie beyond — a dungeon, like the one in the Cornelian Tower, or worse. Smaller, a lower ceiling, nowhere to breathe. Or vaster, wider, endless and dark in all directions.

"Delara." Hugon held the door open, watching her.

The door opened to a staircase leading down. White stone steps, worn low with age. Ru's fingers knotted in her skirt. She reached for the artifact by habit, hoping for some comfort, but its vibrating presence wasn't enough to soothe her.

"*Delara.*"

She didn't move. Couldn't. She knew she should go along with it, that she had *asked* for this. But in the face of reality, she found herself frozen. This was the inevitable, the descent to the fate that would repeat itself again and again. The reflection of a reflection, distorted as it was. White-robed figures, a flash of blade, a gush of blood. Wherever these stairs led, the artifact would be waiting for her there.

"N—" she tried to speak, to refuse. Her mouth was fused shut, her muscles atrophied. *Taryel,* she cried silently, clinging to the feeling of the artifact.

Lord D'Luc went to where Ru stood fixed and unmoving in the corridor. He pressed one palm to her back, the other taking her hand. Firmly, with no hint of gentleness, he half-pushed, half-pulled her to the door.

"You must do this," he muttered, easing her onto the stairs and closing the door behind them. "There's no stopping it now," he said as they went. Ru was ahead of him, the lord bracing a hand against her back, presumably in case she tried to flee.

The stairs seemed to go on forever. They were a nightmarish corkscrew, leading down and down into some dank, old part of the palace. Ru's panic abated gradually, enough that she could think clearly. But that cold fear would not let her go.

"What if I refuse?" She spoke after a long period of silence, the only sounds their breathing, the movement of her skirts against the close walls, footsteps on stone. "What if I change my mind?"

Hugon made a dismissive sound. "It would change nothing."

Ru stopped in her tracks, turning to level a hateful stare at the man. He halted, his eyes wide. "You can speak plainly to me, *Hugon*," she said, her words venomous. "I know what you and your lady want me to do with the artifact. But it will be the same as before, at the Tower. I don't know how to control it. I never have." She bit her tongue; she would not cry. "It won't react to me unless..."

"Continue down the stairs, Delara."

"Why?"

He returned her hard gaze. "You know very well *why*."

Ru bit her lip hard, resisting the tears that pricked at her eyes. Lady Bellenet had frightened her, set her off-kilter, yet put everything in sharp focus. And Ru was hard put not to let her own emotions take her, to allow the anger and dread to swallow her whole. Perhaps that was what they wanted. For her to lose herself in despair, to become easy and pliant.

Biting back a sob, she spun on her heel, continuing down the stairs.

The air grew colder as they descended, stale and old. It was different from the air in the dungeon of the Tower, deeper and earthier.

After what felt like an eternity, they stopped their descent. The stairway opened out into a cavern of white stone, no larger than Ru's bedroom in the palace. Water fell from stalactites into tiny pools at the room's edge.

She didn't see the Children until it was too late to turn and run. Hugon's fingers gripped her elbow, viselike, in the same moment the trio came into view. Inda, Ranto, and Nell were just as they had always been — inanimate, empty, as if the humanity had been drained from them, leaving only a husk behind.

Ru shuddered. If she had experienced just a fraction of what Lady Bellenet was capable of, she couldn't bear to think what it was like for the Children.

A flash of memory, blood in the dungeon, Lord D'Luc's knife. What would it be like to watch your friend die and not feel a thing?

Her throat was closing up; she couldn't breathe. The last time she had been alone in an enclosed space like this, with Lord D'Luc and the Children looking on, something in her had broken. She had watched someone die.

And then she saw it. In the center of the cavern stood a table, simple, hand-carved. The sort of table that might have been used in her childhood home, where her father might have placed a loaf of fresh-baked bread or served tea by the fire. But the thing on the table, naked and shining black, was of another world entirely — another life. The dark one that existed within Ru and Ru alone, tormenting her until she would one day, inevitably, crumble under the weight of herself.

It all came flooding back — every demonstration, every death, every painful press of Hugon's hand against her skin, as if it were happening now, over and over, forever.

"I don't want to," Ru said, nearing hysteria. She fought Lord D'Luc's grip like an animal held captive. Her voice sounded faraway, a shrieking thing, some helpless creature. "Please. *Please*, don't make me. I'll do it. I'll do it at the solstice. Not now. Please."

The Children flowed around the table like specters, moving toward Ru and Lord D'Luc in case they might be needed. Their vague eyes stared out at Ru.

Her legs were losing feeling. They were going to buckle, and she would fall to the floor, or into despair, or both at once. As she always did. Falling, again and again. Helpless in the dark. She might have taken the artifact in her hand then, if she could reach it, and put an end to things once and for all.

Ru's pain was unbearably heavy.

Hands caught her under the armpit. They lifted her, preventing her inevitable crumpling to the floor.

"Get out," said Lord D'Luc.

Inda opened her mouth in unspoken protest. Water dripped like a metronome in that cold, deep cavern.

"*Out*," Hugon spat. An order from a lord, sharp and wild-edged.

They did not disobey this time. One by one, the Children moved away from the table, from the artifact. And one by one they passed Ru, not once catching her gaze, or pausing as they went. And in a moment, they were gone, and the cavern was empty.

Empty but for Ru, and Hugon, and Taryel's heart.

Somehow, Ru found her feet. She wrenched herself from Lord D'Luc's grasp, crossing the cavern and huddling against the wall like a cornered animal, unable to stop the overwhelming surge of memories and feelings, a poisoned well overflowing. Vividly, in her mind's eye, she watched as Hugon twisted her wrist, as he choked her, as he drew blood.

"Stop," Hugon said, running a hand down his face. He did not pursue her. His shoulders slumped. "I'm not going to hurt you."

"Why did you send the Children away?" Ru asked, terrified of what he planned to do.

He stared off toward one of the pools on the floor as if transfixed by the dark water.

"D'Luc is a Mekyan name," he said quietly.

Ru tasted blood and thoughtlessly lifted a finger to touch her lip. It stung, and she hissed through her teeth. Had she bit it?

Hugon didn't react. "It comes from a long line of rich Mekyan blood. An aristocratic line. I am the oldest son and the last. My father entrusted me with the family's legacy. Our lands, our homes. There was a hill where I grew up, thick with cypress trees. I would lie beneath them, feeling the dance of sunlight on my face. Ants would walk across me. Once, a hummingbird alighted on my knee as if I were safe. Not threatening in the least. I felt… free, then."

Ru wrapped her arms around herself tightly. She shivered; the fear had kept her warm, alert, but now it was fading.

A subterranean draft caught Hugon's hair. He did not turn to face Ru but continued speaking as if to the walls or stalagmites. As if, in acknowledging her presence, he would be unable to go on.

"When I was a younger man," he said, "no older than twenty, I met a girl. She was… beautiful, though that seems a paltry word to describe her. She was radiant. A girl who could have charmed the world if she'd tried. But instead, she focused her attention on me. Me, a young man with no accomplishments, a reader of many books, and still a boy in so many ways. But she said that I was kind. That I made her feel safe."

For a moment, he paused, rubbing his eyes with two fingers. Ru thought he might be done with the story, that he'd lapsed into a trance of some kind. But—

"Delara," he said suddenly, "you understand what love is. Don't you?"

She said nothing.

"It's ingrained in us from birth," he went on, apparently not needing a response. "Love. A need for connection. It is biological. Chemical. Nothing more than that. And yet… when I fell in love with this girl, it felt as if I were the first person in the world to experience joy at the sight of a young woman's smile. To want to be near her every minute of the day. I don't know why she loved me back. I was intense, opaque, my conversations dull and overly complex. But she seemed to adore me nonetheless. She was so unlike me, so open to the world and so ready to… to *share*.

"But I was not. I was greedy."

Finally, he looked at Ru. He caught her wide-eyed gaze

across the room, and she found that she couldn't look away. She wanted to know what happened — to the girl, to Hugon. What, or who, had made him who he was?

"We never married," he said, a clearly painful admission. "I asked her time and time again. I knelt before her, offering my hand, my name, my lands... but she refused. I knew she loved me. I couldn't understand why. I loved her more than..." he stopped, biting off his words.

Then he said, "We had a child together. In secret, of course. Her father hid her from society while she was with child, kept her away from prying eyes. The truth would have ruined us both. I tried to give her what she needed. Support, love, a husband, gold. She refused all of it. She always was *unfettered*, often talking of traveling the world. She claimed she would leave, sail to Solmaria on the western coast of Navenie, and seek a new life with some distant cousin, someone who might claim the baby as their own while she stayed on as a doting aunt in the eyes of society."

Ru knew, somehow, that he spoke of Lady Bellenet. She saw it in his eyes, the pain he revealed to Ru when his mask slipped. And something else, some gnawing emotion she recognized but couldn't quite name.

"I lost her for years," he went on, speaking faster now, beginning to pace by the window. "She disappeared. I tried to track her down, wrote letters, even asked her family. They wanted nothing to do with me. I was the father and equally the enemy."

"Did she come back?" Ru asked, the question spilling out despite herself.

Hugon flashed a glance toward her, then looked away again. "Seven years later. She found me in my country home, drunk and alone. My father had died the year prior, and I was the last to bear the D'Luc name. And here came this woman, the girl I'd loved, who would have been my wife, had she only..." He shook his head, schooling his features. He lifted his chin, slightly. "Our child, she said, was gone. Dead those seven years. She had to tell me twice, I was in such a drunken haze. I told her to go, pleaded, begged her to leave me. To forget about me. I couldn't bear the pain of her return and this revelation that our child was lost."

Ru had never seen Lord D'Luc like this, had never seen his expression so open, his agony so palpable. "Did she leave you then?" Her voice was low, muffled by the wail of the wind.

"No," he said. "She did not. She claimed that she had somehow changed, been reborn. She wanted the same for me. She wanted to help me."

"And did she?"

He looked at Ru for a long, unguarded moment. His fingers flexed, a thoughtless, nervous movement. "Yes," he said at last.

"And you forgave this woman?" Ru said, hating Lady Bellenet even more, if such a thing were possible. "She abandoned you and left you to rot. Whoever she was, she obviously didn't care about you."

Lord D'Luc met her gaze. "I didn't care about myself, Delara. I'd thought that much was obvious. I had nothing to my name but a house and a vast misery. And here she was at last, the woman I loved, ready to take me back. To be with me. She had been young, confused, when she…" he trailed off, his expression hardening. "I needn't explain myself to you."

Ru clenched her jaw, emboldened by Hugon's vulnerability. "Fine," she said. "Then tell me how I fit in. And Festra, and Taryel, and the artifact. All of it."

He regarded her thoughtfully, smoothed his hair, and arranged the lace at his cuffs. "You are but a player in the story that Fate has been telling since the birth of the gods, Delara. Lady Bellenet *saw* the Destroyer's heart buried in the scorched earth. A physical manifestation of Festra himself. And she *saw* you arrive there; saw the spool of thread unfurling between you and the heart."

"What does that mean, she *saw*?" Ru asked, careful to sound contrite so as not to break this spell. Afraid that Hugon would close up again, locking her out.

He smiled ruefully, a wan curve at the corner of his mouth. "Through the eyes of Festra."

"A vision?"

"Something like that."

And even then, Ru saw his eyes hardening, the lines of his jaw stiffening. She would lose him. "But… what if Festra has nothing to do with it?"

"Has nothing to do with what, exactly?"

"The artifact, what it can do, my connection to it, Lady Bellenet's powers…" she trailed off, realizing how she sounded. *How could all of this obvious magic, these inexplicable things, be explained by something as far-fetched as a god?*

Hugon raised an eyebrow as if understanding exactly what she meant. "Do you have a better answer? After all that reading, all those studies you conducted in the Tower, do you even have a hypothesis? Or are you beginning to accept the truth?"

Ru stared defiantly. "Magic is science we can't explain yet. It's *real*. Gods… just aren't."

"How many times must we discuss the difference between magic and religion, Delara? When will you get it through your head that they're the same? Once upon a time, your ancestors believed in both."

She knew it was true, but the academic part of her, the one that demanded explanation, resisted. But it would do no good to argue with Hugon now; he was back to his usual self, prim and distant.

"What do you get out of this, anyway?" Ru asked.

Hugon's gaze bored into hers, his blue eyes mirrors of sapphire. "My lady is capable of more than you know."

Ru peered back at him, trying to see the truth in his eyes. But his walls were solidly back in place. "Is she hurting you?" she asked, taking a small step toward Hugon. "Coercing you, using her powers to manipulate—"

"You overstep your bounds," Lord D'Luc interrupted, his voice cold. "You needn't ask these mawkish questions. There is but one thing I need from you, Delara, and it is not your sympathy or your inquisition. It is for you to do the right thing at the appointed time. That is all."

Ru didn't dare speak again. The ice in his eyes, the cruel glint, was too much like the Lord D'Luc she'd seen back in the Tower dungeon. A feral thing pushed to the limit.

After all, he was right — she had crossed yet another

line asking those questions. She'd stopped playing the game, forgotten her role. As she remembered Hugon's pained gaze, the vision of a man whose facade had cracked, a horrible realization hit her. Because she recognized that emotion in his eyes. She had felt it herself: the piercing ache for death.

CHAPTER 23

"**B**e honest," Taryel said, "have you ever seen anything like this in your life?"

Ru took in their surroundings — a circular room with a domed glass ceiling, full to bursting with elegant smiles, courtiers in fine raiment, and footmen carrying plates of food. A harpist played an enchanting melody, while a trio of contortionists performed at the center of the room. And above it all, settled on an ornate golden perch that hung from the apex of the ceiling, was a sky mouse. At least, that was what Lord Edelliar, its keeper, had called it — some exotic mouse from the forests of southern Mekya, which he had claimed could actually *fly*. And the cause for all of this celebration, according to Lord Edelliar, was the creature's birthday.

Had she seen anything like it in her life? Ru had to admit that she hadn't.

"What do you think?" she said, tilting her head toward Taryel.

He glanced down at her from the corner of his eyes. "You tell me. For all I know, you've been hiding a menagerie of beloved sky mice in your rooms since we met."

"And in my pockets, I suppose?"

"Maybe that's why you're so enamored with cinnamon buns. You take them back and feed them to your flying mice." His expression turned to faux shock. "You don't even like pastries at all, do you? It's the *mice*."

Ru snorted, smiling despite herself. Taryel had been in charming form that day, and she was grateful for it. A heaviness had clung to her since the descent to the cavern with Lord D'Luc. While he had not made her demonstrate, had led her back up the stairs after his revelation about his past, it had felt like a punishment nonetheless. Somehow the knowledge that Hugon was tied to Lady Bellenet by the force of a hopeless love made him seem more dangerous to her, more unpredictable.

"What are you thinking about?" Taryel said, always attuned to her.

"Nothing," Ru said, pushing the thoughts away. "Just... I have something to tell you, after the party."

"Is it that you're finally warming to me?"

"No." Her mouth twisted in an attempt not to smile.

"Not even when I send you cake?"

She turned. "I haven't received any cake."

He grinned. "Not yet."

"Well don't. It would look desperate."

Taryel only laughed, a low chuckle in his chest. Ru couldn't help the way her traitorous body responded, the way she yearned to laugh with him, lean into him, move her hands over his velvety waistcoat, eager for the hot skin beneath.

"And now," said Lord Edelliar's shrill voice, startling Ru, "Dionyse Milliottia Edelliar, apple of her father's eye, shall come and have her cake!"

The gathered partygoers cheered, watching with rapt attention as Lord Edelliar reached up with a hook at the end of a wooden pole, unfastening the door to the sky mouse's cage. Everyone gasped as the tiny creature, its orb-like eyes shining like onyx marbles, leapt from the great height.

Ru watched, awed by the tiny thing, as it soared, all four of its tiny legs spread wide, revealing webbing between them. It drifted down to Lord Edelliar's shoulder, gripping his silken jacket with tiny clawed feet.

"There we are, Dionyse," crooned Lord Edelliar. "Are you ready for cake?"

A cheer erupted as a cake was wheeled into the room, a majestic thing of pink and white with edible pearls scattered across its sugary surface. The crowd shifted, and Ru reached out for Taryel's hand, unthinking, so as not to lose him.

It occurred to her then how nice it was, not being the center of attention. She and Taryel had been invited to the party as honored guests, but the star of the show was Dionyse Milliottia Edelliar. Ru felt safe in that brief moment, allowed to be just Ru Delara, academic, amazed by a strange new animal.

"What do you think?" Taryel said, turning to Ru and smiling. "Shall we wish Dionyse a happy birthday?"

While she knew she should let go of his hand, stand firm in her determination to keep him at arm's length… she didn't. She threaded her fingers with his and said, "It would be rude to keep her waiting."

∽

IT WAS another hour before Ru and Taryel were able to say their goodbyes and tumble out into the dusk-lit corridor. Ru's eyes were bright with wine and cake, and Taryel's smile seemed lighter, more carefree than Ru had seen it in ages. She wanted to live in this moment forever — a quiet corridor, Taryel's hand in hers, the fading ache of laughter in their cheeks.

But as they walked through the palace, nodding at tittering courtiers as they went, Ru found herself slipping slowly back into the pit of fear, the gnawing dread that was ever at her core.

"Don't," Taryel said, pausing to face her, to curl a finger and lift her chin. "Stay in the moment a little longer."

As he spoke, the artifact's presence in Ru began to expand, to warm her, comfort her in the way it so often had. But she didn't want it. She didn't want to forget about her worries, about the people who would suffer or die because of her. Lord Edelliar with his Dionyse, all those joyful courtiers whose only crime was to embrace enthusiasm with abandon.

"I can't afford to," Ru said. "Time is running out, and you know it."

"I know," he said.

"So let me try to fix this before it's too late. I have to show you something."

They went back to Ru's rooms. None of the guards who shadowed Ru protested or asked what they were doing. This was all within the confines of Ru and Taryel's roles, after all — why shouldn't they retire to her rooms together?

As soon as they were alone, Ru's heart sped. She caught Taryel's gaze and held it, knowing that he wanted her as much as she wanted him. It would have taken so little. Just the right look, a touch… she swallowed, trying to ignore a sudden spike of feverish want. He was hers, if she wanted him. Nothing and no one stood in the way.

Nothing but Ru herself.

"You keep putting up walls," Taryel said, studying her face. "Let me in. Tell me."

"It's…" she said, hesitating. She wanted to tell him what Hugon D'Luc had revealed about himself, his relationship to Lady Bellenet, but something held her back. Somehow, she felt protective of it, this strange glimmering shard of her jailor's past. What difference would it make to Taryel, to their goals? It changed nothing. And it wasn't her secret to share.

"Wait here," she said, gesturing to the sofa facing the fire. It was warm and bright; Pearl must have come recently.

While Taryel settled himself, Ru went to retrieve *Gods & Glories*. She had shoved it beneath her mattress in a fit of paranoia after the ball, worried that it would be taken from her before she'd had a chance to read it. She hadn't had a chance to sit down and study it, not until now.

"Here," she said, returning to the parlor and handing it to Taryel.

He raised a brow, studying the book. "Where did you find this?"

"I didn't. A young woman gave it to me at the ball."

Taryel's brow rose a fraction higher. "Is that so? I've never heard of it."

"She said it is the only copy in existence, but apparently it used to be all the rage in Ordellun-by-the-Sea. Maybe before your time?"

"We'd better take a look," said Taryel, patting the cushion next to him with a smile. "I thought I'd read every book in the world by now, how unlike me to miss one."

Ru narrowed her eyes in an attempt not to laugh. Did she *really* want to cuddle up next to the Destroyer by a crackling fire, huddled over a book, their faces no doubt leaning closer by the moment? She had to admit to herself that she didn't know *what* she wanted.

"I won't try anything," Taryel added innocently.

With a long-suffering exhale, Ru relented. The sofa was already warm from the fire, and Taryel's solid presence put her at immediate ease. An ease that wasn't earned or deserved, she thought, but she melted into it all the same.

Taking the book from Taryel, Ru flipped through it randomly, stopping to study illustrations here and there. It was a collection of short stories; accounts of gods interfering with humanity. But nothing stood out as being related to Festra until Ru's eyes lit on a chapter heading near the back of the book: "The Isle of the Sun."

Ru stiffened. "Lady Bellenet talked about this," she said. "It's where she believes we'll go after the Cleansing."

"The plot thickens," Taryel said, leaning close to read.

They read the story together, Ru turning the pages and Taryel murmuring the words aloud, almost soothing in the depth of his voice, his accent. The story told of a mythical city on some lost, forgotten island that was said to house the gates to the afterlife. Many kings, adventurers, and faithful men and women attempted to find the island. None ever did but for one explorer.

Her name was Solia. And when she returned to Navenie, steeped in the joy of that discovery, she visited every temple, every church, every town square. She told them of what she had seen on that island, asking believers and nonbelievers alike to join her and pass through the gates to paradise.

But no one believed her. The Isle of the Sun was a story, a children's tale.

Solia was cast out from each city and village, a laughingstock, a madwoman. Until finally, she traveled to the very last temple, a temple belonging to one of the most ancient gods, a god nearly forgotten, even then: the Temple of Festra.

Ru's heart quickened as Taryel read. They glanced at one another, pausing only to share wide-eyed glances as they read on.

It was said that when Solia spoke to that nearly-forgotten god, at the foot of his looming statue, he alone believed her. He alone believed that she had visited the Isle of the Sun and returned for the sake of humanity. And so taken was Festra by Solia's true and honest soul, her unerring faith, that he descended to earth at that moment, kneeling before her. He offered himself to her, his love and devotion. She "drank of it," though the story didn't say how — whether he had given her some blessed tonic, or whether the drink was a metaphor. Images of delicate wounds and blood-soaked lips flickered in Ru's mind.

And then, before his kindred, the gods, and their children who had cast out Solia, Festra made a vow to her.

Then he took Solia in his arms and flew with her to the Isle of the Sun, and there, they wed, living out their lives in that sunbathed, golden city until they were ready to die. And when they eventually had their fill of life and all it had to offer, they would pass hand in hand through the gates of paradise.

But before they went to the Isle of the Sun, Festra upheld the vow he had made. He was known, in those days, as a vengeful god. He believed himself to be fair, but his "fairness" often resulted in bloodshed. And those who angered him, even for the smallest reasons, were dealt whatever punishment he deemed just. So Festra unleashed his anger on the people who had ignored and rejected Solia. He engulfed every town, every village, every temple she had visited with white-hot cleansing flames. Not a soul survived the destruction of Festra.

Exactly as he had promised.

"Have you heard this story before?" Ru asked, flipping back to skim it again.

Taryel shook his head. "Never. King Alaric may have known the story, but if he did, he never shared it."

Frowning, Ru flipped back to the final page of the story. A footnote read that in some ancient religious texts, it was said that those who proved their faith in Festra would be rewarded. That they would be imbued with Festra's love and devotion, and when those devotees were deemed worthy, they, too, would walk through the gates of paradise on the Isle of the Sun.

"Do you think Lady Bellenet has read this?" Ru said, flipping through pages thoughtlessly. "She spoke of the Isle of the Sun. There must be something in it."

"And the line about *imbuing* with Festra's love…" said Taryel, lips curling in distaste.

"Lady Bellenet's powers," Ru finished. "It has to be. But it explains nothing about us, your heart, the artifact. All it confirms is that Lady Bellenet isn't speaking complete and total nonsense."

"Or that she's already read this book," Taryel said.

Ru chewed her lip, reading the footnote again. But it revealed no new secret, no insight into how they might stifle Lady Bellenet's powers. "Taryel," she said slowly, a horrible realization coming to her. In the fog of dread after meeting with Lady Bellenet and Hugon's revelations, she had completely forgotten — the drunk courtier she'd spoken to at the ball. "Have you ever been to Prayer?"

He shifted, angling sideways so he could meet Ru's gaze head-on. "No. Have you?"

"You'd think they would want us front and center at that kind of thing, right? Lord D'Luc refused when I asked to go." Her heart sped. "Taryel, that courtier, he told me Lady Bellenet does something at Prayer. That she lights up the whole chapel."

Taryel blinker. "What courtier?"

"Oh, never mind. It doesn't matter. All I know is he said

Children come out of the chapel looking *empty*. We need to see what happens there. She must be doing something at Prayer, something to change people."

Taryel clearly didn't share Ru's sudden enthusiasm. "It'll be crawling with Children."

"Then I'll go in disguised as one."

He pressed his mouth into a thin line. "If what you're saying is right, if they catch us defying them after all the work we've done..."

"And look what we've accomplished so far," Ru said, growing impatient. "Nothing. This game of playing along isn't opening any doors for us. We need to dig deeper, get our hands dirty. Don't you want to stop all of this?"

Taryel let out a soft breath. "The last thing we need is either of us taking a risk like that."

"All we have to do is play our parts," Ru insisted. "Please? Simon can get us white robes, and if we're discovered, we say we just... got caught up in the fervor. Play innocent."

Taryel's brows lowered a fraction. "You're severely underestimating Lady Bellenet and Lord D'Luc's ability to smell a rat."

Ru pursed her lips. "Fine. Never mind. Forget I said anything."

"Well, now I don't want to."

"I'm tired," Ru said, and she realized it wasn't a lie. Her eyes ached from reading in the low light, and she was beginning to feel the effects of all that food and drink at the sky mouse's party. "Let's talk about it some other time. You're right, it would be a needless risk."

He eyed her, his grey eyes soft in the firelight, his expression so caring it hurt Ru's heart. Reaching out a hand, he tucked a stray curl of hair behind Ru's ear, leaning forward as he did. Her breaths quickened, her heart in her throat.

"Do you want me to stay?" he asked.

Ru thought about the way they'd joked at the party, his hand in hers, the warmth of his body as they read *Gods & Glories*. There was no reason to say no. She could give in.

Open herself to him, close the distance, taste him again at long last.

"No," she said, not meeting his eyes. "I'd rather be alone tonight." *And every other night,* she thought bitterly, wondering how much of her distance from Taryel was still anger and hurt and how much was pure stubbornness.

CHAPTER 24

I f Ru never again attended a courtly party in her honor, it would be too soon. The Marchioness of Cantilla was the night's host, presiding over her garden party with an air of smug pride. Ru had to grudgingly admit that the party *was* resplendent, a show of wealth and excess, its festivities overtaking a vast courtyard with every topiary and hedgerow strung with lamps. Tables and chairs clustered near outdoor fires lit in delicate braziers. Fur blankets lay draped across benches and piled about on stools, ready for the taking. A low-hanging sky of grey clouds muffled the starlight.

It had only been a day since Ru and Taryel had read *Gods & Glories*, and there had been no opportunity to share what they'd learned with Gwyneth and Archie. But even her friends were at the back of Ru's mind — because at the center of the courtyard, surrounded by awe-struck courtiers and blank-eyed Children, was a deeply off-putting ice sculpture. It took Ru a moment to recognize it as Taryel. He was glowering, holding the artifact in one hand and gesturing with the other as if he were about to cast a spell.

"What on *earth* is that monstrosity?" said a voice just to Ru's left.

Ru spun, heart leaping. It was Gwyneth, bundled in wool and fur, her cheeks pink in the cold.

Just behind her was Archie, wrinkling his nose. "You've

got to hand it to them," he said, snatching a trio of steaming mugs from a passing tray and handing one each to Ru and Gwyneth. "Aristocrats certainly know how to create a bizarre and unsettling atmosphere."

Ru tried not to look at the statue, wondering who in the world would have put time and effort into creating such an ugly thing.

"Isn't it delectable?" said a familiar voice, husky in the chill air. Lady Bellenet drifted out from a cluster of courtiers, draped in white furs and flanked by a trio of Children. The regent trailed after her, an empty-eyed reminder that Lady Bellenet held her leash.

"It's… delectable," Ru said, trying to smile through the coil of dread that was pulsing in her belly at the sight of Lady Bellenet. It was the first time she'd seen the woman since their tea, since Ru's emotions had been temporarily stolen from her.

The fur-draped lady only smiled, an indulgent curve of full lips, a knowing glance as if she were bestowing some gift upon Ru. "The Marchioness of Cantilla had it commissioned especially for the occasion. She is a true believer if ever I met one."

"Is it a likeness of Festra," Ru asked, despite herself, "or Taryel?"

"Are they not one and the same?" a new voice interjected, jovial and enthusiastic.

Ru and her friends all turned to see the Marchioness herself, a vision of colorful fabrics, furs, and jewels. Her silver hair erupted outward from the sides of her head, while a fur-trimmed tricorn perched perilously on top. She extended both hands to Ru, who allowed the Marchioness to clasp her fingers in welcome.

"Aren't we the luckiest court in the continent," the Marchioness enthused, gazing up at the statue. "To learn that the Destruction was never about death, but life… eternal life." she shook her head, eyes shining. "A blessed day, a blessed time. Miss Delara, if there is anything you need, anything at all. Simply ask, and you shall have it. Tonight is for you, and the heart, and *Taryel*." She beamed, still looking as if she might burst into tears at any moment.

With great self-control, Ru managed to refrain from twisting her face in disgust. Instead, she forced a half-hearted smile and murmured words of thanks. At last, the Marchioness let go of her hands, and with a slew of blown kisses, departed to greet more guests.

"You see," said Lady Bellenet, with cool satisfaction. "She understands the truth of it. Not death, but life."

The hairs on the back of Ru's neck stood on end, and not from the cold. "I still find myself struggling to understand *how*," she said, forcing a sweet, naive tone. She knew better than to question Lady Bellenet, but the woman had spoken only nonsense and vague rhetoric since Ru came to the palace. And Ru was running out of time. "You say the Great Cleansing won't bring destruction," she went on, "but... the Destruction of Ordellun-by-the-Sea resulted in the loss of countless lives. Simply *saying* that it was never about death... well, words don't make a thing true."

"Don't they?" Lady Bellenet cocked her head. The Children's heads moved in concert with hers, a decidedly unsettling tableau. "As an academic, I would have thought that you, above all, revered knowledge and the spread of it. Words alone can change the world."

"Even the ignorant can speak," Ru said, unable to stop herself.

The lady's eyes flashed. "Be careful, Delara. You tread dangerously close to heresy." Her gaze then turned to Gwyneth and Archie, who had remained frozen in silence throughout the exchange. Lady Bellenet smiled serenely. "Remember that it is by my grace alone that your friends are here, that they are safe and content."

Gwyneth turned to Ru with wide eyes.

"Forgive our Delara," Archie said with a winning smile. "She's sleep-deprived. She'll say absolutely anything without her beauty rest."

Ru swallowed her anger; it tasted bitter. "Apologies, my lady," she murmured. "I *am* tired."

"Enjoy the party," Lady Bellenet said, and it was as much a farewell as a warning. She and the Children drifted away like ghosts in the frost-bitten night.

Archie and Gwyneth spun on Ru.

"You're supposed to be playing along," Gwyneth said, her voice a low warning. "What was that?"

"She thinks she's educating the populace," Ru spat, overwhelmed with anger. "Did you hear what the Marchioness said about the Destruction? They're rewriting history, they're undoing centuries of scholarship. It's absurd. I…" she trailed off, unable to find the right words.

"Drink your wine," Gwyneth urged. "We'll sort this out."

"And remember," said Archie, blowing on his steaming mug, "their god is on our side."

Grudgingly, Ru sipped her spiced wine. She knew her friends' hearts were in the right place, but they hadn't spoken one-on-one with Regent Sigrun. They hadn't seen the vast sadness in Lord D'Luc's eyes, hadn't been on the receiving end of Lady Bellenet's powers. They were not the ones whose hands would deliver the killing blow.

Cardamom and cinnamon-spiced warmth slowly filled Ru, and at last, some measure of calm returned to her. "Listen," she said, steering her friends away from the statue and anyone who might overhear, "Taryel and I read a book last night."

Archie and Gwyneth shared a look.

"Is that what they're calling it these days?" Archie asked, arching a brow.

"*Arch*," Ru spluttered. "An actual book. A courtier at the ball gave it to me, the only one of its kind. *Gods & Glories*."

"Sounds intriguing," said Gwyneth, leaning closer. "And?"

Ru told them everything she and Taryel had learned last night and caught them up on her tea with Lady Bellenet. She told them how Lady Bellenet had explained her powers, that they erased emotions, turned people into Children. She left out the part about Lady Bellenet using her power on Ru — she knew it would disturb them, and she didn't have the heart or energy to reassure them that she was fine.

"Talk about bringing down the mood," Archie muttered, sipping his wine with a deep frown.

"Arch, really," Gwyneth said, shooting him a withering

glance. "As if the mood was anything but horrible." She turned to Ru. "We know what we have to do now, don't we?"

"Don't tell me," said Archie. "Sneak into Prayer?"

Gwyneth beamed. "Exactly."

"No," said Ru, shaking her head. "Absolutely not. If anyone goes, it's me, alone."

"Why?" Gwyneth demanded.

Before Ru could answer, a tall figure across the courtyard caught her eye, and all other thoughts fled. Taryel drifted through the snowy landscape like a scarecrow, all sharp edges and messy hair and a flowing black cloak.

"Delara," Archie said, peering at her. Then, following her gaze, he snorted. "Taryel just got here, and you've already forgotten about us."

"Leave her alone," Gwyneth said.

"Go away, Arch," Ru said at the same time.

Then, as if Taryel felt Ru's presence, his gaze snapped to hers. A group of courtiers came up to him, teary-eyed and curtseying, but his attention was on Ru alone.

She clutched her mug of wine, wishing he would come speak to her, yet hoping he wouldn't. It was easier like this — him at a distance, fulfilling his duties, placating the courtiers while she sought the comfort of her friends.

But they didn't feel much like comfort anymore. They reminded her of the danger they were in, every second of the day.

Simon appeared suddenly from around a frosted hedgerow, strumming his lute. Fur adorned his collar and cuffs, and a decadent furry hat perched at a jaunty angle on his head. "Good evening, fair academics," he said, still playing as he spoke. "Looking a bit glum, aren't we?"

"How could we possibly be glum," Ru said, "with a towering ice statue of Taryel looming over us at all times?"

"How amusing you are when plagued by existential fear," Simon said, winking at his sister. "Did you see the life-sized chess set? Also, funnily enough, carved from ice."

"What on earth for?" Archie asked, peering around in search of it.

"It's over there," Simon said, waving a hand vaguely toward the other end of the courtyard. "A veritable work of art. Will be remembered for ages. Practically beyond words."

"What are the black pieces made of, then?" Gwyneth asked. "Stone?"

"They'd be too heavy," Archie mused. "Wood, maybe."

"I've a novel idea," said Simon, "why don't you go and look?"

When Archie and Gwyneth were gone, clearly entranced by the idea of the ice-carved chess set, Simon turned his piercing gaze to Ru. "Now then," he said, "what will it take to mend your infectious and, quite frankly *unattractive*, bad mood?"

Ru lifted her mug, inhaling the sweet vapor of her spiced wine. "Nothing *you* could do."

Simon looked indignant. "I could very well move worlds for you, sweet sibling. Though I do hope you ask for something a bit less... heavy. Your favorite tune, perhaps? More wine? A dance?"

"Robes," Ru said. "White robes. Like the ones the Children wear. Three of them."

The corners of Simon's grin quivered, the only sign of his distaste. "And whatever would you want with those hideous things?"

"Do you really want to know?"

He made a face like he'd swallowed a fly and refused to admit to it. "Of course not," he said, his tone clipped. "Wouldn't dream of it." He glanced away, and his expression changed to one of gleeful anticipation. "Speaking of *dreams*, guess who's coming this way? Want me to get rid of him for you?"

Ru glanced over her shoulder and saw that Taryel was striding darkly through the lamplit courtyard, his furry cloak billowing out behind him. The hair on her neck prickled, though not in fear.

"I'm perfectly capable of handling him myself," Ru said, almost believing it.

Shrugging, Simon began to strum a new tune and sauntered away into the party. Ru watched him go, the picture of colorful gaiety, and her chest tightened. She hoped he would come through for her and not ask questions.

"What's your brother saying about me now?" Taryel asked, coming up to stand beside her. A smile played at the edge of his mouth. Like everyone else at the party, he wore thick layers of fur, though, unlike Ru, he was bare-headed. A few stray snowflakes clung to his hair, crystal against black waves.

Staring pointedly into her wine in an attempt to avoid falling into his gaze, Ru said, "Take a guess."

"Nothing good," Taryel said, chuckling. "Shall we make the rounds together?"

She glanced up at him, and couldn't help but return his smile. "We ought to give the people what they want."

"Taryel Aharis and the Keeper of his Heart," he said and offered his arm. "The Marchioness will be overjoyed."

"The Marchioness was happy about the Destruction, so I'm not sure she's exactly difficult to please."

Pain and mirth creased his face in equal measure as he choked a laugh. "She came up to me earlier with tears shining in her eyes, going on about how wonderful I was. Called me one of the great artistic voices of our time."

"*Artistic* voices?" Ru echoed, allowing Taryel to lead her in a slow, almost aimless route through the party. Simon's music drifted past them, light snowfall painting everything in glowing ethereal hues.

"She's having difficulty transitioning from the mindset of a progressive patron of the arts to religious fanatic, apparently."

Ru snorted.

"Ah," said Taryel, stopping short. "Here she comes now. Want me to distract her while you escape?"

The offer of escape was unexpected, a small kindness. She tightened her fingers around his arm. "No," she said. "We'll do it together. Give her a little show."

And then the Marchioness caught them both in her bright gaze. "Aha!" she cried, rushing forward. "Look at you both, a vision. Astounding. Heavenly." She pressed a hand to her bosom. "I cannot bear to look upon such beauty, such power, such *romance*."

Taking Marchioness Cantilla's hand, Taryel bowed over it and kissed her knuckles. "We are honored, your grace."

As the three of them exchanged greetings, a small cluster of party guests began to form around the Marchioness, watching with expectant, wide-eyed gazes. Ru realized that they had stopped in front of the ridiculous ice sculpture of Taryel.

"Won't you kiss her for us?" the Marchioness said, glancing eagerly at Taryel. "How holy such a kiss would be, a passionate embrace between Taryel and the very Keeper of His Heart."

"Yes!" cried out some of the gathered party guests, the number of which was growing by the moment. They were in raptures at the prospect, some of them pulling at their clothes in agitation, others fanning themselves with limp hands.

"Kiss her, Lord Aharis!"

Ru's stomach curdled in sudden dread as Taryel's arm snaked around her and pulled her close. He wouldn't, would he? Not like this, in front of all these people. After all the parties they'd attended, never once had he crossed a line like this.

She stiffened against him.

"Yes, Lord Aharis!" came the cry.

And then, when Ru was certain he was about to pull her into an unwanted embrace, Taryel lifted his hand from her waist and settled it gently on her shoulder. Leaning down, he murmured in her ear. "You're safe, Ru. Breathe."

She looked up at him, at those eyes she knew like the depths of her own soul. The sounds of the party faded, the music and laughter, until she was alone with him in the darkness. He smelled familiar, like a winter forest. Something caught at Ru's heart, a memory, a voice in the dark. A stranger draping a cloak over her naked shoulders in the Shattered City. And glancing up at the man at her side, she saw neither the Destroyer nor Taryel.

Instead, she found herself gazing into the clear grey eyes of the man she had always known.

You're safe.

Then Taryel spoke louder so everyone gathered could

hear. His tone was jovial, but Ru caught an undercurrent of granite. "My lady is tired and needs a moment to rest. Forgive us for taking our leave." He bowed deeply and swept Ru away from the crowd without another word.

She allowed him to steer her away from the music, the laughter, the lights, and toward a quieter part of the garden. Her heart was a rapid staccato as they walked in silence. Even the small distance between them was a strained ache.

Ru felt desperately, all at once, that she'd been wasting time. Because as they walked together, snow crunching under feet, Ru realized that she trusted him. That somehow, maybe, she always had. He wasn't Fen, this man at her side, but... he was not the monster she had believed him to be.

In the end, it didn't matter if he was Fen or Taryel — he was the man she loved.

CHAPTER 25

They came at last to a small gazebo at the far end of the courtyard. It was surrounded by tall hedges, with a stone path leading up to it. Music and laughter drifted through the chill night, but here it was muffled, like a memory or a dream. Lamps and candles burned at strategic places on the gazebo floor and along its low balcony.

"I think about it often," Taryel said without preamble. His gaze was far away, his brows drawn together. "When I wake, or in a moment of joy cut short. I dream of it almost every night. And when I'm nearing sleep, or hungry, or… any time my walls come down, I remember how it felt."

There was no reason to ask what he meant. It was the same for her. The day the artifact called, and she answered. The day she became Destroyer.

"Even in a thousand years," he said, turning his gaze to her, "the pain hasn't faded. I remember what the air smelled like that morning. There was a heavy fog, and I was hungry. I hadn't eaten breakfast yet. I remember hearing the sounds of the market being set up, the clatter of wheels on cobblestones, shouts, laughter. There was a celebration planned for the king's birthday. The whole city was alive with so much vibrancy, and I…" he bowed his head, his fingers tightening around Ru's.

"You don't have to do this," Ru said. "You don't have to relive everything just to prove something. I understand."

His gaze, when it met hers again, was tortured. "You don't, Ru. This was my city. My *home*. We lived on a country estate, but I spent my childhood running up and down those streets. My mother, when I was very little, took me to one of the only bookshops in Navenie, a cramped place that reeked of leather and dust, and from the street outside you could see the ocean. I had cousins in the city. Friends and colleagues. And Ru, the Destruction… it reached beyond the city walls. Entire farms, villages… my own home. It was as if they never existed."

He would not meet her eyes again, but she reached up to him, brushing a thumb across his jaw, curving her fingers around the back of his neck. There was nothing she could say to comfort him.

She knew what he had done. She had thought about it, from the distance of academia and all the centuries that stretched between her life and the Destruction. But this was the first time since the proclamation in the throne room that he had spoken about it in detail. Ru's own pain was great, but Taryel had lost everything. And he had only himself to blame.

Ru could not fathom his torment.

"I'm sorry," he said. "I don't like talking about it. But… I wanted you to understand. Before everything goes to shit, in case we don't…" he swallowed. "I lied about who I was, kept my past from you, because I'm ashamed. You deserve better than this. Better than a broken, centuries-old killer. Far better than a man with a cursed heart."

"Don't be ridiculous," Ru murmured. "We're made for each other." The words weren't planned. She bit her lip immediately in the wake of speaking — she hadn't meant to give herself away. But time was running short.

Taryel paused, studying her with an expression of something like hope. "You should have run away with me when you had the option."

"I never had the option," Ru bit out. "They would have hurt people until I gave in. They're fanatics. Lady Bellenet's power is—" she shuddered, not wanting to verbalize it.

"I know," Taryel said. "I wish there was something I…"

He reached for her, pulling her close, her cheek against his chest. "We will think of something," he murmured into her hair. "We'll find a way to stop this. I don't have faith in many things, but I have faith in you."

"But I don't know what I'm doing," Ru said, fingers digging into the back of his jacket, eyes closed tight against the night. He smelled as he always had: of cold mountain air and comfort. Ru realized that she was in immediate danger of crumbling. "Time's running out, and I'm no closer to learning how to stop her. What if there *is* no way? And there's no telling how many people she aims to change, to turn into Children…"

She closed her eyes tight, willing herself not to cry. It was too easy in his arms. Too easy to fold.

Taryel put a thumb under her chin, lifting her face so that she was gazing up at him.

"You are Ruellian Delara," he said. "Archaeologist. Keeper of my heart. Destroyer. If anyone can find an answer—"

Ru interrupted him with a kiss.

She stood on tiptoe, burying her fingers in his hair. He returned the kiss with a soft groan. She needed this. To give in, to let someone else take charge, to let go of control, and lean into trust.

Against all reason, she still loved him. He had betrayed her, lied to her, hurt her. There was a wound in her heart that still bled because of him. But she was no longer afraid of him. And her heart was beginning to knit itself back together, bit by bit.

So she surrendered to him, and that alone was healing.

Gently, almost reverently, Taryel lifted Ru into his arms and spun her, settling her on the gazebo railing, between flickering lanterns. His arm around her was the only thing holding her steady, and she savored it.

So, too, did the artifact, flaring suddenly and brightly between them. She felt as if she were lit from within, so intense was the growing wave of her desire.

She wanted him. Every part of him.

His mouth moved to her neck, hot and soft. He pulled her collar aside, undoing the top two clasps of her dress to bare her shoulder to the cold. His lips left burning marks on her as he kissed her there, his fingers gently pulling her dress down, even lower, until she was shivering not from the cold, but with anticipation.

Anyone could have come into this secluded corner and seen them, Ru's legs wrapped around Taryel's waist. Anyone could have seen him running his hand up her thigh, pushing her skirts up around her waist, exposing her stockinged legs. All so he could press his body against hers, bring them closer, tighter.

In that moment, Ru didn't care if anyone saw. There was nothing but her and Taryel and the fire of lust between her legs, the growing tightness at her core, the artifact blazing alongside.

Why had she fought him? Why keep him at arm's length for so many weeks? She now understood that from the moment she had first heard his voice, from the moment she had first felt his touch, he was hers. Whether he was Fen or Taryel, he had always been hers. And no matter what reason told her, she could not hold back the tide any longer.

Then he hooked his hands under her knees, holding her steady while he rolled his hardness against her, and the feel of his body against hers stopped her breath, stilled her heart. She moaned into his neck, overcome by him. She had lost herself with him before, in that golden light of the dungeon. In the dark forest on her way to the palace. *Was this the same?* she wondered, even as he lowered his head to kiss her throat, to press hot lips to her exposed collarbone. As he hooked a finger over her bodice and pulled it down, down, until her hard nipple was exposed.

No, this was different. Before, she had been distracted, hadn't understood the inexorable need between herself and Fen, hadn't understood the artifact's effect on her. This was a conscious surrender to Taryel. She *wanted* this.

The artifact mirrored her feelings, her desire, but did not overwhelm her. And she could see in the steadiness with which Taryel had unlaced her bodice that he felt the same.

She gasped at the heat of his tongue on her breast, at

the intensity of it, the sharp explosion of pleasure that spread outward from between her thighs at the knowledge that she needed him. That he needed *her*.

"Taryel," she breathed, holding him for dear life, her chest heaving, his tongue circling her nipple. "Please."

He paused, lifting his head to meet her gaze, his pupils blown wide.

"I'm sorry," he said and then glanced down at her bare, heaving breast. Hurriedly, he pulled her bodice back into place. Deft fingers secured the clasps on her collar. He lifted her from the railing, avoiding her gaze, smoothing her skirts. All respectful movements, apologetic, almost embarrassed.

"Taryel," she said again, aching at the absence of his touch. "Why are you apologizing?"

"The artifact," he said through heavy-lidded eyes. "I want you, Ru. Badly. But when I feel like this around you, when my heart... I can control myself, but I can't control the artifact. I can't stop it from compelling you. My actions are my own now, but yours..." He glanced away again, lip curling as if he were disgusted.

"It's not compelling me," Ru said, reaching up to cup his face with a cold hand. His cheek was rough with stubble, but his skin was warm, a familiar balm. Her words were hurried, her breaths still coming quick and shallow with unspent pleasure. "I want this. I've wanted this since the moment I met you, Taryel. Don't you?"

"Of course I do," he said, his expression tortured. "My heart keeps pulling you toward me because I want you, and I've no idea how to save you from it."

Ru couldn't help it. She laughed, and Taryel shot her a hurt look.

"You don't get it," she said. "I've never been compelled to *like* you. Maybe I wouldn't have touched the artifact without its coercion. And maybe... *yes*, it encourages me sometimes. All right, a lot. Like that night in the woods when you asked me to leave with you. But when my mind is clear, I still like you. More than that, I *want* you. Ever since that night in the dungeon, it's almost as if..." she swallowed, unable to put into words the way she felt, how their souls were somehow entwined beyond life or death.

She stood on tiptoe and kissed the corner of his mouth softly. "It doesn't matter why we're bound, or what it is that binds us. Fate, Festra, your heart… I don't care. Do you really believe that I'd give in so completely to something I didn't truly want?"

Taryel's eyes were shadowed in the night. "I'm not a good man," he said. "I'm a god of destruction. My very existence has put you and your friends, your family, the entire world in danger."

"I know," she said.

"I'm not Fen Verrill."

Her throat tightened. "I know. But… I don't think I want you to be."

His eyes widened, disbelieving. "Ru…"

"You're Taryel Aharis," she said before he could protest. "But you're also the man who gave his cloak to a naked, helpless woman in the middle of the Shattered City. I should have seen it sooner. I didn't want to accept it at first, that you were still the man I knew. I was angry with you and hurt, and stubborn. But your name doesn't matter. And your heart's effect on me has nothing to do with the fact that I *want* you. Badly."

His face broke into a grin, and he kissed her, as reverent as a prayer.

Ru could have stayed in that lamplit gazebo, wrapped in Taryel's arms, for a lifetime. But the night chill had begun to numb her fingers, and even enveloped in his body heat, she shivered.

"It's late," he said, taking her hand, "and you're cold."

They made their way back to the palace, winding through the brightly lit garden party, and Ru felt that she might have done anything to make the night last forever. From a distance, she caught sight of Archie and Gwyneth laughing, the massive black and white shapes of a chess set behind them. Simon's lute sang a soft melody in the night.

Soon enough, she and Taryel were back inside, awash in the light and warmth of the palace, along with other couples and groups of courtiers, all moving slowly and with the air of people caught in a dream. As if the magic of that snow-bright night might follow them if they allowed it to.

Lyr had peeled away from the wall to join them when they re-entered the palace, and the shadow of his presence brought Ru back to reality. She was under guard, and this was a beautiful prison.

They made their way back to her room, and Taryel bade her good night with a deep bow and a sweet kiss on her knuckles. She wanted more, ached for it, but Lyr was there. And it was late.

She watched him stride down the hall, a tall black shadow, and when he spun around to wink at her before turning the corner, she smiled.

"Damn," said Lyr. "I owe Rosylla a drink."

Ru turned on him. "Excuse me?"

"Said I owe Rosylla a drink. She bet me you'd be in love with that bastard by the end of the first month."

"Lyr!"

He shrugged. "I said you'd never take him back. Joke's on me."

Ru scoffed indignantly. "Good night. Stop making bets about me."

"No promises," said the King's Guard.

CHAPTER 26

At some small hour of the morning, Ru finally accepted that she wasn't going to fall asleep any time soon. She had tossed and turned for hours, her nightgown clinging to her limbs uncomfortably, her pillow not soft enough, the blankets too hot. Worst of all, she couldn't stop thinking about grey eyes, dark hair, and purposeful hands.

Before she had time to talk herself out of it, she was slipping out of bed and pulling on her dressing gown, shoving her feet into slippers. Then, hoping she wouldn't regret this, she rang for Pearl.

The maid was there within minutes, looking bleary-eyed.

"I'm sorry to wake you," Ru said hurriedly, before she lost her nerve "But...I need to go somewhere. Using your hidden servants' passages."

The maid took on a knowing expression. "Where are you hoping to sneak at this hour?"

Ru hesitated.

Pearl smiled as if she knew exactly where Ru wanted to go. "Well, Miss?"

"Taryel's rooms?"

The maid grinned. "You can count on me, Miss Delara."

As they made their way through narrow corridors, well-lit and warm, and with more foot traffic than Ru would have expected, the artifact rippled in her chest. It somehow knew where she was going, urging her. She needed this release. To let go, fully. If only for a moment.

At last, after several twists and turns and flights of stairs, Pearl stopped before a nondescript door. They had passed countless others like it, each marked with a brass number. Pearl had explained that when someone rang for a servant, a bell next to the room's number would ring further down in the palace where the servants lived.

"This is Taryel's room," Pearl said when Ru made no move to open the door. "He's always awake. Rings for tea at all hours of the night." She smiled. "Do you need anything else, Miss?"

"No," Ru said. "Thank you, Pearl."

Feeling suddenly shy and foolish, all alone now in this part of the servants' corridors, Ru hesitated. What would he think of her showing up like this? She swallowed, pushing away her anxieties. Then she lifted her hand and knocked.

If it weren't for the artifact's insistence, its warm bloom of comfort within her, Ru might have bolted.

But her self-consciousness fled as soon as the door opened.

A tall figure with hair in wild disarray, shirt hanging open, stood in the doorway, backlit by a dying fire. His face, bleary with sleep, split in a slow grin.

"Ru," Taryel said.

"I..." she trailed off, lost for words. Why had she come here? *Because you want him,* she thought. *You always have. And you're tired of waiting.* But all she said was, "I didn't think you'd be asleep."

He said nothing, lifting a hand toward her. He moved slowly, as if frightened of scaring her away. His thumb brushed her cheek, and he cupped her jaw gently, burying fingers in her loose hair. Her heart threatened to burst open in her chest like a blooming flower. It had been only hours ago since they were entwined in the gazebo, but this... this felt entirely different. Slow and deliberate.

"I was dreaming of you," Taryel said.

In that state of near half-sleep, his gaze was unguarded, his eyes clear. Ru overflowed at the sight of him. There was too much feeling inside her and not enough of her to hold it in.

"Taryel," she said, curling her fingers around his wrist, holding him there as if afraid he might let her go. The artifact spoke a bloom of joy in her belly, spreading outward like flaming gold, filling her with a certainty that seemed impervious to questioning. "I missed you."

These three words were the truest she had ever spoken. It was as if the world had unfolded and come together in a shape that was deeply and indescribably known to her.

He swallowed visibly, and the relief on his face was so palpable that Ru's chest hurt. "I missed you too," he said.

Then he was sweeping her into his arms, closing the door behind her, and pressing her up against it with gentle ferocity. His body felt as if it were an extension of her own, though they were both fully clothed. Her legs wrapped around his waist, and while his chest was flush with hers, his breath hot on her neck, his hands holding her tight against him, there was nothing salacious in it.

The artifact burned in her, repeating: *Yes, yes*; a songbird greeting the dawn. And it was not coercive, nor was it overwhelming in its need. It was as if the artifact, once so determined to aim her in its chosen direction, had finally found contentment. With Taryel, she was herself, her whole self, and the artifact was a reflection of them.

Ru felt, in that moment, her arms wrapped around the Destroyer, her face buried in the warm space where his neck met his shoulder, as if their bodies were shrouded in a bright light. Their embrace, lit from within by the cursed thing that bound them, was holy.

She hadn't felt so vibrant, so alive, in months.

Taryel was beaming as he carried her to the bed, as if he couldn't believe their luck. And when he tossed her onto the blankets, her dressing gown falling open just enough to reveal a sliver of her thin silk nightgown, the look on his face made her heart shudder happily. He stood over her and hesitated, and with his open shirt and mussed hair, the circles under his eyes, he appeared strangely young, more vulnerable and human than he'd ever looked.

Ru sat up and took his shirt in her impatient fingers,

pulling him down to the bed. He kissed her sweetly at first, pure revelry. But soon, the kisses slowed, his mouth more purposeful. Hungrier.

She had dreamed of this a thousand times, both waking and asleep. Had imagined with great detail how the weight of him might feel, how his fingers would touch her skin, how he would go about pushing her to the brink of her pleasure.

But this was not something she could study or break down into parts. Taryel's slow undoing of her was unfathomable. It was as if she were meeting him for the first time, this man who said he belonged to her, and who, until now, had always seemed hidden in the shadows of his past.

Now, at last, Taryel was *hers* entirely. He deepened his kisses, teeth nipping and tongue seeking. Unable to help herself, Ru arched her body upward, yearning for more of him.

Her body was painfully eager, but Taryel still seemed hesitant. His knees bracketed her on the bed, and his elbows kept him firmly above her, a tantalizing few inches between their bodies.

Fine. Ru would do it herself. She moved her hands down his body, her fingers brushing through his curling chest hair, trailing lightly down his sides. He moaned, pressing his face into her neck.

"Ru," he said, muffled and desperate.

"What?" she said, pulling at his shirt until it came free from his trousers. She pushed it off his broad, lightly muscled shoulders and down his arms until he sat up and wrenched the shirt off, tossing it across the room.

His expression was so lustfully devious that Ru's breath caught.

Then his mouth was on hers again, and gradually, almost painfully, he lowered his body to hers. When he began to kiss her neck with lips and tongue, she gasped, her hips bucking against him. Pleasure bloomed in a searing ache as his hard length pressed against the most sensitive part of her, so much so that the pleasure was almost unbearable.

"Not yet," he breathed, hot in her ear, and he raised

himself onto his knees again, leaving her bereft. He looked at her with a tenderness she'd never been privy to before. She had been in bed with young men before and even sometimes thought herself in love. But this… the way he looked at her was pure, almost sacred.

Taryel said quietly, "Ru, you are… beyond description."

She laughed, and as she did, her dressing gown shifted further, revealing her bare shoulder and the hint of a nipple.

He groaned, crashing into her. He caressed her neck, shoulders, and mouth with worshipful lips. With slow, deliberate movements, he untied her dressing gown. And with one hand, he eased it open all the way, sliding his palm over that thin, silk nightgown, so sheer she knew he could feel the heat of her want. His hand skimmed up her lower belly, making Ru's hips rock upward involuntarily. And his palm slid upward still, ever so slowly, his thumb circling her navel, until his fingertips brushed the edge of her breast.

She gasped, a quick intake of breath, as he moved his fingers deliberately over her nipple, one by one, a touch so delicate it was almost nothing, but the ardor of his caress ignited her like a wildfire.

Taryel drew back, breathless. "Tell me," he said, his gaze raking over Ru so hungrily she could hardly keep from writhing beneath it. "Tell me you want this."

She reached for him, burying her fingers in his hair, ready to pull if he refused her. "I want this," she murmured, and her heart ached as she spoke. "I want you. I've wanted you since the moment I met you."

He lit up like the sun. With a hum of pleasure, he lowered his head to trace a wet circle around her nipple with his tongue. It was as perfect a response as Ru could have hoped for, and she knew with more certainty than she'd known anything that she was exactly where she wanted to be.

"Taryel," she pleaded, between gasps of pleasure as he kissed his way down her stomach. "Please."

He exhaled hotly against her belly, and she shivered. His kisses descended further until he was lightly nipping the insides of her thighs. She closed her eyes, her heart beating a heated staccato in her chest, the pressure of desire building within her, tightly coiled.

And then he kissed her at her most sensitive part, his lips gentle at first, almost chaste, and she gasped, the pleasure in her tightening, sharpening. His tongue swept over her, and the perfect ache of it was almost unbearable.

She knew how debauched they must look — her, still in her nightgown, writhing on his mussed bedclothes, one breast bared to the night. Taryel, his dark head nestled between her thighs.

But his tongue spoke shapes of prayer against the heat of her. His fingers traced devotion on her skin. And if it was depraved, the Destroyer's mouth worshiping her like this... then she would happily live a life in the darkness.

As Ru's pleasure built, she took his hair in her fingers like an anchor, her back arching. She gasped his name as the feeling reached its peak, waves and waves of white-hot pleasure, intense and all-consuming. As if the world had fractured outward from her, beams of bright light angling through the broken shards, and she was bathed in it, wrapped in that aching glow. And when she was whole again, gasping for breath, she found herself in Taryel's smile.

He swept her into his arms, kissing her neck, and she fumbled at his trousers, pulling at them clumsily. She wasn't finished with him. Not nearly.

"Haven't had your fill yet?" he murmured in her ear. "Greedy."

She was impatient now, still thrumming with the pleasure of her orgasm, and she wanted more. *More.* She wanted all of him, as much as he could give, as often as he allowed.

Her fingers shaking with anticipation, Ru, at last, undid the clasp on Taryel's trousers. And when she finally curled her fingers around his full erection, he paused in kissing her to groan, his teeth against her collarbone.

"Ru," he gasped, stilling in his movements. "I'm... let me. I'll lose control if you don't..."

She grinned, giving him a slow, lazy stroke. "If I don't what?"

"*Fuck*," he said, biting her again until it hurt. "Stop. Or I'll…"

"You'll what?" She asked laughingly.

He made a sound, something like a growl, and sat back, taking Ru's hands in one swift movement. Then he clasped both her wrists in one hand, stretching her arms above her head, pinning her to the bed beneath him. She was utterly at his mercy. A wanton smile curled across his face.

"Ru," he warned, breathless, his eyes dark and hungry, "what did I say?"

She bit her lip, and his sharp intake of breath told her that this small gesture was having the desired result. "Do it," she said, taunting.

He arched a brow. "What, exactly, is *it*?"

She couldn't help smiling, hoping he would take her at her word. "Whatever you want."

It was as if a new Taryel took over then. Where before he had been slow and reverent, savoring every taste of her, now he was single-minded, lustful in his precision. With one quick movement, he freed himself from the confines of his trousers. He pressed a hot, wet kiss to Ru's breast, his tongue laving her nipple.

She bucked against him, desperate, but he held her wrists firmly in his hands.

"Impatient," he chuckled, nipping at her ear. "Hold still."

Ru was about to protest, to make some pithy comeback, but then he pressed his hard length between her legs, teasing her.

"Taryel—" she pleaded, needing him, desperate for him.

"What did I *say*," he murmured, his grip tightening on her wrists. "Don't move."

She nodded once, breathing hard, her wide gaze fixed on his. Finally, with agonizing slowness, he entered her. She lay perfectly still, overwhelmed by the sensation of him, how perfectly he filled her.

At last, after an infinite haze of slowly burning plea-sure, he was buried to the hilt inside her.

"Taryel," she gasped.

He kissed her, and as his lips took hers, he began to move his hips, slow and rhythmic, grinding low over her sensitive part. And because she couldn't touch him but to kiss him back, she was overwhelmed by the feel of him inside her, hot and firm and so, so perfect. She rocked her hips in tandem with his, her back arching.

The pleasure of it, the scalding gold of desire began to build again in her, a coiled-up ribbon that was ready to unspool.

"You are perfect." Taryel's words were hoarse, cut through by his own desire, his loss of control.

She saw that he was losing himself in her, his eyes closed, utterly vulnerable, and focused on what they shared in that moment. That alone made her fall over the edge again, her sweat-soaked thighs tightening around his hips as she came, a tide of pleasure overwhelming her until there was nothing and no one but Taryel.

And when he finally shuddered against her, thrusting hard again and again, he spoke her name softly, once, a benediction.

They lay together in a tangle of sweat and legs and nightgown, breathing hard, coming down from that celestial height. Taryel rolled onto his back and pulled Ru with him so her head was nestled on his chest. He wrapped his arms around her. Kissed her forehead. Stroked her hair.

"Ru," he said, almost awed, as if he would never tire of saying her name.

She only laughed gently, her cheek stuck to his chest with sweat, still breathless, still soaking wet between her legs.

She had not, she realized, felt so content in a very long time.

CHAPTER 27

F rost clung to the palace facade like a thin layer of crystal shining in the pale sunlight. Ru stifled a yawn as she walked with Lord D'Luc in a courtyard that seemed to be made of glass.

She and Taryel had finally slept an hour or so before dawn, her head nestled in the divot of his shoulder. But not until after hours of research, case studies, and experiments. Ru had needed to know every inch of Taryel, what made his heart beat faster, what made him groan with unselfconscious pleasure, what made him gather her in his arms and throw her down to the mattress, devouring her with kisses.

She had to know *everything*.

And he had conducted his own experiments as well, tasting her, driving her near out of her mind with lust, using his fingers and his mouth in ways she had never experienced, with that heavy warmth in her heart. With such tenderness in her partner's eyes.

She had only just returned to her rooms when Hugon was due to arrive, and she knew her appearance wasn't up to his usual standards. But it didn't matter — she clung to the memory of last night, a bright star in her chest, the first true happiness she had felt in this place.

"Aren't we going to the cavern today?" Ru asked after they'd been walking through the courtyard in silence for a time. The lord's silence unnerved her, made her worry that he had something worse in store.

"Hmm?" he said, glancing sidelong. "Did you say something?"

Ru stopped and turned to face him. "You haven't commented once on the state of my hair. Which is awful, by the way. Or my gown, the same one I wore yesterday. What's wrong with you?"

"Ah," said Hugon, giving her a distracted once-over. "I hadn't noticed."

Strangely, the lord's lack of interest in Ru agitated her. "Aren't you going to berate me? Remind me of my fate as the Destroyer? Push me further into despair with every word?"

He sighed, running a hand through his hair. It was such a human gesture, so unaffected that it seemed wrong on him. "Delara," he said, "would you *like* to go to the cavern?" He had yet to meet her gaze, as if his thoughts were leagues away. But she thought she caught a glimmer of that ache of fear and sadness in his eyes.

"No," she said. "I'd like to know what's bothering you."

At last, his gaze snapped to hers, and she was stung by the despair in it.

"Do you want to know?" he said, his voice low. "Do you truly? You'd like to see into the mind of your keeper? You'd like to know what dark thoughts swim beneath the surface, what ailment plagues me, who's been twisting my arm behind the curtain?"

Ru hesitated, not knowing what to say.

Hugon laughed mirthlessly, shaking his head and gazing into the distance. "I thought not. Who am I to you, to anyone? A man of science, once. The regent's advisor, an honor long since discarded. And the things I…" his words cut off suddenly as he turned his back to her, walking a few steps in silence.

"Am I supposed to pity you?" Ru asked, watching him warily in case he spun on her in some sudden rage. His movements and speech seemed erratic, strange — a Hugon D'Luc she'd never seen before.

He turned slightly to gaze at her over his shoulder. A

light snow began to fall. "I'd rather you didn't," he said. "Your pity would only drive the blade deeper, I'm afraid."

"I don't pity you."

He turned away again. "A wise choice."

But she couldn't leave it there. "You can tell me. No more lies between us, remember?"

"Don't look at me like that, Delara. Like you care." He turned to look at her again, a man in pain, armor shed. She had never seen such an empty gaze, such a wretched soul in such elegant trappings. "There is nothing to tell," he said. "We'll return to the cavern tomorrow."

~

ON THE WAY back to her rooms, her thoughts clouded by the conversation with Lord D'Luc, Ru was startled by a young pageboy dashing toward her. He skidded to a halt before her, bowed, and held out a folded slip of parchment.

"Miss Delara," he gasped out, "Regent Sigrun wishes to see you urgently."

Turning to share a slightly bewildered glance with Lyr, Ru unfolded the paper and read it. It was as brief as summons came, and exactly as the footman had said — Regent Sigrun requested Ru's presence immediately.

"Follow me," said the pageboy, color high in his cheeks from the exertion, "if you'd be so kind."

And so it was that Ru found herself in the regent's office for the second time. A clock ticked solemnly in the corner. The regent sat at her desk just as she had before. And, just like before, Inda perched on a nearby chair, scratching notes with a quill.

"Thank you for joining me on such short notice," said the regent, waving a hand at the tea things that were laid out on a rolling cart. "Sit."

Regent Sigrun's face remained impassive, her eyes glazed as if from sleep.

As it always did, the sight of Sigrun made Ru feel sick. She reminded Ru of the helplessness of her situation, an ache of dread in her gut that would not relent.

But there was nothing she could do; not yet. So Ru sat and poured herself a cup of tea. Her fingers shook slightly.

"Your control of the artifact," said the regent, not wasting time with niceties. "How is it progressing?"

Ru wanted to remind the regent that Lord D'Luc wrote up daily reports, and why didn't she simply read those, but it would achieve nothing. Ru understood the real reason for these meetings with the regent — it was a chance for Lady Bellenet to assert her control over Ru.

"Slowly," Ru answered. "I'm sure you've seen the reports. I have not yet succeeded in obtaining a reaction from the stone."

"None whatsoever?" asked the regent blandly.

Ru thought of the night before, the way the artifact had not coerced her to be with Taryel — almost as if her acceptance of him, at long last giving up her resistance, had been what the artifact had wanted all along. But it was impossible to know if her theory was sound, not without tests and experiments.

"No reaction," Ru replied.

Inda scratched away with her quill as if Ru had uttered an entire essay rather than three words aloud.

Meanwhile, the regent rested her face on one curled fist, like a stiff simulacrum of a person. "Your brother Simon," she said.

Ru's mouth went dry. "What about him?"

"He has befriended Taryel Aharis. We have seen them together in shadowed corners. What is the nature of this alliance?"

"I'm not sure what you mean," Ru said, forcing herself to pause and sip her tea. To ignore the unsteadiness in her fingers, the thrum of her heart. "They met last time I was at the palace. As you've said, they're friends."

"I see," said the regent. "What is the nature of said friendship?"

Inda glanced at Ru with an unsettlingly hollow expression, then went back to her note-taking.

It was like sitting in a room of puppets and knowing exactly how their strings were pulled. Ru tried not to shiver with dread. "As far as I know, they discuss... philosophy. Music. Art. Whatever it is minstrels and gods have in common."

"I see," said the regent.

Inda wrote furiously, dipping her quill into the inkwell with sharp little thrusts of her fingers.

There was a long moment in which no one spoke. Ru twisted her fingers in her lap. If Lady Bellenet's gaze had fallen on Taryel and Simon, did she suspect them of working against her? Did she suspect Ru? Her gut was in knots, her palms sweating.

"What was I going to say next?" said the regent suddenly, tilting her head.

"Hill and Tenoria," prompted Inda, not bothering to look up.

Ru's stomach gave a horrible lurch.

"Yes," said the regent. "Hill and Tenoria. They were caught wandering the halls last night. Why?"

Ru froze. Wandering the halls? Why on earth would her friends take such a risk, and how? They were supposed to be guarded at all times. Maybe they had managed to use the servants' corridors, like Ru. Or maybe this was all a lie, a game, a way to put Ru on the defensive, to unsettle her.

"We're academics," Ru said at last, forcing a smile. "We're used to the Cornelian Tower, where we're free to roam the halls at all hours of the night or day. It's not in my friends' nature to be constricted. I'm sure they were only looking at the architecture, or… something."

"I see," said the regent.

Ru gripped the arms of her chair as if to rise. "If that's all, I have to—"

"That is not all," said Inda, cutting her off. "Remind Miss Delara of the new regulations."

"Yes," said Sigrun. "Ruellian Delara, henceforth, you shall be accompanied at all times by a contingent of three King's Guards, in addition to Lyrren Briar. This is for your own safety. And that of the artifact."

"And the kingdom," added Inda, watching Ru with an empty gaze.

"In addition," said the regent, ignoring Inda's remark, "you will no longer be allowed to visit your friends in private. You may see them at public events only. They are a distraction."

Ru opened her mouth to protest but bit her tongue at the last second. She needed to play along. There was nothing else she could do. She tamped down on a rising fear, tinged with scalding rage. The walls were closing in with the passing of every day.

"Thank you," Ru said, her voice unsteady. She knew that if she said anything more, she would give herself away.

"You may go," said Regent Sigrun.

Lyr stood waiting for Ru in the corridor, looking more perturbed than she'd seen him before. Three King's Guards waited with him. He opened his mouth as if to speak, but upon seeing Ru's face, decided not to.

There was nothing to say. But Ru knew what she had to do now. There was no time to delay in attending Prayer. It was her only lead, the only chance to learn how Lady Bellenet's full power worked. The only way to try to stop it.

Flanked by four guards, Ru returned to her rooms. She had no intention of speaking to anyone for the rest of the evening and only summoned Pearl to bring her dinner and a tray of tiny cakes, and to send a note to Simon. The note, written in Ru's best attempt at a coded message, reminded her brother of her need for white robes and impressed on him the importance of speed and discretion.

Ru felt untethered as she often did, helpless and alone, afraid to summon Taryel for comfort. Her meeting with the regent hung heavy and cold on her shoulders, a reminder of her place in the world now and the speed at which her fate was rushing toward her. And most heavy of all, the reminder that Lady Bellenet was always watching.

~

IN THE SMALL hours of the morning, long after she had crawled into bed with a heavy heart, Ru was awakened by the prickling sense of someone in her room. But even in that hazy doze between wakefulness and dreaming, she knew instinctively that it was Taryel. In the darkness, she heard the soft rustle of boots being unlaced, of clothes falling to the floor.

Then her blankets were lifted gently, and he joined her in that sleepy cocoon. He wrapped his arm around her, pulling her against him, her back to his warm chest. His breath on her neck and shoulder, the sudden surety of his affection for her, flowed through Ru like a strong salve.

"I'm here," he murmured in her ear, a reassurance.

She made a small sound, still half clinging to slumber.

He moved her hair out of her face, pulled the blankets close around them, and settled his head next to hers on the pillow.

Ru was floating toward sleep when Taryel spoke again. His voice was so quiet, so low and gentle that she wondered if he had meant for her to hear him at all. But the words, how easily he spoke them, cradled her heart. They held her. The yawning distance between Ru and the world, the emptiness around her, faded away. And in its place was Taryel.

"You're not alone."

CHAPTER 28

Ru woke with the sun on her face. It fell through the window in a pale cascade, doing little to warm her nose and fingers in the chill of the morning. She sat up, peering out at the light. It was late, later than she had risen in ages. Hugon had not come for breakfast despite his promise to subject her to the cavern today. And Taryel was gone.

An uneasiness flickered in her, a sense that something wasn't right. But she shoved it aside — why should she be concerned about Hugon? His unexpected absence was a blessing.

Disoriented by the late hour, Ru struggled into a simple woolen dress and the most functional shoes she could locate in her wardrobe. She found that Pearl had brought in coffee at some earlier hour, but it had long since gone cold. Braiding her dark hair into one long plait, Ru went to the sitting room to warm herself by the fire.

Then, she supposed, she would seek out breakfast… but the concept gave her pause. Her breakfasts with Lord D'Luc were consistent and unending, and until now she had considered them a curse. But at the memory of Hugon's broken gaze yesterday in the courtyard, a strange feeling seeped into Ru's heart — concern.

She was so caught up in her thoughts, wondering if Lord D'Luc had come to some harm, that Ru didn't see the note at first. It lay on a side table near the fire, a neatly folded piece of parchment.

> *Ru,*
>
> *I've gone to attend an early-morning godly duty, a breakfast for some Duke or another. I simply couldn't bring myself to wake you. Did you know that you snore? It's incredibly endearing.*
> *Yours,*
> *T—*

Ru couldn't help the smile that crept across her face, the warm ache in her chest. She wished he had woken her; she wanted more time with him, away from the rest of the world, alone and in bed.

Someone knocked on the servants' door, putting an end to this fantasy. Ru frowned; Pearl had never once knocked before entering. Sliding the note into her bodice, Ru went to answer. She pressed the door gently, and it swung inward to reveal a coppery-haired fop carrying a large wooden case.

"Ah lovely, you're here," said Simon. He pushed past her, all bright eyes and sky-high hair and colorful silks. Then he paused, giving her a searingly judgmental once-over. "Well… it's not perfect, but as my sister and a denizen of the Cornelian Tower, I'm certain your sartorial state will be overlooked." He grimaced slightly. "Though… really, Ru? Wool?"

She closed the door behind him, spinning on her brother with crossed arms. "How else am I supposed to stay warm?"

He sighed dramatically, waving a dismissive hand. "Fine, fine. I suppose there's no accounting for taste, and we haven't much time. Are you coming or not?"

"To what?"

"Your *party*, naturally. The one I sensed you might need right about now, considering you and your friends are being guarded by a veritable regiment of soldiers between you. Oh, and don't tell anyone, but I heard Hugon D'Luc is *under the weather*." He smiled conspiratorially. "Think that means he's dead? I'm taking bets at the party."

Ru blinked, trying to catch up. "Where are my robes, by the way?"

Simon's response was withering. "I'll get you your robes, ungrateful sister. Patience. I'm a minstrel, not a sorcerer." He paused then, giving her another once-over, his expression pained. "I beg of you, before we go, at least don a hat of some sort. I happen to know there's a tricorne in your wardrobe that will match this drab woolen thing perfectly."

Knowing there was no escape from her brother now, and honestly relieved for the distraction, Ru went to her wardrobe. After a moment, she uncovered a black velvet hat with an upturned brim and a dark purple plume.

"The one with the *buttons*," Simon protested.

Ru sighed, opened a series of drawers, and at last found a grey tricorne with gold button fastenings. She held it out for Simon to see.

"That's the one," he replied.

When the hat was pinned in place, Ru's appearance was finally deemed appropriate.

"I'm fine, by the way," she grumbled. "You don't need to throw me a party."

Simon sniffed. "Of course I do. You're my sister. And we might all be dead in a matter of weeks, so why not enjoy our last days while we can?"

"How uplifting," said Ru.

Winking in response, Simon opened the servant's door and gestured for Ru to go first. In the distance, she could hear the clatter of what sounded like a tea tray being wheeled along.

"Isn't it lovely?" Simon gushed, moving to walk alongside her. "One of Lady Bellenet's many weaknesses is her upbringing. She hasn't spared a single thought for the servants who inhabit these halls, and thus, not one of them has fallen under her control. They are loyal to the regent, and, by extension..." he waved a hand to indicate himself and Ru.

They continued, taking sudden turns and going up narrow stairs at odd intervals. Simon greeted every servant they passed with joviality. All of them smiled in return or shared a few words of greeting. Ru found herself in a small kind of awe of her brother. He cultivated allies with those others might overlook.

Then again, she supposed, that was his job. She and her brother tended to underestimate one another, to their detriment.

Ru remained silent for the rest of their walk, her steps keeping time with the lute case softly bouncing against Simon's thighs. When at last they emerged into one of the palace's main corridors, albeit a rather remote and disused one, Ru was winded from the speed of their walk.

"Just across the hall," Simon said. "If anyone sees us, well… be quick."

They darted across the hall and through an unassuming door on the other side without incident. Even so, Ru's heart was hammering and sweat beaded her forehead.

"How do you live like this?" she hissed.

"With far more aplomb than you, that much is clear." Simon grinned, holding out an arm. "Welcome to your party."

The room they had just entered was high-ceilinged with white walls and golden trim, shining in the lamplight. The velvet rose-colored curtains were drawn. Without any natural light, the room had a cozy, cave-like quality even with its opalescent pillars and opulent trimming.

Luxurious furniture took up most of the space, though it appeared to be slightly threadbare and covered in a thick layer of dust. At one end of the room was a small stage, upon which sat a stool and a few empty chairs, also dusty. This must be some disused room, Ru thought, glancing around. Perhaps it belonged to a courtier who had stopped visiting the palace. There were roughly a dozen people in attendance, many of whom were familiar faces. The rest appeared to be courtiers, who Ru could only guess were Simon's friends and allies.

Before Ru had a chance to take it in, Rosylla appeared at Ru's side, crying, "She's here!" Not waiting for a response, she threw her arms around Ru and squeezed. "Happy birthday, Ru."

"It's not…" said Ru, glancing at Simon. He shook his

head almost imperceptibly. "I mean, thanks," Ru amended, trying not to laugh.

Simon leaned in and hissed, "I had to use *some* sort of leverage to convince everyone to come at horribly short notice."

"Happy birthday!" came a chorus of greetings from the party attendees. Gwyneth and Archie were there, and Sybeth was lurking near a table of food with Lyr. Even Pearl was in attendance, holding a glass of wine and looking as if she were about to receive a reprimand.

"How did you…" Ru said, lost for words.

Simon shrugged. "It's shocking what one can accomplish when morale is in dire need of boosting. But look," he said, flitting through the room like a butterfly. He led Ru to a table laid with tiny cakes, cinnamon rolls, sugared berries, and wine. Bowing slightly, he gestured elegantly to the decadent spread. "Enjoy, dearest sister, the fruits of your own brother's thieving prowess."

Pearl, who stood nearby, coughed pointedly.

Simon pursed his lips. "Pearl helped a bit. And now, I must serenade you all with my talent and originality, though there's hardly enough of you to make it worth the effort."

Grinning, Simon set off to the other side of the room, his hair bouncing as he went. Feeling strangely self-conscious, Ru plucked a tiny cake from the table with two fingers and popped it into her mouth. This party was ridiculous and far too risky — Simon shouldn't have done it — but she couldn't help feeling bolstered by the support. Maybe she *had* needed this.

"Happy birthday," said a laughing voice from behind Ru. She turned to see Archie and Gwyneth, both beaming.

"Didn't realize we were celebrating birthdays on any old day," Archie said, swirling his wine. "Can it be mine tomorrow? These secret get-togethers are rather exciting. Didn't think I'd take so readily to espionage."

"I'd hardly call it espionage," Gwyneth said. "But, Ru, are you all right? We hadn't seen you since the garden party, and then we woke up yesterday to an army of guards outside our rooms."

"We're running out of time," Ru said. "There are more eyes on us than ever. As soon as Simon comes through with disguises, we need to find out what's going on at Lady Bellenet's Prayer."

Archie crossed his arms, still managing to balance his wine glass expertly. "Does this mean you've changed your mind? You'll let us come with you?"

Ru's mouth twisted. "Only because I need your scientific minds, not because I think it's a good idea to drag you both into danger."

"We're already in it, if you hadn't noticed," Gwyneth said, primly sipping her wine.

"So what's the plan then?" Archie asked eagerly. "Disguises, you say? I love a disguise. Does mine involve a mustache?"

Ru snorted. "No, it does not involve a mustache. We're dressing up as Children, obviously. The only thing is, I strongly suspect that Lady Bellenet's power will be most potent at Prayer. We have to be ready to slip out of there at any moment—"

"Lest we get turned into empty husks ourselves," mused Archie, gazing into the distance. "Yes, yes... could be tricky."

"Tricky, or suicide?" Gwyneth said, looking wan. "I'm with you, Ru, but remember what Lord D'Luc said. Once the change is made, once someone *becomes* one of the Children... it's forever."

"I know," said Ru, putting on a brave face despite the ripple of dread in her stomach. "But—"

At that moment, a chord was struck from the stage, and everyone turned to see, conversations fading. Simon perched on a stool with his lute propped on one knee, the fingers of his left hand curled against its neck.

"Good evening, all," he said, his voice ringing pleasingly through the now-silent room. "Thank you for attending the rushed and secretive birthday party of my dear sister Ru, an insufferable pedant, yet beloved all the same. If you do not spend the remainder of your evening making every attempt to make her smile, you will be punished."

"How?" asked Lyr.

Simon beamed. "In whatever way I deem fit, handsome guard." Lyr's face turned a deep shade of red. Laughing, Simon began to play.

There were few things in the world that filled Ru with such a longing ache as music. And Simon's music touched her most poignantly. It was the reason she had come to believe in magic.

She believed in the magic of the soul, the incredible way that a song could unravel her and restring her like a violin, play her in a major key. As she listened, her friends all around her, she was surprised to find she couldn't stop smiling.

But where was Taryel? Had he really been summoned to some other duty?

As soon as the thought crossed her mind, as if by thinking of Taryel she had cursed them, the doors to the room swung open. There was no sudden crash, no sound to announce their presence. But Ru felt them immediately — a cold drag of unease across the back of her neck.

And as Simon's fingers stuttered on the strings, as the melody broke, Ru turned to see. There in the doorway stood Hugon D'Luc, and flanking him were his three Children.

Ru reached for Gwyneth's hand and found it was warm against Ru's, whose fingers had gone ice cold. They gripped each other as if they feared being torn apart forever.

Lord D'Luc surveyed the room with haughty authority. "Don't stop the party on my account."

CHAPTER 29

Simon stood slowly, smiling at Lord D'Luc. To an unpracticed eye, he would have appeared entirely at his ease, relieved, even, at the lord's arrival.

"On the contrary," said Simon, holding out a hand in welcome. "We have only just begun. Won't you join us, Your Grace?"

The lazy smile that crossed Hugon's mouth was a thinly masked threat. Ru knew that expression all too well and had been on the receiving end of its cruelty. Hugon snapped his fingers, and the Children moved like specters, taking up residence at either side of the door.

"And what sort of party," Hugon said, moving into the room with the grace of a predator, "would I be joining, exactly?"

"Ru's birthday, of course," said Simon. Ru saw in the tense set of his shoulders, in the strain around his mouth, that he was ready to spring into action. What that action might be, she couldn't guess.

"How strange," said the lord, drifting past the refreshments and selecting a glass of wine for himself. "I never received my invitation."

Everyone in the room remained frozen. The only evidence of unease was a hurried shared glance, the odd clearing of a throat. Hugon moved through the small gathering undeterred until he came to an empty chair. He sat, leaned back, and crossed one foot over his knee.

Ru could not take her eyes off him. He, like Simon, vibrated with anticipation as if ready to strike. His eyes glittered darkly, and his mouth hinted at a sneer. She had rarely seen him more arresting or more terrifying.

"My apologies," said Simon, once again taking a seat on his stool. "I was certain I had sent it. Only the most intelligent and thoughtful members of court are invited. Perhaps it was a mistake."

The insult was clear. A few intakes of breath mottled the silence, but Hugon and Simon were utterly focused on one another. The minstrel strummed a cord, never once removing his gaze from the golden-haired lord. Lord D'Luc sipped his wine and smiled, catlike.

"Hmm," Simon said, "Perhaps we ought to start with something everyone knows. Why not a folk song?"

Ru's fingers tightened against Gwyneth's. How could Simon be so reckless? For a moment, a strange sensation filled her, as if she were a vessel overflowing, suddenly too full with no way to empty herself. She glanced down, almost expecting to see blackness seeping out of her body, as if she were the artifact herself, overcome with rage and helplessness, erupting outward.

But she saw only her drab woolen gown and her hand clasped tightly with Gwyneth's.

"A folk song," Lord D'Luc said, sipping his wine thoughtfully. "And what song would suit me best, do you think?"

Don't, thought Ru, seeing Simon step willingly into the trap as he lifted his lute, knowing there was nothing she could do to stop him. He couldn't help himself, couldn't pass up a chance to be insolent. She wished she could jump on stage and strangle her brother, but there was nothing she could do.

"I know just the one," said Simon, smiling serenely. He began to play.

It was a Navenian folk tune, one every member of court knew by heart. It was the kind of tune sung at pubs in Mirith, a rude, bawdy tale. It told of a lord, a cruel, thoughtless brute, who spent his time pawing at other mens' wives and ignoring his own.

Usually, when this particular song was played, everyone sang along. There would be hearty knee-slapping, and beer-swilling, and plenty of jokes and drunken laughter. But this time, the room was silent as a grave. Not a soul dared move as the last chords faded.

Still seated, Lord D'Luc downed the last of his wine and set it aside. "You have my thanks," he said. "I was in need of some amusement."

Ru and Gwyneth shared a tense, fleeting glance.

"But I'm afraid," the lord said, rising to his feet, "that the time for amusement is over." He snapped his fingers again, and the Children moved as one toward the front of the room. Toward Simon.

Ru knew what would happen next. The Children would take Simon. They would bring him to Lady Bellenet, accused of some unimportant crime, and she would change him. Ru was more certain of it than she was certain of anything else in that moment.

"Amusement," Simon was saying, making a show of how carefree he was, despite the lines at the corners of his mouth, despite the restless tap of one finger against his lute. "Over? Whatever can you mean? Surely the amusement ought to continue."

The Children had reached the stage, and one by one, they moved to surround Simon.

"These three, I daresay, desperately need a laugh." Simon's grin was as strained as Ru's silence. She bit her lip until she tasted blood.

Lord D'Luc was no longer playacting. He waved a hand almost dismissively, rings flashing in the lamplight. "Take the minstrel," he said, his voice ringing through that horrified silence. "Leave the rest for now."

Ru's mouth was dry, her palms sweating. She could hardly maintain her grip on Gwyneth's hand.

Ru realized with a sudden swoop in her gut that she was the only person who could stop this. She was the only one with leverage.

Inda and Ranto took Simon's arms, and she saw from her brother's grimace that they were not holding back. She remembered those viselike fingers on her own arms, marble statues squeezing her flesh.

"My *lute*," Simon protested, "for god's sake."

But it was too late. The Children were pulling his arms back behind him, wrenching his body to obey their commands. And as they did, he dropped the lute. It fell in one shuddering, twanging crash, bouncing from the stage and onto the floor.

Ru couldn't have cared less about Simon's lute. She just needed her brother safe. But his face crumpled with devastation, and she bit back a cry of protest.

"Do you know how much that will cost to repair?" Simon demanded.

"Wait."

Ru hadn't meant to speak. She knew her brother would be silently cursing her for it, but she couldn't watch this happen. Not if there was some way to stop it.

Every eye in the room turned to Ru. Hugon D'Luc's was the only face that showed an expression other than mute horror. Instead, he gave her a lopsided smile, his cheek dimpling. "Delara. How charming. I suppose you have something useful to say?"

Ru dropped Gwyneth's hand. She did this alone. Her chest was tight, her throat twisted up with dread.

She said, "Let Simon go."

Lord D'Luc blinked. "I beg your pardon?"

Simon's gaze was boring into Ru, but she ignored it. She saw only Lord D'Luc, clearly already calculating, guessing what she might be doing, putting himself one step ahead.

"Let Simon go," she said. "Keep your white-robed lackeys, your threats, *and* Lady Bellenet away from him. She doesn't touch him, doesn't harm him. *Promise* me."

Simon shot her a sharp, horrified look.

Ru ignored it.

Hugon crossed one arm over his chest, the other propped by the elbow so one hand rested delicately under his chin. "And why," he said, danger in his cool voice, "would I agree to that?"

Ru turned so that she couldn't see Simon at all, even at

the edge of her periphery. She couldn't bear to see his disappointment, the betrayal, or — worst of all — the worry. She didn't need it. She could handle herself with Hugon.

"Because if you keep this promise," Ru went on, "I'll stop holding back. I'll do whatever you ask of me in our demonstrations. Anything."

An understanding passed between Ru and Lord D'Luc then, an unspoken exchange. For all intents and purposes, Ru already belonged to Lady Bellenet. But Ru saw Hugon as few others did. And she saw him now, the conflict raging in his eyes, the frustration clawing behind his expression of calm.

Please, Ru thought, desperate for Hugon to spare her, to take her deal.

After a moment, the lord shrugged, looking away. "Very well," he said, as if this were all suddenly boring him. He snapped his fingers once more, jerking his head. "Let the minstrel go," he barked.

Simon collapsed to his knees on the stage, the Children's grip on his arms suddenly slackened. He reached down for his lute as if by instinct, pulling it into his arms.

Hugon caught Ru's gaze again, and for a moment, she tried to understand. As if to ask him, through force of will, *Why?* She knew he could have refused, and pushed her harder anyway. She had no leverage. He gained nothing from this agreement.

With a gesture so small she could have written it off as a trick of the light, or a shadow, Hugon lifted one corner of his mouth in a rueful smile. He and the Children made their exit, a flurry of white robes and golden hair. Ru wondered if this had been his plan along, if he had manipulated events for some unknown purpose, just to see what she would do.

Otherwise, she might have to accept that Hugon D'Luc was capable of mercy.

CHAPTER 30

Subterranean water dripped incessantly in that horrible cavern, which was somehow smaller than Ru remembered since the last demonstration. Or maybe the earth was closing in on her, slowly, an inevitable burial, and there was nothing she could do to stop it.

"I know what you're capable of, Delara." Hugon's voice was hardened by the storm of emotion that raged behind his eyes. He seemed miles away, as if living his own torturous demonstration somewhere else entirely. "I've seen you do it. Did your promise mean nothing? I can still fetch your brother…"

"I can't," Ru said, her voice cracking. They had been in that wet cavern for what felt like a lifetime, though it couldn't have been more than two hours since Simon's party. There were no Children with them, no blank stares to seep into Ru's psyche like the festering of a wound, but Hugon himself proved to be monstrous enough.

"You're holding back," Hugon said.

"I'm not," she lied.

Blood crusted her nose and upper lip, evidence enough of Ru's internal struggle. But not for Hugon D'Luc. Her skull was on fire, and her body wouldn't stop shaking. She *had* tried, delicately, gently.

But her fear had awoken the artifact, and its sudden presence, loud at the corners of her thoughts, threatened to overwhelm her.

Unlike her demonstrations at the Tower, now the artifact was eager, aggressive in its assault against the walls of her mind. The more she held back, resisting the artifact's mental and emotional overwhelm, the more of a toll it took on her body. And all the while, she was trying to suppress her fear, her pain, her rage. She was afraid to lose control.

In the depth of her pain, as a rebellious rage crackled to a steady roar in her chest, part of Ru almost *wanted* to let go and coax the heart to life. To destroy Hugon and the kingdom out of spite.

"*Try,*" Hugon spat. "I have seen you draw power from the artifact. I've seen the stone in your hands, wreathed in darkness. There is nothing left of the Shattered City dig site. That was your doing."

"Well, it isn't working now," Ru croaked. "If you keep pushing me, I'll destroy us all by accident."

She caught his eye then and was shocked to see a strange eagerness in his gaze. *No,* she thought. *I'm not putting you out of your misery yet. Push me to breaking, and I'll make sure we break together.*

Ru clenched her fingers where they were braced on the simple wooden table, bowing her head. Loose tendrils of hair hung raggedly over her shoulders. In this position, she couldn't see Lord D'Luc where he stood across from her. She could see only the artifact, black as night, once a cherished object and now an inevitability, as precious as a soul but just as easily turned to darkness.

So when she spoke a thought to it, a simple word — *please* — she felt the presence in her grow searingly taut, as if the artifact were saying *Yes, I'm here.* And the force of that connection, the artifact responding to her so vividly and with such clear intent, nearly made Ru pass out.

Listen to me, she thought, gritting her teeth as she swayed. *Do what I say. I'll let you out if you just control yourself,* she begged then, pushing harder, even as her vision began to blur, and her skull screamed in agony as she resisted the crushing darkness she knew was there, waiting for her to let it out. *Just a little,* she thought. *Just a little tendril of darkness is all I need. Let me control you.*

The artifact showed no sign of listening, of allowing Ru's thoughts to curb its wildness, its vast, consuming dark. Instead, it pushed, prodded, looked for cracks in her psyche.

A thick droplet of red dappled the wood table. Ru rubbed her nose, smearing blood across the back of her hand. Hugon watched her without expression.

"I'm running myself against a stone wall," she said shakily. "I don't know how to control it. The artifact is all or nothing — either we all die now, or there's no darkness. That's it."

"Think back to the Shattered City," he prompted, eyes narrowed. "How were you feeling? What did you do?"

"I touched it," Ru said. "You know that."

"So touch it again, for the love of god." Hugon's lips curled in a patronizing sneer. "Don't play stupid with me. Maybe I *will* call for Simon after all. Your brother might enjoy watching, might prompt a stronger reaction…"

Ru caught and held the lord's gaze. He was clearly desperate, frightened. What would he do if cornered here? What if she presented him with no choice but to hurt her in the worst possible way?

"Fine," she said. "Bring Simon. Do whatever you need to do to push me to the breaking point. But I'm done for the day."

Hugon's eyes narrowed for a breath, and he seemed momentarily lost for words. Then he said, "You don't know what I'm capable of, Delara."

She raised her chin. "I think I do, Hugon. Why did you take my deal at the party? I could have been lying. And you could have taken Simon, done whatever you liked with him, and *still*, I'd be in this cavern with you, nose bleeding. I have no leverage. So why?"

Though he stood stock still, Ru could see a slight tremble in the lord's jaw; he was clenching his teeth, hard. "The minstrel would be more trouble than he's worth," the lord said at last, each word bit out as if through pain.

"Interesting," Ru said, spitting red onto the floor. Her head was screaming in pain, but she had to get through to him. She *knew* she was widening the cracks, about to shatter his mask once and for all. "Tell me, why did you stop the demonstrations back at the Tower?"

Lord D'Luc bared his teeth. "The danger was too great. You would have lost control—"

"Then why," she interrupted, "would Lady Bellenet resume them? Surely, she knows something I don't. Is it safer here, in the palace?"

He jerked his chin, staring down at the floor where tiny pools of water collected near his feet. "I did not cease demonstrations by her orders."

A distant flare of hope rose in Ru. "Then why?" She wanted to add. *Because you didn't want to hurt me? Because you're merciful, and there's a remnant of humanity still left in you?* But she couldn't push him too hard or he'd shut down.

Hugon sighed impatiently, and Ru saw his facade hardening again, the curtain beginning to fall. "You may ask as many questions as you like," he said, "but you'll never get the answer you're looking for."

A horrible lump rose in Ru's throat. She'd been so close. She *knew* there was more to him, things he wasn't telling her. Pain he was suffering on his own. "Hugon," she said, growing almost desperate, "isn't there anything… *anything* you want to tell me?"

He met her gaze, and as they studied one another, Ru watched the mask slide fully into place, his expression utterly closed off to her. "You are useless," he said.

She froze, and a tickle of rage threatened to spark into a flame. "Excuse me?"

"I said, you're useless. A fool. If it weren't for me, lifting you up from the dregs of academia, you'd still be a laughingstock in the scientific community. Or perhaps even worse than that — a nobody. Utterly irrelevant. The only thing that sets you apart, the *only* reason anyone gives one whit about you, is the artifact. Is Taryel, and Festra's name."

Ru opened her mouth to retort, but Hugon wasn't finished.

"What are you, Delara?" he said, taking a step toward her. "If you can't even wield Taryel's heart, after it was handed to you on what amounts to a silver platter, what are you? A merchant's daughter. An unaccomplished, inconsequential, homely, bad-mannered girl."

He was wrong. Ru *knew* he was wrong. But the barbed arrow of his words had struck true. Who *was* she without the artifact? A failure. An archaeologist who studied pottery, and those were a dime a dozen at the Tower.

"What," said Hugon, stepping toward her again, "struck dumb by the truth?"

She backed away instinctively. "No, I—"

"Do you really think that your life matters beyond these walls, Delara?" he went on, still advancing. "All these fawning courtiers… they believe it's a game. You are but a trifling entertainment to them. The only reason you matter is because I give you purpose. The artifact gives you purpose. Festra gives you purpose."

Ru continued to back away, stumbling, all of her bluster and all of her rage replaced by a sudden despair, seemingly amplified by the low ceiling, the small cavern, the *drip, drip* of water on stone.

"Well?" Hugon demanded, looming over her, crowding her until her back was pressed to the wet wall. "What are you without me, Delara?"

She swallowed hard. *I'm me*, she thought. *I don't need you*. But after all her work with the artifact, her nerves were frayed to the limit. Her head was pounding in agony. She could hardly breathe through the caked-up blood in her nose. And Hugon had resisted her attempts to see past his walls, had pushed back, and now had her fully in his grasp. All she wanted was to get out, to go back to her rooms, to sleep, and never wake.

"I'm nothing," she breathed, her voice small.

"That's right," Lord D'Luc said, smiling. "You are nothing and no one. Now get out of my sight."

~

RU WAS CURLED on the sofa by the fire, staring out at nothing, when Taryel knocked. She knew it was him by the flutter in her chest, the artifact's now delicate touch. It took her a moment to gather herself, to pull her thoughts away from the dreary forests they'd been wandering in. It took her so long that when she finally opened the door, Taryel's expression was all concern.

"Good lord," he said, touching her face gingerly. "What happened? Are you hurt?"

Ru started, remembering. "Oh," she said. "My… sorry, I forgot to wash. Just a bloody nose."

Taryel took her chin in a gentle hand, tilting her face up to meet his gaze. His eyes were glittering dark. "What did he do to you?"

She swallowed. "A demonstration. It's fine. I mean, it's not fine. But I'm fine. It was just… worse than usual."

Without another word, Taryel went into the other room. When he returned, he guided Ru back to the sofa and held a warm, wet cloth to her face, cleaning up the dried blood. When he was finished, he pulled her into his arms, cradling her as she buried her face in the soft part of his chest, just below the shoulder.

At last, she let herself cry. She let out wet, wracking sobs, clutching Taryel like a lifeboat in a storm. He kissed her head, murmuring sweet words and stroking her hair. And when she was finished, dried her eyes, and sat up again, blinking and sniffling, he didn't push her. Didn't ask what had happened, didn't demand explanation. He only waited.

"Taryel," she said, her voice breaking on the name, as if she'd been desperate to call for him and hadn't. "You must have heard what happened. At Simon's party. And I thought… I tried to see Hugon D'Luc as a prisoner like me, hoping he might have some shred of decency left, an explanation for why he does what he does, but he…" she sniffled loudly.

"You don't have to say anything," Taryel said, pulling her close. "I know. Simon told me. He also told me about the deal you made — no, don't worry, I'm not going to scold you. You're brave, Ru. Braver than most. Not many people would tell such a bald-faced lie in front of all those people."

Ru laughed, which came out as a muffled choke. "I don't know why he agreed to it. He's frightened; I can see it in his eyes. I think he's been going easy on me. But Lady Bellenet found out, and… well, someone's been hurting him." She rubbed her own wrist where she'd seen Hugon's bruise. "He's terrified. All the time."

"I'm sure there is some shred of mercy left in him," Taryel said, "buried deep. Unsalvageable at this point. It's not worth trying to get him to turn on Lady Bellenet if that's what you want. He'll never budge. He's obsessed with her."

Ru sighed, a long and mournful exhalation. Then a thought came to her, as obvious as a sunrise, and yet somehow, it had never occurred to her before. "Taryel," she said, sitting back. "How does your power work?"

He shrugged. "You're the scientist."

"You mean you don't know?"

His mouth curved in a half-smile, as if he couldn't help it. "Absolutely no idea. Why?"

Ru made a sound of frustration. "But you said it had limitations."

"Well, yes, but I don't know *why*. I've found my power to be something like a well. The more I draw from it, the faster it empties. If I use it all up too quickly, I have to wait a week or so before I'm able to travel again. But—"

"*Taryel*," Ru interrupted, sitting up straight, eyes wide. "What are Lady Bellenet's limitations?"

"Exactly the question we've been asking this whole time."

"No, I mean… not a counter-spell. Not a way to stop her altogether. Her *limitations*. Is there a way to empty her well and keep it empty? We might not save those who are already turned, but… it could slow her down."

Taryel nodded slowly. "Possibly. But if she's dropped any hints as to what her limitations might be, I haven't seen them."

"If it's a similar sort of power to yours," Ru mused, her mind working to form hypotheses even as she spoke, "I could run experiments on you. Some of the ones I ran in my paper but with an actual *magical* test subject. I wonder, could your powers be cellular, biological? She alters the brain, while you alter… the fabric of space in some way.

No, maybe not biological… but *definitely* physical. The effect of Lady Bellenet's power is emotional, but the cause must be physical. I might be off track; I'm an archaeologist, after all. But if her power is drawn from within, then…" she trailed off, recognizing Taryel's expression. He was humoring her in listening but hardly following at all. "My paper," she said. "You read it. Any ideas?"

"It's ingenious," he said. "I wasn't lying when I told you that. The theories are complex yet sound. But whatever *this* is," he gestured to himself, "and whatever Lady Bellenet's working with, I couldn't begin to explain within the context of your paper."

Ru chewed her lip, staring past Taryel, her eyes unfocused.

"Ru."

She blinked. He was watching her, one dark eyebrow raised. "Taryel?"

"You may have to accept that some things can't be explained by science."

"Then how…" she persisted, angry with herself for wanting to cry again, "how are we supposed to stop Lady Bellenet?"

"We will go to Prayer, and obtain more information, and eventually find a way to stop her," Taryel said, "I'm certain of it. If anyone can put an end to all of this, it's you. But not tonight. You're in no state to be scheming."

"I'm in a perfect state for—"

But he interrupted by pulling her to him, silencing her with a kiss. She melted readily into him. She needed this, solace in his strength and calm. When she pulled away for a moment, breathless, she saw that his eyes were dark and hungry. He kissed her again, deeper this time, his fingers making deliberate circles against her skin, his mouth unyielding. The knowledge of his desire made Ru shiver, an ache already forming between her thighs.

They spent the rest of the night in each other's arms, in various states of undress, all hands and skin and sighs. Ru didn't tell him she had tried to coax the artifact to life in the cavern, that she had spoken to it, that she was being pushed closer and closer to some unknown limit, the edge of a chasm.

But he knew. She felt it in the tenderness of his caresses, the slow warmth of his mouth on her breasts. This was how he would try to heal her.

And when Taryel had brought her to the luxurious peak of her pleasure not once but three times, her fingers laced in his hair, legs wrapped around him as she gasped his name, she found peace. A brief respite, but sorely needed.

Taryel was, in that moment, enough.

CHAPTER 31

The opportunity to attend Prayer came the next day, exactly two weeks before the winter solstice. Lord D'Luc had sent a note in the morning that he was unable to attend their demonstration, and with no other parties or dinners to attend, Ru had a whole day that was hers for the taking.

She did not tell Taryel about her plan to attend Prayer without him. He would only worry or demand to come with her, and Simon had only given her three robes. They were exactly like the ones the Children wore, including the gold sashes and white hats. He'd left them with Pearl, who had been terribly reluctant to hand the folded garments over to Ru, pleading with her to be careful.

Ru didn't need telling twice.

That afternoon, as Ru prepared to go, Pearl gave her a roughly drawn map of the relevant servants' passages with a look of disapproval. "I don't think it's a good idea," she said.

"Of course it's not," Ru said, smoothing her robes and tucking the white cap under her arm. "But it's all I've got at the moment." She smiled, hoping it would mask her anxiety. "Wish us luck."

"Good luck," the maid grumbled. "You'll need it."

The walk to Gwyneth and Archie's rooms was quick enough. Ru passed servants in those narrow hallways, but nobody stopped her or asked where she was going. Nor did any of them react as if she were one of the Children. Pearl must have warned them what she was up to. By the time she came to the door that led into Gwyneth's room, Ru found that she was shaking — with fear or eagerness, she couldn't tell.

Ru lifted a hand and knocked softly.

A moment later, the door flew open, and Gwyneth stood blinking, dumbfounded, at Ru. "Ru! We've been so worried, thank god you're—" her eyes narrowed. "What on earth are you wearing?"

"A disguise for Prayer," said Ru, holding up the remaining robes. "Come on, get dressed or we'll miss it. Is Archie here?"

"Yes, hello," Archie said from where he lounged in an armchair by the fire. He reminded Ru of a cat, suspiciously eyeing the white robes as she unfurled them, yet not moving from his warm spot by the fire.

"You want me to *wear* one of those things?" he said, watching Gwyneth as she pulled the robes over her clothes and fastened the tie belt.

Gwyneth gave him a withering look. "Oh, I'm sorry, were you expecting Prayer to be a fashion show? Put it on."

She hurled the third robe at Archie, who caught it with a grimace. "It's just that I'll feel like a prick."

"How do you think we feel?" Ru said, pulling her cap on. "Hurry, we're going to miss the procession."

In their disguises at last, the three friends bundled into the cramped servants' corridor. They made their way, breathless, toward the corridor where Ru and Lord D'Luc had seen the procession of Children on their way to Prayer.

"So what are we looking for, exactly?" Archie asked as they walked.

"Anything, really," Ru said. "Lady Bellenet will be using her magic to change people, I'm sure of it. If we can see how she does it, we can try to extrapolate how to counter her power. It's possible we might even be able to drain her of it altogether, like Taryel's. Her power *must* have limits, and I mean to find out what those are."

"Easy enough," Archie said sarcastically.

"I have a good feeling about this," said Gwyneth, and Ru was grateful for her optimism.

When they finally came to the door that was supposed to open onto the procession corridor, Ru paused, checking her hat to make sure it was securely in place. Then she opened the door a crack, peering out. There they were, the Children, walking in single file with their backs to Ru.

"Right, let's go," Ru murmured. Then she glanced back at her friends. "Don't forget to look... empty inside."

Gwyneth and Archie nodded, checking that their robes were pristine. And then, when Ru was sure no courtiers were looking, and no guards were in view, she slipped into the hallway and went to join the procession of Children. They fell in line easily. None of the Children turned to glance at them, no questioning stares were aimed their way.

It was an eerie sensation, drifting reverently through the palace with a stream of Children. It made the hairs on Ru's neck stand on end. They were hardly human anymore; they were ghosts, husks of what had once been laughing, feeling people. And now they were devoid of emotion, the vivacity of life. Forever.

Soon, the procession came to a courtyard, the Children all flowing out into the frosted grass like a ghostly river. They filed into an old chapel in the middle of the courtyard, surrounded by cold-bitten foliage and a few skeletal trees, their branches blackened with frost. Candles lined a stone pathway to the building, its facade shining angelically, all white stone and spires soaring upward. It was lit from within, and Ru could hear the strains of a lonely melody drifting outward. Ru recognized the chapel as a historical fixture, once visited by the spiritual members of court, now tainted by Lady Bellenet and her Children.

In a few breathless moments, they were inside the chapel, surrounded by Children. Ru's stomach was in knots, her heart thrumming with nerves. They stood in a small lobby, from which Children were filing into the chapel beyond. Ru caught a glimpse of myriad candles and row upon row of white robes within.

"This way," she hissed, motioning for her friends to follow. Instead of going with the rest of the Children, they turned sharply to the left, where a narrow staircase curved upward, leading to what Ru imagined must be a balcony. They traipsed up the stairs one after another, robes swishing in the dim light.

As Ru had guessed, they found themselves on a small balcony lined with pews, so dark in contrast to the lower level that nobody looking up would be able to see them in the gloom. Ru moved down toward the front of the balcony, hoping to more clearly see what was happening below. She waved a hand, beckoning Gwyneth and Archie.

The balcony was empty but for them. When they were all close enough to the edge of the balcony, Ru lowered herself into one of the pews to watch.

At first, it appeared to be nothing more than a religious service. Such gatherings had been waning in popularity for more than a century in Navenie, so Ru had never attended one. But she had read about them, had stood in the ruins of ancient temples, pressed her palms to their stones. This chapel spoke of a rich history of deity worship, its walls painted with colorful murals of angelic figures, men and women with frothing wings bursting forth from clouds, images of death and rebirth.

Ru was entranced by the colors and the light — candles were strewn on every surface, from stained glass windows to the chapel's center aisle, to the dais at the head of the room, upon which stood a glowing golden throne.

It was unlike any throne Ru had ever seen, far larger and more opulent than the regent's or even the king's, and it appeared to be entirely encrusted with gold. It was all organic curves and whorls, as if its makers had somehow frozen and gilded billowing smoke. At the throne's apex, the smoke-like whirls of gold gave way to a series of spikes, reaching up to the ceiling like rays of sunlight. Or a crown.

And seated on the throne was Lady Bellenet.

Ethereal notes from an unseen harp sang alongside a low prayer that emanated from those gathered in the pews below. Every seat was taken by a figure in white, heads bowed, each of them reciting the same chant Lady Bellenet had recited in the throne room, what felt like so long ago.

Together, we will discover the mysteries of the universe. We will journey together to paradise. You only have to choose it. You must simply give in to the will of your god.

She leaned toward Gwyneth, who had seated herself next to Ru, watching the quiet spectacle. "Who does she represent in all of this? Some kind of high priestess?"

"High rubbish, if you ask me," came Archie's hushed reply from the other side of Gwyneth.

"Quiet," Gwyneth murmured. "We can't miss anything."

Ru frowned, watching the service. She found herself unable to look away from Lady Bellenet. Seated on that throne, she appeared almost inhuman. As if, with such angelic features, she had come down from the heavens themselves. Her hair shone like dark honey in the candlelight.

The harp's music swelled, and in that moment, Lady Bellenet lifted one hand aloft. In her bare palm was the artifact.

Gwyneth gasped.

"What the devil…" Archie breathed.

Shaking, Ru looked inside herself, ran an imagined finger along the artifact's cool surface. And as she did, she realized that the stone in Lady Bellent's hand was not the artifact. It was a fake. Taryel's heart was safe somewhere else.

"It's a decoy," Ru murmured.

"How can you tell?" Gwyneth asked.

"I can feel it."

The woman then stood, descending from the dais with a stoic expression. The chanting stopped, and the room seemed to still, as if the Children all held their breath, as the music faded.

Ru watched, riveted. "Why aren't I part of this?" she wondered, feeling inexplicably like a child left out of the game she had invented. "Why isn't Taryel?"

"Probably because it's a load of drivel," Archie whispered.

Then, facing the gathered parishioners, Lady Bellenet began to speak.

"I, Lady Solia," she intoned, as if reciting by rote, "came to Festra as a maid, abandoned by the world. Now, I am a wife. Upon the wicked and the nonbelievers, I bestow my light. And thus the chosen few, Festra's Children, will journey with me to paradise in the Great Cleansing."

The was a long pause as Lady Bellenet bowed her head, still holding the artifact aloft. Ru held her breath. And then the music started again, and the congregation murmured in unison. Another chant.

"What now?" Gwyneth asked, her fingers twisting in the fabric of her robe.

Ru couldn't move, sickeningly enraptured by the sound of the Children's voices, atonal and eerie.

"Let's go down there," Archie suggested. "Nothing useful to glean from up here but ominous chanting."

"You're right," Ru said, standing. "I want to see this up close."

They hurried downstairs to the vestibule. Light spilled out from between double doors, where the Prayer was taking place. Without pausing to question, to extrapolate every outcome that might occur as a result of her decision, Ru pushed through the doors and into that candlelit sanctum.

Everything was lit up within, golden and white. Children, white-draped and docile, filled every seat in the room. There were dozens standing in the aisles, lining the walls. There were too many to fit, and it seemed strange to Ru that they would not use the balcony. But even in her confusion, she was relieved — there were so many white-robed figures there that no one seemed to notice as three more joined the crowd.

As they situated themselves at the back of the room, Gwyneth hooking one finger around Ru's in a quiet bid for comfort, Ru began to understand why the entire congregation was gathered together in one room.

A single Child was moving down the aisle toward Lady Bellenet, and by the time Ru and her friends had found a place to stand, the lone Child had lifted an earthen jug, allowing Lady Bellenet to make what Ru guessed were signs of blessing over it.

Lady Bellenet took the jug, holding it aloft. This was some kind of communion. The earthenware jug — its wide lip and the pattern of carvings at its base — Ru recognized it. She had dug up pieces just like it in ruined churches. Held those pieces in her hands and wondered what must have been poured out, what faith it must have watered.

The Children surged forward. Lady Bellenet tipped the jug against the first Child's lips, and as she did, she placed a hand on the Child's head. Then a strange thing happened — an explosion of light, blindingly white, burst outward from the Child as they drank. For a split second, it was as if every face in the chapel were lit up by the light of a star.

Ru's finger tightened around Gwyneth's. The courtier at the ball had spoken of the chapel lighting up. And as Lady Bellenet touched each of the Children reverently, with each explosion of light, the lady herself seemed to emit a dim glow.

The Children drank and drank, and each of the Children was engulfed in horrible blinding light, one after the other. Ru had to close her eyes each time, the light was so painful. It was so unlike Taryel's crackling black magic or the honey-gold coils the artifact had once shown her. Lady Bellenet's power was harsh, unrelenting.

Ru saw even deeper hollows in the Children's eyes as they filed back to their seats; it was as if they had been scraped clean from within, over and over. And then, with horror, Ru began to recognize some of the faces. Faces she remembered being full of laughter, courtiers' faces. Men and women who had bowed to her, cheered for her and Taryel to kiss. Fingers of ice gripped her chest as she recognized Lord Leon, his expression glazed. Georgina, so talkative at the ball, now silent and dead-eyed.

They were all empty, expressionless, with no hint of a soul within.

Desperate as she was to see the end of the ritual, Ru wanted to leave. Badly. She closed her eyes, which were streaming now from the bright flashes of Lady Bellenet's power.

Gwyneth's finger, clamped tightly around Ru's, began to tremble.

Ru opened her eyes again, blinking, her vision dappled with green and yellow motes. Then her breath caught. Lady Bellenet, at the center of the chapel, *glowed*. She radiated light as if she had become a star herself. Every Child in the room had become oddly colorless; their skin faded to grey. Ru thought for a wild moment that she could see *through* some of them. As if they were transparent.

As if the lady had leeched some core force from them, a life-giving energy.

Despair clawed at Ru's throat. How could Ru find some weakness, some way to empty Lady Bellenet's well, when her well was seemingly endless? With every Child she made or remade, the woman glowed more brightly. There was but one explanation that Ru could think of — Lady Bellenet's power became stronger every time she used it.

This was how she bolstered her power. There was no faith or love in this communion. It was control at its most basic. Lady Bellenet fed from the Children like a hungering creature, stealing their devotion at the moment of highest worship.

And here Ru was, standing in the midst of it with her friends, the only three Children who had not given communion.

CHAPTER 32

They needed to leave. Immediately. Ru was certain of nothing else, only that if they were caught witnessing this, she wouldn't be able to protect Gwyneth and Archie.

"Let's go," Ru hissed in Gwyneth's ear. She tried to keep her voice steady, but her nerves were on fire, her gut in knots.

Archie heard her whisper, his expression questioning.

Ru jerked her head back toward the exit, her eyes wide with unspoken meaning.

"How is she *doing* that?" Gwyneth murmured, looking stricken.

"I don't know," Ru said, already inching her way backwards. "But we need to go."

Ru's heart hammered against her ribs, terror at being recognized by Lady Bellenet. The walls seemed to be closing in around them, the scattered candle flames blurring brightly to fill Ru's vision. The Children's voices were rote, chanting, like animated corpses. Staring, empty eyes gazed out from beneath countless identical hats.

Ru did not realize she had been moving, backing out of the sanctum, until the double doors swung closed in front of her. It was like a music box slamming shut. The muddle of her mind began to clear, her blind terror fading in the absence of Lady Bellenet's bright presence.

She turned to Archie and Gwyneth, who looked frightened but curious, academics to the core.

"What exactly did we just witness?" Archie asked.

"Later," Ru breathed. "We're not safe here."

They nodded, trusting. A surge of warmth rose in Ru. Her friends' faith in her was stronger than she deserved. They hurried across the vestibule to the exit, three sets of footsteps on marble.

And then, echoing in that empty room, a fourth set of footsteps joined the sound — hurried and deliberate.

It was too late to escape. Too late to rush through the door and flee. Inda slid in front of them, stoic and hard-eyed, blocking the way.

Ru stopped short, reaching for her friends' hands with shaking fingers.

No one spoke.

Like a rodent in the sights of a snake, Ru's muscles seemed to atrophy. She could neither move nor speak. Then came a soft creak of footsteps, and three more figures descended from the balcony into the vestibule.

Hugon D'Luc was flanked on either side by Ranto and Nell. He strode almost lazily, knowing his quarry had nowhere to flee. "Delara," he said, "how kind of you to join us."

"The pleasure's hers, I'm sure," Archie said.

Gwyneth exhaled sharply through her teeth.

Hugon ignored them. He came to stand in front of Ru, the Children a few steps behind. He studied her face, his brow creasing slightly, as if trying to discern her motivations by expression alone. Apparently coming up empty, he said, almost reluctantly, "I suppose now is as good a time as any for you to learn the depth of Festra's devotion to his Children."

Bile rose in Ru's throat. Would he force them to succumb to Lady Bellenet's powers, turn them into automatons like the empty shells who shadowed him? There was no denying what they'd seen.

"I'll kill you," Ru said, her voice a breathless rasp. It was a useless threat. The only power she had ever held over Hugon was the artifact's. But she had not so much as summoned a wisp of darkness from the stone since arriving at the palace. What evidence was there that she could do it now, even with a forced hand?

Hugon only smiled, a mirthless baring of teeth. "You must think I'm an utter fool. Have you forgotten your promise?"

Simon. Cold gripped Ru's heart. To keep Simon safe, she would do anything. To defy Hugon now, in front of the Children, would force his hand. There would be no mercy.

Gwyneth and Archie shifted, glancing at Ru. She knew they wanted her to resist, to fight. But their lives weren't a price she would ever pay.

"I'll go with you," said Ru. "Without a fight. But my friends have nothing to do with it. I made them come. Give me your word you won't hurt them."

Hugon sighed, pressing his full lips together as if this exchange bored him. "We've no interest in your friends. Not yet." He waved a hand, his gaze never leaving Ru's. "Inda, take the academics to their rooms. Double their guard. Delara, with me."

~

THEY WERE GOING to Lady Bellenet's rooms. They had passed the stairway that would have led them down toward the cavern and the artifact. It was the only other place Hugon might bring her, the only place she could imagine that might scare obedience into her.

It will be like the last time you saw her, Ru thought. *At worst, she manipulates your feelings. She wouldn't hurt you. She needs your soul, your emotions intact. It will be a mind game, and that's all.*

The words circled in her head like a prayer, but the benediction lost its meaning as she walked with Lord D'Luc, cold fingers balanced on his silken arm. Her body knew the truth of it. Lady Bellenet would siphon the life from her, one way or another.

Your friends are safe. Taryel is safe. Simon is safe. She clenched her jaw, as if the motion might forcefully ground her. *As long as you do what is asked of you.*

A pair of King's Guards joined them as they went,

looming. Ru wondered vaguely if Lyr was still outside her door, unaware that he guarded an empty room.

Hugon was silent as they made their way through the palace. Ru couldn't begin to guess what he was thinking. She avoided his gaze, and had no idea which Hugon D'Luc was leading her through the corridors now — the jailor or the prisoner.

"Pull yourself together," Hugon said, as if reading her mind.

Ru shot him a poisonous look. They had come to a stop in a vacant, elegant corridor. Beautiful doors stood closed before them, closed — Lady Bellenet's rooms.

"I am pulled together," Ru said.

"You look green in the face," said Hugon, with a hint of disgust. And then he faltered slightly, straightening his cuffs, his gaze falling away from Ru's. "If it's within your power, Delara, be compliant for once. For your own good." He nodded sharply at one of the guards, who returned the nod stoically.

Lord D'Luc spun on his heel and left, the clack of his shoes echoing in that quiet hallway.

The guard produced a key from within her uniform and unlocked the door, holding it open. "Lady Bellenet will join you shortly," she said. "You are free to make yourself comfortable in the meantime."

Ru couldn't fathom comfort in that room. It was lit by the fire and a few lamps, but was otherwise deeply shadowed. Ru drifted through the space, trying not to form complete thoughts for fear of panicking. She didn't even risk reaching for the artifact for comfort — it might somehow alert Taryel that she was in trouble, and she wanted him far away and safe. To ground herself, Ru ran her fingers over the soft silk brocade of a cushion. Breathed deeply the scent of burning wood, spices, and the faint aroma of brewing tea. A thick rug cushioned her footsteps.

It occurred to her, staring into the large marble hearth, that she was still wearing the white robes of one of the Children. As if the cloth would suddenly burn her, she tore the robe from her body, tossing it into the fire. The flames were nearly smothered in the process, and a sickly thick smoke began curling up into the flue.

"Trying to asphyxiate us both, I see."

The deep, resonant voice struck a chord of fear in Ru's chest, and she spun, her back now to the flames.

Lady Bellenet stood serenely in the middle of the room, her delicate white hands folded in front of her. She had removed her veil, and now looked little more than a young woman of Ru's age, the remains of youth in her plump cheeks and bright eyes. Ru's dark and unkempt hair, mussed dress, and barely contained fear and rage were a stark contrast to Lady Bellenet's well-groomed calm.

"You seem stubbornly intent on harming yourself," said Lady Bellenet. "Have you not thought of what it might mean if you simply—"

"Gave in?" Ru interrupted, her voice shaking. "Accepted my fate and became the villain you so desperately want me to be?"

"There is nothing immoral in letting the current carry one toward one's destiny."

Ru closed her eyes for a moment, staving off a frustrated ache that pressed against the back of her eyes. "You're a tyrant. A prison warden. Your followers have lost their minds in the most literal sense. I know what you're doing to them. I saw you at Prayer. You're not just taking their emotions, you're… stealing their life force and taking it for yourself, to bolster your power."

Lady Bellenet cocked her head. Her dainty brows furrowed. "What you saw at Prayer was a blessing. A holy sacrament. Those who follow Festra give their faith freely."

She seemed determined to drive Ru into a blind rage, her answers consistently vague, never addressing the question.

"Do you truly believe that?" Ru asked, almost pleading. "You remove the Children's free will. Is that what Festra wants? Mindless followers who have no choice in the matter?" Ru's voice became more urgent as she spoke, as if truth was power, as if words alone could wrench her free from Lady Bellenet's grip.

"How fascinating," was Lady Bellenet's reply. "You scientists will fight tooth and nail against what you see with your own eyes, simply because it is not in your books."

"I believe in magic," Ru said. "I don't believe in controlling people with it."

"How quaint," Lady Bellenet said. Her indulgent tone made Ru's skin crawl. "But these philosophical conversations, this *nonsense* you and Hugon have made such a pastime of indulging in..." her lip curled, her honeyed voice souring as she spoke. "It is superfluous. Festra gifted me with this power not to encourage scientific banter between intellectuals. No, he did so knowing I would gather followers to his cause and present them to him in the Great Cleansing. I've done as he asked so that all of us might travel together to paradise. What you see as control is simply... release from the constraints of an ordinary life. A gift from Festra. Just as his heart was gifted to you, in the knowledge that you would use it to bring a new world to fruition."

Ru had naively thought that in the face of the truth, Lady Bellenet might crumble. Admit to everything. Fall to her knees, weeping. But Ru now saw that this had been silly, a child's wish. Lady Bellenet truly believed in Festra — that he had given her these powers, that he wished for her to build a veritable army of Children and then sacrifice them at his altar.

"Why did you bring me here?" Ru asked, brimming with hateful energy and nowhere to spend it. "Punishment?"

Lady Bellenet sighed, and her eyes shone as if she were about to cry. "If you see only punishment, that is what you will receive."

Ru tasted blood as she gnawed her lip in frustration. "And that means... what?"

The lady smiled almost pityingly. Then she spoke in a bold, resonant voice: "Enter, Lyrren Briar."

At once, the door swung open, and a tall form entered, his dark brows hung low over questioning eyes. His gaze fell on Ru, and he relaxed slightly at the sight of her.

"Lyr," she said, the name tumbling thoughtlessly from her lips. "Don't—"

He shook his head almost imperceptibly, but it was enough to silence Ru. If she said the wrong thing, it would put them both in danger. She couldn't guess why Lady Bellenet had brought him here, unless...

Ru's throat constricted.

She studied the King's Guard, intent on memorizing any details she had missed before. There was a tiny white scar on his left cheek. His fingernails were clean, his knuckles cracked and dry. The firelight cast shadows across his face. Ru imagined him as he might have been as a youth — gangly and awkward, with large joints and hands and limbs he hadn't yet grown into. She watched his throat move as he swallowed. A small patch of stubble stood out on his neck where he had missed shaving. He shifted his weight from one foot to the other, a sign that he was uncomfortable or impatient.

"Why is he here?" Ru asked, her own voice sounding far away in her ears.

Lady Bellenet held out her hand to Lyr, the picture of a priestess offering absolution.

"Why is he *here*," Ru said again, her voice breaking on the last word. "Lyr, don't."

The lady ignored her. Turning her palm to face upward, her fingers unfurled toward Lyr. A faint light emanated from her hand, and Ru's heart turned to ice. "Take my hand, Lyrren Briar."

Ru stepped forward, shaking. "Don't. Please. I'll do anything you want."

"You made that promise once before," said Lady Bellenet, never taking her eyes from Lyr. Her voice hardened. "And you broke it. You crept through the servants' corridors, you came to Prayer, and you lied to Hugon. You are not putting your all into the demonstrations, Delara."

To Ru's abject horror, Lyr took a step toward the lady's outstretched fingers. He was already under her sway. Then he lifted his hand, laying his palm upon Lady Bellenet's.

"Lyr," Ru cried, her voice cracking. "Stop. Turn around and go. *Go!*"

He glanced at her, and a glint of some distant understanding passed over his eyes. Ru knew there was nothing she could do to stop this short of murder. Her mind raced. If she could wrench a poker from the fire, rush at Lady Bellenet, and run it through her heart…

"There is no pain where you are going, Lyrren Briar," said Lady Bellenet, closing her eyes. "There is no end to the beauty and the joy. Revel in Festra's love. Show Ruellian Delara that there is no reason to continue resisting."

Ru stumbled backward, hands outstretched behind her toward the fire. She fumbled for the steel poker, the tongs.

"Kneel," said Lady Bellenet.

Lyr knelt. Lady Bellenet placed a hand on his head.

Ru's fingers closed around metal. She pulled the poker free with a sliding clang.

Lyr closed his eyes.

Blinding white light erupted from Lady Bellenet like a silent scream. The light cut through Ru like a blade, pure condensed pain, as if a still-blazing star had fallen from the sky.

Just like in the chapel, the radiant burst was a twisting knife in Ru's temple, a blind shriek of horror. She fell to her knees, the poker clattering to the floor. She closed her eyes in a vain attempt to shut out the light and that terrible vision — Lyr, knelt as if in prayer. Lady Bellenet, blessing him.

It only lasted a moment. The room was as brilliant-white as the core of the sun, and then it wasn't. Ru opened her eyes, blinking, tears streaming down her face.

"Lyr," she croaked, her voice hollowed out. Spots danced in her vision. She was on her hands and knees on the carpet, her head in agony.

The two forms before her solidified slowly. Lyr, still kneeling, and Lady Bellenet, her hand resting on his hair. Slowly, the lady stepped back. Blinking, Lyr got to his feet.

Ru hardly dared to breathe. "Lyr," she whispered, grasping desperately at some remaining mote of hope.

He turned. "Ru."

Something broke in her. A piece of her heart or the worn-off edge of a ragged soul, falling into a dark abyss. The King's Guard was alive, safe and well. His scar remained. And there was that patch of unshaven stubble at his throat. But the familiar glint in dark eyes, the affectionate curve of his mouth, features that had been so dear to Ru, were gone.

Lyr regarded her with a look of vacant boredom. No, worse than boredom — emptiness.

"What," Ru said slowly, each word heavy with rage, "was the *point* of this."

And as she spoke, unable to contain her emotions, the artifact responded in kind. It boiled up into her throat, hot and bitter, encouraging her.

I should have killed her, Ru thought, burning with hatred for Lady Bellenet. And choking with self-loathing, for not stopping this. Lyr was gone. What stood facing her was an empty thing, a reminder of a man who was lost forever.

Ru let out a strangled sob.

Lady Bellenet turned to her. Her cheeks were pink, her eyes bright, as if she'd just finished eating a filling meal. "You see what your lack of obeisance has brought, Delara? Do not question Festra. And now let us rejoice, for Lyrren Briar has found eternity. He will join us on our journey to the Isle of the Sun on the solstice. It is a gift."

Ru choked on another sob. Her voice wouldn't come; she felt as if she were engulfed by a raging flame, unable to move, hardly able to think.

The lady smiled sweetly in the face of Ru's pain. "Do not attend Prayer again. Do not contradict Hugon. Do not evade my guards. It is for your own good, Delara. You must perform the Cleansing. There is no escaping your destiny."

A seemingly endless stream of burning tears blurred Ru's vision. She clenched her hands, fisted against the floor where she still sat half-sprawled.

"Lyr," she murmured, unable to think of anything else.

"Ru," he said. But her name on his lips was meaningless. It rang empty in the room, devoid of feeling, of *Lyr*.

Lady Bellenet went to the door, flinging it open. She turned back to Ru, eyes flashing. "The Solstice falls in two weeks. If you do not show clear progress with Taryel's heart in the interim, I will be forced to bring more of your loved ones into Festra's fold. Use your time wisely. Now begone."

So dismissed, Ru stood and left the room in a grief-stricken haze until she stood alone in the empty corridor. Lyr and the King's Guards — But no… not Lyr. One of the Children, the shape of him only, a dark emptiness where Lyr had been. She didn't know how long she stood in the hall, weeping into her hands, snot hanging from her nose, sobbing until she choked.

When she was finally exhausted enough to lift her head, forcing herself to wipe her nose and breathe, Lyr was still there. He had been watching her as she cried, his expression uninterested.

CHAPTER 33

Somehow, Ru made it back to her room. Her contingent of King's Guards followed. And Lyr, no matter how many times she screamed at him, sobbing at him to go away, trailed after her. It was as if Lady Bellenet had known, understood that Lyr would haunt Ru like a specter. A nightmarish reminder of what she could do. Of what would happen to Gwyneth and Archie, to Simon, if Ru tried to rebel.

When she at last slammed the door in Lyr's vapid face, Ru found herself feeling utterly lost. Untethered and un-knowing. Prayer had shown her what Lady Bellenet was capable of and how she fed her power. But there was no hint of how it might be stopped. What could Ru do? Empty the palace of people so Lady Bellenet had no one else to change? Such a thing would be impossible.

Alone in her room, with the reality of Lyr's loss crashing down on her, Ru sat unmoving for what felt like an eternity, staring into the fire. She couldn't let this break her. She could not give up. Taking a long, rattling breath, Ru began to think.

She tried to wrack her brain for hints that the lady might have dropped, anything to indicate a weakness. But all Ru could picture was how horribly steady the woman's gaze had been, how avidly she truly seemed to believe what she said about Festra. Ru held nothing over her — Lady Bellenet had every opportunity to be honest, to admit that she was nothing but a sorceress with a desire for annihilation. But she stood by the Festra story. She truly believed.

Ru couldn't accept that Lady Bellenet's faith was based in truth. She railed against the possibility. Because if Festra was real, if all of this was celestially planned, then Ru's world as she understood it would be upended. Like a puzzle, scrambled up and reassembled, perhaps into a similar shape but a new image entirely. Science, facts, her own free will — all would become meaningless.

In all her studies at the Tower, Ru and her friends had found almost nothing of Festra. If he was a god who routinely interfered in the lives of mortals, then surely there should have been records. She would have believed that Festra had been invented by Lady Bellenet altogether had she not seen *Infinite Night*, a painting in a book from the Cornelian Tower. Had she not read *Gods & Glories*.

There had to be more to learn, more to understand. So she would go directly to the source.

Taryel found her there in her rooms, tear-stained and shaking. It took coaxing, soft words and softer touches, to open her up. She didn't want to recount what happened to Lyr. But Taryel saw it in her eyes, had seen the guard in the hall, and had drawn a line between points.

Ru held him as if he would save her while she recounted the Prayer, and what had occurred in Lady Bellenet's rooms after. She cried until his shirt was soaked with her tears, at last allowing herself to open up to grief.

Taryel sent for a late supper, and afterward, Pearl brought dainty cups of melted chocolate. Ru ate dutifully, not tasting anything.

"It's not your fault," Taryel said over and over.

"It *is*," Ru insisted. "I could have stopped her." There was no consoling her.

The night passed slowly, and Ru remained curled against Taryel, catlike, engulfed in his warmth. Morning crept along the eastern horizon. The fire was only embers, and rising sunlight softened the edges of Taryel's face. Ru's eyes stung, and there was an ache in her chest that would not ease.

But Ru now knew what she had to do next.

"I'm not sure about this," said Taryel after she had relayed her plans with breathless fervor.

"I am," she said. "Tell me why we shouldn't. It won't take more than an hour. I need to understand it." She sat up, moving back to see Taryel more clearly.

His eyes were shadowed, lids heavy, and his hair stood up in odd places where she'd dug in her fingers for dear life. He watched her, almost wary, as if she might burst into tears again or worse, dash headlong into harm's way.

"You know this about me," she continued. "I need to understand things. With understanding, with the right information, I can stop her. I just don't have all the facts yet."

His face softened, and he sighed. "Ru, if Hugon comes and finds you gone—"

"He won't. An hour. We'll go now, before the sun's fully risen. No one will miss us." She saw him waver in the face of her grief and desperation. *Please.*"

He groaned, rubbing a hand over his face. "There are limitations to my power. I can only travel a few times without it burning out, depending on the distance."

She sat up, brightening slightly. This was something she could do, a line of action she could take, a way to feel less helpless. "Is that a yes?"

"It's a *fine*, if it's what you really want." He stood stiffly and held out a hand. "Come here, I need you as close as possible. And… as a warning, it's not a pleasant sensation."

Ru let him help her to her feet and pull her into a tight embrace. Then he made a complex gesture with his fingers, one arm still wrapped tightly around her shoulders. A strange smell like ozone and metal and earth filled her nostrils, and then, all at once, the room around them was gone.

And then she was falling, weightless and simultaneously pulled violently in every direction, surrounded by darkness, lost and spinning. For a moment, she thought she might never stop falling, but there was a buzz or a crack, and she stumbled, clinging to Taryel, who still held her close.

The first thing she noticed was the air. It was thick and

wet in her lungs, unseasonably warm. Birds sang an early morning chorus, and pale colors flooded the eastern sky. There were no lingering lights on the horizon in any direction, nothing to indicate civilization, only the sweep of hills dotted with trees. And somewhere, Ru thought, the distant roar of the sea.

They were in Mekya.

"Turn around," said Taryel.

And there it was: a lone construction in that soft, quiet landscape: the temple of Festra. It jutted up like defiance, perhaps long forgotten but still beautiful in its decay. Not much bigger than a house in the city, it was narrow and tall, with columns at its entrance and ivy winding up every edge of its crumbling stone walls.

Ru found it strangely sad. Abandoned and lonely. As if those who followed this god were remnants of a time long past, clinging to some memory that had long since faded to darkness. But that was the archaeologist in her, the Ru who sought stories in every ruin, every crumbled facade.

There was no longer time for such fanciful thinking.

"One hour," said Taryel. With his long black coat and tousled hair, he looked every bit the wandering historian he had once professed to be. It had been a persona, a way to keep Ru from learning his truth, but it suited him. He caught her watching him and smiled. "You'd better find something useful *now* because I'll need at least two weeks before I can travel again after this."

Ru nodded, only half-listening as she set off toward the temple. Her silk shoes were soaked with dew by the time they came to the temple's entrance. There were no windows, and a seemingly depthless cavern of blackness stared back at Ru.

"Do you have a candle or something?" she asked.

"A candle?" Taryel replied at her side. "What am I, a pack horse?"

Ru shot him a look. "How should I know what gods carry around with them?"

He rolled his eyes affectionately. "I'll check inside." Moments later, he returned with a torch, and after muttering and rifling through his pockets, produced a tiny silver tinderbox.

Taking the lit torch, Ru pushed past Taryel and into the temple's quiet darkness. She was impatient and eager, and she only had an hour. She would find something here; she had to. Scanning the walls, she quickly found more torches in aged sconces. Lighting them one by one until the temple was lit with a flickering orange glow, she paused in the center of the room.

The temple was not large. Nothing like the grand ruins of an ancient temple she had once stood in on the western coast of Navenie.

It consisted of one rectangular room; a line of columns ran along either wall, set a few feet out from the walls. Between the columns were altars, clumps of melted candles, and small offerings that might once have been flowers but were now lumps of brown or reduced to dust. At the far end of the room stood a statue, a man with palms upheld, as if catching the sunlight. The statue was bearded and stern, and Ru disliked it immediately.

"Looks nothing like me," said Taryel, studying the statue.

"Oh, shut up," Ru said, biting back a laugh despite herself. "Help me look."

"For what?"

"I don't know," said Ru. "Anything. Inscriptions, prayers, items of note. I want to understand the people who worshiped him once, and those who still do. To find something that connects to Lady Bellenet, or you, or your heart."

"Right," said Taryel, still peering up at the statue. "What secrets are you hiding, you big stone lunk?"

Meanwhile, Ru's intuition took her to the edges of the space, the shadowed corners where secrets might dwell. At the first alcove she came to, she knelt to see a book leaning against the stone wall. Dusty stumps of candles surrounded it in a crescent. The temple was ancient, but had clearly been in use until quite recently. It might still receive visits from time to time.

Unwilling to remove the book from its place against the wall, Ru leaned forward, torch held aloft, to read.

...and he said, follow me to the golden plain, to the sunlit fields beyond, where together we bask in joy. I ask so little of you. Only that you become who you were meant to be, that your footsteps trace the words of a story I have written since the world was new, that you fall upon the rapids of the river and be swept away. Only in the letting go will you see. Only when you see will you become. Only in becoming will we drench the world in light.

This sentiment was familiar to Ru. It was a verse from the chant the Children had intoned at Prayer, of faith and belief and cleansing light. Yet here, in this temple, on the pages of this worn old book, the words didn't feel sinister. On the contrary, as she read them, Ru felt oddly reassured. If she had been someone else, a lost soul looking for meaning, she might have found respite here.

She stood and moved along the wall, stopping to inspect, to read. At another cluster of old candles, she found a locket lying open to reveal a painting of a young boy. Beside it, a polished pink stone the size of a knuckle. Further on was another book, also lying open. This time, a love poem. And when she had made it almost all the way along that wall, she saw a folded piece of parchment underneath a grey stone. A single candle, now nothing but a melted waxy shape with a blackened wick pricking its center, flanked the paper.

She moved the stone and set it aside. Plucking the parchment between her fingers, she unfolded it, ever so delicately. She didn't know how old it was, whether it would disintegrate at the touch of her skin, or whether its ink had long since faded.

But upon handling it, she estimated that it was new, probably no more than a decade old.

I have traveled far and wide. You are my last hope, Festra. If you are listening, if you are here, please watch over my daughter, who was taken far before her time. Before I had a chance to properly love her. Due to my circumstances, I fear she is destined for the fires of the underworld. Yet I would do anything to know that she is joyful in eternity. Free. Happy and loved, as she ought to have been. If it is my life and my love you must take in exchange, so be it. I give myself to you wholly. I am your vessel. Do with me what you will.

D.B.

Ru read it again, but she had already guessed its author. The plea for a lost child, a woman turning herself over to Festra, to be used as a vessel. *I have traveled far and wide.* The hair on the back of Ru's neck stood on end. Lady Bellenet.

"Taryel," she called out, still studying the paper. What did the D stand for? Dorothea? Diana?

No response.

Standing, Ru neatly tucked the paper into her pocket. At the last moment, she paused, changing her mind. Gingerly, she placed it back where she had found it, in a square of shifted dust underneath the stone. A sentimental gesture, but in that quiet temple, something in Ru urged her to be respectful.

She found Taryel on the far end of the temple, crouched behind the statue. He was squinting at a plaque of some kind, hair curtaining his face so he didn't see her coming.

"Taryel."

He looked up, smiling at the sight of her. The curve of his mouth seemed so natural, a habit born of familiarity. Her chest ached.

"What's that?" she said, settling into an uncomfortable crouch beside him. She peered at the stone plaque. It was part of the statue, carved into its base near the back of Festra's heel.

"An inscription," said Taryel. "In ancient Mekyan."

Ru blinked. "You know ancient Mekyan?" It was a language no longer spoken, fallen to memory and scholarship in a world that valued trade and easy communication. Navenian was the common language now, with so many ancient tongues having long since died.

It struck Ru just how old Taryel was, how many hundreds of lives he had lived.

He grinned proudly. "Centuries of life give a man plenty of opportunity for developing hobbies. I've learned eleven languages in that time. This one is particularly familiar to me. It's Festra's favorite."

"His favorite *language?*"

"The preferred language of prayer, anyway. No one spoke it in Ordellun-by-the-Sea, even then, except to praise Festra. King Alaric learned it, and he taught me."

Ru reached out to run a finger along the stone and found that it came away clean. She frowned. "Do you think many people still come here?"

"Seems that way," he said. "Though I can't imagine who."

"What does it say?" Ru asked, still fixated on the tablet. Something about it attracted her, the strange curve and angle of letters unfamiliar to her. A puzzle, a riddle to be solved.

"I'm not *exactly* sure. I've never seen it before or heard of anything like it, despite my brief dalliance as a follower of Festra. Oddly enough, it mentions a heart. Or a stomach or liver, a word to indicate a large organ, but it's used synonymously with—"

"Taryel."

He shot her a sheepish glance. "You rub off on me. I think it says something like, 'at the heart of me lies resurrection.' Or that word could mean freedom, or even death. It's... not a very precise language. Anyway, then it says, 'Keep me and resolve me.' No, that can't be right. Resolve..."

"Compromise?" Ru suggested.

"Maybe. It's incomprehensible poetry. Pretty, but probably meaningless."

Ru caught his sleeve as he tried to stand. "Maybe not. It mentions a heart, resurrection, and... *keep me.* I'm the Keeper, Taryel. Is that all it said?"

He hesitated, then turned back to the stone. "No," he said. "There's one more line. 'I give it to you. Resolve me.'"

"That *can't* be the word," Ru muttered, pushing Taryel's

hand aside as if she might understand the language just by staring angrily at it. "Resolve me… no, something else."

Taryel hummed, chin pressed against folded fingers. Then he inhaled once, a soft, quick breath through the nose. "*Absolve*," he said. "I read it wrong."

Ru recited the lines, already memorized. "'At the heart of me lies resurrection. Keep me and absolve me. I give it to you. Absolve me.'"

"It doesn't have much of a cadence," Taryel said. "Let me…" He recited the words in their original language, a strange, beautiful series of sounds that fell like music from his lips.

"That sounds better," Ru said, moved by it despite herself.

Taryel stood then, offering his hand to Ru. "I suppose you've already come to some academic conclusion?"

She took his hand and got to her feet, her legs stiff from crouching. "It can't be a coincidence, the mention of his heart. But what absolution would Festra be seeking?"

Taryel shrugged, and seeing her shiver in the morning chill, pulled her to him. His warmth enveloped her, and she relaxed against his chest, though her thoughts were running at full speed.

"Absolution," she said. "Keeper of his Heart. Resurrection. Lady Bellenet… I think I found her here. Evidence of her, I mean. She left a note, offering Festra her life in exchange for her daughter's place in the afterlife. That could explain her devotion to him, but…" She faltered. "There are so many missing pieces."

Taryel was quiet for a moment, his chin resting on Ru's head, his arms around her. "I asked you once if you believed in fate. I asked because I feel, often, as if I'm caught in it. As if I'm constantly walking in a circle, crossing my own footsteps again and again. As if there's no escape from what *will* happen, no matter how I try to alter the course."

Ru stepped back, looking up at him. His expression was distant, thoughtful, and seemed to tilt on the edge of an understanding.

"You think everything is predetermined?" she asked, unable to hide her incredulity.

"Not everything. But… me, yes. And maybe you. At the Shattered City, when I told you how I'd felt you calling me, as if I'd known you would be there, all those months ago… I wasn't lying. There is no scientific explanation for what I felt. What else could have guided me to you but fate? What else could have called you to my heart?"

"No," Ru said, frustrated. "Magic, I believe. Gods… maybe. But there's no such thing as fate. I mean, how would it work?"

But her thoughts, almost against her will, constructed layers of meaning from the chaos, and she began to see a shape. Taryel, in the name of Festra, trying to save the world but destroying a city. His heart, turned to stone, wrenched from his body and buried in the earth, cursing him to live forever like the hero of some dark fairy tale. A rebirth, of sorts.

At the heart of me lies resurrection.

And then Ru, called to the heart by some means she had yet to fully comprehend. Was it magic or Festra? Or was it the strings of fate? And whose fingers pulled the strings, if anyone's?

Keep me and absolve me.

Ru wracked her brain, trying to find a connection. Ultimately, Ordellun-by-the-Sea had fallen because of King Alaric's devotion to Festra. And, according to *Gods & Glories*, Festra was a cruel god, smiting those who refused to believe, rewarding only those who followed him without question, leaving a trail of death and destruction in his wake. But what if those stories were exceptions to the norm? Brought to light only because the god was acting out of character somehow?

Ru gnawed her lip in thought.

Keep me and absolve me.

What if the Destruction wasn't at all what Festra had wanted? What if it was nothing but the confusion of a simple devotee, a mortal man poisoned by power and ignorance?

I give it to you. Absolve me.

If Taryel's translation was accurate, if the poem spoke of the artifact like Ru suspected it did, then the heart had not been stolen from Taryel's breast. It had been *given* to him.

"Taryel," Ru breathed, as understanding began to glimmer, "had you considered the possibility that the artifact isn't your heart at all?"

Morning was dawning in pale hues over the shimmering hills, accompanied by a distant cacophony of birdsong. Ru and Taryel emerged from the dim interior of the temple just as the sun began to crest the horizon, and watched together as the sky warmed to purple, then pink.

"It can't be about *me*," Taryel said at last. His overcoat collar, black and gold-embroidered, was turned up against the cold. "This temple is thousands of years old."

Ru said nothing, even though she knew the structure could be no more than eight or nine hundred years old. Now wasn't the time for pedantry.

"It's just a silly poem," he continued. Turning, he frowned at her over his coat collar. "But you disagree."

"Is it really that silly?" Ru said, almost sheepish. "I know I'm supposed to be the scientific one of the two of us, but... I'm beginning to think I've been too narrow-minded. Consider where we are, everything that's happened. What if the poem isn't about you specifically, but a general sentiment? It's likely this isn't the first time someone has destroyed something in Festra's name, or... at least done something terrible."

"Of course it isn't," Taryel said, almost scoffing. "People have been committing atrocities since the beginning of time, almost always in the name of some god or another."

"Then what if that plaque is part of Festra's doctrine? Something that's been lost over the centuries, or forgotten by his followers, or ignored." She was embarrassed to theorize as if the god were real, and even more ashamed to admit that she was starting to believe it. She wrapped her arms around herself as much to stave off the cold as to hide. "You told me so many things back at the Shattered City. None of it made sense, not really. No — don't try to argue, you know it didn't."

He grinned, his interjection swallowed.

"So let me just… let me say it. I need to voice this theory, even if it's madness."

Taryel's hair blew across his eyes, and he pushed it aside, watching her intently in the pale light. His skin was so fair in the early morning, in contrast to the black of his rough beard and his unkempt hair. She drank in the sight of him as if desperate to drown.

"Tell me," he said.

"Let's assume, for a moment, that deities are real," said Ru. "Festra is an ancient god, no longer worshiped by any modern religion. His remaining followers are few and far between. For that reason, he's misunderstood. The story I read in *Gods & Glories*… Consider the possibility that it's, well, inaccurate. It depicted Festra as a god of righteous fury, cleansing disbelievers with fire."

She pushed her hair out of her face, twisting it impatiently and tucking it into her collar. "But what if that's not true? What if he was a loving god, and it was his followers who twisted things? Humans are nothing if not selfish and ignorant. I mean, could King Alaric, could others long before him, have worshiped a Festra who didn't exist in the way they envisioned? And what if Festra knew the way humans are, knew his followers would stray toward evil, and did something other gods hadn't? He made a contingency plan."

A long fingertip tapped Taryel's chin as he frowned, thoughtful. "I'm trying to keep up. What's the contingency, then? The artifact? I'd say it's done a bit more harm than good so far."

Ru shook her head, impatient. Thoughts crowded at the edge of her mind, all out of order. "Yes. I mean, no. You said that in the Destruction, your heart was ripped from your body and buried. Meanwhile, Festra's plaque speaks of resurrection. What if your immortality is the resurrection? And what if Festra feels responsible for the crimes committed by his followers?"

She was speaking faster now, her words barely able to keep up with her thoughts. "Taryel, what if Festra didn't remove your heart at all — what if the heart is *his*? Keeping you alive this whole time, just waiting for the chance to… I mean, what if…" Ru began to gesticulate, grasping at empty air as if it might demonstrate her thoughts aloud. "You and me, Taryel. We were called to the artifact on the same day. Whether it was fate or the hand of an ancient god, it wasn't a coincidence. We're tied to it. Tied together. I know you agree with that, at least."

"I do, but—"

"We're meant to absolve him, I think."

"Who?"

"Festra! Taryel, keep *up*."

He laughed, shaking his head. "Your mind works ten times faster than mine. You talk about resurrection, absolution, but all the artifact has done is cause us pain. Look at you, Ru. I see the vitality draining from you, day by day." His voice faltered as he spoke. "If anyone needs absolving, it's me. But I don't deserve it."

"Yes, you do," Ru said quietly. "You're a good man, Taryel. You were naive, young, and misled. But now we have to figure out what Festra wants, how to absolve him, how to absolve *us*." She hesitated, heat rising in her cheeks. "If any of this is even close to accurate."

Taryel frowned more deeply, and a strange, almost guilty look crossed his face for a brief moment. "But why you?"

The wind picked up, and Ru moved toward him thoughtlessly, drawn always into his tenebrous orbit.

"I don't know," she said, her voice muffled against his chest. And with those three words came a crashing wave of uncertainty. Either Ru had been born to walk these very steps and speak these words, had lived with her entire life mapped out in advance by the hands of a god… or it was random, fate was but a fiction, and *anyone* could have stumbled upon the artifact.

Anyone could have found themselves joined to Taryel, soul to soul.

Neither option comforted her.

"I'm cold," she said.

Taryel tightened his arms around her, and together they fell through the sky, spinning into the darkness.

CHAPTER 34

Lord D'Luc arrived late that morning, and the sickening knot in Ru's stomach returned. Lyr waited outside in the hall, as he always had. Hugon dismissed the King's Guard, and Ru tried not to look at him, but her gaze caught his for a fleeting moment — less than a breath of time — and the pain of it was crushing.

Lyr was gone, and an emptiness gazed back.

"Forget about him," Lord D'Luc said lightly, steering them in a different direction than usual. They were headed away from the cavern, and he had instructed her to wear boots and to bring an overcoat and mittens. "There's no point clinging to that which is gone."

Ru's throat burned from the effort of holding her emotions in check. She wished for Taryel, wished that they were still tangled together in her bed.

"Where are we going?" she asked, more to distract herself than out of actual curiosity. She felt the oppression of loss slipping over her again, and she gnawed her lip. *Don't let him see you breaking,* she urged herself. *Be strong.*

"We're going outside," said Hugon. He held up his gloves, fur-lined leather.

She didn't push him. His lips were tightly drawn, his eyes darting, as if unhappy thoughts pulled him out of the present moment and kept him moving with brisk steps through the palace. When at last they came to the garden,

Ru was too warm from the walk, and the burst of cold air on her face was a relief.

It had snowed in the night. Ru hadn't noticed; she had been so caught up in Taryel. Soft white powder crunched under their boots. Caps of snow perched on rounded topiary. A light snow still fell, though the flakes were so light that they drifted in swirls of wind, seemingly never quite reaching the ground.

Lord D'Luc bent to scoop up a handful of snow, molding it into a sphere.

The garden was expansive. Ru had thought at first, in the heavy grey, that they were in a very large courtyard. But now she saw that they were outside the palace entirely, and that if she squinted, when the wind shifted, she could see a sliver of the sea to the south.

"These are the pleasure gardens," Hugon said, continuing onward.

Ru had been to the palace once before in winter when she was very little. Simon had wanted to play chase in the garden. *This* garden, she realized. The snow had been fresh, like today. But instead of a wide blanket of white, little walkways had been carved into the powder by the shovels of servants, rising early to clear the garden's many paths.

But that had been what felt like a long time ago, back when the palace was free and joyful and full of light. Now, the palace had become something like Inda or Ranto or Nell, elegant yet empty. A remnant of a thing that had once been vital.

Ru and Lord D'Luc continued through the snow, tufts of white kicking up as they went.

"As much as I love a pleasure garden," Ru said, "I have to ask the obvious question."

"Why have I taken you out into the snow rather than to the cavern?"

The thought of that damp place, the dripping stalactites, filled Ru with sick dread. "Yes," she said. "Lady Bellenet said…"

"That two weeks remain," he interrupted. "I know."

She trailed in his wake. Snowflakes landed on her eyelashes, melting on her cheeks. She pulled on her gloves, glad to have brought them. The kingdom's imminent fate seemed almost unbelievable now. A horrible joke in the wake of Lyr's loss. She said, absently, "Two weeks until a new Destruction."

Hugon glanced sideways at her. "Until you fulfill your destiny." As if these were two different things.

"If by destiny, you mean finally submitting to what you believe is Festra's will. Killing everyone."

"If that's how you'd like to think of it."

She stumbled, her foot catching on an uneven surface, and he caught her elbow easily, stopping her fall. They stood glaring at one another. Ru was annoyed by how well the snow suited him, how the gold in his hair softened against it. His cheeks and nose were pink in the cold.

"What if you have it all wrong?" she asked, careful not to give herself away, knowing that her visit to the temple must remain a secret. "What if Festra was appalled by the things you've done? By what you plan to do?"

He regarded Ru with an expression that hovered somewhere between confusion and awe. "Do you mean to tell me you believe in Festra now?"

She paused. "No, but..."

He laughed once, a sad huff of an exhale. "It doesn't matter anyway."

Ru studied his face, and as he met her gaze, her breath caught. His eyes were honest and infinitely sad. He was no longer Lord D'Luc, the regent's advisor; no longer Lord D'Luc, her jailor. He was Hugon.

"It doesn't matter?" she repeated, momentarily lost for words, hoping desperately to keep the real Hugon with her.

"No," he said. "It doesn't. I wonder, over the course of history, how many men have truly believed the rhetoric they so righteously spout?" He tossed the snowball, which Ru had forgotten he was holding, out into the dreary garden. "Don't mistake me, Delara. I have made every choice while in full possession of my mind. But it was not in the name of Festra. Like you, I wonder if he isn't simply a fairy tale."

Ru stood almost witlessly in the snow. Had Hugon ever spoken like this before? Been so frank with her? She worried that if she asked the wrong question, she would startle him from this transparency, and he would be gone again.

But she couldn't help herself. Maybe part of him wanted to be asked. "In whose name, then?"

His expression lost its last vestige of ice then. A young man still in his twenties, a man who had lost so much, stared back at Ru. "Dulcie Bellenet."

Dulcie. The snow was falling thicker now, and the palace had faded to a ghostly-spired behemoth in the distance. Ru waited.

"At first, it was to prove that I loved her," he said, his gaze drifting past Ru, perhaps to some memory that belonged to him alone. "That I was worthy of her. In the hopes that she might love me back one day. And then I stayed because I had nowhere else to go, no one else to go to. And now..." He turned back to Ru, studying her face as if he had only just begun to see all the facets of her. "For the same reason as you."

"I stay because I have no choice," Ru said.

"You could leave at any time," Hugon replied, almost dismissive. "Taryel could take you. You could don a disguise and sneak past the guards. Run to Mekya, or Rothen, if you can handle the cold. You could even murder Lady Bellenet, slit her throat, and then mine. There are ways. But that's not why you stay."

Ru knew that what he said was true. She did have a choice.

"Fear," she said quietly. "I'm terrified of everything. Of what she'll do to my friends, to the world, if I flee. If I fight back and fail. I'm afraid of the artifact and losing control."

"There," he said, lips curling. "Now you understand me."

Ru stared at the lord. "I would never do the things you've done."

He exhaled through his nose in loud impatience, turning away for a moment before facing her again.

"Delara," he said, holding her gaze, "back at the Tower, I saw something begin to break in you, and it frightened me, what I was doing to you. I stopped the demonstrations then, against my lady's orders. For you. Here at the palace, I've handled you with kid gloves while my lady would have had me flay you alive. I spared your brother. I've turned a blind eye to your scheming and defiance whenever I could. I have held back, resisted, done everything in my power to keep you whole when my lady would have seen you fall apart."

Ru's mouth fell open. "Wh…"

But he continued, speaking faster now, his blue eyes almost wild with intensity. "I saw your edges fraying. You were crumbling. If I had done the things she wanted me to do, said the cruelest words, pushed you to the physical and emotional limit that *she* desired, you would no longer be Ru Delara. You'd be hers, utterly. A thing of darkness, ruled by fear and rage. We know the artifact responds to you when you're hurting. She wanted you to be in so much pain, all the time, that there would never be an end to it. So that the artifact would finally awaken. She wants it *still*."

"I *am* in pain," Ru said, almost reflexively. "You haven't saved me from anything." She didn't know how else to respond, what to feel. She thought of the way he'd been since coming to the palace, distracted, afraid. Had he truly been defying Lady Bellenet all that time?

She thought Hugon might argue with her, or that he might disappear forever behind his carefully curated facade. Instead, he closed his eyes for a moment, snowflakes collecting in his hair. "I'm keenly aware of that," he said. "If I were less of a coward, I would save us both. But I am not that man."

"You could be," Ru said, her voice breaking, knowing how delicate this moment was, how liable to shatter, and how badly she needed to keep it intact. "You could stop her if you wanted to."

"There's nothing I'd like more," he said, "but you must know by now that I am not a brave man. I lost myself long ago."

Something in Ru reached out to Hugon, a tendril of affection, some part of her that wanted to understand him, on a distant and profound level. "Is this why you brought me out here? To tell me I should pity you after all, or be grateful to you?"

Hugon laughed sadly. "No, Ru. You should hate me for what I've done. But…" He moved closer to her then, easing past the limits of propriety until she could have stood on tiptoe and pressed her cold lips to his with ease.

He lifted her chin with a gloved hand, and for a second, Ru saw her reflection in the blue of his eyes.

"In another lifetime," he said softly, "you and I could have built such a kingdom. I see it so clearly. Our minds, our ambition… your goddamned idealism. We would have been the glory of Navenie."

He paused, closing his eyes. Ru stood frozen, sharing breath with him, and in some distant, bright part of herself, beyond her anger and bitterness and fear, she saw the faded golden vision of a life unlived.

"If not for the manipulative fingers of fate," he said.

It was as if the ground fell away for a moment, and Ru hung suspended, caught between this life and another. She imagined Hugon D'Luc as a child, laughing under Mekyan cypress trees. Bare feet in summer, reading by firelight in winter. A life free of Dulcie Bellenet, a life of wonder and discovery, of science and understanding. She imagined him as a young man at court, the elegant Lord D'Luc, his lips brushing her knuckles tenderly. In this world, there were no Children. There was no artifact, no Festra. Just a lord and a young academic meeting for the first time.

So easily, she reached for him. Her hand curled around the back of his neck, and she stood up on her toes.

So easily, she pressed her lips to his. He stilled, and for a moment, she thought he would push her away. Then he parted his lips for her and returned the kiss, slowly, carefully. As if they stood balanced upon the edge of a knife.

Ru spoke a eulogy in the kiss. He yielded to her with precision, and she filled the gaps with everything they could have been.

It was only a moment. A brief intermission. And yet it spanned for what felt like a lifetime, and when Ru broke away, she found that tears had formed in the corners of her eyes. Lord D'Luc stared at her, his lips parted. They stood together in the snow, a silent understanding. A farewell.

Then, as one, they moved apart, the distance between their bodies a widening gulf.

He straightened his coat, brushed smooth the wrinkles where Ru had grasped it in her fingers. The mask fell into place. Another edge of Ru's heart crumbled and fell free, tumbling into the abyss.

She knew that had been the last time she would ever see the real Hugon.

He said, clipped and matter-of-fact: "You will do what is required of you, Delara. That is all."

With ten days left until the solstice, Lady Bellenet hosted an exclusive dinner party in her personal chambers. It was the first time Ru had been back since losing Lyr. Simon was in attendance, playing uplifting tunes on his lute. A sullen snow fell outside. Normally, Ru would have reveled in the cozy atmosphere, the plates of tiny cakes, the music and candlelight, warm inside while winter's fingers tapped at curtained windows.

Instead, she was anxious, agitated like a caged animal. Even with Taryel at her side, even with a steady, comforting warmth from within — the artifact's soothing presence — Ru could not stop herself from seeking out Lady Bellenet wherever she was in the room. And always nearby, Hugon D'Luc.

They hadn't spoken more than a few words to one another since that morning in the snow. Demonstrations with the artifact played out by rote, with Hugon urging her and Ru holding the artifact at bay, desperate not to lose control.

Ru told no one what had been shared between her and Lord D'Luc. It would accomplish nothing. And part of her wanted to keep it for herself, a moment of truth between her and her enemy. It felt too private, too honest to share. So she held it close and tried not to despair.

Because not once has he let the mask slip, not once has she seen the true Hugon looking out through those ice-blue eyes. Not once since that fateful morning. Knowing he was there, yet unable to reach him, made her chest ache.

As if understanding what she needed just then, Taryel wrapped an arm around her, pulling her close. The gleeful remarks from nearby courtiers had become so common they fell into background noise, Ru hardly noticing.

"You're worrying," Taryel said, his voice low. He and Ru stood near the hearth, and firelight warmed his dark features as he studied Ru's face. The obvious love in his eyes made her heart feel as if it were too big for her ribs.

"When am I not?" she muttered. "Ten days, and I have nothing. The only way to drain her power is to deprive her of victims. What do we do, empty the palace?"

"It's not… *impossible*," Taryel said.

"It may as well be," said Ru.

Taryel bent his head to hers, as if he was going to kiss her or murmur some comforting words. But before he could do either, Lady Bellenet swept into the center of the parlor, pinging a tiny silver spoon against a glass. Every eye in the room went to her — she was radiant and deadly.

"Good evening," she said, smiling warmly at those gathered. "It has been too long since I held one of my dinner parties. Don't you agree?"

An exultant cheer went up from her party guests, all except Ru, Taryel, and — Ru noticed — Hugon D'Luc.

"Then come forward, friends, if you wish to be blessed in the name of Festra." Lady Bellenet's words rang in that elegant room like a death knell.

At once, breathless courtiers lined up before her, everyone in attendance. Ru scanned the crowd for Simon, knowing he wouldn't be there but anxious all the same. He would be creeping from shadow to shadow for a while yet, avoiding the gaze of Lady Bellenet and her Children. Ru let out a slow breath when she was certain of his absence.

"Kneel before me," said Lady Bellenet, gazing down at the courtier first in line.

"She's not…" Ru said, pressing closer to Taryel. "She won't. Not here, surely."

He said nothing. There was nothing he could have said to reassure her.

The "blessings" didn't take long. One after another, Lady Bellenet placed her hand on the head of each courtier, or pressed their hand, or gazed into their eyes. It seemed she didn't need to touch them in a certain way, all she had to do was connect with each soul. And then came a flash of light, blinding and horrible, before she moved on to the next.

"I ought to have brought my tinted spectacles," one courtier remarked laughingly to another as they waited to be blessed. "Terrible on the eyes."

Ru watched Lord D'Luc with something like hatred. He stood across the room, leaning against the wall with a glass of wine in one hand, watching the blessings with an expression of detached disinterest. Ru wondered if he went to bed with Lady Bellenet, if she made herself vulnerable to him. She wondered how many opportunities he'd been presented with, how many times he might have slipped a blade between the lady's ribs or across her throat. Yet there he stood, simply observing. Useless.

"There's nothing we can do," Taryel murmured. "If you intervene... she'll take your friends."

But there *was* something she could do, Ru thought, shaking uncontrollably as she watched the last of the courtiers receive Festra's blessing. Lady Bellenet glowed in the candlelight. *There is always a choice.* She hated herself in that moment, as much as she hated Hugon.

Dinner was served to a table full of empty shells, Children in courtly regalia, yet to don their white robes. The woman across from Ru had been so full of joy earlier in the evening, a beautiful young Countess who excelled at chess. Now she was gone, a body going through the expected motions, lifting a glass to her lips and drinking, a simulacrum of life. They all were.

"What a lovely evening this has been," said Lady Bellenet, smiling around at her guests.

Everyone gazed back at her, expressionless. Ru and Taryel, at the other end of the table, held each other's hands tightly under the tablecloth.

"Indeed," said Hugon, holding up a wine glass. "Festra's

flock grows so quickly, soon the chapel will not hold them."

"It won't need to," said Lady Bellenet, smiling directly at Ru. "In ten days, there will be no need for a chapel."

Ru didn't touch her food during that eerily quiet dinner. She was sick to her stomach, hardly able to sit at the table, let alone eat. Taryel managed to eat both her dinner and his own, which she couldn't possibly fathom, but she was grateful for his steadiness. Perhaps it was all those years of misery that had made him impenetrable. Or maybe he was simply used to it.

When at last the settings were cleared away, Ru and Taryel took their leave, and he walked with her to her rooms. As they approached her door, a pair of hurried footsteps rang through the hallway.

"Wait for me," came a voice from behind them.

They turned to see Simon, trotting after them with his lute in tow.

"Where did you go?" Ru asked, relieved at the sight of her brother.

The minstrel dipped a playful bow when he reached them, his copper hair flopping over his forehead as he did. "Evening, Keeper. My lord Taryel." He eyed the King's Guards in their periphery. "Thought I'd take my leave when the party was at its zenith, you know. Why, what did I miss?" His expression said that he knew exactly what he'd missed and why he'd left early.

"Nothing," said Ru. "Dinner."

Simon darted a glance at Taryel. "My lord, if it pleases you, may I have a few moments alone with my darling sister?"

Ru bit back a sound of annoyance — Simon was hamming it up for the guards, but his ham always went too far and came out looking ridiculous.

"Of course," said Taryel. He turned to Ru and pressed a kiss to her cheek. "I'll speak with you later."

"Lovely," said Simon, offering Ru his arm. "A bit of tea by the fire? It will only be a moment."

The guards seemed reluctant, but allowed Ru and Simon to enter her rooms unimpeded. Simon flitted about immediately, setting down his lute and calling for tea, talking as he went. "Nightmarish business, from start to finish," he said. "Do you know how much it costs to fix a lute? It's nothing to sniff at. Had to replace two strings, the bridge, and a tuning peg. Not to mention my *ego*."

Ru slumped onto the sofa facing the fire. "At least you're not… empty inside."

Simon paused, a tin of cookies in his hand, which he had procured from who knew where. "I'm sorry," he said, his tone unusually serious. "I heard… about Lyr. If there was something I could have done—"

"Just don't throw any parties from now on, all right?" Ru said, feeling strangely bitter. How could her brother go on joking, acting like he hadn't been outright threatened by Lord D'Luc and the Children? Ru had put herself on the line for him, was tormented every day, and he had only a broken lute to fix.

At last, the tea came, and Simon settled himself next to Ru on the sofa, handing her a cookie with some force. "Eat."

She took a reluctant bite, chewing slowly. She *was* hungry.

"I see that you're angry with me," said Simon, shifting uncomfortably as if his clothes were too tight. "That's why I wanted to talk to you. I wanted to, well, apologize. For putting you in a situation that required you to stick your neck out for me." He poured a cup of tea and handed it to Ru. "And to thank you for doing so. I might be in a bit of a pickle if you hadn't."

Ru took the tea, but her hands shook, spilling hot droplets onto her knees, and she had to set it down again. The thought of Simon like that, his mind gone, everything that made him *Simon*… gone. It made her sick. A hard lump formed in her throat, and she had to close her eyes to keep from crying.

"Oh, no," said Simon, "don't. Please don't cry. I thought you were *angry*, Ru. Get angry again. I can deal with anger."

"I don't want…" she began, nearly choking on a sob.

Simon groaned.

"Shut up," she said, speaking through a sudden and steady stream of tears, "I'm going to cry if I w-want to. I just... I don't want to lose you. Or anyone. Lyr was too much. I can't even think about it. I can't—"

Muttering to himself, Simon pulled Ru into an awkward one-armed hug. "There, there," he said, patting her hair as if he'd never encountered a crying woman in his life before. "Let it out, or whatever you'd like to do. Just don't get snot on my jacket like last time."

Ru hiccuped, laughing, and overwhelmed with affection for her brother. She sat up, wiping her eyes.

Simon tilted his head, regarding his sister with an assessing sort of fondness. "You know," he said, "the painful knowledge of one's impending demise is hardly reason to let oneself go."

She made a face. "Do I look that bad?"

He laughed, a musical, uproarious thing that warmed Ru's heart. "God, Ru. Yes. I know for a fact you own gowns in colors other than drab gray. Let me braid your hair, at the very least."

He hadn't braided her hair since they were children. Before she left for the Cornelian Tower. Before he took up the lute. Ru could think of nothing she would like more. "Please," she said.

Simon's fingers were deft, the precise movements of a musician. Ru leaned back against his bent knees, his feet propped on the sofa as if they were children again. The tug of his hands in her hair was calming, the repetition soothing.

And then something occurred to her, something she should have wondered at before. "Simon," she said, "you know things. Do you know how Lady Bellenet changed the professors at the Cornelian Tower?"

He paused in his ministrations. "I thought you knew."

"I thought it was poison, but now I know how her powers work. Did she travel to the Tower in secret?"

"Exactly," Simon said, almost too quickly. "They *were* sedated with some herbal tincture, held captive until she could jaunt up to the Tower and change them."

"But..." Ru said, her thoughts turning over like stones

to reveal what was beneath. "The travel alone would have taken days. We would have seen her carriage." And then she understood. The truth landed like a stone in her gut. "Taryel took her."

"You ought to consider not using your brain for a while," said Simon, still braiding, slowly and fastidiously. "I think you'd find it relaxing."

"*Simon.*"

His voice softened. "Don't be too angry with him. He had no choice, did he? Playing along, and all that. And stop fidgeting," said Simon. "You'll make the braid crooked. I'm almost done."

When he was finished, he took Ru by the shoulders and spun her around to face him. He smiled, though there was a faint sadness in his eyes that Ru wasn't used to seeing there.

"Acceptable?" she asked.

"Only just," he replied, the edges of his eyes crinkling. "And now I must depart." He stood, smoothing his frock coat and neckcloth, patting his hair to ensure that he remained the very picture of perfection. At the door, he turned, his features pinched in thought. "You only have ten days," he said. "What will you do with them?"

Ru reached back and ran her fingers over the braid. It was neat as a pin, not a single lock of hair misplaced. Just as it had been when they were children.

"I'll find a way to stop her," she said. "Or, I suppose… I won't. Either way, we'll find out soon enough."

Simon grinned, pride shining in his hazel eyes. "Grim and somewhat hopeless. That's my Ru."

Snow fell through the night. And when the sun rose, a southern wind pushed the clouds toward the mountains. The sunlight on the snow made the palace shimmer like a sugary confection. Ru couldn't help but admire the sight through the tall windows to her left, the beauty of it, otherworldly in its quiet.

"I had intended for us to take the air together," said Lady Bellenet, "but fate had other plans."

Turning back to her breakfast, Ru avoided the woman's gaze. She had risen with the sun that morning, finding herself alone. And when Lord D'Luc didn't come to fetch her, she at last dressed and, strangely worried, went out to find him. Instead, she had found Inda waiting outside her door.

"Lady Bellenet has summoned you to her rooms for breakfast," Inda had said with heavy indifference, and that had been all.

"Where is Lord D'Luc?" Ru asked now. The question was innocent curiosity laced with fear, but Ru saw in Lady Bellenet's expression that she *knew*, somehow: two opposing forms, drawn together in the snow.

"Where he'll be useful," she said. "Away from you."

Ru willed herself to remain relaxed, to appear untouched by the words, the threats that dripped from them. She did not need to waste her worry on Hugon D'Luc. "And the demonstrations?"

"Drink your coffee before it cools," said the lady, daintily sipping her own. "The air is chilled this morning."

They finished their breakfast in stiff silence. Ru forced herself to chew and swallow a fresh scone, dousing it in cream and jam to help it go down.

Her appetite wasn't what it had been. And while she had braided her own hair today, even coiling it around itself at the crown of her head and securing it with pins, she had seen herself in the mirror. Simon was right — she looked like a ghost of herself, hollowed out.

Ru waited for Lady Bellenet to speak, to make some impossible request of Ru, to threaten, to cajole. Instead, after a time, the lady rose from the table and went to the window. She wore a dove grey dress, and her hair hung loose around her shoulders. To Ru, she appeared almost childlike in that moment, framed in sunlight, squinting against the sparkling snow.

At last, she turned back to Ru, her expression unreadable. "You went to the temple."

This caught Ru off guard. She had believed it was a secret between herself and Taryel. Had he told her?

"I saw you," Lady Bellenet said, as if understanding Ru's thoughts. "In a dream. I see many things. They are often vague and unclear, these messages from my god. But this one, I understood. Ask me."

Ru fumbled for a response. "Ask you? I…"

"About my daughter."

The room was warm, heated by a roaring fire in the hearth, but goosebumps formed on Ru's arms. "The one in the note."

Lady Bellenet said nothing, her hands folded perfectly in front of her, her face still half-turned toward the sun.

"What happened to her?" It was the only question Ru could think to ask. She knew that the daughter was Lord D'Luc's, that she had died as an infant. She knew that the infant's death had led to Lady Bellenet's faith, her power, and, in some tangential way, to the artifact and Ru.

"She was sent away," said Lady Bellenet, casting her gaze toward a not-so-distant past. "She was beautiful. So sweet, a perfect child. Always smiling. I named her Dulcinea, my name, and my mother's name. She used to hold my thumb in her tiny hand, and refused to let go." She tilted her head as if in thought. "I never wanted to marry. I had never yearned for motherhood. But when she came, it was as if my life had found its purpose. I would, I thought, be happy forever."

She paused for such a long time that Ru began to wonder if she was waiting for a question or a prompt. But no words seemed right.

Finally, Lady Bellenet touched the tip of a finger to her eye, as if to staunch an unshed tear. Then she continued. "Hugon was devoted to her. Devoted to me. He would have given anything for us. But it wasn't enough. I had always wanted *more*, you see. I had imagined Dulcie and I traveling the world. Seeing distant shores together. Hugon wanted me at home, doing needlework, speaking soft words, and doing soft things."

Ru couldn't imagine Lord D'Luc expecting such a thing from a woman he loved. He was drawn to ambition, to progress. But that had been nearly a decade ago. Perhaps, she thought, the loss had changed him. "So you refused him," she said. "But Dulcinea…"

Lady Bellenet turned at last to look at her. Grief shone bright in her eyes. Her fingers twisted. "I wanted to keep her. But he wouldn't have his reputation sullied by a bastard child. He wouldn't see *mine* sullied. I didn't care. I would have made do without my social standing. As long as I had my Dulcie, and the world at my fingertips. But he…" A tear ran down her cheek, catching the sunlight. "He and my father overpowered me and sent Dulcie away. There was a home for orphans and bastards, not far from Hugon's country estate. He promised to be generous, to send yearly payments for her upkeep. That she would have a comfortable life. No one but our families ever needed to know. It was best for us, he said. Dulcie had only been there for two months when I received word."

She brushed the tear from her cheek with hurried fingers, and it was the first time Ru had seen her shaken. It was the first time her movements had not been practiced, poised, delicate. She was, after all, a young woman. Not much older than Ru.

"What happened?" Ru asked, suppressing the irrational urge to reach out. Lady Bellenet needed no one's comfort, least of all Ru's.

"A sickness," the lady replied, lifting her chin. "It took a quarter of the children at the house. All of the infants were lost."

"So you left," said Ru, remembering. "But why didn't you tell Hugon?"

Lady Bellenet's jaw tensed. "He had not earned the courtesy. It was he who had sent Dulcie to her death, *he* who insisted. He might have discovered the fate of our daughter for himself if he hadn't drowned himself in drink immediately after sending her away. He never read the letters the orphanage sent, never bothered to check in. His accountant had continued to send yearly payments, all that time, to a dead daughter." She took a long, unsteady breath. "For many years I called him a murderer. It was only when I found faith in Festra that I..." she shook her head, glancing at Ru. "That I found it in myself to forgive."

"He didn't tell me," Ru said, and the admission stung. He had painted himself the victim, a man abandoned. "About the orphanage, I mean."

The other woman let loose a bitter laugh. "Of course he wouldn't. You know as well as I that Hugon D'Luc acts for no one but himself. It will be his downfall. But I didn't bring you here for your sympathy."

Ru understood now, on the most basic level. Lady Bellenet had been a woman with no escape from her grief. There had been no one she could turn to for comfort, her sadness wrapped tightly and concealed beneath a veneer of ladylike poise. Festra, somehow, might have been the first and only being to grant Dulcie Bellenet some measure of comfort. Of relief.

It was no wonder that the woman clung so tightly to her faith. She had written a note, pleading for her child's peace in the afterlife. And Festra had given her a power beyond mortal reckoning.

"I envy him," said Lady Bellenet.

The words startled Ru. They were broken and raw, as if she spoke with a voice that was her own for the first time. "Lord D'Luc?"

Lady Bellenet's face twisted. "No. Taryel Aharis. He and I are more alike than you might guess. Both touched by a god, each of us unworthy of forgiveness. His heart, like mine, broken and hardened beyond recognition. Both calling out for a thing it cannot have. But his…" she looked at Ru, and her eyes were aflame. Warring emotions seemed to dance across her face, and color rose high in her cheeks. "His heart found its counterpart. Its anchor."

She reached out one hand, shaking fingers brushing Ru's face. "That is why," she said, deep voice catching, choking on emotion, "your Cleansing will be more powerful than Taryel's Destruction could have ever been. It will draw from the love between you like water from a bottomless well. It will spread like a dark flood from one end of the world to the other. No one and nothing will be left to defy it."

Dread rose in Ru like the dark flood Lady Bellenet so reverently spoke of. She had thought that maybe this vulnerability from the other woman had been a crack in the facade. That it might all come crumbling away at last, like the storybooks from childhood — the tortured villain turns to love, accepts that she can change, and then does.

Ru took a step back from Lady Bellenet. This was no storybook.

"It doesn't have to be like this," Ru said, dread winding its way through her and suffocating logic. "Hugon loves you. He told me. You say your heart has no anchor, but it does. The man is utterly devoted to you. The happiness you seek, you can have it. Here. Now. With him. You don't have to do any of this."

Lady Bellenet's ice-cold wall did not melt despite Ru's desperate efforts. She only smiled, an empty quirk of the mouth. "Don't patronize me with this nonsense," she spat. "There is no love left in Hugon D'Luc's heart. He is driven by fear and selfishness alone. A coward."

"You're going to kill people. You've *already* killed people." Ru's words came out as a half-sob.

Lady Bellenet's eyes flashed. "Kill? You think the Children are dead? For a scientist, your mind seems unable to grasp anything but the smallest concepts. After the Cleansing, Festra's true followers will not die. They will journey to the Isle of the Sun and through the gates of paradise. The gates that *you* will open."

"You're deranged," Ru said, her common sense long since fled.

"You're the hand of a god," said Lady Bellenet, her eyes wild. "What you say means nothing. You're a conduit. A tool."

"I can't," Ru said, voice breaking against the words. "I can't do it, even if I wanted to. I've *tried*."

"You have not tried." Lady Bellenet's voice was growing deeper, wilder, as if each word were tearing at her esophagus, flung violently at Ru like a bludgeoning weapon. "Hugon has admitted to being lax with you, Delara. He does not understand you like I do. He didn't see you at the Shattered City, the way you fell in love with Festra's heart, the power you wield. A god's power. He never understood the darkness in you."

The lady seemed to grow taller as she spoke, as if a stormcloud were building around her figure.

"What darkness?" Ru said, almost flinching away.

Lady Bellenet took a step toward Ru, her gaze growing less human by the second. "The artifact responds to your innermost desires," she intoned. "The deepest, most hidden wants. All you need to do is let go, Delara. Give in. Accept that nothing you can do will stop me; nothing you can say will put an end to Festra's Cleansing. Accept that you are nothing without Festra. *This* is what you were born for." The lady pressed a hand to her chest. "To serve me, and by extension, Festra."

"You're mad," Ru said as rage boiled inside her.

"Lyrren Briar," said Lady Bellenet, "pledged his soul to Festra for you. For *you*."

"Because he had no choice," Ru said, choked with anguish. "Because you would have hurt me or my friends. He was loyal to *me*." She nearly doubled over with the pain of remembering that last image of Lyr, kneeling before Lady

Bellenet. "You're a monster," Ru breathed. "Everything you do is for yourself. For power."

But Lady Bellenet loomed before Ru then, holding up a hand, her eyes flashing like a vengeful goddess. Ru bit her tongue, but it was far too late. She had gone too far, miles and miles past the limit. *Strike me down then,* she thought. *Bless me like you blessed Lyr and all those people at your party. See how well I use the artifact then.*

But the lady only twisted her mouth, an ugly grimace of rage. And then, in an instant, her eyes softened. Her mouth curled into a serene smile and she seemed to diminish in height. "I thought you might say something like that," she said.

Ru's heart slammed in her chest. She watched as Lady Bellenet went to a door at the other end of the room, flinging it open. From within, three forms emerged. Lyr came first, escorting Gwyneth and Archie. The two friends held hands, their heads held high, defiant, their faces un-flinching.

No, thought Ru, and her knees nearly buckled beneath her. *Not this.*

She didn't need to ask what they were doing here. She knew — they were here to die.

CHAPTER 37

"Kneel," said Lady Bellenet, when the pair of academics came to stand before her, Lyr at their heels. Lady Bellenet spoke with the voice of a queen, a woman who would not be disobeyed.

Gwyneth and Archie stared, clearly frightened and confused. Ru thought she saw Archie brush a thumb across Gwyneth's hand, an intimate and soothing gesture.

Ru began to crumble.

"I beg your pardon," Archie said. "You want me to kneel in my best trousers?"

Tears streamed down Gwyneth's cheeks. "You don't have to do anything, Ru," she said. "No matter what happens to us… Don't let her get to you."

"No," said Ru, panic hastening her words. "You don't need to… Lady Bellenet, bring the artifact. You've pushed me enough. I'll stop resisting."

"No need," Archie cut in. "Don't worry about us, Ru. We've got everything handled, as you can see." His freckles were dark against a paling face; even his sarcasm fell flat, limp, and impotent.

If Ru had been a better person, she thought, more accomplished, more competent, she might have lunged for Lyr's weapon and wrested it from him. She might have driven the blade through Lady Bellenet's heart, twisted it deep, reveled in the strength it took to cut through bone and sinew and organ meat. She would have savored the crack of bone, the rush of last breaths, the spurt of blood.

But just like before, when Lyr had knelt before Lady Bellenet, Ru couldn't bring herself to fight in the way that her loved ones needed. Because she was not that person. She'd never even held a sword. She was only Ru Delara.

"Please," she croaked helplessly, realizing then that she, like Gwyneth, was crying. "I'll do anything. Anything."

"Yes, you will," said Lady Bellenet, breathing hard and eyeing Ru as if she were a disobedient dog. "But you defy and *defy* me. You lack the proper motivation. Hugon failed to push you over the edge." Her eyes flashed. "Let me remind you of your place here, Delara."

Ru didn't know what to do. What *could* she do but watch in abject horror as her friends were lined up before their executioner? Archie had the audacity to smile at Ru, a crooked, wan thing. As if he were reassuring *her*. Gwyneth sobbed once, broken and loud.

Lyr, glassy-eyed, shoved the academics to their knees.

Lady Bellenet placed her hands on their heads. And as the blinding white light poured forth from her like a scream, Ru fell to her hands and knees and wretched.

When at last the light was gone, and Lady Bellenet lowered her arms, Ru knew she would never see her friends again. She tried to catch their gazes, her most beloved companions. But they were only dark silhouettes, her vision still blurred and spotted from the burst of power.

Ru blinked until she could make out her friends' stony faces, desperate to catch a glint of recognition.

Gwyneth turned to Ru, her face no longer crumpled in anguish. Tears still stained her face, but they had ceased to flow. Her expression hung slack, vacant.

They were gone.

"Bring me the artifact," Ru said, her words grazing a sore, tattered throat. Had she been screaming? It didn't matter. All she wanted was to end this. *Fine. You want me in the darkness? I'm here.*

Lady Bellenet opened her mouth to respond, advancing on Ru like a demonic specter. But the lady paused at the sound of a door opening. Ru turned to see Lord D'Luc sil-houetted in the doorway, his face shadowed.

"What's this?" he said, his prim voice at odds with the situation. The door swung shut behind him, and at last Ru could see his features. They were handsome and cold — he gave nothing away.

"She required motivation," said Lady Bellenet, who had become once again the delicate lady with rosy cheeks and shining eyes. But Ru saw malice behind that innocent gaze. "It is nothing to fret over."

Hugon strode forward, frock coat billowing. He knelt before Archie and Gwyneth, one knee to the floor, and took each of their faces in turn, gripping their chins and staring hard into their eyes. Then he stood, smoothing his waistcoat with a tight-lipped expression.

"You risk pushing her too far," he said at last, not once acknowledging Ru's presence. "We had agreed—"

"An agreement long since forfeit," Lady Bellenet spoke over him, half-smiling, though her voice had a frozen edge. "I will do what I must to ensure the success of the Great Cleansing."

"As will I, my lady, but surely this was… unwise."

A storm cloud settled over the lady's face. "I see," she said. "Unwise, you say. The great Hugon D'Luc says that I have been unwise. Is he certain he'd like to stand by such an accusation?" She stretched her fingers, and though her hands hung at her sides, they had begun to glow once more.

Hugon took a step back. "No, my lady," he said quickly. "I only meant the timing… but you were right to do it. For-give me. I was wrong."

"We will go to the artifact," Lady Bellenet said. "I want to see what you've been doing these long weeks. If I find that either of you has failed me in some way…" she looked at Ru, her icicle gaze penetrating the soft tissue of Ru's heart, "it's your brother who will be next."

The cavern was a reflection of Ru's nightmares. The subterranean room, dimly lit and stale, was frigid and lifeless. Ru would have shivered anyway, her skin and muscle clenching in the gasp of cold air that came seeking through that unseen draft. But the violence of her reaction to returning to this place — teeth chattering, hands clenched and fingers clenched, a blur at the edges of her vision — was more than just a chill.

She could not stop replaying the moment over and over in her mind. Archie and Gwyneth kneeling, the flash of light. Their blank, empty eyes. She hadn't been able to save them. And the artifact waited for her, cold and black.

Shame overtook her, and she cried out, a sound of anger and frustration, self-hatred and helplessness.

"I can't do this," she rasped.

Lady Bellenet said, "You will. The Cleansing approaches, and you still have not mastered the artifact."

Lord D'Luc said nothing.

Ru glanced hopelessly at Lyr, who had stationed himself at the base of the stairs. She imagined rushing at him, taking his weapon and turning it against him. The thought choked her. As long as he looked like Lyr, sounded like him... she would never be able to harm him. And he, no longer the guard she so deeply cared for, wouldn't hesitate to fight back.

Out of options, Ru went to the table and stared down at the black stone. The artifact, gleaming in low light. There was only one option, one choice.

"Lyr," said Lady Bellenet, her voice echoing harshly. "Stand beside Delara. Watch her. The moment you see the artifact react, I want her unconscious. Is that clear?"

The guard said nothing but took up his station, flanking Ru. Lady Bellenet had faith. She believed that Ru could do this from the depths of her despair. And for the first time, Ru wanted to prove her right.

She couldn't lose Simon.

Please, Ru thought, the shadowy fingers of her mind reaching inward, drifting along the artifact's coiled energy. *Give me something. The golden light... show it to them. Not the darkness. I don't know if I can hold it off this time.*

The artifact seemed to hum in response, but that was all.

Ru closed her eyes, breathing slowly. She could not stop shaking.

I'm angry, she thought. *Feed on that rage. You used to be so angry, too. You used to push me. Do it again but don't overwhelm me.*

Nothing happened.

"You're not trying," Lady Bellenet said.

"I am," Ru bit out. Had her friends put up a fight before they met their end? Had Inda, Ranto, and Nell dragged them bodily from their rooms in the palace? Or had they come willingly, foolishly, in some vain attempt to save Ru? Out of some horribly misplaced loyalty?

The fire in Ru surged; her anger, her pain catching in her chest like a jagged piece of glass, clambering into her throat, choking her.

Taryel, she said the name silently, as if she could call him by thought alone, as if her desperation was acute enough to be felt through their shared tether to the artifact, as if he might know exactly where she was and how to save her.

"You continue to defy me," said Lady Bellenet. "Hugon, send for the minstrel."

Ru's gaze shot to Lord D'Luc. He could still save her. He could prove himself brave instead of a coward. *Hugon,* she pleaded internally. *You can stop her.*

But he avoided her gaze, turning to the door.

"No," Ru said, desperate. "Let me try again. One more time."

Lady Bellenet said nothing, but Hugon paused by the door, waiting.

Ru's fingertips scraped the table as she gripped it for dear life, as she pulled and pulled on the connection between herself and the artifact. *Just enough,* she thought. *Just show them enough to be satisfied.*

This time, the artifact seemed to jerk against the margins of her mind, a sharp acknowledgment, sudden and bright. It took almost everything Ru had to hold it within herself, to staunch the flood of destructive energy that was suddenly writhing, pressing at the edges of her mind, begging to be let out. If she gave way to the artifact for a moment, there was no telling what would happen. Lyr could be gone before he had a chance to knock her unconscious.

Blood dripped from her nose and into her mouth. She wiped it with the back of her hand, and the thick tang of iron cut through her thoughts.

Taryel, she pleaded again, wishing he could hear her, that the artifact would somehow warn him.

"Hugon," said Lady Bellenet, her voice ringing. "Go and bring the minstrel. I wish to bless Simon Delara."

Lady Bellenet's words were no longer a threat. They were an execution order.

"If we push her too far, too soon..." Hugon's words were distant, in the periphery, as Ru slipped further inside herself.

"You defy me even now?" Lady Bellenet's words were shrill, maniacal.

Hugon said something in reply, but Ru didn't understand it. She was worlds away. She closed her eyes and saw her friends' faces, so beloved, the faces of two souls who had been like family to her. Closer to her than even Taryel, the brightest spots in a world that felt increasingly gray. But their lights had been snuffed out. Their faces drained of all familiarity, their souls devoured by Lady Bellenet.

And for what? To punish Ru? To push her to do this thing that even now, even at her most despairing, she couldn't manage to accomplish? Anguish rolled in her like waves, marrow-deep, congealing and coiling along with her rage.

She had been teetering at the brink, fighting against the inevitable. But Lady Bellenet's words cut through the haze: "Your brother will look charming in white, Delara."

And so Ru tilted and fell over the edge, just as Lady Bellenet had wanted.

She plucked the artifact from the table, bare skin against cool stone. Lady Bellenet watched, eyes bright and wild, as if she had driven herself to some madness as well, both she and Ru in the grips of a mania.

Hugon faded into the shadows like a slinking vermin.

And Ru held the artifact above her head and screamed, a guttural howl of anguish, ripping through her throat until it stung, until it bled.

And at last, the darkness came.

She looked up and saw it seeping outward from the stone, between her fingers. It filled her vision like a thick fog, and soon, she was blanketed in rage and death.

And when Lyr's blow came to the base of her neck, when she should have fallen unconscious, a horrible reverberation shook her body, and she watched in detachment as Lyr's sword clattered to the floor. And then the man himself collapsed, the force of his own blow rebounding back to him.

Somehow, the artifact had protected her.

Good, she thought. *Destroy them, then. Turn them to ash. Everyone. Everyone.*

Vengeful anger and pain flooded her and left nothing behind. Ru saw nothing but darkness, misery, and a world that would burn no matter what she did. All she knew was that Gwyneth and Archie were gone, and Ru would destroy everything in her path until she was either stopped or ran out of souls to reap.

CHAPTER 38

Taryel

He felt her call for him at the back of his neck, where spine met skull. It rattled through him like a bell of onyx, the artifact thrumming in echo. A loud and dire warning.

It was a wild thing, his connection to Ru. He thought of it as a jagged slice through the veil, a seething window that she could open and close at will, and reach through with loving fingers to pull him anywhere.

And he let her do it gladly.

But she did so very rarely. She had only called for him a handful of times in the months he'd loved her, unaware that she was doing it.

Had there ever been a time when he didn't love her?

But her call now was tormented, wrathful, despairing. It slammed against the corners of his mind, tore at his heart with thrashing limbs and fingers, clawing and screaming. The pain of it was visceral, a pounding against his skull, a fist closing on his heart.

It terrified him. Something was terribly, unspeakably wrong.

Moving purely by reflex, he ran to her. Skidding through corridors, breathless and panicked, his breath loud in his ears. He cursed himself as he ran, hating that he couldn't travel directly to her, that his powers had reached their limit. If she hadn't been so adamant that they needed to visit that horrible temple…

But she had asked, and so he had taken her. As if he was supposed to refuse her. As if he *could*. She could have asked him to put a knife to his own throat and press until the skin broke, until he was drenched in red, until his blood stopped flowing and his heart stilled. He would have done it. Without question.

He would have *loved* doing it, for her.

Ru's scream was wordless and unending, and he needed to save her. He pushed past courtiers, his boots slamming on wooden staircases as he barreled through the palace, down and down, toward Ru's agony.

Wait for me, he thought desperately. *I'm coming.*

He followed Ru's call all the way to a downward stair, narrow and claustrophobic. He skidded down the stairs, nearly falling as he went, his footfalls echoing. Because Ru was tormented and pained, but there was something else, a sickly and bitter thing that stuck like tar in Taryel's throat.

Something was very, very wrong.

As he came to the bottom of the stairs, the scene there stopped him dead. Lady Bellenet and Lord D'Luc cowered against the far wall, Hugon white with fear, his lady's eyes blazing wildly with hunger. Lyr lay crumpled on the floor, half lying on his sword pommel.

"Stop her," Lady Bellenet hissed, her voice shaking. "It is too soon. *Stop her.*"

Taryel took everything in with a glance.

All he cared about was Ru. His counterpart, the other half of him, the goddess at whose altar he worshiped.

She held the artifact above her head like a beacon. A sphere of inky darkness expanded from it like a tide. Her hand was fully engulfed in the darkness, and so was her arm down to the elbow. Her eyes, usually a lively brown, shone solid black, as if her pupils had expanded to fill the irises, the whites.

And she was screaming. A wordless shriek of pain and

rage, a howl of horror. Blood flecked her lips and encrusted her nose.

"No," Taryel said, his own heart gripped by fingers of cold terror. "No, no, no," the word tumbled from his mouth, over and over as he went to her, taking her in his arms. "I'm here, it's me," he murmured. He touched her face with anguished fingers, desperate to bring her back. What if it was too late? What if she was lost to him, consumed at last by her own despair?

"Ru," he said, trying to keep his voice steady. He would be her anchor, holding her in life, in joy, in love. "Ru. Ru. You don't want to do this."

But her scream was unending, as if she wanted to devour the world and spit it out, bloody and gnawed.

The darkness had expanded from Ru's outstretched hand to her shoulder; her entire arm wreathed in swirling blackness. The sphere of destructive magic was halfway to the stone ceiling and had already begun to erode the table and a low-hanging stalactite. A pile of ash gathered on the floor where the darkness ate away at the wood and stone.

Taryel's universe was Ru, and Ru alone. He had to stop her. Not because the world needed saving, and not because Lady Bellenet demanded it. He had to stop her because he couldn't bear to lose her.

He pressed his nose to Ru's cheek, letting his breath brush her skin. She was molten hot, even in that frigid room.

"Ru," he said, his lips against her ear. "Please come back. For now, at least. Remember, your friends are here in the palace. Your brother Simon."

An unbidden image came to him then, of a life without Ru in it. He knew that life well; he had lived it for a thousand years. He had simply existed from moment to moment, often wishing for death but too cowardly to end his own life. And then he had felt her, though he hadn't known it at the time. A shimmering beacon at his core. And when he saw her for the first time, he saw a frightened woman with the power of a god's heart at her fingertips. A woman he knew by heart, soul-deep.

From that moment, he had loved her.

There was no choice but to love her. Not because the artifact urged him, though it had brought them together. Not because he felt with every part of his being that he was meant for her. No, Taryel loved her *despite* all that.

Because in Ru, he saw, for the first time, a kindred soul.

The sphere of darkness had expanded now to caress Ru's hair, and Taryel knew that in a moment, it would begin to consume him, too.

Part of him wanted to let her end it, to burn them all. It was what he deserved. He and Hugon D'Luc and Lady Bellenet. But their time would come soon enough. And perhaps Ru hadn't found her solution yet, a way to save the world. But she would. He had faith in her, at least.

"Remember your brother," Taryel murmured in her ear. "Sybeth, Rosylla. You're losing control. If you don't stop, the artifact will kill them. *You* will kill them. You'll kill me."

A shudder ran through her then. Ru gasped, then crumpled. Her full weight fell into Taryel, and he caught her, cradling her head as it lolled against his shoulder.

The artifact tumbled from her hand, clattering to the floor. And as it fell, the darkness dissipated, so quickly and completely that, in a moment, it was gone, as if absorbed back into the stone itself.

"Ru," Taryel said, brushing her hair out of her face. Her eyelids fluttered, and she scowled as if dreaming.

"Don't destroy the world just yet," he murmured, smiling in broken relief. "Not without me, anyway."

CHAPTER 39

Everything hurt. Her arms and legs, her eyes, her head; her throat burned as if she had been guzzling scalding water. Ru whimpered in pain, forgetting where she was. Had she fallen asleep? Then she heard the steady *drip drip* of water on the cave floor, and everything came rushing back.

But something was different, something strange. She hadn't fallen to the floor unconscious, as she had so often done in demonstrations. Something held her. Something… Someone warm.

"You're all right," said a deep voice, faintly accented.

Her eyes flickered open, but she saw only darkness. She started, heart beating wildly in her chest. "Taryel?" she gasped, reaching blindly for him. "Gwyn, Arch, where…"

"They are safe," said another voice, resonant in the quiet. Lord D'Luc. "As is the rest of the palace, thanks to Taryel."

Ru wanted to leap up and strangle Hugon, wanted to take the artifact in her hands again, and burn them all. But she couldn't see, couldn't move. And as she tried to sit up, a wave of nausea stopped her.

"What happened?" she murmured so that only Taryel could hear. She felt his arms around her and knew that she was sprawled on the floor, propped against his chest. "When did you get here?"

"You called me," he replied, and something in him sounded broken. "You lost control."

"I didn't mean to. I didn't… I wouldn't."

"I know," he murmured. "I know."

"Taryel." Lady Bellenet's voice was like cracked glass.

Ru shuddered at the sound. "Give me the artifact," she breathed, clutching at Taryel. "Let me end this."

"Later," he said gently. "You're delirious."

Then he stood, lifting Ru and helping her to a sitting position, where she curled around herself on the cold stone. She blinked hard, trying to see. She heard his booted footsteps moving across the room, and death seemed to echo at his heels.

There was a scrape of stone on stone — Taryel retrieving the artifact.

I need to see, Ru thought. At last, shadows began to form in her vision, dark shapes moving against a murky field.

"Well done, Aharis." Lady Bellenet's voice was cold. "She shows great promise. She was stronger than I had expected. The guard was unable to subdue her, as you can see. But I am gratified by the progress we've made today."

"Are you indeed," Taryel said, anger lacing his words. "Fascinating. Tell me, what did you do to her? What pushed her over the edge?"

"The academics," said Lady Bellenet. "They were irritants. Delara defied me. She needed to be controlled."

"Do you forget," Taryel said, and Ru could tell that he was holding back, could hear his anger threatening to burst through clenched teeth, "that they're her closest friends? Do you think she'll do anything you ask of her now? You played your hand too soon."

The woman hesitated, then said, "There was no other way."

"No other *way*?" Taryel demanded.

As the two of them argued, one of the shadows in Ru's vision edged closer to the far wall. The shape's height, its movements — it was Taryel. And the other form must be Lady Bellenet, retreating in the face of him.

"I've been obedient," Taryel growled, "despite your threats against her, the fact that you held her friends as hostages… and now you hover on the cusp of asking too much."

Lady Bellenet scoffed. "Too much of you, the avatar of a god? Surely, you jest. Ru is a tool. A *conduit*. There are greater things at stake. I thought you understood me, Aharis. None of this matters. Her friends are not *dead*." She paused. "Or is it that you never embraced the concept of eternity? That you've played along like a good boy, only to lose your faith at the end?"

"I'm not a *good boy*—"

The argument turned from heated words to traded insults. Ru's attention turned to a sudden movement at the edge of her clouded vision. Squinting, as colors slowly resolved, she realized that it was Hugon. He approached her slowly, with careless movements, perhaps to check that Ru was still there, still breathing.

He crouched at her side, and she jerked away.

"Be still," he muttered. In her half-blindness, the hollows of his eyes seemed to swallow his face, as if a skull were watching her.

Ru spat, an attempt at derision, but the wad of blood and spit fell only inches from her face. She coughed, spluttering.

"Charming," said Hugon.

The voices on the other side of the room grew louder, sharper. They were speaking over one other, the argument reaching a head.

"What do you want?" Ru croaked. Her throat still stung as if she had swallowed nails.

"Listen," said Hugon, his voice just above a whisper, "if I'm right, Taryel is about to reach his breaking point. No doubt he'll brandish one of the many knives he keeps hidden on his person. If my lady had known he was so armed, she would have confiscated them, of course, but… I never told her."

Ru blinked hard. "What…"

But Hugon pressed a finger to her blood-encrusted lips, glancing over one shoulder.

Why was Hugon doing this? Ru couldn't wrap her head

around it. He was a coward. Too afraid to save himself, let alone Ru.

"*Now*," he hissed, hooking his hands under her arms, lifting her roughly to her feet. "Go. Now."

Ru stood frozen, her mind trying to catch up to reality. She could hardly see, and the stairway was nothing but a hollow black blur.

"What?" she pleaded. "Where?"

"I don't *care*." Hugon let go of her and moved between her and the others, blocking her from sight. Ru's senses seemed to heighten then — she could feel the taut tremble of Hugon's muscles, his labored breathing. He was putting himself in danger, taking a risk, at long last, for her.

There was an unmistakable sing of steel, a drawn blade. Lady Bellenet must be armed as well. Taryel made some sarcastic, laughing remark.

Ru took one hesitant step toward the stairs, then stopped. He had spoken of sparing her from pain, shielding her from Lady Bellenet's punishment. But to defy his lady right in front of her... "Why are you doing this?"

The shadow of Hugon, ghostly and dim, was impossible to read. "It ought to be obvious by now, Delara." Pain laced his words. "For love."

She heard in his voice that he spoke the truth.

It was enough.

Ru ran, dashing for the stairs, stumbling, not knowing where she would go or how she would get there, half-blind. Her focus was on escaping, on getting out, on finding safety. Gwyneth and Archie were gone now. Taryel would find her. She would seek out Simon. He'd know where to hide her, how to keep her safe, how to...

"*Stop.*"

She had just made it to the stairs when Lady Bellenet's voice cut through the din of her thoughts. The words caught Ru like a fish on a hook, and she froze. She turned slowly, and the sight that met her deflated her utterly.

Her vision was clearing with every moment, and while the tower room was still shadowed, every detail a smear or a blur, she could see enough.

Taryel stood unarmed, his back to Lady Bellenet. He seemed to be leaning back, and in a moment, Ru realized why — Lady Bellenet gripped his hair, wrenching his head back. Her other hand was curved around his front, pressing a shining thing to his throat. A dagger.

Perhaps it was her rage, or her fear, or her self-preservation instinct. Whatever it was, Ru's vision finally cleared, the shadowed forms resolving sharply. Her throat constricted with terror.

Lady Bellenet's gaze briefly flickered to Lord D'Luc, and then her gaze fell to Ru like a hammer slamming down.

"One more step," the lady said sweetly, "and Taryel dies."

"You won't kill him." Ru's voice was hoarse and cracked, hardly a voice at all. But her certainty was clear.

He's your god.

"Maybe not," said Lady Bellenet, tilting her head. Slowly, she dropped the hand holding the knife. But her other hand remained in his hair, pulling so his chin tilted up to the ceiling. His chest heaved with quick breaths, and Ru knew it must be tormenting him — this helplessness. "But I can *bless* him," the lady continued, a smile creeping across her face. "I have so much power in me and so many souls to touch."

"You won't," Ru bit out.

Lady Bellenet's eyes flashed. "Won't I?"

Ru had fought and fought. She had kicked and screamed and clawed and bloodied herself in the process. And even after all that, she hadn't been able to stop Lady Bellenet. She hadn't even saved her friends. What had her resistance accomplished? Taryel couldn't save her now, but Ru had the power to save him. She would not say goodbye to anyone else today.

Ru held up her hands in surrender.

"There we are," Lady Bellenet cooed, as if this was all a game and Ru was but a stubborn child. "Was that so hard?"

Lady Bellenet let Taryel's dagger clatter to the floor. Then she rummaged in his pockets, ignoring his grumbles of protest until she unearthed the artifact. Wordlessly, she held it out, and Lord D'Luc came to fetch it.

Like a pretty little lapdog, Ru thought, watching him return it to its place on the half-ruined table. He was too weak to truly defy his mistress. He had tossed Ru a ragged lifeline that would never be offered again.

At last, Lady Bellenet released Taryel, shoving him toward Ru. Her expression was carved in ice. "The Solstice approaches," she said. "I expect you to be ready."

Ru could not have said how she had made it back to her rooms without shattering, her atoms falling to ash and nothingness. Taryel held her as best he could, but she was weak, her legs like jelly.

When, at last, Ru was undressed, bathed, and carried to sit by the fire by a murmuring Taryel, his hands so caring and his kisses sweet against her hair, she closed her eyes and found that she saw nothing but the blank faces of her friends staring back. There would be no peace for her, not even in sleep.

As she lay there, staring vacantly at the fire as Taryel stroked her hair, she wished she could remember… were her friends' hands still twined together when she left Lady Bellenet's rooms?

Or had they lost even that?

CHAPTER 40

Taryel held Ru late into the night.

Held her tightly as she screamed, sobbing, lost in grief. He pressed soft kisses to her head as she cursed herself, over and over. And when she threw the teapot against the wall and it shattered in a hail of porcelain shards, he took her hands in his and kissed her fingers.

When she howled and swore at him, cursed his name, told him that she hated him, that she never wanted to see him again, he listened silently. It was *his* fault the artifact existed, she screamed. His fault that Gwyneth and Archie were gone. His fault that Lyr was, too. It was his fault that Ru was hurting. His fault. His fault.

She hated him.

And when Ru had finally worn herself out, when she lay staring numbly out at the snowy night, he settled behind her and wrapped her in his arms. His quiet tenderness, his steadfastness in the face of Ru's darkest moment, his persistence in loving her — it was the only thing that kept Ru sane. At last, for a while, she was able to sleep.

But her nightmares were endless, one fading into another, death and endless skies without stars. Her loved one's staring eyes, their bodies here, and their souls ripped away like flesh from bone.

She woke in the night.

"Taryel," she said, reaching for him, needing him. She pressed her face to his chest, curling hair tickling her nose.

She breathed him in, shaking with the remnants of her dream. "I'm sorry."

He pulled her against him, stroking her hair. "There's no reason to apologize."

She should have said it then. It should have been a given, tripping from her tongue with such an easy lightness. But feelings had never been easy for Ru. She had never professed her love before; she wouldn't have known how. And in her pain, she clung miserably to what she had, this lovely, quiet thing with Taryel. She couldn't bear to change the nature of it, to risk it, as if not speaking the words might keep him safe.

~

Taryel Aharis and the Keeper of His Heart were summoned to a ball. The summons from Lady Bellenet left no room for refusal, and six empty-eyed guards came to escort them.

Three days remained until the Solstice. Ru had regained her composure and settled into a sort of quiet hopelessness since the loss of her friends. Lyr, Archie, and Gwyneth were gone. No one could bring them back. She found, with a sort of detached interest, that she no longer recognized herself.

She had donned a silk and velvet gown as if it were mourning attire, staring into the mirror like she might find reassurance there. But all she saw was a reminder of everything she'd lost.

Simon had come to her once, climbing through the window. "Chin up," he'd said, handing Ru a tin of cookies that would sit on the table uneaten. "We'll think of something. Don't lose hope until you're standing in a kingdom-sized crater that you created. On the bright side, by that point, you can do whatever you like; nobody will be around to care." His smile was too big, and his one-armed hug too tight.

Ru had asked him to leave just once. To go to their father's house in Mirith or Archie's country estate, anywhere he might be safe. But she had known he would refuse. He wouldn't abandon her.

Other than the clack of slippers on marble floors, the palace was tomb-quiet as Ru and Taryel made their way, hand in hand, to the ballroom. The last time they'd paraded together to a ball, they were surrounded by the titters of courtiers, clusters of laughing aristocrats in bright clothes.

But now, the halls might as well have been empty for all the atmosphere the courtiers provided. At first, Ru thought they might not have noticed her and Taryel. And then, as they approached the ballroom doors, she saw Rosylla and Sybeth stationed on either side. Their gazes were vacant, and when Ru lifted a shaking hand to wave a greeting, they only stared, as if she were some distant and uninteresting curiosity, before turning away.

Ru started back, tripping over her gown, nearly falling. Taryel was there to catch her. "It's all right," he said, even though his voice was unsteady. "Don't look at them."

But as they entered the ballroom, Ru gripping Taryel's arm as if it would save her, she found it impossible to see anything but her friends' emotionless faces. Every visage became Archie, Gwyneth, Lyr, and now, Rosylla and Sybeth. It was all she knew anymore. There was no respite. All around them, standing at the edges of the room, dancing in strange, slow movements, were courtiers. And every one of them, as far as Ru could see, had been *blessed* by Lady Bellenet.

"They're all Children," Ru said, almost choking on the words. She couldn't move; she had to leave. A strangled panic fluttered in her chest.

Taryel drew her to him, holding her close. "Don't forget to breathe," he said. "I won't leave you."

The artifact mirrored Taryel's words, trying to warm her with an unseen caress. But it was cold comfort, a bandage over a wound that would never heal.

"Look," said Taryel gently as he led her into the ballroom. "The musicians."

Across the room, an ensemble played a lively song. And — a rush of relief flooded Ru — Simon was there, and his eyes were as bright as ever. The other musicians were just as emotive, though they looked more anxious than joyful. They played for what amounted to a roomful of ghosts, after all.

"She didn't change the musicians," Ru breathed. "Of course she wouldn't."

"Why do you say that?" asked Taryel.

She glanced up at him. "Music comes from the soul."

As if sensing that glimmer of relief in Ru, Lady Bellenet made her entrance then, half a dozen Children in her wake. Her gaze swept over the ballroom, the dancers, and landed on Ru. A faint, hard smile tugged at her lips. And then she turned, ascending to the dais at the far end of the room and settling herself on the throne that perched there. Hugon D'Luc was nowhere to be seen.

"Will she make us do something?" Ru wondered. "More ridiculous playacting?"

"There's no one left to impress," said Taryel.

Ru watched, only half aware, as bodies danced in a blur before them. It was like watching a puppet show, a horrible cursed play put on by marionettes. And then, as faces spun past her vision like an endless parade of specters, Ru caught sight of golden curls. A freckled face.

Gwyneth and Archie danced past, unaware and uncaring that Ru was right there — so close she could have reached out and brushed a finger against Gwyneth's gown or Archie's fine coat. The pair twirled by so quickly, they were soon swallowed up by the rest of the dancers.

Ru had seen enough to stop her heart for a beat, to remind her of the truth: She was already at the bottom of the deepest well, and darkness had engulfed her. She could not climb out. She could not even think. All she felt was a weight, infinite and crushing, and a ghost of light at the end of a tunnel: the inevitable end.

"Ru." Taryel's voice came from what sounded like a great distance.

Let me disappear, she thought, the ballroom muddling into smudges of color in her vision. *She wanted me broken. I'm shattered.*

Taryel's arm went around her, and she vaguely sensed

that he was steering her away from the dancers, away from the crowd, closer to the music. She focused on the sound of Simon's lute, sweet notes undercut by violin and harpsichord. Simon was alive. He was safe.

"Ru," said Taryel again, turning her to face him. "Don't give up. There's time."

"Time for what?" she said, keenly aware of the guards stationed nearby, lining the perimeters of the room, watching silently. "What can we do?"

"There's a reason we found each other," Taryel murmured. "Festra didn't give you his heart for nothing."

"That's assuming my theory is correct," Ru said, her attention flitting about the ballroom as if she were a hunted creature. "So what, we say, *dear Festra, please tell us how to absolve you?* For all we know, he wants another Destruction."

"Don't think like that," said Taryel, but his tone said it all — he felt the same, but wouldn't admit it.

And then, like the first warm breeze of spring, the musicians began to play a new song. The lute's voice was strongest and led the way, a sweet dance that took Ru's broken sinews and sought to mend them. It was her favorite song, a melody that Simon had played for her when they were young, in dappled sunlight in some Mirithan garden.

It was a balm for Ru's soul, a light in the darkness of her despair. She turned her face to the music. *There is still beauty,* she thought. *There is life and light and music beyond the palace. We're not lost yet.*

Inda and Nell appeared like specters, emerging from the dancing bodies and descending on the musicians.

"Not that song," came Inda's voice. "Play another."

But the musicians only played louder, and Simon's gaze was a fire of defiance. So Inda had no choice, it seemed, but to wrench the lute from Simon's hands, its strings twanging a cacophony.

The hope that had blossomed in Ru withered, scattering to nothing like seeds in the wind.

"The music is over," Inda said, and she and Nell took their leave, Simon's lute still held in Inda's iron grip.

Simon remained, his expression obstinate, until his gaze met Ru's. *I'm fine*, his eyes seemed to say, *don't worry about me.* But Ru knew better. Simon would die at the Solstice, or — more likely — his soul would be stolen from him, just like the rest of them.

Ru caught sight of Lady Bellenet across the room, watching with a grim smile. As if she enjoyed watching Simon's failure, as if she relished Ru's crushed spirits. Ru wondered vaguely if Lady Bellenet had planned it; if she let Simon remain himself just to torment Ru, to watch her grasp at hope and then rip it away at the last moment.

The dancers in the room seemed unperturbed by the sudden silence, their movements continuing as if they were wind-up dolls.

Ru and Taryel returned to her rooms after the ball. Ru was reading to fall apart, and she needed him to hold her together.

As if understanding what she needed, Taryel caught her in his arms, pulling her to him. His hand moved down her back, settling in the divot at the base of her spine. "Exist in the moment with me," he said, nuzzling her neck. "Let me distract you. Let me soothe you if I can."

A spark of desire flared in Ru, so easily lit by Taryel's voice, his fingers, his smell. She leaned into him, trying to forget who she was, just for a moment. He lifted her effortlessly, carrying her to the bed and setting her gently down. She watched as he undressed, her pulse quickening, her fingers pulling at the laces of her gown, loosening and undoing.

There was no hurry in their movements. It was a shared intimacy, a moment of sweetness in the quiet before a storm.

When Taryel pulled off his shirt, breath caught in Ru's throat. His form, so pale and lithe, the dark curls of his hair climbing up from his trousers, scattering across his firm chest, stoked the flame in her. She gathered her skirts up to her thighs, hooking her thumbs under her stockings and sliding them off, and he groaned deep in his throat.

Nakedness with Taryel was dreamlike. Ru had experienced desire, pleasure, the build-up and release. But he was different. More. There was a deep understanding between them, as if they knew exactly what the other wanted, moment to moment and breath to breath. Ru felt weightless under his caress, losing herself so deeply in him that she forgot everything.

His fingers dug into the flesh of her thighs, and he kissed her there, wet and hot. She let herself melt into him as he suckled her neck, tongued nipples, hands warm and precise. His body was an escape, but it was also a salve. That she was still allowed to have this, after everything, was a quiet miracle.

He moved inside her, unyielding, as the tide of pleasure rose in them both.

With a breathless word, he rolled her over, he on his back, her legs pinned to his sides. Tears pricked the corners of her eyes at the sight of him like this: his hair spread around his face, his lips parted, his eyelids heavy. The tips of his fingers dug into her backside as she rolled her hips against his. Her hair fell around her as she leaned down to kiss him, curtaining them in shadow.

"You," he said, breath hot on her lips. "You are all I want. You are the reason…"

Ru bit his lip to silence him, her climax taking over. With a series of gasping sobs, she overflowed in blinding pleasure. And he was coming too, riding that same wave. She tasted blood where her teeth claimed his mouth.

Only later, curled together on the bed, their once sweat-slick bodies now dry, did Ru speak again. "Don't say those things unless you mean them."

She couldn't see Taryel's face from where she was nestled on his shoulder, but she felt his frown, the tensing of his body. "What things?"

"Beautiful, romantic things."

His finger drew a pattern along her back. "Why not?"

"Because it might be…"

"One of our last nights together?"

She sat up. "Don't say it like that."

His expression was gentle. "How else should I say it?"

She flicked his stomach with a finger, where dark hair met his navel, and he winced. "I'm serious. If you want to say… if you want to express affection, I need to know that it's not just some attempt to cheer me up. Or out of obligation. Or… a goodbye."

"Fine," he said, his grey gaze clear and soft. "You, Ru, are all I want. Or haven't you guessed it yet? You, in any lifetime. With or without the hand of fate. I draw breath because of you. I wake up in the morning for you and you alone. It will always be you, Ru. It always has been."

She licked her lip and tasted the remnant of his blood. The tang of it made her ache again, made her want to taste every part of him. "But what if we've just been pawns in a game? Moved across a board by hands we can't see, all this time?"

He sat up slightly, bracing himself with an elbow, and regarded her tenderly. "You've been manipulated. Controlled. The artifact has compelled you again and again. But you've come to recognize when it's happening. You know when you're acting with free will."

"Yes," she said, hesitant.

His knuckle brushed her jaw, her mouth. "Then you know it's the same for me. I've betrayed you. I've hurt you. I don't deserve you. But I've never lied about the way I feel. I love you."

Ru valiantly fought the urge to cry with relief. She had thought, wondered, but… *love*. She was overflowing with emotion, almost too much to bear. "Oh."

"Oh," he echoed, pulling her down to him, kissing her slow and deep. And in the quiet between the night and the dawn, she was Taryel's. And he was hers.

CHAPTER 41

On the morning of the Winter Solstice, Ru slid from under the covers and padded across her room, leaving Taryel asleep in bed, softly snoring. She pulled on her warmest dressing gown and a pair of fur-lined slippers. The sun had not yet risen, though it was not fully dark outside. Snow and heavy clouds softened the world in hues of grey.

In the two days since the ball, Ru had been confined to her rooms. Only Taryel was allowed to see her, and there were always guards in the corridors, at the door. Always eyes watching. Ru had no desire to leave her rooms anyway. And no one had summoned her or demanded things of her. At first, it was a tiny comfort. But now, the Solstice looming heavier than ever on her mind, Ru found even the confines of her room to be more prison than refuge.

And so, when only a few hours remained until she would destroy the world or, by some miracle, save it, Ru woke before sunrise wondering where Hugon D'Luc had gone. It was a sudden thought, surprising her in its insistence. He hadn't been at the ball. The last time she'd seen him was in the cavern, when he'd tried to save her.

That seemed like a lifetime ago, to Ru.

But the wondering wouldn't subside — she couldn't silence the nagging feeling that something had happened to Hugon. It shouldn't matter. It *didn't* matter. But she remembered, so clearly, the way he'd looked at her in the snow: Like someone who, in another world, could have been a home.

Taryel would have stopped her, told her it was pointless to seek him out. She'd only see Gwyneth or Archie in the corridors, or someone else she knew, and plummet further into her well of darkness. If such a thing were possible.

But Taryel was asleep.

And Ru needed to know what had become of Hugon D'Luc.

She drifted through the palace with a veritable army of soulless guards in her shadow, none of them questioning her destination, the empty shape of Lyr among them. One led the way, a young woman who knew where Hugon's room was located. None of them spoke, only responding when spoken to or when given orders. Ru was utterly alone.

She moved past gorgeous rooms and through quiet hallways. She saw Children here and there, early risers, ghostly under crystal chandeliers. Did they drift about by some guidance, she wondered, the unseen hand of Lady Bellenet controlling them, even from a distance?

After a while, Ru passed a painting of a fox hunt, its hunters lovingly rendered in white and red, the fox a restless orange, so free in its dash toward death. The painting was half again her height, and she paused, admiring the scene. Who had painted it, she wondered. Were they alive still, or had they long since passed into memory? She would never know.

Ru's thoughts turned unhappily to the Cleansing. It would be at midday, when the sun was at its pale zenith, as if to defy the long darkness that Ru was destined to bring. The longest night of the year, and it would never end. Lady Bellenet had sent a note explaining it all: the ceremony, the sequence of events. Ru would be escorted to the chapel, the artifact taken there as well. And Taryel…

"There," said the guard who had led the way. She nodded toward a doorway down the hall. "Lord D'Luc's room."

As Ru approached, she saw that the door was ajar. Chill air caught at the hem of her dressing gown.

"Wait here," she said, not bothering to glance back. The guards would stay as ordered. As long as she had no means of escape through that room, they would stay.

Heart in her throat, she pushed open the door.

The space beyond was cold, far too cold. Ru was glad she had worn her warmest dressing gown. Across the room, a window hung open. Dread crawled up her spine, settling at the base of her skull. It was too quiet, too still. No lamps were lit, and black cinders lay cold in the hearth. Some ashes had scattered on the floor, no doubt blown there by the wind.

Under the open window, a drift of snow had collected against the wall.

The dread coiled around Ru's throat, tightening as she moved to the window. There was no reason to fear it. It was only snow, and the sun would rise soon. Tensing her fingers against the open window, she began to close it.

And then she stopped.

She had a horrible itching urge to look outside. Unable to resist, she ducked her head, leaned out, and peered into the dimness. She saw nothing, only rooftops and snowflakes — the window was at least eight stories up, maybe higher.

Her gaze caught on something far below, something on the ground, a shape on the flagstone pathway. She shouldn't have seen it, let alone recognized it. She was too far up, and snow was thick on the ground. But she knew, somehow, that the shape didn't belong there. It was a body.

She inhaled sharply, withdrawing her head. Closing the window firmly, she moved away from it, as if the body might appear there, pressed to the glass, watching.

She didn't *need* to go outside, she didn't need to closely inspect the shape in the snow. She knew whose it was.

But she had to see for herself. To be certain.

Ru asked the guards to bring her outside, to just below Hugon's room. They traipsed down several staircases and through a ground-floor corridor, armor clattering as they went.

It felt like they walked for hours, though it must have only been a few minutes. Ru refused to allow her thoughts to drift toward the body in the snow. She didn't want to lose her nerve. At last, they came to a door that led outside, and they shuffled out into the snow, Ru's toes growing instantly numb.

Ru wondered whether the regent would be at the Cleansing ceremony, whether her friends would be there. Would all the Children gather in that small chapel, shoulder to shoulder, and watch with disinterest as Ru destroyed them?

The body was easy to find. As she approached, her movements seemed to belong to someone else, a separate entity that she was watching from far away.

The snow had all but stopped falling, and the body hadn't been there long. It had landed on flagstone, its slumped shape now starkly visible against the powdery white, the towering palace wall. Ru kicked at the snow near the body and saw that below the fresh powder, the snow was stained with red.

The body seemed to be turned away from her. She did not want to see the rest of it, the ruined face. So she knelt, her knees forming divots in the snow. The cold didn't bother her now. It was the least of her problems.

Her guards hovered nearby, watching, but none moved to stop her as she reached out to the body. She brushed the snow away from its head, oh so gingerly. She didn't want to feel the skull beneath its hair, terrified that it was shattered, that she would feel things where they shouldn't be. She only wanted to be sure.

But she already knew what she'd see: pale gold hair, familiar and soft. Swallowing hard, she swept more snow from Hugon's back. She couldn't have explained why it felt so important to know what he had been wearing when he died.

Deep blue silk, embroidered in silver.

Ru sat back on her heels. There was no way to tell from there, his body obscured in snow, how he'd died. Had his body been tossed from the window, a final punishment? Was he pushed? Or perhaps he had climbed onto the windowsill himself, balancing half-in and half-out of the room, alone in the night, gazing below at the ground that would rush up to him and rob him of his life.

Ru knew what that pain felt like, that despair. She'd seen her own reflected in his eyes. It was just as likely that he'd seen a way out and taken it.

She realized that she was shivering uncontrollably, her feet utterly numb. Her fingers were bright red from the cold. But Ru couldn't bring herself to leave him just yet. The last time she saw him, he was trying to save her. A weak, last-ditch effort, maybe. Too little, too late. But he'd done it for her, knowing, maybe, that he was forfeiting his own life in the act. Or maybe, he had planned to end it anyway.

It wasn't right, thought Ru. That this would be the last she ever saw of him, a crumpled form in the snow. He had been so much more than that, a vivid, cruel, beautiful, frightened creature. But he had also been merciful.

And even in his mercy, he couldn't save you, thought Ru. *There is no one left.*

Whoever Ru was now, whatever she would become, no matter the doom she brought down on the kingdom, Hugon D'Luc's hands had helped to shape her. Should she be grateful? Should she hate him for it?

Neither felt right.

Closing her eyes against her tears, Ru imagined his keen blue eyes, his dimpled cheek, that quick and deadly tongue. He had been a monster, yes. But so was Taryel, and so Ru would be.

The sun began to rise, pale over the palace. When it caught on his hair, glinting like spun gold, Ru eased to her feet. She was stiff, aching with cold, and her eyes stung.

"You were happy in another lifetime," she murmured, and it was the last time she ever spoke of Hugon D'Luc.

CHAPTER 42

Ru was draped in white for the Cleansing ceremony. Lady Bellenet said little as she twisted Ru's dark hair, as she fastened it at the nape of her neck. There was a horrible understanding between them now, it seemed. After seeing Gwyneth and Archie's lives ripped from her, the empty courtiers, and Hugon's body in the snow, Ru had finally settled at the bottom of a black well. And seeing no more reasons to continue, no possibility of a happy ending, she had simply given up trying to escape it. Lady Bellenet saw, of course, that Ru was a broken creature. Hateful and bitter, perhaps, but unwilling and unable to put up a fight.

"The veil," Lady Bellenet said, draping a gold-spun swathe of lace over Ru's head, "represents innocence. The unsullied heart, offered up to Festra."

Ru said nothing. The words were nonsense in her ears.

The world seemed to be drenched in fog, drifting past and eddying about her. The dress, the veil, the chapel; they were all figments of a nightmare. She wondered if Lady Bellenet missed Lord D'Luc. If she had lain awake at night wondering where he'd gone, or whether she had pushed him to it, had been the hand that tipped him over the edge. Had she, too, looked upon his crumpled body in the snow? Knelt and spoken words of comfort to a man who couldn't hear?

It didn't matter.

Taryel had been quiet that morning. Ru had wanted to tell him about Hugon's body, its shape in the snow. But she didn't know how to explain it to him, her need to find him or the subsequent grief, not when she should have been relieved by the discovery of her dead jailor.

There was, Ru believed, no such thing as an evil soul. Monsters were made, not born. Taryel had murdered thousands. She had murdered dozens. Some had lost their souls because of Ru's failings. If this was a just world, no one would mourn them when they passed — Ru, Taryel, Hugon D'Luc, Dulcinea Bellenet. And if absolution truly did wait at the Isle of the Sun, through the gates of paradise, Ru felt sure it wouldn't be enough.

It would never be enough. Not for Ru. Could she ever be redeemed after this? Would she, standing in a blackened crater that stretched out and out across the world, have any desire to draw another breath?

She doubted it.

Before Ru left for the chapel, Taryel had pulled her to him. He kissed her, held her reverently. "It's not over," he had said, his voice firm. She supposed centuries of life gave a man a sense of confidence. "Don't give up, Ru. All you have to do is fight it. There will always be a way out. Always a choice. I know you'll make the right one. Lady Bellenet is not all-powerful."

But Ru knew the truth — she could no longer fight Lady Bellenet. The woman held a card, the highest in the deck, and when she called it, Ru would fold. She hardly dared to think of the possibility, refused to worry in the superstitious fear that it would come to pass. Because as long as Taryel was alive, as long as he could be hurt, Lady Bellenet held Ru suspended like a fly in a web. Caught, enraptured as the spider approached.

"The sun is almost at its zenith," Lady Bellenet said. "Come, my child."

It was suddenly *my child* today, as if Ru were no longer held at the end of a blade. As if she were now pressed to the bosom of Festra's most devoted follower.

Ru followed the lady into the chapel, obedient as one of the Children. Her guards had departed, taking up their stations at each entrance to the chapel, leaving Ru at the mercy of Lady Bellenet. Ru considered asking where Gwyneth and Archie had gone, where the rest of the Children were, but thought better of it. They were all no better than dead, and to pretend any different was to twist the knife in her despair.

The chapel's sanctum glimmered brightly. Sunlight streamed through its multi-colored windows and glanced off the myriad of white-robed figures that were crammed into the room. Children filled the pews, pressed against the walls, and crowded the aisles. They were everywhere, watching as if with one set of eyes, and utterly silent.

Unable to look at them, Ru turned to Taryel, where he waited at the dais. He stood leaning on the golden throne, one hand hooked over its sunlike spires. He caught Ru's eye and smiled. She couldn't understand his lightness, the faith he had in her. How had she earned it? Why had he ever believed in her, loved her? She was weak, cowed by her own fear. Look how easily she'd given in.

But even as she wallowed in self-loathing, some tiny speck of defiance still flickered in her, and she pointedly pushed it away, pleading with it to leave her alone.

There is nothing I can do. I want this to end. Maybe we really will end up in paradise. Maybe she's been right all along.

"Sit," said Lady Bellenet, holding out one hand, fingers outstretched.

A ridiculous surge of amusement rose in Ru as she drifted forward in her veil, her vision obscured by gold lace. She sat on the throne, which was fit for an empress or a true god, not some half-starved, horror-stricken academic. The throne was as uncomfortable as it looked, cold and unyielding. She glanced up at Taryel, who laid a comforting hand on hers. She imagined how they looked — Taryel Aharis, the Destroyer, clad in black, consort to the woman on the throne. And Ru, sickly under the weight of her veil, of everything — the Keeper of His Heart. The new Destroyer.

Lady Bellenet knelt before them, producing the artifact

from the depths of her robes. Like Ru, her raiment was simple and white. The artifact was wrapped in a bundle of cloth, but Ru saw it so clearly, its black shape beneath the fabric.

"Beloved Festra," Lady Bellenet intoned, "we entreat upon you. We call upon the sun and the stars, the fires of the souls that love you. In this cleansing fire, we declare our devotion, our unending loyalty. And in return, we beg that you show us to the Isle of the Sun, that you open the gates of paradise. We beg that you welcome us into the after with loving arms."

Ru waited, her gut in knots. She might have retched, had there been anything in her stomach to eject. She turned her hand so that her palm faced upward, twining her fingers with Taryel's. She could not stop shaking.

"And now," said Lady Bellenet, rising, "the conduit, Ru-ellian Delara, the glorious Keeper, will you take the Heart? Will you set it alight, let it consume you, and bring forth a rebirth, the likes of which has never been seen before?"

"Sure," said Ru. She hadn't been taught any lines, or if she had, she recalled nothing of them. Hesitantly, she held out her free hand.

Lady Bellenet's eyes narrowed in disapproval as she set the artifact on Ru's upturned palm. "And now," she said, turning to the dead-eyed congregation, "we raise our voices in prayer."

As one, the Children began to chant. It was the same droning words they had sung at Prayer, an eerie sort of tune that made the hair on Ru's neck stand up. She wished they would hurry. Midday was only minutes away. All she wanted was for all of this to end.

Something in the sea of Children caught Ru's eye then. A flash of golden curls amid the white. And squinting against the light, Ru saw that it was Gwyneth. Archie sat beside her, his freckles visible even from the dais. A surge of nausea passed through Ru, and she remembered the way they'd held hands before Lady Bellenet's blessing. She had to see. She stood slowly, craning her neck to stare over the rows of expressionless Children. Blood drained from her face. Between them on the pew, partly obscured by their robes, Gwyneth and Archie's hands were clasped tightly together.

Ru sat again, her legs giving way beneath her. The chanting continued, loud and sonorous. Her ears began to ring.

They were holding hands. Ru had seen Lady Bellenet's power, had seen them lose their souls to her. But here they were, together, skin to skin. And they'd danced together at the ball. Surely, this meant that they weren't all gone. Some part of them remained, however small. What if Hugon had been wrong? What if the change wasn't irreversible?

Gripping the artifact in her palm, vice-like, Ru tried to keep her breaths steady as the possibility took hold.

What if they could all be saved?

The chanting ended, one awful note hanging in the air until it was silent.

Lady Bellenet turned to Ru and Taryel, her eyes shining brightly, predatory. "It is time," she said, kneeling at the foot of the dais. "Festra looks upon us with great pride. He has spoken to me. It is time. The gates will open for the Keeper when at last the dark flames of the Heart engulf her. You are ready, Ruellian Delara. Bring us home."

Ru held up the artifact, letting its shroud fall away. Its black surface reflected in every pair of eyes that gazed up at her, vacant and waiting.

"I don't think I will," she said.

Slowly, Lady Bellenet turned. Her eyes slid from the artifact to meet Ru's gaze, obscured by the veil. "The sun is at its zenith," she said, a warning flickering in her words. "Festra demands that we not delay."

"Fuck Festra," Ru said, her crass words ringing through the holy sanctum. "The Children's souls can be returned, can't they? Their life force. They're not *gone*. You wanted me to believe they were lost. That *hope* was lost."

"Taryel," Lady Bellenet spat. "Control her."

The tightness of the woman's mouth, the hint of fear in her eyes, was all the confirmation Ru needed. Clutching the artifact, she drew it to her chest, as if Lady Bellenet might try to take it by force. It was Ru's only leverage now, the only power she held.

Taryel, chuckling slightly, as if all of this were some amusing misunderstanding, turned to Lady Bellenet. His hair fell in black waves over his forehead, his grey eyes shining. He didn't belong there in that chapel, in that place of filtered light. He belonged in the forests, in a dusty library, in Ru's bed. But here, he was all wrong.

Ru's heart ached.

"Give her a moment," Taryel said, stepping off the dais to extend an arm to Lady Bellenet. He spoke as if he had the power to reassure her, the voice of Festra, an immortal creature of death.

And Ru saw in his movements that he believed the woman defeated. That she would fall supplicant and give up, just like Ru had done.

But Ru guessed that Lady Bellenet was at her most dangerous now, when her plans hung in the balance, a knife's edge from ruin. Her body grew taut as Taryel reached for Lady Bellenet, and Ru opened her mouth to warn him.

Because Taryel was the trump card, and Lady Bellenet was about to call Ru's bluff.

Before Ru could speak, before Taryel could react, Lady Bellenet pulled him to her. It was a swift, easy movement, a practiced disarming. She had done it before, after all. She kicked him expertly behind the knee.

He hadn't been expecting it. His leg buckled, and as he stumbled to his knees, the woman withdrew a blade from within her robes. In half a breath, the knife was at his throat, glinting in the stained glass light.

It had all happened so quickly. One minute, Taryel was there, at Ru's side, his fingers twined with hers. And the next, a line of red was on his neck, one thick droplet forming at the tip of a blade.

Ru held the artifact as if it were an anchor in a storm.

"Refuse again," said Lady Bellenet serenely, "and he dies. If you do not obey the will of Festra, he'll be condemned to eternity in the underworld. You will never reunite in paradise."

"Taryel," Ru said, her voice wary. Had he somehow guessed this would happen? He wasn't so naive as to put himself in danger like that. He must have known Lady Bellenet would turn on him, use him like this. Was this his plan all along, to force Ru to kill him and Lady Bellenet in some twisted moment of… what, self-discovery?

Taryel smiled sadly. "It's all right, you know. All you have to do is let me die."

CHAPTER 43

"I'm obviously not going to do that," said Ru, still shaking so hard that her teeth almost chattered as she spoke. "Are you insane?"

"Probably," said Taryel, grimacing as Lady Bellenet's knife pressed against his throat. "But I think it needs to happen. I'm ready to go. It's all right."

"*Silence*," Lady Bellenet hissed.

No, Ru thought, pressing the artifact against her chest. She wasn't going to let him die. But she wouldn't destroy the world. There had to be something. *Anything*. There was always a choice.

The chapel glowed brightly in the noonday sun, glimmering in colors and shapes cast down through stained glass windows. It would have been a beautiful place to die, Ru thought. And while that minuscule spark within herself, that speck of hope continued on, she knew it would only take Taryel's death to snuff it out.

Ru held the artifact aloft, turning it this way and that in the light. She schooled her features, trying not to show her fear. "I don't think you understand," she said, only just masking the tremble in her voice, "that I'm the one who holds the power."

She pulled the veil from her face, watching it flutter to the floor, landing in a little heap on the dais.

The artifact was cold and heavy in her palm, skin to stone.

"On the contrary," said Lady Bellenet, and Taryel winced as the blade cut deeper. "You would do anything for him. I've seen it. Loving him makes you weak. I always knew you might fail me in the end, and that your love for him might be the one thing that would force you to obey me."

"It doesn't matter," Taryel said, his gaze never leaving Ru's. His hair was a mess, his chest heaving. He swallowed, and Ru could see the pain in his eyes as he bled steadily from the shallow wound at his throat. His expression began to crumble. "It's all right, Ru. It will be all right. She won't harm you. You don't need me."

His words made Ru sick. Let him die? As if that were a choice at all, as if it would accomplish anything. She would have fallen on Lady Bellenet's blade herself if it meant saving Taryel. He was more important to her than anything, than breathing, than the world itself.

"Let him go," said Ru, despite knowing she'd lost her leverage. She stood, the artifact still cupped in her hand.

"I'm not afraid to kill," said Lady Bellenet, pulling Taryel's head back, his neck exposed like an animal at the slaughterhouse. The blade pressed into his flesh, a dark line of crimson rippling down his throat. "There's no point in defying me. Where will you go? What can you do? We are at an impasse, and you have one choice left. Festra's Great Cleansing. Save us. Send us through the gates of paradise and reunite with your lover there."

Ru imagined herself doing it. She imagined an explosion of blackness, bursting outward from her body. She imagined waking up naked in a plain of death, knowing she had done it. If she were a different woman, she might have. If only to avoid the visceral sight of Taryel's neck opening up, of his blood spattering the floor, of his body going limp.

"You could change your mind," Ru said, stepping forward to the edge of the dais. And as she did, she reached a delicate thought toward the artifact and found it waiting, a vibration of energy against her mind.

"You could let him go," said Ru, "turn away from here and leave, go back to Mekya. Return to your family. Marry someone else, have another child. Live a happy life, free of Festra, of your past, of whatever this is. You could move on."

"Move *on*," sneered Lady Bellenet, her gaze growing wild. "You think I'd abandon my faith so easily?"

"No," Ru said. "Only alter what you're willing to do for your god. Did he truly give you this power, imbue you with this incredible gift, only for you to use it for death and destruction?"

"You see only death," said Lady Bellenet, "where I see rebirth. I might have tried harder to convince you of how wrong you are, but it is your despair that feeds the artifact. Your pain makes its darkness flow. It is the nature of the thing. Agony is all I've ever needed from you, agony to bring about our salvation."

A horrible, choked sensation caught in Ru's throat. No matter what she did, Lady Bellenet was going to kill Taryel. It would be the thing that pushed her over the edge, down into the black mire of anguish, until the artifact engulfed her. Just as Lady Bellenet had said it would.

But instead of ending things right there and then, the lady continued talking as if caught in a reverie, her voice taking on a bizarre, detached quality. Her grip on Taryel, on the blade, did not falter. "I remember when I first saw the heart," she said. "When Festra showed it to me. It was spring, and I was praying. He bestowed a vision upon me. A wide black crater on the edge of the southern sea, dotted with spires of stone, and at its center… a beating heart. *His* heart. And then he gave me a name: Ruellian Delara. We connected the dots from there, Hugon and I. We discovered that you were an archaeologist, a believer in magic. So we traveled to Navenie and settled ourselves comfortably in the court of Mirith. My powers helped us ensconce ourselves in places where we might affect real change. Hugon as the regent's advisor, myself as a powerful aristocrat."

"But why?" Ru asked, gripping the stone with white-knuckled fingers. "Why unearth the artifact? Why do *any* of this?"

"The vision, child."

"You dreamed of a crater and extrapolated the rest?" Ru

spat, her face growing hot with anger. "What about Dulcie?" Taryel looked as if he might speak, but any movement would drive the blade deeper.

Wait, Ru thought, catching his eye.

Lady Bellenet frowned, her delicate brows drawing together. "My daughter is irrelevant."

"Is she?" Ru said, her words dripping with contempt. "Or did you pledge yourself to Festra to save her from torment in the underworld? Isn't that what all of this is really about? Dulcie?"

For an instant, the other woman's eyes fell away as if caught by a memory long past. Then her gaze returned to Ru, and pain darkened her eyes once more. "I asked for my daughter's happiness, that she would be sent to paradise, to be loved in the after."

Then Lady Bellenet began to speak in a singsong voice, as if chanting a child's rhyme. "*At the heart of me lies resurrection. Keep me and absolve me. I give it to you. Absolve me.* Festra gave me this power to pave the way to absolution. The absolution that was attempted a thousand years ago and failed."

"The Destruction?" Ru said, not expecting this.

Lady Bellenet nodded, and Taryel hissed in pain as the knife slipped down his neck, leaving raw skin in its wake. "Yes. Taryel Aharis was to cleanse the world, just as you are today. But he failed. And as his punishment, he walks the earth undying, faced with the lost souls that Festra could not reap. This is his opportunity to absolve himself, and, by extension, Festra. To do what should have been done long ago."

Ru was silent for a moment, realizing that one of them had fundamentally misinterpreted Festra's poem and hoping it wasn't her. "You're wrong about the heart, you know. And Taryel isn't the one who needs absolving. It's Festra."

Lady Bellenet's lips pursed, her face pinching in impatience. "Why should Festra seek redemption? He is a god. You understand nothing, girl."

"I understand enough," said Ru, and a sudden memory came to her. She and Taryel, in the dungeon of the Cornelian Tower. The artifact before them, their hands entwined. And as they touched, a golden light that leapt forth from the stone in gleaming ropes. "The artifact isn't meant for this Great Cleansing. It's not a punishment; it's a gift. You're misusing it."

"You speak nonsense," said Lady Bellenet, her lips turning white as bright red splotches of color began to stand out on her cheeks.

"Do I?" Ru said, a hesitant excitement taking hold of her. "Taryel and I were called to the artifact. I heard it, felt it, long before I ever saw it. And we can *feel* one another; we can communicate through the artifact. Through Festra's heart. He gave it to *us*, not to you. He brought us together to break this cycle of destruction. You are the one we're meant to stop. You, because you've misused Festra's gifts."

Lady Bellenet's eyes were wild, red-rimmed. "You know nothing of Festra," she breathed. "The heart is for *me*. I was chosen. *I* will cleanse the world, and I will do it for the love of my Dulcie."

"You can't murder an entire kingdom," Ru said, "and call it love. It's the opposite of what Festra wants. It absolves no one."

Taryel grunted, and Ru saw that the blade had nicked him in another place on his neck; Lady Bellenet's grip was faltering, her movements uneven.

"Let him go," Ru said quietly. "You want to show how much you love your daughter? Obey your god's wishes. Let Taryel go."

"He's only a figurehead," Lady Bellenet growled, and her voice was almost inhuman as it echoed in the chapel. "He is nothing. All I need is for you to fall, to plummet into the dark."

"Don't," said Ru, her grip on the artifact faltering.

Lady Bellenet's fingers tightened on the knife as she plunged it deep into Taryel's flesh, and Ru's world stopped.

CHAPTER 44

Lady Bellenet did not hold back. Her knife cut deep, and Taryel's blood flowed thick and fast down his pale throat, onto the white of his shirt, the black of his waistcoat. In seconds, he would fall unconscious. In minutes, he would die.

Ru recited these facts in her mind as if they might offer up some rationality, some saving grace. Her strength was fragmenting, her knees giving way. The fingers holding the artifact were stiff and cold, numbing as she watched.

But in the haze of a grief she refused to accept, Ru knew that Lady Bellenet had wasted her final card.

And Ru now had the upper hand.

Because Ru would not let despair take her, she wouldn't let the current of sadness pull her down into the depths of darkness. She understood now — as if she had always known it — that the golden light was the artifact's true nature. A power born of care and affection. The darkness was a manifestation of Ru's own pain and hurt and confusion. But when she looked at Taryel…

The golden light was love incarnate.

The artifact's truth was as simple as unlocking a door and pushing it open. Ru loved Taryel. She had loved him as Fen Verrill. She had loved him at the Cornelian Tower, and the artifact had known it, had done its best to show her.

But she'd been a coward, afraid to admit it even to herself.

"I love you, Taryel," she sobbed, a desperate declaration.

Taryel crumpled to the floor, his hands stained crimson where he'd tried to staunch the flow of blood. Lady Bellenet dropped the blade. It clattered metallically, echoing in the quiet chapel.

The only sound was Taryel choking on his own blood.

Ru had never seen so much of it, so much red. Taryel was supposed to be immortal. He was supposed to live forever. But he seemed to bleed for each lifetime he had lived, a sea of thick crimson spreading across the floor.

Lady Bellenet stepped sideways to keep her dainty slippers clean.

Ru stumbled forward, slipping in his blood. She half-knelt, half-fell into him.

"Taryel," she pleaded, fumbling for his neck where the wound cut deep. She pressed the skin together, but her fingers slipped, hot and sticky. His eyelids fluttered.

"*No,*" she cried, a wracking sob.

He was no longer there with her. His vision would have blurred and gone. He might hear her voice in some distant way, but in a few moments, there would be no life left in him. He would be nothing but a broken shape, like Hugon in the snow.

Lady Bellenet stood watching, her eyes wide, as if she hadn't foreseen this. As if it hadn't been her plan all along.

Ru screamed a painful, guttural cry, pressing her face to Taryel's chest. It no longer rose and fell beneath her. She could not imagine living after this. She couldn't accept that his light was gone while hers remained. His soft kisses on her neck, his arms holding her close, the way he smiled at her... she would never... she sobbed, unchecked, into his blood-soaked waistcoat.

"Get up," ordered Lady Bellenet. "The sun has passed its zenith, but we may still perform the Cleansing."

Ru only cried out again, a muffled, plaintive wail.

"Get *up,*" Lady Bellenet nearly shrieked, and before Ru had a chance to react, she was yanked away from Taryel, dragged by the armpits.

"You'll stain the ritual garments," Lady Bellenet hissed, once more brandishing her knife. "You must do it now."

Ru sat hunched over herself, sobbing. The artifact was somehow in her hands again, though now it was sticky with blood. Blood was everywhere. On Ru's dress, her hands and hair, dripping from Lady Bellenet's blade.

Ru shook violently. Everything she loved was gone. It was only Ru Delara now, and Dulcie Bellenet. Alone together at the end of the world.

"Do it *now*." Blood flecked Lady Bellenet's desperate face. Taryel's blood.

The artifact seemed to fit so perfectly in Ru's palm, blood and all. Her fingers curled around it as if seeking salvation.

"I want to be very clear," Ru said, her voice as hard as granite, "that I'm not doing this for you."

Who for, then? a thought drifted in from the darkness. *For me.*

With no effort at all, Ru's mind reached out and ignited the artifact. Without the weight of fear, the need to hold back, it was as easy as breathing. She simply stretched out a fingertip of affection in her mind, and it responded.

Golden light burst in Ru's vision like an exploding star. It was endless, swirling, both glowing within the artifact and radiating outward from it, enveloping the chapel, the world, in millions of rivulets of luminous gold. Ru held the stone in her hands while her mind seemed suspended in an infinite night, as if her mind was gone and replaced by a dancing web of light.

For the first time, Ru *saw* the artifact as it truly was. The power that had lain within it, dormant, waiting. It now lay open to her, yearning for more. A god's heart, aching for forgiveness. A thing of beauty, its power unending.

But even in that glorious epiphany, she could only think of Taryel: The man she loved, whose soul had found its counterpart in hers. The man who was now gone.

And *god* she loved him, she loved him.

She fell forward, one hand braced against the blood-wet floor.

The other held the artifact. *Yes*, it said, thrumming against her consciousness.

Her only thought was of Taryel. And as her mind seemed to drift further and further from the present moment, swept up in the power of the artifact, she found that she *was* Taryel. She was standing with King Alaric II in the early morning. Ocean wind whipped at her hair and skin. It seemed to her that she was offered a choice: a small death for the sake of the many?

Or an annihilation?

She opened her eyes, and through the artifact's shimmering glow, she saw Taryel. Limp and lifeless, his hair matted with blood. One hand lay across his belly, the other palm upward, by his face.

From what seemed like miles away, a chapel full of Children gazed at her. A hopeless scene.

Ru took a shuddering breath. She was Ruellian Delara, Destroyer. Doomed by the hands of fate. Hugon and Dulcinea had taken everything from her. They had found her and molded her as they liked, pushed her. As if she were nothing but an experiment, a tool, a simple *conduit*.

She had nothing left.

In the end, Lady Bellenet might have succeeded. She might have driven Ru to utter despair, even now. She would have made Ru the Destroyer a second time over.

But Gwyneth and Archie were still holding hands.

A small death? Or annihilation?

Ru clenched her fist around the artifact, sticky and blood-wet.

Neither, she thought.

CHAPTER 45

Ru's world lit up.

The artifact exploded in an infinite array. Again and again, waves of boundless golden light surged outward from Ru and the stone until the chapel was gone and all Ru could see was the artifact's power, filaments and ropes of gold weaving through a sea of energy.

She reached out a hesitant hand and found she could feel the golden strands. She ran her finger along a thread of power, and it vibrated at her touch.

It was the same golden light she had seen before with Taryel's hand in hers. *Taryel.* She remembered exactly how his voice had sounded in the dark of the Shattered City all those months ago, the voice of a stranger. Yet he had never felt unknown to her.

Somehow, there in that liminal space with her senses engulfed by the artifact's energy, Ru found that the idea of Taryel's death seemed distant. Impossible. How could he have died, when so much bright love was flowing through Ru, through Taryel, through the whole world?

I'm sorry, Ru thought. *I couldn't save you.*

But as she watched, several golden filaments from the artifact seemed to move toward her, as if offering themselves to her. As if the mountains would have marched for her or the sea would have overflowed if she asked. And she saw it all spread out before her — the palace, Mirth, Navenie, The Tower, the Continent, the world.

Ru's every nerve and tendon and bone and vessel *brimmed* with the artifact's power.

The strangest thing happened then. A voice spoke. No, an energy, a nudge against the edge of Ru's mind, like the artifact but infinitely louder. The voice spoke words she couldn't understand, but Ru was certain that it was Festra.

I can fix this, Ru thought at once, as if the god himself had given her the knowledge and the power to do it. *I'm not the conduit. The stone is, and I'm the one who wields it.*

Ru saw the world through new eyes. The golden light enveloped her, fire-bright and ready. It flowed from her core to her fingertips: the power of a god's heart. And then the world before her changed, and she saw it not for what it was but for what it *could* be.

She saw a blackened crater, stretching across a continent. She saw death, grief, and a myriad of souls mowed down in an instant.

But she also saw the possibility of life, growth, and love. She saw the palace as it had once been, joyful and lively. She saw Professor Obralle at the Cornelian Tower, muttering to herself as she flipped through a leather tome. She saw Lyr and Rosylla and Sybeth, bickering good-naturedly on the road, a red sun setting behind them. She saw Gwyneth and Archie, firelight warming their faces, smiling at one another. She saw forests rising up from the Shattered City, flowers touched by rain, a world built and rebuilt and molded… however Ru saw fit. The power was at her fingertips.

Yes, she thought. *There. Just like that.*

～

THE SUN HUNG high in the sky, less than a quarter-hour past midday. All was quiet in the chapel.

Ru lay on her side, stiff and aching. She blinked as sunlight lanced through the chapel windows, glaring in her vision. Slowly, gingerly, she sat up. She pushed a mess of blood-matted hair out of her face, tucking it behind her ear.

Her hands were empty; the artifact was gone.

Ru had done it.

Had... *had* she done it?

She tried to remember what had happened — light bursting outward, blindingly bright, a new world re-molded from the old. And now, here she was. Had anything changed? Had she dreamed it?

Turning slowly, Ru took in the empty sanctum. She remembered now: there had been Children here, sitting in the pews. And Lady Bellenet had been... just there. But the lady was gone now. And the pews were empty. It was as if the Children had vanished into thin air. No, they hadn't vanished. They were themselves again, their minds restored, as if Lady Bellenet had never been. Ru knew it as certainly as she knew that she had used Festra's power to do it.

Taryel.

There was a body on the floor, wreathed in still-wet blood.

"No," she breathed. This couldn't be right. She had used Festra's power for good, she had rebuilt everything, she had fixed it. Ended the cycle. This wasn't right.

She crawled to him, too weak to stand.

"No," she said again, her tears falling hot on his chest. She whispered, her voice breaking, "I fixed it. I set everything right. For you. *Because* of you. Because I love you."

She let out a dry, echoing sob.

Clutching his body to her, she kissed his cold hands. She pressed her hot cheek to his pallid one. She kissed his temples and brushed the hair from his eyes. She did all this through the fog of tears until her head began to ache, her eyes swollen from weeping.

And then, like a distant mirror catching the sun's rays, a shimmer of energy flickered within her. The last dregs of Festra's power, fading. But not gone. Ru called it forth, and it took every bit of her energy. She was so drained, so weak from rewriting the world. She pressed her lips to Taryel's forehead, one palm against his chest, and let the full force of her love for him surge forth. She was done holding back.

"I love you," she murmured. The power inside her leapt

between them, joining her and Taryel in vibrant ropes of light. "I love you, I love you," she said, over and over like a prayer, willing the last of Festra's power to knit him back together, to fill his lungs with air and set his heart beating again. His mortal, precious heart.

She didn't notice it at first. The change began slowly, the gradual movement of magic. And then Taryel himself began to glow, brighter and brighter by the second, until he was fully embraced by the gold.

A burst of sudden light blinded Ru, and she raised her arm to block it, tears still streaming down her face. And when the light was gone, and Ru lowered her arm once more, Taryel still lay there, bloody and limp. His chest rose beneath his blood-soaked waistcoat, then fell.

Fumbling, her own heart beating a mad rhythm against her ribs, Ru touched her fingers to his throat.

The wound was gone. Blood remained, but the wound was gone.

"Taryel," she said, hardly daring to believe. She kissed the corners of his mouth and caressed his brow. She murmured his name again and again until at last he sighed and — so, so slowly — opened his eyes.

"Ru," he wheezed. He lifted a hand to touch her cheek. "Did I die? I thought I died."

She laughed, a sobbing, choked sound. "You did," she said. "But Festra's heart... I fixed you. I fixed everything"

He frowned, and the divot between his brows, the downturn of his lips, was the most beautiful thing she had ever seen. "How?" he looked around, raising himself onto one arm. "Where did she go?"

"She's gone," Ru said. "The artifact is, too. I think... I think we broke the cycle. The heart, Festra, all of it... it's over. I—"

"Ru," he interrupted, turning back to her, his face splitting into a soft grin. "Explain it later. I'm not feeling too—"

"I love you," she said, the words spilling out of her. She would not wait to say it, not now or ever again. "I've been in love with you since the day we met. I love you even more now that I know who you really are. I love you, Taryel Aharis. I forgive you for everything. I'm sorry I didn't tell you sooner." She took his face — his beloved face — in her hands. He watched her with clear grey eyes, and she could have doubled over with the ache of it, the overwhelming joy of having said it. "I know you. I know it's not my place to forgive, but… you're a good person, Taryel."

"I love you too," he said. "If I'm forgiven in your heart, then I'm satisfied."

She grinned, not caring that they were both coated in drying blood, that her hair was a tangled mess, that snot and tears and blood caked her face and mouth.

"What do we do now?" She asked.

He sat up, reaching out and pulling her to him. He pressed a kiss to her forehead, burying his fingers in her hair. She could feel his heart beating, a lively rhythm in his chest.

"I don't know," he said. "But we have time to figure it out."

A lifetime opened up before Ru, of love and long summers, of long winter nights spent in Taryel's arms, of laughter and music. They were free. They had all the time in the world.

EPILOGUE

EXCERPT FROM THE INTRODUCTION TO
"RUELLIAN DELARA: THE UNAUTHORIZED
BIOGRAPHY" BY SOPHIE HILL

Published 1791, archived at the Cornelian Tower.

Upon my own visits to the Shattered City, I found little evidence of the desolate landscape so described by those who had visited prior to 1748. My grandmother, Gwyneth Hill, insisted upon it being a drab wasteland with nary a blade of grass or flower to be seen; that it had been that way for a millennium. Yet even from a distance, one can see that only lush forests and verdant meadows blanket the crater. I told my travel companion, with some measure of mirth, one cannot refer to it as *Shattered* at all anymore.

Similar, though smaller, changes seem to have occurred throughout Navenie on the Winter Solstice of 1748, discussed in their entirety in this text, as a result of many interviews, letters, and accounts from those involved. The most eager participant, perhaps not to the surprise of those who know him, was Simon Delara, our subject's older brother. While I found it rather daunting attempting to decipher fact from overt fiction, as the minstrel has a way of exaggerating things in his own favor, I found his insights about the sudden disappearance of Mekyan aristocrat Dulcinea Bellenet to be most enlightening. To this day, her body has not been found.

One might pronounce such a thing as mysterious; however, I seek to present the events of Ruellian Delara's life, in particular the days surrounding the 1748 Solstice, as accurately as they were relayed to me by not only those close to her, but by the woman herself.

Even so, many things about the story remain unconfirmed, both scientifically and factually. Delara is terribly reticent to share the finer points of what many of her scholarly peers have described as "an obvious whimsy, fantasy verging on madness,"* but after attending several of her lectures at the Cornelian Tower and in Mirith, I feel that I might, with authority, put forth the assertion that all of it is true.

* See: *Ruellian Delara: Genius or Madwoman? A Discussion of Magic's Role in the Scientific Landscape* by Grey Adler, Buford Hennes, et al. 1750.

ACKNOWLEDGMENTS

This was a very hard book to write. I'm not lying when I say it's the most challenging thing I've ever written (not counting grad school research papers, those were hell). I knew where the story was going, but it took a full rewrite, some *hefty* revisions, and lots of crying to get the manuscript just right. So if you're reading this, thank you for being here, and for waiting so long for the conclusion to Ru's story. It was a labor of pain and misery... but it was also a labor of love.

Thank you, firstly, to my wonderful editor Rachel Wharton. She served as both editor and therapist for an entire *year* while I edited and cried about *Sanctifier*. Sequels are no joke! At some points I seriously contemplated throwing in the towel, canceling the book, changing my identity, and moving to a remote location in the Swiss Alps to live off-grid and herd goats. But Rachel put a stop to the madness and reminded me it wasn't that serious (it never is)! So, as usual, you have her to thank for this book's existence.

To Brooke, you believe in me like no one else and I love you so much. Thank you for reading my terrible early drafts and not calling the author police on me. Your support while writing this book was invaluable.

To Rose, you'll always be My Reader. You get it. Always.

To all my positivity readers, you kept me afloat when I was convinced this book sucked ass. You're all angels and deserve sainthood. You know who you are!

To Adam, thank you for listening to me whine about this book for literally two years. More than two? Let's not do math. I love you. Also, thanks for yet another banger of a cover.

To my readers, what can I say? You're the reason I do this. ILYSM. x

ABOUT THE AUTHOR

Meg Smitherman writes romantic stories about magic and world-ending stakes. Based in Los Angeles, she shares her life with a chihuahua, a cat, and a handsome Englishman.

If you love Meg's books, please don't forget to leave a review!

If you want to keep up with Meg's upcoming releases and sneak peeks, subscribe to her newsletter: https://au thormeg.substack.com/

Follow Meg on social media:
Instagram: @megsmitherman
TikTok: @megsmitherman